# DEDICATION

*To all those wonderful people who keep the home fires burning.*

# TABLE OF CONTENTS

# BUILDING TIES

## BOOK 4 OF THE
## A SEAL TEAM HEARTBREAKERS

Teresa J. Reasor

Building Ties

COPYRIGHT © 2014 by Teresa J. Reasor
Print Edition

Contact Information: teresareasor@msn.com

Cover Art by Tracy Stewart
Edited by Faith Freewoman

Teresa J. Reasor
PO Box 124
Corbin, KY 40702

Publishing History: First Edition 2014

ISBN 13: 978-1-940047-02-7
ISBN 10: 1940047021

# CHAPTER ONE

**M**ARY STUBBEN WAS scared. Really scared. Tess Kelly didn't need any special reporter skills to recognize it. Mary's hands shook visibly as she spiraled her napkin into a thin tube. Twisted shreds of paper littered the small table in front of her.

Tess had done her usual quick character study, and nothing about Mary's appearance, demeanor, or background even hinted that she was an attention-seeker. In fact, just the opposite. Her beige blouse and skirt did nothing to enhance her petite figure and the neutral shade leached the color from her fair skin. Her medium brown hair tucked under her chin like a brown football helmet, and her face was as clean of makeup as a five-year-old's.

Despite her mousy appearance, this soft-spoken, nondescript secretary knew everything about what went on in the office of Chanter Construction, and she wanted to talk about her suspicions.

During their phone conversation the night before, Tess had noted the fear in Mary's voice, so she chose a time when the downtown San Diego Café Curiosite' would be less busy, so they could talk freely. Hoping to make Mary more comfortable, she'd selected a table to one side of the restaurant, hidden from direct view of anyone coming in the front door. It hadn't helped. The woman was so shut down, so frightened, the charming atmosphere of the unique Café—its glass-fronted display cabinets full of antique jewelry and knickknacks, the eclectic, oddball furniture—was completely lost on her.

A waitress swung by their table, scooped up the shredded paper, asked if they needed anything else and dropped a fresh stack of napkins next to them.

Tess waited for her to wander away before asking, "Was Mr. Frye aware of how many bids they were competing against for the Ellison project?"

"Yes. Thirteen." Mary stirred her cold coffee but didn't attempt to drink any. "But he knew their stiffest competition was Hamilton Construction and the Brittain Development Corporation."

"How did he plan to outbid them?" Tess asked.

"He couldn't afford to undercut them. He could only propose an amount equal to Hamilton's or Brittain's. No one but the planning commission knew what the bids were, because they were sealed and confidential. But they did release the names of the corporations who were competing."

"So he knew who his competition was, but not how much they bid, no details of their proposals?"

"Well, he wasn't supposed to." Mary scrubbed at an imaginary spill on the table. "Somehow he found out how much the bids were. I heard him talking to Mr. Sullivan."

Tess drew a quick breath. Who in the planning commission had he paid off? "When was this?"

"A month ago. When Mr. Sullivan started coming around the office."

"Who is Mr. Sullivan?"

"Henry Sullivan. He says he's a private detective, and he may be, but there's something about him that raises the hair on the back of my neck when he looks at me."

"And?"

"They went into Mr. Frye's office and stayed in there a long time. When Mr. Sullivan left, there was a look about him. He seemed excited."

"When did you find the report?"

"Two weeks later, just before the accident at one of the Brittain Construction sites."

"You said you were going to bring me a copy of the dossier."

Mary bit her lip. "It's an investigative report on Hamilton and Brittain." Mary started folding a fresh napkin into smaller and smaller squares. "Mr. Sullivan found out Mr. Hamilton was having an affair with one of the girls in his office. There are explicit photos of them in the file. I think he's dropped out of the bidding now. But there wasn't any dirt on Mr. Brittain."

Tess covered Mary's hand. "Do you believe Frye had something to do with the accident, Mary?"

"I'm afraid he did. But I didn't find anything in the office to prove it."

Tess caught her breath. The woman had put herself in a dangerous position. If her suspicions were correct, she could lose her job, but also, if Frye was as ruthless as she described, she could be in physical danger as well.

Mary withdrew her hand from Tess's and rifled through her purse. She pulled out a small flash drive shaped like a rubber bracelet with a logo on it and slid it across the table. "I know Mr. Frye's computer password and copied this information one morning before he came into the office."

Tess's heart skipped a couple of beats. Hopefully Mary had covered her tracks. "Why haven't you gone to the police, Mary?"

"And tell them what? I suspect my boss might have sabotaged a construction site and caused two men's deaths? That he might have blackmailed Mr. Hamilton? Without hard evidence they wouldn't listen to me."

"Why did you come to me?"

"I read the articles you wrote about the terrorist attack on that family. I knew since you had taken on a terrorist, you wouldn't be afraid to look into Mr. Frye's background and follow whatever trail you uncovered."

If Mary only knew. It had taken Tess weeks to get over the incident. The injuries Captain Jackson had sustained from the invaders' brutal beatings still horrified her. And Tess could only imagine how his wife, Marsha, was recovering after being terrorized for three days, and threatened with rape, while knowing that at any moment she might be forced to watch them murder her husband and child. The lead terrorist, Tabarek Moussa, had even dropped their baby into the deep end of their pool and then stood there, watching him drown. Thank God Brett had been there. Captain Jackson, Marsha and baby Alex had only survived because of him. They were all working to put the experience behind them.

"I didn't really take a terrorist on, Mary. My fiancé did."

"But you were there. And you helped him."

"I just did CPR on the baby."

"You still kept your head in an emergency, and you stood up to someone even though you must have been scared."

Tess had found Brett's gun in the car and followed him into the house with it when he didn't reappear. She hadn't had to use it, *thank God*. Brett had been the *real* hero. Facing Moussa unarmed. Fighting him in the water. Where did he find that kind of strength and courage?

And where had Mary Stubben found the courage to sneak around her boss's office and ferret out information? They both had more bravery than she did.

"Are there key people in Mr. Frye's organization he depends on? Certain foremen and workmen he hires consistently on important jobs?"

"Yes."

"If he hired someone to sabotage the Brittain site, they'd either be someone really close to him, or someone he's never hired before."

"They vet every person. Anyone with a record, their referral has to go directly through Mr. Frye."

"Is there any way you can send me a list of people recently hired? And the key people he keeps on his payroll all the time? Only if you can do it without putting yourself in the line of fire, Mary."

"I can do it. I have to pull together info like this all the time."

"Okay. Please be careful. Once you send me the information, I'll do a thorough background check on Mr. Frye and the employees, as well as this P.I., Henry Sullivan. And I'll do some digging about the accident at Brittain Construction. I have some contacts who might be willing to give an opinion about how it happened." Tess studied Mary's anxious features. "But I want you to be careful. If your boss catches you snooping, you'll certainly lose your job. If he's as ruthless as he sounds, he might get physical or even take legal action against you."

"Two men lost their lives in that accident, Ms. Kelly. If Mr. Frye did have something to do with it, someone needs to be told."

"Take your suspicions to the police, Mary. Then you'll at least be on record, and they might look into it. The accident is still an open investigation."

"If I go to the police, Mr. Frye might learn it was me who reported it, and I'll be in the same boat. It's better if you investigate. You're a public figure. He won't be able to come after you."

Obviously Mary had an exaggerated view of Tess's importance at the newspaper. But it couldn't hurt to look into Mary's allegations. And, since she'd been transferred to crime news, her stories were getting wider readership.

If she found anything she could always go to the police herself.

Mary gathered her purse and stood. "I'll keep in touch. And if I find anything else, I'll email you."

Tess stood as well, and offered her hand. She was startled to realize how much smaller Mary seemed standing next to her. It intensified Tess's concern. "Be careful, Mary. I'll keep you posted on my progress."

Mary's handshake was brief, her grasp cold. "Thank you. If it looks like I need to find a new job in a hurry, I'd appreciate a heads up."

"I understand."

Tess watched Mary weave her way through a group of new customers and disappear out the café door while a niggling uneasiness settled in the pit of her stomach. She toyed with the rubber bracelet flash drive Mary had given her, staring at the logo from a local bookstore. She tucked the flash drive into her pocket. She'd check its contents once she had some privacy at the office.

Saraphina Rollins, the coffee shop manager, stopped by Tess's table just as she gathered her things to leave. "Hey Tess, I didn't want to interrupt your conversation, but before you leave, I wanted to say hi and thanks again." They'd spoken at length after the shop was burgled some months before.

Tess smiled. "I've been covering stories in another part of town and haven't been around in a while. Things going okay here?"

"Better than okay." Saraphina's large, expressive eyes sparkled in her beautiful, café au lait face. "At first people came in because they were curious about the break-in. Now they're coming in because they like our muffins and lunch specials. So I guess there's an up side to every situation. Is that handsome hunk you're engaged to home yet?"

"No. Not yet." She hadn't heard from Brett in almost a week. Was he okay? All she wanted was to know he was alive and well.

Worry over his well being warred with the pressure the wedding represented.

"He's cutting it close, isn't he? Isn't the wedding in just a few weeks?"

"Yes. He'll make it." She hoped. But there was never a guarantee. SEALs' lives revolved around deployments and training rotations. After eighteen months of being engaged to a SEAL, she was going into this marriage with her eyes wide open, but it would be hard to take if Brett missed the wedding. "Brett's never let me down," she said, as much for her benefit as Saraphina's.

Saraphina smiled. "Then you're doing the right thing. Not many of us can say that about our guys. It's good to see you."

"You too."

After paying the tab, Tess left the café. She shoved the worry about Brett's continued deployment aside, and thought about her meeting with Mary while she walked to catch a trolley to the parking structure. She got into her car, locked the doors, and spent ten minutes writing detailed notes of the interview while the conversation remained fresh in her mind. Then she called to check in at the office and let them know her next stops. She wove through the downtown San Diego area, hit the I-5, and headed south for an interview in National City.

Her concern for Mary's safety slipped to the back of her mind, to be replaced by another worry; yesterday's offer from the Washington Post. Her call with the managing editor had lasted more than an hour.

They wanted her. She hadn't even applied. The offer had come out of the blue because, the editor said, they'd read her coverage of the hostage situation at SEAL Captain Jackson's house the year before. Her article about Senator Rob Welch and his connection to some shady political maneuvering related to a SEAL team deployment might have had a little to do with it, too.

Had her father also had something to do with it? She'd tried to call him right after her conversation with the editor, but Ian was out of the country and his number was out of the service area. Not an unusual occurrence. But she needed to talk to him about the offer.

She couldn't take the job, of course. Brett was based in San Diego, and Washington was on the other side of the country. But the idea that the *Washington Post wanted her...* Every time she thought about it, her heart rate shot into the stratosphere and she couldn't catch her breath. It was flattering, exciting, and terrifying all at once.

What did she have to be terrified about? She wasn't going to accept. She was getting married in three weeks. And Brett's permanent duty station was here. She had to stay with him. To be associated with a major publication like the Washington Post—it was her dream job. And it would once and for all prove to her father she was a serious journalist.

She loved Brett. She'd known all along she would have to make some sacrifices because of his work. She could freelance for any number of publications. She could cover national news from anywhere in the country and maintain her home base here with Brett. She was young. There would be other opportunities.

But what if there weren't? She pressed a hand against her throat, where a knot tightened. What if she never got to cover a major story because of this decision? There was no guarantee she would even if she took the D.C. job. The thought eased her panic, and she could finally settle down enough to plan the next interview on her schedule.

Three hours later she was headed back to the office. She turned her phone back on and the instantaneous beep alerted her to a voice mail. She glanced at the screen and opened the message when she saw Mary Stubben's number.

"I think someone followed me when I left the café," Mary whispered. "Or it could just be my imagination. But I'm afraid. I've sent you the information you needed. It includes background checks on the employees as well. I've deleted every email I've sent you from the server, just in case. I found something else, too. I'll get it to you as soon as possible." Then Mary gasped. "Talk to you later."

Tess pulled over quickly and keyed in Mary's number, letting the phone ring for more than a minute. No one picked up. Her earlier fears resurfaced with a vengeance, and she keyed in Mary's name, and found her home address. Tess started the car and merged into traffic, fighting the urge to break the speed limit. An image of Mary shredding the napkins, her hands trembling, rose up to torment her. She needed to check on her right now. If something had happened to Mary, she'd never forgive herself.

7

# CHAPTER TWO

T HE MORE YOU *sweat in training, the less you bleed in combat.* The saying was at the forefront of Brett Weaver's mind as he crept down the hall behind Petty Officer Martin Swan. Swan reached the door, swung around the narrow entrance into the room, and fired. Brett double-timed in behind him and covered his quadrant of the interior space. Spotting a paper target representing one of the cartel members in the midst of photos of the hostages, he fired. Three more SEALs rushed in, and for a millisecond the sound of discharging automatic weapons was deafening.

"Clear!" Swan yelled.

"Clear," Brett echoed, as did the other team members.

Brett breathed in the familiar smell of spent gunpowder, wood and rubber lingering inside the structure they called the glass house. He eyed, with satisfaction, the image he'd double-tapped between the eyes. One bad guy down in the midst of several innocents. Now if only the actual op went as smoothly tomorrow.

He was certain they'd done everything they could to make sure it did. They'd used cheap plywood to convert the interior of the block building into a rough replica of the house they would breach tomorrow. Old tires lined the walls to absorb sound and spent rounds, a major difference from the real deal. But the place provided a stage to practice their maneuvers.

The lives of six American hostages depended on the timing and skill of his team. Their mission was to save and free the hostages, some of whom had been held in captivity for over a year. They'd take out every guard if necessary, but hoped to capture at least one to gather some intelligence about the Sinaloa Cartel.

As their time in Nicaragua wound down, and this last mission rushed at them with the lumbering weight of a tank, Brett was eager for it to be over. In fact, if they could load up now and go, it wouldn't be too soon for him.

He hated the last weeks of deployment. They were always dominated by the anticipation of seeing family and home. Something else he tried not to acknowledge. The anxiety that some bad guy's bullet might find him and steal his future.

His promise to Tess intensified those feelings. Even though he knew something could happen to fuck it up, he'd sworn he'd get home in one piece and in time to say "I do" on April tenth. He damn well meant to do both if humanly possible.

At Senior Chief Ryan Engle's whistle, Brett fell in behind Swan again. The squad straggled out of the building to join Engle, 'Book' Ashe—their communications expert—and Lieutenant Sam Harding, their CO, in a nearby patch of shade.

"Final briefing in five." Engle said and disappeared inside the plywood structure to check their targets.

Now practice was over, the men, still pumped on adrenaline, traded trash talk about how well they'd done. Brett only half listened, instead studying his new teammates while they walked to the abandoned hangar they'd made their headquarters.

Petty Officer Clyde 'Squirrel' Rosenberg was a cutup and prankster during down time, but he was all business when they went into action.

Seaman Frank Denotti, the team medic, knew his stuff. During the last mission, one of the Nicaraguan soldiers they sometimes worked with had taken a ricochet to the calf. Denotti had popped it out, patched him up, shot him full of antibiotics, and the guy had recovered without a doctor. Good thing, since they'd been out of touch with civilization for a week. As an endnote to this deployment, of which there would be many, it read pretty well.

Seaman Josh "Arrow" Aaron had an arm like a major league pitcher and could lob a grenade with just as much accuracy. Brett would take his pitching skills over any grenade launcher. More important, Arrow served as Brett's spotter when his sniper skills were needed.

Petty officer Martin Swan was as sharp an operator as Brett had ever worked with. He could do anything on a computer and was also fearless in battle.

Seaman Elijah 'Book' Ashe could fix a COM system with bailing wire and Band-Aids. He kept them connected to their intel guys and extraction crews no matter how much lead flew over his head.

Lieutenant Sam 'Hardass' Harding reminded Brett a lot of Hawk, his brother-in-law and past squad leader. The Lieutenant could be a hardass, which was why they were doing drills they'd done thousands of times before. No one on the team second-guessed their CO. Not with six American civilian lives and their own at stake.

Though he missed the men he'd lived and fought with in Iraq, Brett was as confident of these guys' skills as he'd been with his old team. This squad had been sent here because of their ability to be flexible and their special training. Everyone had taken turns in the glass house, done the drills, and familiarized themselves with the hostages through pictures.

They were ready.

Some of his tension drained away. Soon he'd be winging his way home to Tess soon.

The team trooped to the back of the hangar where a battered table and chairs waited for them. Brett dropped his gear in its assigned place against the wall, checked the safety on his rifle, and found a place at the table with the rest.

Five minutes later Senior Chief Engle joined them. The guy looked wiry and thin, but in a firefight, Brett would take him as a backup over any other guy on his team. The guy had balls the size of boulders and smarts to back it up. That's why he was in charge of reconnaissance for this op.

"New intel, guys," Senior Chief called the briefing to order.

"So far it looks like at least four of the hostages are ambulatory. The other two may be incapacitated in some way. We won't know until you get in there. Thermal readings show both groups are being confined in the back west corner of the structure." Engle pointed to a schematic on the wall of the church where the hostages were being held indicating the room.

"Surveillance reports ten targets with automatic weapons. And we've seen at least two Mk5 machine guns. These guys are as well-armed as any army, because they operate like one."

"For the most part, the tangos stay under cover inside the building while two two-man teams walk the perimeter. Cutter, even though you've practiced with the fire team, your sniper skills are even more important this time. You'll take out those guards before the breach."

"Roger that, Senior Chief," Brett said.

"Since you'll be outside the building, you'll also be in charge of maintaining contact with the extraction team. One Apache and one Chinook will be en route as soon as the team breaches the building. There may be more bad guys living in the village, so once gunfire starts they'll be on you like ticks on a coon hound."

"Understood, Senior Chief. Arrow and I can handle things until the extraction team gets there."

"Good. By the time you have the targets down and the hostages under your wings, the birds will be there to extract you."

"Hooyah, Senior Chief!" the men bellowed.

"Two women arrive with food for the group every day at zero five hundred, but they don't stay. When the women are out of range of the action, we'll hit the targets as soon as they settle in to eat." Engle looked around the group. "Any questions?"

When no one spoke, Senior Chief nodded. "You have your assignments. We move out at twenty-four hundred." Engle turned to Lieutenant Harding. "Anything else, Lieutenant?"

Harding stood. "Thanks, Senior Chief. I've got news. Even if this op goes as planned—"

That got a chuckle from several of the men. Things rarely did.

Harding flashed a brief smile. "It will be at least two more weeks before we head home. There's been some additional intel on these guys. If we have the opportunity to break the back of this organization, we will take it."

Brett stifled a groan. Two more weeks! That left him only six days leeway before the rehearsal dinner.

There'd be no guarantee he'd make it home even then. Ops like this always took longer than planned. Why had he put Tess through the aggravation of planning a wedding when he knew damn well this shit might happen?

If she had to cancel her big day, there wouldn't be a wedding. Not a formal one, at least. That was only if he could persuade her to marry him after the disappointment wore off.

He'd warned her shit like this happened, but hearing it and experiencing it were two different things.

They should have locked lips at the county courthouse before he left and arranged something at the church after he got back.

But Tess wanted something more. She deserved more for all the shit she'd have to put up with in the years to come.

Being married to a SEAL was no picnic. The separations weren't the worst of it. There was the stress of being alone so much of the time. Then there was always the worry that he might not make it back.

That she'd said yes when he proposed was a freaking miracle. He was lucky. Damn lucky.

The briefing wound down and Brett allowed himself a quick glance at his watch. As soon as it was over, he'd call Tess. He hadn't heard her voice in seven days, and he needed to give her some reassurance he wasn't blocking her out intentionally. A hard thing to do when he was in *fucking* South America in the *fucking* jungle where cell phone service was non-existent, and he only got a few minutes satellite phone time every week.

Lieutenant Harding dismissed the men. Brett headed for the COM room and see if he could get some SAT phone time.

"Cutter."

Brett turned to see Engle bearing down on him. "Yes, Senior Chief?"

Engle waited until he was right in front of him before speaking in a low voice. "I know you have a wedding planned for the tenth."

"Yes, sir."

"You may want to give your fiancée a heads up that your arrival time may be tight."

"I was just about to go to the COM room to see if I could do that, sir."

Engle handed him an unwieldy SAT phone. "Take care of that ASAP, and when you're done I'd like a word."

"Roger that, Senior Chief." He watched the man walk away,

wondering what the phone call was going to cost him. Did Engle have some special detail he needed taken care of?

Brett took a seat on the floor in a more or less private corner of the hangar, leaned back against one of the metal walls, and dialed Tess's number.

"Hello."

At the sound of her voice he smiled. "Hey, hon. How you doing?" He closed his eyes and thought about how she smelled like orange blossoms and she tasted even better. Thinking of her shot his heartbeat to double time and gave him an instant hard-on.

"Brett! Are you okay? Oh—I'm not supposed to ask you that, am I?"

He grimaced. The wives and girlfriends of his previous team members had obviously warned her not to mention anything that would worry him or say anything that would show she was concerned about him. "Aside from where I am, you can ask me anything you want, honey. You don't have to watch what you say. I'm fine. I just wanted to hear your voice. I don't get much time to call. How's everything going?"

"Fine. The restaurant we booked for the rehearsal dinner was damaged by fire and canceled our reservation. Zoe's helping me find another. Other than that, everything else is taken care of."

He wasn't ready to tell her his trip home had been delayed. Not yet. He'd save that bad news for later. "Good. Between you and my sister, you'll have everything squared away in no time."

"Zoe really is a wonder. She stays so organized and seems to take everything in stride."

Brett chuckled. "Zoe has you snowed, Tess. She worries about everything." Should he have told her that? "It's okay to be upset and worried. In a way, deployment is easier for us. We just concentrate on what's in front of us and try to block out the rest."

"The chances of something happening to me are substantially lower than they are for you, Brett."

"Yeah, but shit happens, Tess. And some of the people you associate with now are pretty—"

"Are you talking about the wives and girlfriends of other SEALs I talk to most days or the people in my office?" Her tone of voice turned brusque and controlled. "Those are the people I associate with, Brett."

"People you interview, then. I just want you to be careful, honey." He tried to keep the concern out of his voice, but knew he hadn't quite managed.

"I am being careful. I promise. I got wind of two interesting stories today. Both could be big. The first was about a possible construction company payoff. One of the companies involved experienced a terrible accident where two men were killed. There may be a tie-in with the payoff. The other story is about an honor roll student arrested for robbing the grocery store where he works. There's something strange going on in both cases. I'll be doing some research and interviews tomorrow to see if I can pin down what it is."

He was eager to know what she was up to, but damn if her job didn't make him worry. It wasn't like she was a cop, but she pushed too hard sometimes, just like her old man did. Her drive to get at the truth could piss some people off. "Watch your six, babe. Until I get home."

"Then I'll have you here to watch it for me."

"Roger that. I miss you."

"I do you, too." Her voice dropped and grew husky. "Want to have phone sex?"

Brett laughed. "Yeah, I would." His hard-on just got harder. He glanced across the hangar at the guys standing around shooting the shit. "But I'm not exactly where I could enjoy it." Their last time together before he'd deployed popped into his head to torment him. They had come so far together since they'd met. Instead of holding back, as she'd done in the beginning, she reached for what she wanted from him with both hands. He almost groaned at the pun.

She was beautiful, sweet, and giving. And he loved her like crazy. He switched subjects, hoping to distract himself, and bent his knees to hide the tent in his cammies. "How is everyone?"

"Your nephew, A.J., has grown like a weed since you saw him. Hawk and the team were training down south, but they're home now. Flash and Samantha have moved in together. He's so good with Joy, her little girl. You'd think she was his daughter. He's doing some kind of training right now with his new team. Do you guys ever stop?"

He was so engrossed in listening to her voice he almost missed the question. "No, not really. There's always tech advances, new weaponry, tactics... *something* to learn or refine."

"And always some bad guys in the way of you being home with me."

The note of melancholy in her voice made it tough for him to swallow. "Unfortunately, yes. But I'm at the top of my game. I'm fine and I'm going to continue to be fine, so you don't have to worry about me. And I'll be home soon."

She was silent for a moment. "But you're not coming home yet, are you?"

He hated to say the words. He'd give her the worst-case scenario. And if things went better than he expected it would be a plus for them both. "No, honey. I'm not. I think I'll make the rehearsal dinner and wedding, but I can't promise much time before that."

After a brief pause, she said, "As long as you come home to me, I don't care, Brett."

The unconditional love he heard in those words gripped him by the heart and throat all at once. "I love you. So. Damn. Much. More than I can put into words."

"I know."

Was she crying? Jesus. He didn't want that. "I'm sorry."

"I knew what I was getting into when I said yes. If I need to cancel everything at the last minute, just contact me if you can. We'll deal with it together when you get home," she said.

Brett ran his hand over the top of his head, roughing up the hair he'd cropped so he could tolerate the intense heat and humidity. She was going to be disappointed about his hair, too. "I don't know what I did to deserve you. But whatever it was, I just hope I don't do anything to fuck it up."

She laughed. "I'll remind you of that when you get home."

"You can remind me as often as you'd like. I love you."

"I love you, too."

To keep them both from getting too maudlin he changed the subject. "What're Mom and Russell up to? How's your dad?"

"Everyone is fine. Your mom and Russell had me over for dinner a few days ago. And she has taken some fantastic photos of

San Diego. She's selling quite a few on photo sites. Dad's in India right now. He's due back next week sometime. He's actually been calling me every week. Can you believe that?"

"Amazing, especially with Ian's wanderlust. But it's a good thing. What's the word on Selena and Greenback?"

"She's in remission, thank God. I don't know how she keeps going through it all. We're all doing what we can to help out and keep her spirits high."

Relief unclenched his shoulders. Greenback and Selena were good people. They deserved all the good luck they could get. "Selena's a strong lady." What would he do if Tess got sick? He cut off the thought for fear of jinxing them.

"Yes, she is. The baby's doing well. He looks just like Oliver."

They spent a few more minutes talking about other wedding arrangements, her mom, stepdad, and some of their other friends.

Brett glanced at his watch. If he had his way, he'd spend the rest of the night on the phone with her. He suppressed a sigh. "I have to go, honey. Senior Chief is waiting for me."

"I'm tempted to whine, but I won't. I understand."

She really did. She truly got him. "That's my girl. I understand what I'm asking you to take on. I know how hard the life is for family in the military. But I love you so much."

"I know you love me, Brett. And I really do get it—all of it, you know?"

She'd gotten a real taste of what it was like in the past ten months. He wanted to be there with her. Not in this fucking jungle with the heat and the bugs. But he was needed here, too. The tug of war between his commitment to his team and his country and his heart's commitment to her was constant. "I'll call again soon. And if I can, I'll let you know when I'm on my way home."

"Thanks. I'll be waiting for your call. I love you."

After his final "I love you," he hit the button to disconnect, stood, and stretched. He felt better for having talked to her, but guilty, too. He should be there to help with the arrangements. Not that he was good at those things. Hell, he could shoot the eye out of a sparrow at fifteen hundred yards. How hard could it be to find a restaurant for a rehearsal dinner? Worst case, they could have a barbecue on the beach. Doc would let them use his back patio.

Why hadn't he suggested that?

Because every time he called he was more focused on the sound of her voice than anything else.

*Damn, he had it bad.*

He wandered across the hangar and paused to survey their temporary lodging. At least they had cots, so they didn't have to sleep on the floor. His new team sat around the table eating MREs. It was still strange not seeing the team members he'd left behind, Hawk, Flash, Greenback, Bowie, Doc, Strongman and Lange.

And it still stung that Derrick Armstrong, his swim buddy in BUD/s and one of his best friends—or so he'd thought—refused to man up and admit he'd tried to bash Brett's head in. The man had no honor...or had lost it somewhere along the way. But Derrick was the one who was going to have to live with it, and with his prison term for unlawful imprisonment, breaking and entering, assault, and several other charges.

Brett had moved on.

"Hey, Cutter," Frank Denotti called out and waved an unopened MRE in his direction.

"Hold it for me. I have to speak to Senior Chief. I'll be back in a couple of minutes." He knocked on the door to the office space and went in after Engle barked, "Enter." He offered Senior Chief the SAT phone. "Thanks for letting me call."

"Everything okay?"

"Yes, sir. A bump with the rehearsal dinner, but everything else is on target."

"Good." The Senior Chief took a seat behind a table littered with schematics. "I wanted to touch base with you on your latest round of evaluations. Hell of a time to bring it up, but you're in line for a promotion, Cutter. After this mission, it will probably come through."

Too stunned to speak, Brett, stared at him. "I was out of commission for a long time." Wariness kicked in. It was hard to believe after all he'd been through. Months of speech therapy, months of training to renew and hone his skills. More sniper training. Then this deployment.

"You came back strong. And you did single-handedly take out three tangos at Captain Jackson's house. You've done top-notch work for us here, too."

Brett allowed himself a small smile. "Thanks for saying so, Senior Chief."

Engle eyed him. "Well, how do you feel?"

"I'll think about that after it comes through. Too many good things happening at once might throw me off my game."

Engle chuckled. "You're the least superstitious operator I've met in the SEALs, Cutter."

"Not superstition, Senior Chief. But fate does have a way of balancing the positive with the negative and biting you in the ass."

Engle laughed. "All right. I'll keep it to myself, and you can break the news to the others when the time comes."

Brett grinned, allowing himself a short burst of pleasure. "Thanks, Senior Chief." He reached to offer the man his hand.

Engle smiled as he shook it. "You earned this, Cutter. Not many men would have roared back like you did. That says a lot about what kind of SEAL you are. I'm glad you're on our team."

"Thanks, Senior Chief. I'm glad to be here." Though he missed his old team, he was grateful to still be a SEAL, and to be fit enough to continue doing what he loved. And he did love it.

He left the makeshift office and walked back into the hangar. The team was lingering over their meal. They'd been doing drills for hours, and now that the lull before the storm had hit, they were taking a break before preparing their gear.

"Everything okay, Cutter?" Martin Swan asked.

"Everything's fine. A hitch with the rehearsal dinner. The fucking restaurant burned down. Can you believe that shit?"

"That might be an omen, Cutter." Denotti took a bite of stew from his MRE envelope. "Better call the whole thing off." He grinned, his dark eyes alight with mischief.

"Not happening." Brett shook his head. "I have the perfect woman She's the one."

"You miss the wedding, and she may shit-can you." Denotti looked up from stirring his food, his expression serious.

Lieutenant Harding passed Brett an MRE.

He took the meal from the package, even though the real possibility that he'd miss his wedding leached his appetite. He opened the chemical heating envelope, poured in some water, put his meal in, and folded the top down.

"She said if we have to cancel at the last minute to try and get in touch with her and we'd deal with things when I get home." He put the heating envelope into the cardboard sleeve and propped it up against an empty box on the table so the water wouldn't roll out of the warmer.

"She's more understanding than any woman I've ever dated," Harding said.

Rosenburg made noises of agreement.

"Women say what they want you to hear while you're down range, then get all resentful and shit when you can't come through for them because of the job. You miss that wedding, Cutter, and you're fucked," Swan said, pointing his fork at him, his thin, pale features set in anger.

"Lay off, Swan," Gilly Giles cut in. "Not all women are like that."

Who'd have thought Swan was old enough to harbor that kind bitterness. "If I miss my own wedding, Swan, what kind of universal asshole will that make me? It's a two-way street." "You're not going to miss the wedding, Cutter," Lieutenant Harding said. "If we have to strap you to a drone and fly you out of here, we'll do it."

The guys all laughed and the mood lifted.

Harding's reassurances helped some, but shit happened. In the military a personal life came second to the job. He'd signed on the dotted line and it was his duty. But damn, sometimes it was *hard*.

"You got a picture of her?" Arrow asked.

Brett pulled the Velcro pocket of his shirt and removed a dog-eared photo of Tess. He'd put it in a Ziploc bag to protect it and he smoothed the plastic. She was dressed in her wetsuit because they'd been surfing. The neoprene material hugged her slender figure like a dream. Her dark auburn hair was down around her shoulders, copper highlights shining in the sun. Her dark brown eyes had a gleam of humor.

She'd had his back, when no one but family believed in him. If he missed their wedding, he'd deserve whatever fallout came his way. He'd scrape his knees bloody from groveling if he had to. He couldn't lose Tess.

Rosenburg pounced on the picture before anyone else could reach for it. "Jesus, Cutter, she's freaking gorgeous. Victoria's Secret supermodel gorgeous. Where the hell did you find her?" Hearing the admiration in Rosenberg's voice, the other guys crowded around to get a look.

Brett smiled. "I met her at a luncheon at the Hotel del Coronado. That's where we're having the wedding." They'd decided, since they'd first met in the Hotel del's Crown Room, to have their ceremony there. Sort of bringing the beginning of their life together full circle. And the perfect lead in to their married life. "My former CO sent me there to give a ten-minute Q&A about SEALs to a ladies' group. Tess was there to cover the luncheon for the entertainment-lifestyles section of the San Diego paper. She asked if I'd be interested in being interviewed for a series of articles about SEALs."

There was a lot more to it, but it wasn't something he could ever discuss.

"We started dating, and about six months later I proposed."

"What took you so long?" Elijah Ashe asked.

Lieutenant Harding made a gimme gester. "Let me see that picture, Ashe, before your drool ruins it." Several of the guys laughed.

Why *had* it taken him so long? He'd known she was the one damn near from the moment they met. "I didn't want to scare her off. With the way we operate, all the time we're gone, I wanted to be sure she understood what she was signing up for. Luckily she's independent as hell. She's as career-oriented as I am." But Tess had an underlying vulnerability she tried hard to hide. He'd seen it from the beginning. Although, now they were engaged, she seemed more confident.

"She was promoted to the news section and now covers crime mostly." And he was so darned proud of her, for her. "Her stories end up on the front page all the time."

"Hey, I've read her stuff," Book said. "Tess Kelly. She nailed Senator Welch for having a special interest in military funds."

"Yeah."

"Sounds like she's working her way up to big things, Cutter," Lieutenant Harding said.

"Yeah. She's good."

"Does she hound you to tell her where you're at and what you're doing?" Swan asked.

Brett grinned. "No. She knows the score. She's just like any other girlfriend. She just wants to know I'm okay." Senior Chief came out of the office and wandered over. "I'd like for you guys to come to the wedding if we make it back in time."

"You can't just spring an extra fifteen or sixteen people on her at the last minute, man," Swan said.

"The food will be buffet style, and the dance floor and the bar, open. Bring your girls and come on." He scanned each of their faces. "Seven o'clock, April tenth, in the Crown Room at the Hotel del."

"Count me in, man," Denotti said reaching forward to bump knuckles with him.

"She really is beautiful, Cutter," Lieutenant Harding said, handing the picture back.

Brett smiled as he looked at the photo again. "Yeah. I'm a lucky man." He tucked the picture back in his pocket and reached for his MRE. Learning about his promotion, knowing he was about to marry the perfect woman, and that he was building a reputation for good work with the team was as good as it got.

But he hadn't been joking when he'd made the comment about how too much positive might attract the negative. He had to push all that out of his head until the mission was over. He couldn't allow it to distract him. But it still gave him an itchy feeling, like Fate had painted a bullseye on his back.

# CHAPTER THREE

**R**ELUCTANT TO BREAK her connection with Brett, Tess let the empty silence at the other end of the line stretch out before pushing the "end" button on her cell. Hearing Brett's voice filled her with relief and joy. But every time he called she ran the gamut of emotion from happiness to despair. She wiped at the tears streaking her cheeks and took several deep breaths to try and regain control and stem the flow.

If someone came into the lounge and saw her crying it would make for an awkward moment. She didn't share her personal life with people at work. They were all too busy running around covering stories to get into personal stuff.

Brett's delay in coming home added a special bit of stress. She never should have suggested they have a formal ceremony. He had only agreed because she'd wanted it.

Though he *had* thrown himself into getting as many of the details taken care of as possible before he left for…places unknown. In fact, he'd gone at it like it was a SEAL mission, all focused and serious. The memory made her smile.

They'd both wanted their families there, and that included his SEAL buddies. But it was a crapshoot whether any of them would make it. Even Hawk, his best man, could go wheels up.

She should have told him about the Washington Post job offer, but she hadn't wanted to dump any worries on him. She wanted to share it with him face-to-face. Or did she? If she told him about it—he loved her, he'd want her to be happy. But they couldn't be happy together if she was on one coast and he was on the other. No marriage could survive that kind of distance between spouses. Her father and mother were proof. The thought triggered a heavy, tight feeling in her chest.

Screw it. For the first time in her life, she was crazy in love. *Really* in love. That wasn't going to change. She knew Brett felt the same.

She was going to marry him come hell or high water. If all they got was a trip to city hall to do it, so be it. She wiped at the residual moisture on her cheeks and sucked in a deep breath.

No more tears. She had work to do. Concentrating on something else would help her get back on an even keel emotionally.

Tess left the lounge and wove her way through the crowded news section desks to her own. She ignored the hum of activity, picked up the phone, and dialed the number of Daniel Delgado's court appointed attorney. The honor roll student had been arrested for armed robbery of the store where he worked. But neither a gun nor cash had been found on him, even though the cops captured him only a few feet from his house. They had also searched the route he usually took home and found nothing.

Tess wanted a quote from the boy's lawyer. Fifteen minutes later, when she cradled the phone back on her desk, she was left with a feeling of concern rather than the excitement she usually felt when she was on the trail of an interesting news story. The kid's lawyer had all but thrown him under the bus, identifying him as the brother of Miguel Delgado, the leader of one of the most notorious gangs in the National City neighborhood. He'd said his client was cooperating with the police, which implied strongly he'd snitched on his brother. It would be next to criminal for her to print anything the lawyer had said for fear the kid would be killed in jail before he ever went to trial.

Still reeling from the man's blatant incompetence Tess picked up the files she'd printed off the flash drive Mary Stubben had given her. She could still hear the fear and concern in the woman's voice. She dialed Mary's number again, only to get the voice mail message. Anxiety cramped her shoulders with tension and gave her stomach a twist.

If Mary's suspicions were true, it could be one of the biggest stories Tess had ever covered.

She returned to working through the background checks Mary had emailed—the people Frye had personally vetted and hired recently, and the ones who had worked for him several years.

The reports from Chanter Construction were very thorough, and included a picture of each employee and details of their personal life. Checking the info on the reports was easy, but confirming each person was who they said they were took much longer. It had gotten easier now everyone had social media pages and posted information about themselves *everywhere*.

How any of these people enjoyed any sort of privacy was nothing short of a miracle. No wonder so many people reported their identity stolen, their houses broken into, and their lives disrupted by stalkers.

"I will never have any kind of social media page," Tess murmured to herself and grinned at the irony.

She searched for newspaper stories about each person on the list, and perused arrest records, awards, family obituaries, participation in local groups, and tragedies.

Two stories triggered her reporter's instincts. She set those dossiers aside for further study.

One story detailed a car accident. Forty-five-year-old Brian Gooding, an employee of Chanter Construction, was hit head-on by a drunk driver. Though Gooding escaped with moderate injuries, his sixteen-year-old daughter, Lisa, suffered severe brain trauma and now remained in a vegetative state in a nursing home. The driver, an insurance executive, was charged with DUI and assault and given ten years in jail, but had been released in seven.

She discovered a short article about Gooding bringing a civil suit against the man. Though he'd won enough to pay for his daughter's care for a time, it couldn't restore his daughter's physical and mental health. Two years later the couple sold their home, and the wife, Jessica, filed for bankruptcy. A few weeks later they divorced.

A family wiped out because of one man's decision to get drunk and climb behind the wheel of a car.

Tess typed in Alan Osborne, the man responsible for the wreck…and found an obituary. Alan Osborne, fifty-five, died of alcohol poisoning in a motel room two weeks before the Brittain

Development Corporation accident. The article said he'd remained sober since his incarceration. Speculation circulated it might have been a suicide.

She decided to look into what happened to the Goodings after Osborne's death. She could interview Shelly and Brian and see how their daughter was five years after the accident.

The other story detailed the arrest of twenty-five-year-old Marcus Kipfer. Although he was arrested for cocaine possession twice, he never served time. Tess guessed he'd probably turned evidence against his dealer and wiggled out of a jail sentence, though he had gone to rehab. And Frye hired him to work for his construction company.

Tess studied his mug shot. Kipfer had tattoos on his face and neck and a full beard. In the photo his eyes looked glassy and hard.

She searched for a family connection, but found none. The man worked construction, but his work history was spotty. Why would Frye hire him unless there was something there she couldn't see yet?

Both Kipfer and Gooding could be desperate for money. One to take care of his daughter and the other for his drug habit. But had they been pressured into doing something illegal? And could either be connected to the other corporations?

Her eyes burning, Tess leaned back in her seat, closed her eyes, and let her thoughts range back over what she'd learned. The moment her attention shifted away from her research, her thoughts turned to Brett. He'd sounded okay. Upbeat, comforting, loving.

"I hope you're working on that story about the gangs and human trafficking, Tess," her editor, Elgin Taylor, said.

She suppressed a grin as she opened her eyes. "It's already finished and should have hit your inbox." For a moment she thought she saw surprise on Taylor's face. "I was able to get an interview with one of the girls, and she described what they went through." She shook her head. Talking about it made her feel queasy. "It will have the readers outraged and sympathetic."

"What are you working on now?"

Tess hesitated and bit her lip. She scanned the desks closest to her. Seth Maxwell, another reporter, sat close by. "May I speak to you in your office?"

Taylor's bushy brows hiked up. "Certainly."

She gathered the material she'd printed out, slipped it in a folder, and followed him.

Taylor settled into his chair and she took a seat across from him. Nearly a year had passed since he'd switched her from the entertainment-lifestyles section to the news page and the crime beat. Her series about SEALs—and her subsequent coverage of a terrorist hostage situation involving SEAL Captain and Mrs. Jackson and their son Alex, and Brett's heroic rescue of the family—had gotten her there.

But she'd gotten even more than a promotion from the experience, as dangerous as it had been. She'd gotten Brett.

"A woman contacted me about a story yesterday. It's about the Brittain Development Corporation accident. Most of what she told me was supposition, so I'm doing research to ascertain if what she thinks might have happened could be true."

"What does she think happened?"

Tess took a breath. "She believes that Jonathan Frye may have blackmailed Jason Hamilton, the CEO of Hamilton Construction and forced him to drop out of the bidding for the Ellison Project. He was having an affair with one of the girls in his office and Frye's P.I., Henry Sullivan, found out about it. She also believes that Frye may have been responsible for the accident at the Brittain Development site."

Taylor stared at her, his expression avid. "Who is this woman?"

"Someone close to Frye. An employee. She gave me copies of the P.I.'s reports on both men, as well as reports on all the other people competing against them for the contract." Tess scooted to the edge of her chair. "I've been doing a background search this morning on Frye, Sullivan, and some of Chanter Construction's other employees, as well as following up on the info Sullivan gathered on the others. The man is good. But some of what he's gotten, he had to have an in with several different agencies or a really good hacker. It's very personal information."

"Why hasn't she gone to the police?"

"She's afraid. If she's right and Frye learns it was her…." Tess let that hang. "At the moment it's a collection of suspicious coincidences."

"I don't believe in coincidence," Taylor said leaning forward in his chair. "Why would he target Brittain and Hamilton?"

"They're the only two companies whose bids were even close to competing with his."

"How did he know that?"

"Someone from the city Planning Commission office emailed him a list of the bids."

Taylor straightened from his normal slouch. "That alone would be enough to get his company thrown out of the competition. Whoever emailed him the list could be fired. Why hasn't she contacted someone from the Planning office?"

"And what if the person she contacts happens to be the one who sent the list to begin with? She really is afraid to reach out to *anyone*."

"But you," Taylor deadpanned.

"When readers see your name all the time in the paper, they get the idea you're trustworthy," Tess replied. They also thought she was bulletproof.

"As much as I'd like to recommend you sit on this and do some more research, I think you need to send the info you have to the police."

"If I do, and the police launch an inquiry, Frye will know it was Mary who passed the info on to me. It could put her in danger."

"Or it could just cost her the job."

True. But Tess got an anxious vibe every time she thought about Mary Stubben. "Let me do more research and see where it leads first. If I think her suspicions might be true, I'll send everything I have to the police right away. If I find it's just a crazy conspiracy theory, I'll back off."

She leaned further forward. "We're talking about releasing information about three of the biggest construction companies in the area. Even sending it to the police doesn't guarantee it will stay in-house until they do a thorough investigation. Look at what's happened to the Brittain Corporation since the accident. All three of these companies employ a lot of people. If any of them are forced to close down, it will affect hundreds of people."

"Regardless of what happens, Frye's corporation needs to lose the bid because he had inside information," Taylor said. "That would be news enough."

"He didn't know until the bids were already in. It was unethical, and it could cost him the contract, but it isn't illegal for him to have the information after he's already submitted his own bid. Unless he's conspiring to beat out the competition through blackmail and murder."

"Unless," Taylor repeated with a frown. "I want to be apprised of everything you do, Tess. Everything. I may want our lawyers to look at it when you've gathered enough info."

"Okay."

"Now, what else are you working on?"

She held back the Daniel Delgado story until she did her interview and additional research to see if there really was a story there. "I've turned in the human trafficking story and the drug dealer who killed a family of four."

"Okay, I have a couple more things that came in an hour ago." He wrote information down on a pad, tore it off, and handed it to her. Taylor studied her for a long moment. "Be careful, okay?"

Brett had said the same thing. For the thousandth time, she wished he'd come home. When Taylor seemed to expect some reassurance she said, "Always."

Her cell phone rang and she excused herself and stepped outside the office to take the call. "Tess Kelly."

"Ms. Kelly, this is Detective Scott Buckler from the San Diego Police Department. Since you called Ms. Stubben several times since yesterday, I wanted to return your call."

Tess leaned back against the windowed wall of her editor's office. For a moment, she struggled to breathe. Her voice sounded weak when she was able to speak, "Something's happened to her, hasn't it?"

"I'm sorry to say it has, Ms. Kelly. Ms. Stubben was killed in a hit and run accident on her way home yesterday. A large SUV forced her car into the concrete bridge support and she was killed instantly."

Tess's throat worked as she tried to swallow. Her eyes burned with tears. "I think we need to talk," she managed. "Are you at the Broadway Division?"

"Yes, I am. What time would you like to come in?"

"I need to pull together some information she gave me. Give me half an hour, say four o'clock."

"I can come to you," he said.

"I work in a newspaper office, Detective. I don't think you want to come here."

"So you're *that* Tess Kelly."

"Yes."

"I've read some of your stories. I'll be here at my office waiting for you."

"Give me your email address and I'll forward some documents to you before I leave the office." She grabbed a pen and paper off a nearby desk and jotted down his address.

Tess hung up, but continued to lean on the desk. The urge to cry nearly overwhelmed her, but she beat it back. Crying wouldn't bring Mary back, but she could give the police everything Mary shared, including her suspicions, and it might make a difference. When she was certain of her composure, she shoved into a standing position and marched to her editor's door.

He motioned her in and she pushed the door open.

"Mary Stubben, my source at Chanter Construction, was killed in a hit and run accident yesterday a few hours after our meeting."

Taylor's heavy-jawed features blanked in shock.

"I have a meeting with the detective in charge of her case in an hour," Tess broke the silence.

"Jesus," Taylor breathed.

The reality that Mary's death might be related to her suspicions hung between them.

Taylor collected himself. "I'll have security walk you to your car. Would you like one of them to drive you to the police station or ride with you?"

Tess shook her head. "I think I'll be fine. I'll be going downtown. But I would appreciate having someone walk me to my car."

"Done. Let me know when you're ready. I assume you're turning everything over to the cops."

"Copies of everything she sent me, as well as Mary's original flash drive."

He nodded. "This could be just a coincidence."

"I thought you didn't believe in coincidences."

Taylor shook his head. "I want a security guard to ride with you, Tess."

Brett would want that too. "Okay" she said. "Give me a few minutes to compile everything. I'll call you from my desk."

Taylor nodded. "I'm sorry, Tess."

"Me too. She was small, mousy, and had a soft voice. She was afraid. I could see that. And she was upset about the men who were killed in the accident." An ache settled in her chest as she turned away to pull open the door.

Back at her desk, she forwarded the files Mary emailed to Detective Buckler, and then loaded the files from the flash drive onto her computer, and emailed those to him as well. She compiled the research she had been doing, including the articles she'd run across, into a file but decided to hold that one back. He'd do his own investigation and find the same information. She didn't want to plant suspicion in his mind in cases where nothing could have been going on. She called Taylor from her desk phone and put the flash drive into her purse.

Five minutes later a security guard came into the newsroom and she gathered her purse and rose. "Tess Kelly," she introduced herself as she approached him.

"Sam Cather, Ms. Kelly. Mr. Taylor said you needed someone to ride to the police station with you."

"Yes. Did he explain why?"

"Yes, ma'am."

"Are you sure you want to go with me?"

He smiled. "I think we'll be fine, Ms. Kelly."

All she could do was give him a choice. "You're sure?"

He nodded.

At four o'clock the parking lot echoed nearly deserted. Their steps sounded gritty and loud in the late afternoon sunlight. A man dressed in a dark gray business suit got into his car. She caught a glimpse of a bright orange sticker on the bumper when he pulled through the parking slot and turned toward the exit. His brake lights flashed when he rolled to a stop, then screeched out of the parking lot and merged into traffic.

Halfway across the lot, Tess tugged her keys from her purse and hit the button on the key fob to unlock her car.

Sound hammered against her eardrums. Air rushed at her. Her car levitated, and fire and heat shot out from beneath it. The body flew apart. Tess was lifted off her feet from the blast and thrown backwards. She hit the asphalt shoulders first, hard, knocking the wind from her. A large piece of metal, blackened with heat, landed to her right. She rolled away from it and covered her head.

The security guard writhed upon the ground to her left, holding his jaw. Blood streamed down his face.

# CHAPTER FOUR

**F**ROM THE DROP site, Brett took point on the hike. The reassuring weight of his M 91A2 sniper rifle hung from his shoulder while he periodically checked the coordinates with the GPS and his compass. The constant buzz of insects and the call of night birds covered the sound of their movements through the tall grass, while a quarter moon illuminated their path. The damp, raw smell of greenery permeated the air.

His body armor trapped the heat generated by his activity, causing a sheen of sweat to cling to his skin. A short distance outside the village they paused to report in to their extraction team. After making contact, he took advantage of the break to drag a black sweatband from one of his many pockets and roll it around his head, then clamped his Boonie hat over it.

Although their faces were painted and their individuality blurred, he'd learned each man's walk, the way they arranged the tack on their utility vest, everything about them. Seeing a telltale bulge in the back pocket of Ashe's pants, he shook his head. They called the man "Book" because he was always reading. But to bring a novel with him on this op... Brett shook his head. The man's optimism appealed to him. He grinned to himself.

"It was working fine before we left the chopper," Swan complained in a whisper.

Book tossed aside his Boonie hat and clamped a penlight between his teeth while he went to work on Swan's COM system.

Brett moved in to take a closer position to the group and caught the end of Lieutenant Harding's radio check. He'd stay in touch with Senior Chief at base camp in case any kind of last-minute intel surfaced before they hit the building.

They settled in for a half-hour wait. Brett squelched the urge to pace. There were so many things he loved about being a SEAL, but he hated the waiting. Two hours tops and this operation would be over. He was eager to see the end of it. He'd be that much closer to going home. To being with Tess.

When Harding murmured, "Take us out, Cutter," into his COM, he eased quietly to his feet, used his compass to re-confirm his bearings, and moved northeast toward their target location.

After a twenty-minute hike, they reached a stand of trees. In the distance, the dull glow of two lit windows appeared. The uneven skyline of a small strip of buildings came into view a few minutes later. They wove their way through the copse, circling the perimeter of the village, looking for their target.

When they maneuvered around a curve in the valley's topography, the church came into sight. Located at least half a klick from the village, the structure appeared to be the only two-story building in the area and looked in worse condition than aerial surveillance photos had led them to expect. The roof had collapsed into the second floor, and only part of a small bell tower remained intact. No way could the sentries use the roof or upper floor as a lookout. Even as the thought came to him, movement caught Brett's eye. He signaled for the men to take cover.

A sentry appeared, rifle slung across his chest, walking the perimeter. Brett eased into the tall grass to hide until the tango passed. As soon as the man moved out of sight, Brett fell back to join the squad.

"After the women bring the food, Cutter, you take out the guards on duty, then we'll breach the building," came Lieutenant Harding's low-voiced command.

"Roger that, sir. Let's hope they stay out here instead of joining the rest for breakfast." If their intel was right, with four targets down after Brett completed his assignment, they'd have six tangos between them and the hostages.

Moving slowly, and aware of every sound, Brett attached the silencer to his M 91A2 and opened the bipod. While they waited for the women to show up with the food, he studied the slow rounds the four men made along the perimeter. He signaled to Arrow and they moved west into heavy brush to set up.

As daylight crept over the ridge, Brett got a good look at the building from his position diagonal to the church corner. Nestled back against the hillside, the structure, with its faded beauty, exuded a poignant sadness. The façade's curved lines and shape reminded him of the Baroque structures he'd seen in Europe, its patterned brickwork lending a rolling movement to the roofline. A broken, dry fountain stood in the courtyard.

It was a shame the church had been taken over by drug runners and thugs. Perhaps once they took out this nest of assholes, the villagers could reclaim the structure and restore it to its original purpose.

At zero-four-fifty two women from the village walked up the path, both carrying heavy baskets on their backs. They knocked on the door and an armed man came to the entrance. They exchanged baskets, leaving the ones they carried and taking the others away.

For seven long minutes the women traveled back down the valley toward the village until they were finally out of sight. "You're good to go, Cutter," Lieutenant Harding muttered over the COM.

Brett's heart raced. He took several deep breaths to calm himself while he waited for the first sentry to make his pass. He needed to space the targets so when he took the first one out the next would not stumble upon his fallen comrade and raise the alarm.

The first target wandered right into Brett's scope. The man cradled his M-5 machine gun against his side at the ready. Brett waited for the tango to pass around the shadowed side of the church, breathed in, then out, and pulled the trigger. The bullet passed through the suppressor, making a distinctive pffft sound, and struck the man in the side of the head. The target sprawled facedown in the tall grass, quietly disappearing from sight.

"Target one down." One minute later, Arrow murmured, "Next target approaching northwest corner."

Brett swung the rifle in that direction and sighted the tango. The man spotted the first one lying in the grass. His head whipped around and his rifle came up as he looked for a threat. He zigzagged toward his downed comrade. Brett pulled the trigger and the target fell nearly on top the first tango.

"Target two down," Arrow said, his tone dispassionate, professional. Nearly two minutes passed before he murmured. "Target three approaching."

The next man had barely cleared the northwest corner of the church when Brett took him out.

"Target three down. Target four approaching north side."

Brett swung the rifle toward the front of the church, waiting for the next man to walk around the façade. The tango strode across the uneven pavers at the entrance of the church. Armed with a machine gun, more observant, more wary than the other three, he scanned the surrounding area. He looked directly toward their position.

Brett froze.

He waited for the man's attention to shift away. He shut down any personal reaction as he looked into the target's face through the scope. The tango was three quarters of the way across the front yard when he spotted the third sentry's body. He turned to run and Brett fired. The man's skull shattered a millisecond before he toppled sideways.

Arrow laid his hand on Brett's shoulder and gave it a squeeze, a signal for good job. "Target four down," he reported to the waiting team.

Lieutenant Harding's voice came over the COM, "Breach is a go-go-go-go."

The squad charged from the cover of the tree line and up a slight incline to the front door. They paused for half a second, then rushed the entrance.

Brett turned his attention to the inbound helicopters, ETA ten minutes. Ten minutes could be a lifetime if the extraction went hot.

"We're taking up a defensive position to the north," Brett reported into his COM. He and Arrow hoofed it to the other side of the church. If the enemy staged a charge up the valley, the two of them would hold the line until the extract team arrived to pick them up. From there they could also take out any squirters who escaped the building. They had reached the fountain when gunfire erupted inside the church. The desire to run toward the action was nearly overwhelming, but Brett fed info to the pilots headed their way and held his position.

Four men appeared at the narrow bottleneck of the path, all unarmed. Brett fired at the ground in front of them, kicking up dust. The men sprinted back the direction from which they'd come.

Two minutes later a dilapidated truck rounded the bend. Twelve or fourteen armed men bailed out and took cover in the brush and behind the vehicle.

Bullets kicked up dirt and pinged off the crumbled concrete where he and Arrow had taken cover. Another adrenaline rush hit Brett's system. He rolled to the edge of the fountain, looked through the scope, and took aim while Arrow laid down suppressing fire.

Minutes stretched like hours as they hunkered down behind the fountain. Arrow picked off three tangos with his M-5 while Brett took out another four.

Five minutes later an Apache helicopter flew down the valley, spotted the truck, and blew the vehicle off the weed-strewn path. The shooting stopped. The few remaining tangos bugged out toward the village.

With the area now covered by the Nicaraguan troops inside the Chinook helicopter, Brett fell in with the rest of his squad and searched the church. Finding nothing there other than a few cell phones to analyze for intel, they loaded the six hostages, all men, aboard the Chinook. The SEALs piled in with them and settled beside the Nicaraguan soldiers. The Apache flew a parallel position, covering the transport helicopter.

None of Brett's team were hurt, so Denotti, with Ashe assisting him, went to work on the hostage's worst injuries. One rescue went in and out of consciousness. The smell of his septic wound circulated through the fuselage.

Brett fought against a quick wave of nausea and focused on passing out water bottles. The other injured man, too weak to talk, clung to Lieutenant Harding's hand and wept. The rest of the grimy hostages remained silent, the ordeal they'd endured written on their faces and bony limbs.

Three hours later, after the hostages had been loaded on a large truck to be taken to a hospital in Chinandega, the team settled into a patch of shade outside a small tin building while they waited for transport back to their hangar.

The adrenaline high from the action had long passed and now exhaustion set in. Brett's limbs felt heavy as he stretched and tilted his head back against the metal building. He closed his eyes. He could use a nap.

One more mission down without an injury. Every op they completed without losing a man or having one hurt was a victory. He was one more mission closer to being with Tess. Marrying, Tess.

"Why don't we ever get to follow through and deliver the people we rescue to the hospital?" Ashe asked. He took a long slug from a water bottle.

"Have you smelled yourself lately, Ashe?" Swan asked.

"That was kind of my point. I could use a shower and there are always showers at a hospital," Ashe said.

"Can't argue with that, Swan." Brett chuckled and forced his eyelids open. "A warm shower sounds pretty good to me, too."

He fell silent as he noticed Lieutenant Harding speaking into a SAT phone. his expression grave. When Harding looked in his direction, Brett's shoulders tightened.

"Cutter," Harding motioned to him.

Brett rose and strode toward him. Harding nodded as he continued to speak into the phone.

He hung up and focused on Brett. "As soon as we return to the hangar, you're to stow your gear, and get your passport and other shit together. Transport will be sent to take you to the airport in Chinandega. From there you'll be flown into San Diego."

He was going home! For a moment joy rushed through him, but Lieutenant Harding's expression tamped his elation as quickly as it hit. His heart drummed in his throat. Something was wrong. "Has something happened to my family?"

Harding and Engle exchanged a look. "There's been an incident involving your fianceé. Command wants you in San Diego stat."

Brett had depended on his training to keep him grounded and in control, but nothing prepared him for those words. The blood drained from his head, his ears filled with static, as if he was under water. His breathing became labored. This couldn't be right. If something was going to happen to anyone it was supposed to be him. "Is she—?"

Engle grabbed his arm. "She's okay. A bit banged up. But she'll be fine."

"Oh, Jesus." Tess was hurt. "How bad is it? What's happened?"

Harding's tone was almost harsh. "They think it might be another attack directed at you. Her car was blown up."

# CHAPTER FIVE

TIME CREPT BY with the speed and determination of a blind sloth. Tess paced around her small apartment. From living room, to kitchen to bedroom, then back again required little time or thought. Every muscle protested, but she continued her restless rounds.

Where was Brett? He'd called her the day before and promised to be home by early afternoon. It was creeping toward evening and still no word. She needed to know if he was okay. Where he was. When he would be here.

They'd been apart ten long, lonely months and—her eyes glazed with tears—she needed to feel his arms around her. Hear his voice. Smell his sexy scent. She stomped to the apartment door and jerked it open.

The young policeman sitting in a chair outside the door stood quickly. He was thin, tall, and looked about fifteen. "Is there a problem, ma'am?"

Her head throbbed dully. The doctor said she had a concussion. At the time she hadn't thought so, but ever since she'd woke up a low grade headache beat relentlessly at the base of her skull. Her shoulder blades and her back were a mass of bruises and scrapes. Every move hurt. "I was just checking. You know what my fiancé looks like?"

"Yes, ma'am. I'm Officer Stanifer. I've been briefed by the officer who just left."

"Thanks for being here. I just—I'm just anxious to—"

"I understand, ma'am."

She nodded and closed the door. She leaned her forehead

against it and closed her eyes.

She needed to either go back to bed or work. Either one would help pass the time until Brett arrived.

Since she'd missed her interviews the day before, she decided to deal with them, and sat down at her desk and picked up the phone. Ten minutes later she'd rescheduled her meetings for the next day. Life had to go on. She wouldn't hide inside her apartment indefinitely. She had a wedding coming up and last-minute arrangements to take care of. And she had a job to do.

The police and the FBI were so focused on her position as a newspaper reporter, they'd forgotten she was like any other woman. They'd also shrugged aside her suspicions, ignored the information she'd gathered, and instead fixated on her car going up like a failed moon launch. They had decided the incident was a terrorist attack. All because of the actions taken against Brett and Captain Jackson over a year ago.

She'd bet her next paychecks terrorists didn't have a damn thing to do with her car blowing up. This attack hadn't been directed at Brett, but at her.

Mary Stubben had been killed and someone believed the secretary had passed on important information to Tess. She was convinced of it. Things aligned too precisely for it to be anything else.

But if Mary had gathered more evidence against her boss, where was it?

Tess pushed away from her desk and wandered toward the window, then stopped. She'd been told to stay away from the windows. "Damn!" This was driving her crazy.

A tap interrupted the thought, and she caught her breath. Her heart raced. *Brett.* She rushed to open the door. The same young police officer stood outside. "You're fiancé is on his way up," he said with a grin. "Thought I'd give you a heads up."

Leaving the door open, Tess hurried to the living room mirror. She finger-combed her hair and checked her makeup. She smoothed the sleek shift she'd put on for Brett. The last time she'd worn it he'd told her he loved the way it made her legs look a mile long.

Approaching steps sounded in the hallway, and she hurried to the door again.

Brett shouldered a heavy green duffle. His cammies looked faded and well worn. A heavy beard shaded the lower half of his face. Exhaustion darkened the skin beneath his eyes, but the moment he saw her, he smiled. He dropped the duffle bag in midstride and rushed toward her with the determination of a man who hadn't seen his woman in ten months.

Tess reminded herself she wasn't going to cry, but as she hurried forward to meet him, tears pricked her eyes. Her arms encircled his neck and she buried her face against his shoulder. He crushed her against him, causing both pain and pleasure. She ignored it and clung to him. Emotion spilled over her, and the tears she'd managed to hold back streamed down her cheeks in a rush.

"I've missed you so much," Brett broke the silence, his voice husky.

She couldn't speak, could only continue to hold him. He smelled of outdoors, machine oil, and him. His body, muscular and strong, rested tightly against hers, giving her a sense of shelter and care.

"I dream of how you smell," Brett murmured as he pressed his lips against her throat. "Good thing since I've been living with a group of guys who reek like wet dogs who've wallowed in a swamp. Worse—a stagnant swamp. I may bury my nose in the crook of your neck for the next week. It'll take that long to forget."

Despite her tears, Tess laughed and tipped her head back to look at him.

Brett brushed the wetness from her cheeks with his thumbs, his pale blue gaze trailing over her face, searching and tender. He bent his head and kissed her, the pressure of his mouth, gentle, loving. "Are you okay?"

Tess nodded. "Now you're here I'm better."

He rested his lips against her forehead, then tucked her in close against his side. "We're always stronger together."

"Yes, we are," she agreed.

Aware of the young police officer waiting, witnessing their reunion, she turned to him, taking Brett's hand. "Brett, this is Officer Stanifer."

Brett offered his other hand. "Thanks for keeping my fianceé safe."

Stanifer actually blushed while he shook hands. "No problem. I'll get your bag." He lifted the heavy duffle, set it inside the apartment, and took up his post again. Brett thanked him.

Tess closed the door and leaned against it. The dark rings beneath Brett's eyes stood out in the shadowed apartment. Moved by the need to take care of him, she said, "How does a meal sound? I haven't eaten anything since a bowl of oatmeal early this morning."

"Food sounds good. Later." He stepped close and wrapped her in his arms again. "I just need to hold you for a while, Tess."

Something in his tone gripped her throat with emotion. She nodded and, sliding her arms around his waist, nestled as close to him as she could get.

His voice grew hoarse. "For a moment, when Lieutenant Harding told me what had happened, I thought I'd lost you."

"I'm okay. A bit bruised here and there."

He brushed back her hair, raised her chin and pressed his lips to hers.

Brett had been tender, passionate, and playful with her. She had seen him in every mood, or so she'd thought—until now.

"I love you," he said, his expression serious.

She caressed his cheek. "I love you, too."

"I want you to tell me who *you* think might have done this. I don't believe it was another terrorist group from Iraq or Afghanistan."

"Have the men from homeland security been questioning you, too?" she asked.

"Yeah. I was questioned for about four hours as soon as my plane landed at the Naval Air Station on North Island."

So that was why he was so late. And why he looked so exhausted. He'd come out of the field, then had to go back over everything that had happened at Captain Jackson's house, no doubt in exhaustive detail, and for the hundredth time.

"I'm sorry. I don't think it was terrorists." She ran a soothing hand along his jaw, feeling the roughness of his beard. "I believe it was a man named Jonathan Frye. He's the CEO of a construction company, and I think he's responsible for at least three deaths. But

Homeland Security and the FBI are fixated on terrorists and don't believe anything I'm saying. Or if they do, they're too busy ruling other possibilities out to look into this one."

He sighed. "Once I get some shuteye, eat something, and make love with you about half a dozen times, we're going to chase some truth. How does that sound?"

"Meaning you're going to help me do some investigative journalism?"

"That's exactly what I mean."

Two full days trapped in the apartment had left her with nothing to do but stew about everything. She was ready to go out and kick some journalistic butt. She smiled. "Which do you want to do first?"

Brett laughed. "Sounds like a trick question." He touched her forehead with his lips. "I'd get the job done. Then fall asleep for about a week. I'd rather be in shape enough to talk coherently after we make love."

"How about a meal, a nap and then we'll see where that takes us?"

"Perfect."

"Breakfast or dinner?" she asked.

"Anything. I haven't had a good meal in—a long time."

Okay." She offered her hand. "You can help me." She knew him. He'd fall asleep, take one of his power naps, and be up all night.

Brett smiled and grasped her hand. "My pleasure."

AFTER EATING A quick meal of beef stir fry and rice, Brett stripped off his uniform and stretched out on Tess's bed in his boxer briefs. While he watched her undress, he realized, out of all the things he missed when he was gone, it was the small things she did he missed the most. The way she laughed at his corny jokes. The way she moved, the sound of her voice, the way she slept curled against him, the way she would run her fingernails down his ribs to tickle him.

Tess pulled loose the scrunchie she'd used to confine her hair while cooking. The dark auburn strands had grown since his deployment and now fell down her back. A quick grimace of pain flitted across her features, her normal graceful movements disrupted.

Every time she hesitated while doing something, every time she flinched, the anger trapped beneath his breastbone flared hotter. He *would* find the bastard responsible for hurting her. He wouldn't kill him, though he wanted to. But he planned to *seriously fuck him up*.

"Did you call your mom and let her know you're home?" Tess asked from behind the closet door.

From a glimpse of her movements, he guessed she was slipping out of her dress and putting on something else to lie down in. Was she hiding her bruises from him? The anger tripped over into rage.

She glanced around the edge of the door, and he homed in on her face. The falling sensation hit the pit of his stomach, similar to when Harding notified him about the car blowing up. If something happened to her, he'd go crazy. God, he loved her so much. "I called Mom while I was on the plane and told her we'd see her tomorrow. I knew HQ would want to debrief me before I could talk to you or anyone else. Then Homeland and the FBI met me at the base."

"So you got a triple dose. Poor baby." She flipped her hair over her shoulder. "They asked me the same questions, a hundred different ways. It was a complete waste of time."

At least he'd been able to write his report about the mission enroute and submit it before they landed. He ran a hand over his eyes. He was flagging fast. He'd been without sleep for more than twenty-four hours. Without the adrenaline of physical activity and danger to keep him primed, he craved sleep.

Tess climbed onto the bed dressed in a T-shirt and bikini panties.

"Oh, babe. Why don't you hold that pose for a minute or ten and let me look at you? It's been ten long, *long* months."

Tess laughed and rose on her knees to put her hands behind her head, her movements careful, as she stretched her lean body back in a model pose.

She took his breath away, she was so beautiful. She'd still be gorgeous when she was seventy. The urge to sleep evaporated and his body quickened.

He needed to be close. Real close. And make up for being so far away for so many months. He patted the bed beside him.

"I thought you wanted me to hold the pose." She smiled, a teasing light twinkling in her sherry-brown eyes. Her gaze tracked down to his obvious erection. "Or do you have something else in mind?"

With his cock just begging for attention, Brett said, "I want to get as close to you as I can, for as long as I can. I've missed you like crazy."

The teasing light dimmed. She crawled to him and straddled his hips. Bracing her arms, she looked down at him. "I love you. I've thought of you a hundred times a day and reached for the phone to call you at least that many times. Every day."

"Ditto, honey. I'm sorry—"

"Shh…" She pressed her fingers against his lips. "I love you and I'm so proud of what you do." She seemed to struggle between a smile and tears for a moment until the smile won out. "But while you're here you have to make up for all the sexual frustration I experienced while you were gone."

Brett laughed. "No problem." He ran his hands beneath the satiny weight of her hair to cup the back of her head and pull her mouth down to his. Their lips and tongues meshed, then tangled in deep, slow, kisses. Had he ever wanted a woman this much? He wanted to hold her, make out with her, for hours.

She pulled her T-shirt up just enough to rest her breasts against his chest. He caught his breath at the silky glide of her skin against his. "God, you feel so good, Tess." He cupped the rounded curve of her ass and groaned when she moved her hips to tempt him.

When he pulled up her T-shirt, she tensed. "I have some road rash along my shoulder blades. It's a little tender."

"Let me see, honey."

"Nope. Later. You're supposed to be concentrating on us, not a few scrapes."

From the way she moved, she had more than scrapes. If she wanted to put dealing with them on the back burner—But he couldn't.

He pushed up into a half-seated position and traced the edge of her jaw with his lips. "As much as I want you, Tess, just being here with you is more important to me. If you're too sore, we have time for the other stuff later."

She hid her face against his shoulder and collapsed against him. "You're so full of shit, Brett." She thumped his chest with her fist.

The blow was just a ruse to cover up her quick tears. Tess didn't cry at the drop of a hat. She worked through things. Concern rocked the pit of his stomach. She'd been through a trauma, something she needed to work through physically and emotionally. He needed to focus on that, not on getting his rocks off. Brett nuzzled her neck. She shivered and nestled against him. He relaxed against the pillows and splayed a hand along the small of her back to hold her close, her weight a precious burden he'd support for hours if she wanted him to.

Eventually she straightened her legs and moved to lie along his side. Brett turned with her so their limbs lay tangled and their faces close.

"I'm so glad you're home." Her breath, warm and moist, skimmed along his collarbone. Her voice sounded soft, drowsy.

"Me, too. This is what I dream about when I'm away." Being skin-to-skin with her, knowing she was alive, in one piece, safe, was all he needed right now. He brushed her forehead with a kiss.

When her breathing was finally even and deep, Brett allowed his muscles to relax, but his thoughts raced. She didn't want him to know how badly she was hurt. Now that she wasn't kissing him, he ran a searching gaze over her body. The shadowed impression of a bruise was forming along the thigh bent over his. The elbow resting along his stomach was already marred by a dark blue mark. Why hadn't he noticed her injuries before?

Because he'd been focused on her face, the sound of her voice, and the joy of occupying the same space with her.

But now reality reared its nasty head, and with it the rage came rushing back. As soon as she woke, they were going to talk. And he was going to make some phone calls and arrange some backup protection while they conducted her investigation. The San Diego police wouldn't provide protection for long. And once the Federal guys ruled out an act of terrorism, they'd be gone as well. The FBI or Homeland would figure out who it was eventually, they always did.

He couldn't do anything about catching the fucker, other than keep her safe while she covered her stories. But in the meantime he and Tess had a wedding coming up, and she would be out and about open to attack.

No one was going to get close enough to hurt her again. It wasn't happening. Not on his watch.

# CHAPTER SIX

**B**RETT WOKE. INSTEAD of steel girders supporting the roof, the ceiling hung low and smooth overhead. Realization clicked. He was home. *Thank you, Jesus.* He breathed in the scent of orange blossoms and hardened in a rush. Tess curled tight against his side and he half turned to tuck her closer and nuzzle her neck.

Tess's eyes opened and she smiled.

Her fingers brushed his jaw in a caress. Jesus he'd missed her touch, her body, Her.

The phone rang on the nightstand across the bed from him. She started to turn toward it.

"Let it ring," he urged.

Obnoxious and persistent, it rang again. "It may be the police officers in the building. They've been calling to check on me."

He released her with a sigh. Her movements stiff, she rolled away from him to reach for it.

Whoever was on the other end of that line was officially at the top of his shit list.

He stared at the slender length of her back. Two nickel-sized spots of dried blood stained her white T-shirt at shoulder blade level. *Fuck.* While he listened to her end of the conversation, he struggled with the emotions the sight had triggered. Concern for her hit him in the solar plexus, then rage overtook it. When guilt kicked in, he ground his teeth. *He should have been here for her.*

She hung up and rolled back to him. "That was a detective I'd contacted before my car blew up. He's been waiting his turn to interview me. He's on the way here."

"Of course he is," Brett said dryly.

Tess laughed, then snuggled up to him. "We'll make up for lost time later."

He brushed her temple with his lips. "After I've put something on your back, Tess. You're bleeding and your shirt has stuck to it."

She sighed. "It's just a little road rash."

Brett drew back so he could look into her face. He smoothed her hair from her cheek. "How many times have you pampered me through little nicks and bruises since we've been together?"

"Nicks and bruises? *Nicks and bruises?* Jesus, Brett. It was a *bullet hole.*"

The indignation in her expression, triggered the urge to laugh and he bit his bottom lip to suppress it. If he laughed, she'd punch him. "It wasn't exactly my fault I got shot, honey. I didn't know Moussa was up on the cliff with a sniper's rifle while we were surfing. We didn't even know he was in the country until then." He jerked the conversation back to the point he wanted to make. "What I'm getting at is, I want to be there for you, like you were for me. Isn't that part of being a couple? Being married people?"

Her expression cleared and softened, her sherry brown eyes misting. "We're not married yet."

"That doesn't mean we can't practice the together 'in sickness and in health' part." He leaned forward and kissed her, because in that moment she looked so freaking beautiful he couldn't *not* kiss her. "You don't have to hide your injuries from me. It only makes me feel like more of an asshole for not being here for you when you needed me."

She ran her fingertips up and down his forearm in a comforting caress. "You wouldn't have been able to do anything if you had been here."

"Maybe not, but I'm here now, and you might as well use me."

"Use you?" One perfectly arched auburn brow went up.

He couldn't suppress a grin this time. "For whatever you need, honey, but I was thinking a body guard, driver, and corpsman." He wiggled his brows. "And your own personal love machine."

Tess laughed. She ran the fingers of one hand over his close-cropped hair, moved in and kissed him. "I never laugh as much with anyone as I do you. But that is one of the cheesiest things I've ever heard you say."

"What about your, 'I've handled your weapon, and now I want to touch your gun' comment?"

Tess chuckled. "As I remember, you were all for having me handle your gun."

"Yeah. Want to do it again?"

She dropped her gaze to his chest and ran a fingertip down between his pectoral muscles to the thin line of hair that bisected his abs. His muscles clenched in response and his cock stood at attention.

"I'll even oil it if you want me to," she breathed. "But you're going to have to wait until after Detective Buckler has his interview."

"Do you sense a theme happening here?" Brett asked. "Later, later, later."

Tess laughed.

He turned serious and ran the backs of his fingers against her cheek, while he looked into her eyes. "I'm just happy to be here, close enough to touch you."

"You're going to make me cry," she complained and turned her face against his chest.

He held her for long, sweet moments. "I know you're stalling getting up until I do. You're probably stiff as hell and don't want me to see you. I'll bite the bullet and roll out so I can answer the door when the detective gets here. You take your time."

"Okay." That she didn't deny his speculations about her condition was more telling than how she was sitting on the bed when he came out of the bathroom a few minutes later.

"Ibuprofen helps," he suggested as he put on his camouflage pants. "I can get you some."

"I have some pills the doctor prescribed. They're on the kitchen sink. If you could cut one in half and bring it to me, I'd appreciate it."

"Roger that." Brett grabbed his T-shirt and slipped into it while he moved down the hall to the pint-sized kitchen. He found the pill bottle, snapped a pill in half and grabbed a bottle of water from the fridge.

Tess pulled on a pair of leggings and dragged a long, light-weight sweater from her closet. No way could she wear a bra. The skin on her back felt stiff and sore now that the scrapes had sealed themselves. Thank God her wedding gown wasn't backless.

Brett returned. His pale blue gaze settled on her breasts for a moment and she felt the warm rush of color to her cheeks, and the accompanying tingle down below. All he had to do was look at her, and despite the pain, she wanted to climb right back into bed with him and do more than sleep. A lot more.

"Do you have some kind of medication to put on the scrapes?" he asked.

"There's some antibiotic ointment in the cabinet under the sink and some dressings."

He went into the bathroom and returned with some gauze pads and the ointment.

"How much time will you get off now that you're home?" she asked.

"I have four weeks before I have to go back to work." He ripped open two gauze pads and set them on the wrappers on the bed. When he moved around behind her, he hesitated before he touched her. "It'll take some time for this to heal. It's in a bad spot. Every time you move it's going to pull." He squirted the ointment onto her back, then gingerly spread it out over the spots. "Hold on, I have some rolled gauze in my bag."

He went into the living room and brought back the heavy sea bag. He opened it, dug through the tightly packed clothes, and found his ditty kit. He pulled a roll of gauze wrapped in plastic from the bag and some medical tape, then returned to her.

"I'm not going to ask why you have that in there," Tess said.

"Got to stay prepared for anything, babe." He handed her the end of the gauze. "Hold your elbows out and this between your breasts." He laid the pads over her injuries and wrapped the gauze around her to hold it in place, creating both a bandage and a bra at the same time. "How does that feel? Not too tight?"

"No, not too tight." She leaned into him and put her arms

around his waist. "My own personal medic."

"Always." He brushed her forehead with his lips. "Does that mean I can cop a feel before the police get here?"

Tess grasped the hand he rested on her hip, and tugged it up to her breast and held it there. Even through the gauze his touch set off a sweet, languid weakness in her limbs. The fierce heat in his gaze dried her throat.

Brett bent his head to kiss her when a knock at the door interrupted. He groaned and pressed his lips to her forehead. "I'll get the door."

She smiled as he caught the edge of the bedroom door on his way out and closed it. *God, how she'd missed him.* He had so much energy and wit. When he walked into the room, he nourished her with all that he was. When he was here, she couldn't imagine being without him. When he was gone, she ached to have him back. Was this how her mother had felt with her father? If it was, how had she ever divorced him?

But she needed to tell him about the Washington Post offer. He felt guilty for leaving her, guilty for not being here because of the explosion. He'd feel guilty about her passing up the job. And she felt guilty about not telling him. It was a never-ending circle. But if he found out about the offer before she shared it with him…

She eased into her sweater. Her back felt much better for Brett's care. Her own personal medic. Erotic visions of playing doctor with him made her smile. Reluctantly she went into the bathroom to freshen up and brush her hair.

When she entered the living room, the three men got to their feet and immediately took up most of the space in the small room. Though she'd been interviewing policemen for nearly a year, having the shoe on the other foot was stressful.

The ordeals of having been grilled by both the FBI and Homeland Security in the last couple of days, and now this police visit, seemed suddenly overwhelming. She moved to stand next to Brett and was grateful when he put a protective arm around her waist while he introduced the two. "This is Detective Buckler and his partner Detective Michael Hart, Tess."

"May I see some identification?" Tess asked.

Brett grinned. "I already asked for it."

"That's okay," Buckler said and produced his badge. His partner did as well.

The two detectives were about the same age, thirty-five to forty, and both had dark hair. Hart had a rounded chin and intense, deep brown eyes. Detective Buckler stood a few inches taller than his partner, and had a bulk to his frame which suggested he worked out. The loose-limbed way he stood added the impression that he was laid back, yet he scanned her, Brett, and the apartment in a manner that implied he would later be able to recall every detail.

Tess shook each man's hand briefly. Brett motioned her to take his chair and pulled the desk chair forward to sit beside her.

Hart took out a notebook. "You don't mind if I take notes, do you Miss Kelly?"

Tess shook her head. "No, of course not."

"You've been through an ordeal," Detective Buckler said.

"It wasn't much fun having my car levitate and fly apart, but I was only injured a little. The security guard who was to accompany me to your office got hit by shrapnel and had to have surgery to remove it. He had a scalp laceration that bled pretty badly."

"We've spoken to him." Buckler leaned forward to rest his elbows on his knees.

A knot of tension tightened in her stomach. She slid forward in her seat. "How is he?"

"He's been released and will be back to work in about six weeks."

She breathed a sigh of relief. "I'm glad." She'd been thinking of her own safety, but she'd never dreamed anything would really happen.

Buckler linked his fingers. "How are you feeling?"

"I'm a little bruised here and there, and moving a little slower than usual, but otherwise I'm okay."

"What made you think you needed protection on the way to our office?" he asked.

"I filled my editor in on Mary's concerns. She was scared. And when you called me and told me she was dead…" Tess brushed her hair back. "It seemed more than a coincidence. My boss encouraged me not to take any chances."

"Your editor is?"

"Elgin Taylor. He's been with the paper for a long time."

"Did Mary say she was afraid?" Buckler asked.

"No. But it was in her body language. We'd met for coffee. She spent the whole time wiping the table, shredding her napkin, or stirring her coffee, but barely drinking it. She did say the private investigator her boss hired to do research on his competition made the hair on the back of her neck stand up every time he looked at her. I was worried for her."

"What's his name?"

"Sullivan. Henry Sullivan."

It was subtle, but the two detectives glanced at one another before Detective Hart wrote the name down in his notebook.

She needed to do more research on Sullivan.

Buckler continued. "What kind of information did she give you?"

"She had discovered her boss had access to the bids submitted by competing construction companies for the Ellison Project."

"Why do you think she came to you instead of going to the police with her concerns?"

"I think she was looking for a way to get someone to investigate her boss without having him suspect her of blowing the whistle."

"Why didn't you contact the police?" Buckler asked.

"During our interview I urged her to notify you about the bidding irregularities. She told me if she did she'd lose her job. That they'd know she was the one who alerted the police. She wouldn't speculate on what it might cost her if she was right about everything else. So, I promised her I'd do a little research. The nature of her suspicions could trigger some really big problems for Chanter Construction, and if she was seeing shadows instead of facts…" Tess shifted in her seat, uncomfortable. Would it have made any difference if she'd called the police immediately after Mary left?

"What else did she say?"

"She thought her boss might have blackmailed Jason Hamilton into pulling his bid. And she thought he might have also been responsible for the accident at the Brittain Construction site which killed two men."

Buckler and Hart both shifted forward in their seats. "Did she give you any specific information to back up those allegations?"

"No. She was still looking for proof. After she left me at the coffee shop I went to do a couple of interviews for another story. I turned my phone off while I was busy. As soon as I'd finished those interviews I called to check on her, but it went to voice mail. But she'd left a message on my phone while I was out of touch. She said she thought she was being followed and that she'd call me later."

"Do you still have the message?" Buckler asked.

"Certainly." Tess got the phone from her purse on the desk. She turned up the volume, opened the message and played it for them.

She had encouraged Mary to meet with her. The weight of responsibility rested heavily on her shoulders, her heart. Had she pushed too hard for the story? But Mary had approached her, not the other way around. They had just met. What had she found that could have caused someone to kill her? Or had it truly been just a horrible accident? Was she jumping at shadows now? Had Mary been chasing imaginary shadows?

Mary's soft voice came through the speaker and Tess looked away from the detectives and swallowed as the urge to cry welled up. "I think someone followed me when I left the café. Or it could just be my imagination. But I'm a little afraid. I've sent you the information you needed. It included background checks on the employees as well. I've deleted every email I've sent you from the server, just in case. And I found something else. I'll get it to you as soon as possible." Mary gasped. "Talk to you later."

Brett reached for her hand, and for a moment their gazes met, his dark with concern. Her tears eased back.

"It sounds like something startled her," Detective Hart frowned.

"Yes," Tess agreed.

"And this was the only voice mail she left you?" Buckler asked, his hazel eyes sharp with inquiry.

"Yes."

"What time did it come in?"

Tess picked up the phone. "Five-oh-two in the afternoon. She must have been getting ready to leave the office. What time was the accident?"

Buckler and Hart exchanged a glance. "The call came in about five-forty," Buckler said.

What had Mary been doing during those forty minutes before the accident? Had she been aware someone was after her? Had she been in a panic? Or had this been a terrible accident caused by someone uninvolved with Chanter Construction? She wouldn't know until the police did their job and found the car that had crushed Mary's vehicle. If they ever did.

"We'd like to get a court order to get a copy of her voice mail. We'd prefer a direct line of custody from your phone service in case we need to use it later to build a timeline," Buckler explained. "Would you cooperate with that?"

Giving them access to her phone seemed an invasion of privacy and a threat. Some of the sensitive messages she'd received lately—When he noticed her silence, detective Buckler looked up. She chose her words carefully. "As long as that's the only voice mail you ask for. Mary is…gone. If her message can help catch whoever killed her, I'm willing to give you access. But I have the expectation of privacy for myself and several people I've interviewed lately. In particular victims of a crime I've interviewed."

"That can be stipulated," Buckler said.

"I'd like a copy of the paperwork before it goes to the judge." Tess held the detective's gaze. "So I can see the scope of what you're asking for."

The detective's brows climbed and he studied her for a moment. "I'll see what I can do. Have you received any packages from Miss Stubben?"

She had wondered what Mary had meant that she'd found something else. Had she had the presence of mind or the time to hide it somewhere? Tess would have received it by now if Mary had mailed it. "No, of course not. Otherwise I'd have mentioned it."

"If you do, please contact us," Buckler said.

Tess studied the detective's expression. They hadn't discovered anything in the car. They'd be less excited about the voice mail if they had. And less thrown by the information she'd shared. At least now they'd be on the lookout for something in Mary's possession. And they'd be looking at her death as more than just a hit and run. Could Mary have taken the something she'd found home before her death? Or had she unearthed more data on her computer?

"I'd like to go back over your interview with Ms. Stubben at the café. What was the scope of your discussion?"

Tess closed her eyes, visualizing each moment of the meeting. When she opened them, she described how Mary had behaved after entering the coffee shop. How she'd glanced around her as she sat down, her gaze sliding from one person to another. How her hands had trembled as she placed them palm down on the tabletop. They'd spoken for a few minutes about their backgrounds while the waitress took their order and served their coffee. When Mary talked about her boss and her suspicions, her breathing quickened, anxiety pinched the corners of her eyes, and her nervousness increased.

For twenty minutes Tess shared her observations and repeated every word she could remember of the conversation. When she was finished, her muscles were cramped with exhaustion, as if she'd gone on too long a run. She sank back in her chair and grasped the hand Brett extended.

Detective Hart sat back as well. "Do you have a photographic memory, Ms. Kelly?"

"Not quite. Two weeks from now I wouldn't be able to tell you in as much detail, only the highlights. But I'd still be able to describe Mary's behavior. If the person I'm talking to seems at ease, I write everything down and take copious notes during an interview. I've tried using a digital recorder, but that either freaks an interviewee out or makes them stilted and self-conscious. I couldn't use either with Mary, so I was at my most observant."

"Have you written about your interview with her?" Buckler asked.

"Yes. That afternoon in the car I jotted down some notes right after the interview. Then that evening when I arrived home, while it was fresh in my mind, I fleshed out my observations and impressions. When getting it right means publishing a story or not, I cover all my bases."

"We'd like a copy of your notes."

She didn't mind giving them a copy of her interview with Mary, but Taylor might have a problem with her sharing her work product, and she did, too. They needed to gain their own insights. "I can email those notes to you tomorrow from the office."

"Thank you." Detective Buckler stood to go, and Hart followed.

She and Brett stood as well. Buckler extended a card to her. "If you think of anything else, please let us know."

"Certainly."

Buckler was half way out the door when he turned back to face her. "We'll do all we can to find out what happened to Mary Stubben. The Feds will find out who blew up your car; they're good at what they do." For the first time a small hint of humor lightened his normally somber expression. "Don't quote me on that." His gaze turned intent. "But in the meantime, I'd suggest you give Chanter Construction a wide berth, Ms. Kelly. We'll be investigating these allegations about the construction bids."

Of course he didn't want her doing any kind of interviews while they were investigating. "I'll take that into consideration, Detective."

Buckler's eyes narrowed and his jaw tensed. "We appreciate your cooperation, Miss Kelly. I'll be in touch."

"Thank you." She closed the door and locked it behind them.

Brett turned her to face him. "I've seen that look before, Tess. What are you planning?"

"I won't interfere with their investigation. But I have my own ideas. I'll be going at this from a different direction than they probably will."

"And that is?"

"What I'm known for, the human element."

"That's what saved my butt when you helped me."

"I can't save Mary Stubben, Brett." The pain and guilt for the small, soft-spoken woman burned inside her. "If I hadn't encouraged her to meet with me, she'd still be alive."

He shook his head and ran soothing hands down her arms. "You can't know that."

"Not for certain but—"

"*She* made a choice to try and get at a truth she believed in. *She* chose to take the risks." He hesitated. "Just as you're doing now."

"It's my job."

"Yeah. Covering the news. Not investigating it. I can't tell you to stay on the sidelines. Not when your investigation and your dad's dug out the truth about my own situation." He took a breath. "All I can do is protect you, if you need me to."

He stood against terrorists, drug cartels, and other bad guys to keep the nation safe. And now he was volunteering to do it for her. She slipped her arms around his waist and leaned in against him. If she put him at risk and something happened to him… "Maybe I'll back off and let the police do their thing."

"Maybe you can manipulate them into giving you a scoop in exchange for your cooperation. You're not really going to give them everything you have, are you?"

Tess shot him a look.

He grinned. "Didn't think so."

# CHAPTER SEVEN

**B** RETT STRETCHED HIS legs out, propped his feet on the coffee table, and pretended to focus on the television screen. Though the talk show droned in the background, he had one ear cocked for Hawk's arrival and the other listening to Tess while she circled from one area of the apartment to the other. Briefly his attention was captured by a report on Afghanistan. How many morning programs had he watched in the last seven years? Not many. He'd been too busy training, on post and off. And working to get back to where he'd been before the coma.

He needed to learn to relax and just enjoy, not necessarily the inane show on the television, but…the moment. And just being with Tess.

Though his eyes were on the screen, his attention returned to her as she paced and chatted with her boss about the police detectives' visit the night before.

Listening to her describe her interview with Mary Stubben in such detail… Tess had noticed more about the woman in those few minutes than he probably had absorbed about people in weeks. She had a real gift. She'd been exhausted after the detectives left the night before, jittery and anxious, although she'd tried to hide it. He'd done what he could to sooth her by holding her until she went back to sleep.

Tess slid in next to him on the couch and glanced at the screen. "You're really not into that, are you?"

He looped an arm around her. "I was just thinking how amazing you are."

She smiled. "You're supposed to think I'm amazing. You're going to marry me."

"I'm serious, Tess. You have something special. You really see people. You really hear them. One day you'll earn a Pulitzer or something."

Her burnt sienna brown gaze settled on his face for a moment, then skittered away.

"What is it?" Brett asked.

She drew a deep breath. "Nothing. You said that with such conviction." She rested her head against his shoulder.

"I believe it."

"I could win a Pulitzer as a freelancer, couldn't I?"

Freelancer? A sinking sensation struck his stomach. He studied her expression. "Are you thinking about doing that after we're married?"

"It's just an idea. Dad has made a living that way."

And Ian was gone as often as Brett was, possibly more. The newsman had been from Pakistan to Paris in a week's time when they'd last spoken. Could Tess handle that kind of nomadic existence? Could their marriage? Jesus...could he handle it? He'd worry about her constantly.

Just like she probably did about him.

But hoping she'd stay in one place while he hopped from one global hot spot to another wasn't fair to her, either.

"I want you to do what makes you happy, Tess. I know you need to have more than just me in your life. Especially when I'm asking you to take on—"

She covered his lips with her fingertips. "Since this car thing happened, I just—it makes you think. It was a fleeting thought. I know my strengths and weaknesses. I'd go crazy waking up in a different hotel room, alone, every morning. I need a home. Stability."

Stability. What was stable about having a husband who was gone for ten months out of every year? A husband who could be transferred during any rotation? Or deployed at a moment's notice? Jesus, what was he thinking asking her to put up with that?

Or was something else going on here? Since the police interview, though she had remained composed, she'd been more than wound up. There was something else going on with her, something he couldn't quite put his finger on.

"You don't have to be afraid, Tess. I won't let anything happen to you."

"I'm not afraid. Well, maybe just a little. I haven't been out since I got home from the hospital. I'm a little anxious about how I'll react to going outside."

Of course she'd be anxious. Any civilian would be after what she'd been through. The way she'd been able to recall every detail of her interview with Mary Stubben, she must be doing the same thing about seeing her car blow up. "Why don't you write about the explosion, Tess?"

"The police asked me not to. And Taylor assigned another reporter to the story."

"I mean, write how you feel about what happened to you. You focus on the human element...well you're human and you're the one who experienced it."

"Do you talk about the things you go through?" she asked.

For a moment the face of the last cartel thug he'd taken down flashed through his mind. Damn, she homed right in on exactly what he didn't want to talk about. "I've been through psyche evals, but no, we don't normally talk about it."

"Then how do you deal with it?"

"It's part of our training to think in terms of mission, training, reconnaissance, and targets. We don't let it get close, Tess."

"And when you're the target?"

"You don't give up or give in. You keep fighting until you have nothing left." *You don't give up until you're dead.* But he couldn't say that to her.

He needed to guide her away from that line of thinking. "Hawk will pick us up and drop us at a car rental place, and we'll get a car a little more low-key than my Mustang. I'll be with you all day while you do your thing. The cops will do theirs, and they'll get this asshole. It's going to be okay. While you're busy, I'll make some calls and find us a rehearsal dinner location."

"And if you can't?"

"We can use Doc's back patio or Hawk and Zoe's back yard. Or Lang and Trish's. Trish won't mind if we pitch in to do some of the housework. I thought about it after we talked the other day. I'm sure one of them will volunteer if we can't find a restaurant. It isn't as though people do the fancy dress thing for the rehearsal anymore, do they? Are we?"

"No, it was just going to be casual family thing at an Italian restaurant." She nestled close. "I might do what you suggested and write about things…later."

Tess's cell rang and she reached for it. "It's Hawk. He's at the door."

A brief knock brought them both to their feet. Brett opened the door to his first team leader and brother-in-law. All six foot four inches of him and a duffle bag filled the door. Hawk stepped forward, dropped the bag, and he and Brett hugged and pounded each other in greeting.

"Good to have you home, bro," Hawk said when he stepped back.

"Good to be home."

"Morning, Tess," Hawk gave her a quick, careful hug. "How are you feeling?"

"I'm okay. Just a little bruised here and there."

"Sorry you have to go through this. The two of you are welcome to hole up with us if you want to. I have a state-of-the-art alarm system on the house, with cameras and everything. Flash helped me install it."

Brett wasn't surprised by the offer, but the thought of putting Zoe and the baby, A.J., in any kind of jeopardy made it unacceptable. "We appreciate the offer, but we're fine."

"I expected to see some cops," Hawk said.

Tess explained, "They were here, but when I told them I was going to be interviewing people for stories today, they didn't want to take responsibility for keeping me protected."

Hawk's brows went up, and he gave Brett a quick glance. "I've brought your sig from the apartment and a vest, a jacket, and I found a shirt you can use. I looked around for smaller vest, but we don't have anything that would work for Tess."

"We'll make do." Brett took the vest from Hawk. He put it on over his T-shirt, then put Hawk's shirt on over it. It bulked him up, but it would work. He shoved his shirttail into his jeans. He slipped on his shoulder holster, checked his weapon, and thrust the clip Hawk handed him into the gun. "If you can give us a lift to the rental car place, we can take it from there."

"I can stick around for a few hours and do reconnaissance to make sure no one follows you to your first appointment. Once you get past that hurdle, you should be clear the rest of the day." Hawk turned to Tess. "Anyone know where you're going?"

"Only my editor," Tess said. "But he doesn't know the order of my interviews."

"Good," Hawk nodded. "I'd mix it up if you can, just to be certain."

"Let's do it," Brett said. He slipped on the jacket to cover the shoulder holster.

"One more thing before we go," Hawk said. "Your mother has set up a family thing tonight. You're expected at our place at seven. You two up for that?"

He should have known it would happen as soon as his feet touched U.S. soil. He knew he should be as eager to see his family and friends as they were to see him, but he hadn't had enough alone time with Tess yet. But the get-together would only be a few hours, and they could slip away.

Brett glanced at Tess and she nodded.

"We're good." Brett said.

TESS READ OVER the arrest report for Daniel Delgado for the third time as part of her preparation for the interview. Maria, his mother, believed her son had been railroaded for something he didn't do. The gang-related activity in the area colored the way cops and the public viewed teenagers. The woman had begged Tess to look into it, and after seeing the arrest report, Tess felt there seemed to be some credibility to what the mother believed. Just maybe.

Brett took the 28th Street exit while Tess punched in the address she'd saved on her GPS. Half an hour later they pulled up in the drive. Brett's cell phone rang, and Hawk's voice came across the line about the time his car cruised by the rear view mirror. "It's all clear. No sign of a tail or anything else suspicious."

"Thanks, bro."

"Any time."

Brett took off his seat belt but Tess grabbed his arm. "I'm not sure it's such a good idea for you to go in with me. It's hard enough to get people to talk when it's one-on-one. Would you mind very much waiting here for me?"

"After I've checked the situation out and escort you to the door," he said, his expression serious.

Just because she felt less hunted didn't mean Brett shouldn't continue to take the situation seriously. He and Hawk had sandwiched her between them all the way to the car. Their jackets did nothing to hide the sidearms and shoulder holsters, or the body armor Brett wore beneath his shirt and Hawk wore outside of his. Tess knew Brett had a license to carry. Now she knew Adam 'Hawk' Yazzie, her future brother-in-law, did as well. The police didn't seem to mind Brett was taking over their protection detail. Though they'd kicked up just a tiny bit of fuss to make things look good and had her sign a form waiving their responsibility.

Tess had fought not to roll her eyes. The two officers who'd stood guard all night had looked a little sheepish when she shook their hands and thanked them. Maybe she should write about that.

"Stay in the car, Tess. I'm going to check and make sure we're at the right house." Brett opened the rental car's door and stepped out. He paused for a moment to scan the street.

He climbed the three steps to the front porch and knocked. A man answered, and for a second or two, he and Brett exchanged words. A woman came to the door and stepped out on the porch to speak with Brett.

Brett returned to the car. He looked over the street again before opening her door. Then he squatted down to speak to her, keeping the door partially closed. "This character, the son, looks like a gangbanger. Are you sure you want to go in alone?"

"I'll be fine. I'm here to interview the mom."

A frown worked its way across his face. "I don't like this, Tess. Why didn't you arrange to meet them somewhere public?"

"When you're talking about your honor roll student son being arrested for armed robbery, you don't want to go over the details in public. Part of what I do is sort out the frustrated venting from the truth."

As she exited the car, he positioned his body between her and the open street behind them. For the first time she realized her future husband was protecting her from a bullet. He would actually take one for her if something happened. A knot shoved its way into her throat and tears burned her eyes.

Brett dogged her steps all the way to the front door. He eyed the tattooed man standing at the door.

She rested a hand on Brett's arm. "I'll be fine, Brett," she said, her tone just above a whisper. She stepped toward the storm door and the man opened it. She entered the house and Tess caught the man's brief smirk before he released the door.

Brett laid a hand on it, preventing it from closing, and stepped into the room.

*Damn it, Brett.* She could handle this on her own.

"Why did you bring a cop with you?" the man demanded.

A policeman? That would burn Brett's buns.

Tess had read about Miguel Delgado, Daniel Delgado's brother. Mostly she'd uncovered information about his arrests and seen his picture. He had been taken into custody a number of times for assault but somehow avoided being prosecuted thus far. His history was written on his face, his body.

At the moment his eyes were narrowed, his body tensed, as if he was gearing up for a physical confrontation.

Brett folded his hands in front of him in a relaxed pose, but his eyes remained on Miguel, the planes of his face controlled.

Tess stepped between the two men. "Hello, Mrs. Delgado. I'm Tess Kelly." She offered her hand to the woman, who stood to one side. "This is Brett Weaver." She shot Brett a frown. She wasn't going to offer any personal information to these people. And saying he was her fiancé would not put a professional spin on this whole situation. "He isn't a cop. I've had some threats to my life recently. He's here to protect me."

Miguel's eyes shifted from Brett, to her, then back again. "What kind of threats?"

"I tripped over some sensitive information, and my car was blown up."

"That was on the news." His brows lifted. "They said it was a terrorist attack." His dark eyes skimmed over her in an assessment. "This thing you discovered, was it true?" he asked.

"I don't know, but I'm going to find out." Tess offered the man her hand. "I assume you are Miguel, Daniel's brother."

He eyed her hand for a moment, then clasped it briefly.

"Please come and have a seat, Ms. Kelly," Maria Delgado spoke for the first time, in a husky voice. "You too, Mr. Weaver."

"I'll need to stay here, Mrs. Delgado, so I can watch the car from your front window, if you don't mind."

"No one will steal your ride from my front door, man," Miguel said, a jeer in his tone.

"Having it stolen isn't my concern, Mr. Delgado," Brett replied, his voice quiet.

Tess caught her breath against the sudden image of her car rising in the air as fire scorched the asphalt beneath it. Would they set another bomb while she and Brett were away from the vehicle? Her fingers tightened around her small notebook.

Brett took a position at the front window and turned his profile to the room.

Tess settled on a couch in the small, neatly arranged living room and faced Maria, a woman in her forties, and her son, a known gang member.

Miguel dove in, swearing his brother Daniel had nothing to do with the market holdup. "It has to be mistaken identity. We all look the same to white people." The hard-bitten man of twenty had tattoos down one arm and was working on the other. He'd tied his long dark hair back in a ponytail, baring his flat cheekbones and pointed chin. Though he only stood a few inches taller than Tess, his body seemed taller with all its lean angles and ropy muscle. His deltoids and biceps worked as he punched his palm with a fist over and over in a show of agitation.

"Miguel." His mother's soft voice held a plea.

In reply he stopped pacing and leaned against the open archway leading into an equally small but clean kitchen.

"Not all white people believe Latinos, Asians, or Blacks look alike, Miguel," Tess said, her tone even. The sharp predatory gleam in the man's eyes brought the tiny hairs on the back of her neck to life. She was beginning to regret coming here. She turned toward Maria. "Let's concentrate on Daniel right now. Tell me about him."

"He's a good boy, Miss Kelly. He studies most of the day, then goes to work at the grocery store from six until eleven each night. He had left the store and was walking home when the police stopped him and put him in their car. They wanted to know what he did with the money, but he didn't have any money, because he wasn't the man who held up the store." Tears ran down her face. "Then they came here and searched my house. He was on his way home from the store. He had not been home. Yet, when I got home they were here, tearing my house up, looking for drugs, the money. Anything they could find to arrest him."

Miguel broke in. "They found nothing because there was nothing here for them to find. Daniel is smart. Doctor smart. Everyone in the neighborhood knows it. He wouldn't do anything to jeopardize his opportunity."

"What opportunity?"

Maria spoke, the pride outweighing her tears for the moment. "He's been accepted to University of California on a scholarship. He worked so hard for it. Someone is setting him up to take the fall for this. Maybe someone from another gang."

"Why did the police think it was him?"

"They wouldn't tell us." Bitterness lay heavy in Miguel's tone.

Tess studied Miguel. Could he somehow be involved in all this?

As though he read her mind, his features hardened. "The police already checked me out. I was at a friend's house working on his ride."

If eyes could have been bullets, she'd have been a dead woman. He wouldn't attack her here in front of his mother, but he might later if she pissed him off. Goose bumps marched up her arms, but she tried to ignore them.

"Could they be using Daniel to draw you in, thinking you know who held up the store?"

Miguel shook his head. "They're wasting their time. I don't know who did it. And there's no word on the street. Whoever did this is keeping quiet. But they'll talk, they always do. If I find out who he is—"

Tess cut in. "You'll go straight to the police. Getting the real criminal arrested may be Daniel's only chance to clear his name."

"After I beat the fuck out of him," Miguel said beneath his breath.

"Have you gotten Daniel a lawyer, Mrs. Delgado?"

"He's worthless." Miguel's rage rasped with every syllable. "He went into the interrogation already wanting Daniel to take a plea deal before they'd even charged him. Just because his skin isn't as white as his, because of the neighborhood we live in, he assumed he was guilty."

Tess's wasn't naive enough to interpret everything from their perspective. Buy having spoken to the lawyer herself, she had her doubts, too. She'd check as many facts as she could, and maybe everything would unfold before she wrote the story. But there was enough doubt in her own mind that she felt obligated to look into it. She reached for her billfold and pulled out a business card. "I can't tell you what to do, but this lawyer might be able to help. Call him and see what he says."

Mrs. Delgado bent her head. "Gracias, Miss Kelly."

She spent some time getting names of people she could contact who could tell her about Daniel.

"I need to talk to some of the people you've mentioned who worked with Daniel, Mrs. Delgado. And I'll certainly interview the people whose names you've given me as references. I have to have corroboration for everything I put in my article."

"Will you call me and tell me what you find out?"

"Good or bad. Yes, I will. Also, I'd like to speak with Daniel. If he'll allow me to interview him."

"I will ask him this afternoon." Maria said.

Tess rose to leave. "You have my number. Let me know what he says. I'll speak with you soon."

Miguel was suddenly in her personal space, his brown eyes emotionless and flat, like a shark's. Tess read every year he had spent in the gang, every violent act he had committed, on his face. His voice was almost a whisper. "My mother believes you will help my brother. I do not hold out such hope. You fuck my brother with your story, and you will be sorry."

Aware of movement and little else, Tess staggered back when Brett shoved an arm in front of her to create a space between her and Delgado, every muscle in his body poised for violence. She couldn't read his expression from her position, but his word's held an ice-cold conviction. "Ms. Kelly is under my protection, Delgado. You may be a big fish in this little pond. But you're just another threat to me. You come anywhere near her, and I will take you out."

"Miguel, please." Maria grasped her son's arm, her eyes wide with fear. "She is trying to help Daniel."

Afraid for Brett more than herself, Tess's stomach clenched and prickles of fear raced across her chest and down both arms. She grasped his jacket, but remained focused on Miguel. To show fear would only feed the violence inside him. "I'm not out to screw your brother, Miguel. I just report the facts. Good or bad. If he's innocent, that's what I'll report. If he's guilty, that will be on him."

"Stay behind me, Tess," Brett said, backing toward the door. Though both hands remained at his side, he was poised to deal with Delgado.

"Wait," Miguel said. He spoke to his mother. She went to a small cabinet in the room and returned to him with a pad of paper and a pencil. He wrote something on the pad and tore it off. Maria approached them with the sheet.

"Call that number if you need help," Miguel said.

Tess treated the note as if it might be laced with poison. He was threatening her one minute and offering her his number the next. She looked at Miguel. "Why?"

"You did not think you were going to walk into my mother's house, the big time newspaper reporter, and be trusted without being tested, did you?" He shrugged. "If someone is trying to kill you, it usually means you've fucked them, stolen from them, or discovered information dangerous to them. You may run into the same problem clearing my brother."

Tess sighed. Why did everyone assume that reporters were like private detectives? The days of Bernstein and Woodward were long gone. In today's world no one could pass gas without five other people reporting it online if it was the least bit newsworthy. And worse yet, print papers rarely got the scoop.

Brett opened the door and stepped out.

He grasped her arm and dragged her close while he searched the street and surrounding area. His jaw pulsed, suppressed emotion in the hardened planes of his face, and his eyes blazed a pale, accusing blue. "Stay behind me until we get to the car."

She followed him as he instructed, settled back into the car, and fastened her seat belt.

Brett got in, jerked his seat belt into place, and started the car. His movements measured, careful, he backed the car out of the drive, shoved it into gear, and stomped on the gas.

In her side view mirror, she could see Miguel standing on the sidewalk, watching them drive away, his arms folded across his chest.

# CHAPTER EIGHT

**B**RETT STRUGGLED TO control the rage that lashed and beat inside his skull. He was incensed with Miguel Delgado for jerking them around with his street gang bullshit. And he was mad as hell at himself for allowing the man to get so close to Tess. And he was furious with Tess for putting them both in the situation for the sake of an interview that could have been conducted in a public setting.

Neither one of them had spoken a word since leaving the house. At the moment he needed it to stay that way. At least until he had his temper under control.

A minute later Tess said, "I need to stop at the grocery store where Daniel worked, and afterwards go to Scribe Mercy Hospital to check on someone."

"Anyone I know?" Brett asked.

"No. A girl who was held prisoner by a human trafficking ring for ten months."

"Jesus—" Brett breathed, and rubbed a hand over his hair.

"She was in pretty rough shape when I interviewed her a couple of days ago."

"This crime beat job is different from what I expected, Tess," he said, approaching the subject as if it was a land mine they'd already stepped on and were waiting for it to blow.

"It's not normally like this, Brett. I get there and scope out the scene, interview one or two bystanders while the police are doing their thing. Then I wait for the information officer to release a statement, go back to the newsroom and check to see if anything further has come in. If it hasn't, I write the story. It's not usually so—" she hesitated to find the right phrase, "in your face."

"You don't need the added stress of this Delgado thing after having your car blown up. That guy back there is dangerous."

"I think I got that, Brett."

At her wry, sarcastic tone, he glanced at her. *Damnit.* "What would you have done if I hadn't been there?"

"He wasn't going to attack me in front of his mother. He has more respect for her than that."

"How the—" he cut himself off. "You don't know what he would have done for certain, Tess."

"He was trying to intimidate me, but he wasn't gearing up for a physical confrontation like he was with you when we first arrived."

Brett whipped the car into an empty space between cars on the street and parked. A number of foul swear words worked their way through his mind. Since he and Tess had gotten together, he'd made an effort not to cuss so much in front of her and the other ladies in his life, but the need to voice his displeasure was hard to stifle. "I wasn't going to stand around outside while you were in the house with a violent criminal."

"I understand. And I appreciate your need to protect me. And I love you for it. But this is what I do, Brett."

He understood what she was saying. She had to accept that he faced danger on a daily basis. But she put herself at risk for a string of words people would read and dismiss in a matter of days.

"The girl who's in the hospital, I wrote a story about how these two monsters took her off the street and forced her into prostitution. They beat her brutally and often, raped her, then sold her to other men. Those men abused her so badly she cut off her emotions till she had no will of her own."

She half turned to him, her gaze piercing. "If telling her story keeps one girl from walking down the street at night and putting herself at risk, then it was worth whatever I had to do to get the story and tell it. If that story encourages judges to pass harsher sentences on these animals, then I did my job. If that story encourages one policeman to really look at the woman he's arresting for prostitution and ask if she needs help, then something good came out of a horrible situation."

Tess sat back again, taking a deep breath. "If this woman was brave enough to tell me her story, then I had to be brave enough to write it. It was horrible and ugly and heart-wrenching. And it needed to be told so all the people who read it and are touched, or horrified, or sickened by it, might gain some understanding. Maybe even do something about it."

He threw up an impatient hand in surrender. "Okay...all right...I get it. I'm not trivializing what you do." But he had been. "The thought of you putting yourself at risk drives me crazy. You're working three very controversial stories at the same time. Dangerous stories. And if I weren't here with you...you'd be doing it alone." He swallowed against the rush of emotion that lodged in his chest. "I don't want to lose you, Tess. The thought of that..." He shook his head. He couldn't go there.

"But you are with me, Brett." She grasped his arm and, laying her hand against his cheek, turned his face so he would have to look at her. Her brown gaze, dark with emotion, delved into his. "I have to live knowing you face danger every day. The least you can do is accept that on rare occasions I may have to do the same. Langley realizes Trish has to deal with enraged parents when their children are taken from them. Hawk has to accept Zoe works with the stressed-out post-traumatic patients who may not be stable. My job for the most part is trying to liven up dry information released by the public relations officer at the police station. But when a story falls into my lap I'm not going to ignore it."

With every word, the nails of worry and concern were hammered into his brain and heart—worry about her, Zoe and Trish. Everything she said was true. He and the other men couldn't do a damn thing to protect the ones they loved from what they encountered in their work. Hell, Zoe had almost been killed at the physical therapy wing at the hospital. Brett rested his wrist across the top of the steering wheel. If he loved her, he had to accept this and learn to live with it.

The alternative wasn't even something he could contemplate. And it could be worse. She could be pushing to do freelance assignments.

His eyes strayed to the street and he let the silence stretch between them. "I think we may be close to the grocery store where

Daniel Delgado worked. Ready to go there?"

Tess relaxed back against her seat and rested a hand on his thigh. "That would be perfect."

Brett checked the street, then merged into traffic and circled back down a couple of side streets until the store came into view. At least he could be reasonably sure she wouldn't be in danger wandering the isles of a grocery store. Until she started asking questions.

THROUGH THE WINDSHIELD Tess watched as Brett scanned the parking lot before coming around to open her door. He stood close beside her as they walked to the grocery store and hastened inside.

Tess breathed in the fresh, green smell of produce and her stomach growled. "I'm going to get a few things, like we've just come in to shop."

"I'll get the cart." Brett strode toward the carts only a few feet away.

When he returned, Tess looped her arm through his while they turned right toward the produce section. "I don't think we've ever shopped together. How are you at clothing stores?"

He shot her a deadpan look. "I'd rather have bamboo shoots hammered under my fingernails. That's why they issue me uniforms."

Tess laughed. "I happen to know you do on occasion wander inside a store to buy jeans, shorts and T-shirts."

"Babe, a man's idea of shopping is going into a store, picking out five pairs of pants or shirts of the same style in different colors, then double-timing out of there as quickly as possible."

Tess shook her head at him. "I'd never have guessed you have such an aversion to shopping. You always look well dressed."

He grinned. "I'll tell my mom and sisters you approve, since they're the ones who dress me."

"Really, Brett." She let out an exasperated breath, then caught his smile and wasn't really sure if he was shining her on or not.

A woman was stocking the vegetable cooler with fresh broccoli. Tess focused on her. "I thought we could use some fresh vegetables for a salad. I'm going to talk to her."

"I'll do some lettuce reconnaissance and give you some time."

She shook her head again. Only Brett could turn a shopping trip into a mission. She slipped up next to the woman and reached for some broccoli flowerets from the bin she was stocking. "These smell fresh."

The woman, who looked to be about twenty years old, smiled. "They just arrived this morning."

Tess reached for a plastic bag and put four stalks into it. "I read about the robbery in the paper. I hope everyone is recovering from the scare."

The woman's smile wavered. "Yes. Everyone is fine."

"Were you here when it happened?"

Every expression that flitted across the woman's face was so open, her relief was easy for Tess to read.

"No. Thank goodness."

"I heard it was an honor roll student who robbed the store."

"Daniel Delgado was arrested. But I can't believe it was him. He's always been one of the best workers here."

"Why would he do it, then?"

"He wouldn't. Whoever it was wore a mask."

No one had said anything about a mask before. "Did someone recognize his voice?"

"I don't know. It was Mr. Gordon, the manager, who said it was him." The woman looked close to tears.

Tess nodded. "I'm sorry your friend is in trouble. But it sounds like there's some doubt about the manager's identification. It may never go to trial."

"I hope so. Daniel wouldn't do this."

"Look, I'm a reporter with the San Diego paper. I'm very interested in this story." Tess plucked a business card from her purse and offered it to the woman. "I know one of the employees was there with the manger when it happened. I'd really like to talk to whoever it was. If Daniel is getting a raw deal, maybe I can help get the truth out there. Why don't you give my number to the other employee and have her, or him, call me."

The woman hesitated for a long minute. "I'll see she gets it."

TERESA J. REASOR

Tess murmured a word of consolation and wandered back to Brett.

Why would the police arrest Daniel if the perpetrator had been masked? How had the manager identified him if his face was covered? Did he have some kind of identifying mark the manager recognized?

Brett raised his brows in inquiry when she reached him.

"Curiouser and curiouser." She filled him in on the conversation.

"Something doesn't add up, does it?" Brett commented.

"No. But the woman wasn't here when the robbery went down and she's just repeating gossip. I'll need to speak directly to the manager who was here that night."

"Let's wander around to the customer service department so you can set up a meeting," Brett said.

Tess studied the buggy's contents. It contained every vegetable in the department. "I didn't know we were really going to shop."

"After weeks of MREs, I had a craving for fresh vegetables. We can drop them at my apartment before we go to the hospital."

He'd consumed the stir-fry she'd fixed the day before like it was candy. The thought brought an ache of emotion to her throat. Tess slipped an arm around his waist and leaned into him. "Okay. I'll fix a big salad for lunch and we'll get a rotisserie chicken from the deli. Let's go pick one out."

They circled around to the deli and got the chicken and some sweet Italian bread, and then headed for the customer service department.

"I'll go pay for this while you're busy," Brett said and pushed the cart toward the checkout line only twelve or so feet from the counter.

"Mr. Gordon isn't here right now. He'll come in about five, if you want to come back." The assistant manager tag the woman wore on her jacket identified her as Leslie Hill. About forty years old, Ms. Hill had streaked blonde hair pulled into a ponytail and wore a flowered blouse tucked into dark blue slacks, with a navy jacket.

Tess produced her business card. "I will be back, possibly tomorrow. I'm looking for some information about Daniel

Delgado's work history with the store."

Leslie Hill's lips compressed as she studied the card. "Daniel was an exemplary employee. He never missed a night of work, and he often trained new employees. He's worked in every department."

"In your opinion, do you believe he was the man who held up the store?"

"I wasn't here. I can't state one way or the other. Mr. Gordon said he was."

"So he was able to identify Daniel even though the robber wore a mask?"

"So he said."

"How?"

She shrugged. "I don't know. You'll have to ask him. The police must have believed him, though, since Daniel's still in custody."

"And Daniel's brother is a known gang member who has avoided prosecution several times in the past."

"We all know Daniel's background."

"Yet you still hired him?"

"He had excellent letters of referral from three of his teachers."

"And?" Tess encouraged.

The woman remained silent for a long moment, then finally volunteered, "If you're providing a livelihood to family members, the gang is less likely to cause issues with the business where they work."

"Yet the boy who has every reason to avoid trouble, who has a scholarship to University of California in the fall, just decides to hold up the store?"

Leslie's lips compressed once again and she leveled her gray-green gaze at Tess. "That's what Mr. Gordon said."

And he identified him despite a mask. "Does Daniel have any identifying marks on his hands, arms, or face?"

"No. Mr. Gordon will be here at five tomorrow, too, if you want to talk to him about the robbery."

"Thank you. Just one more thing, is the other witness here today? I'd like to interview her."

"Antonia hasn't come back to work since the robbery."

Tess nodded. It would have been traumatic to have a gun stuck in her face. The arrest record said armed robbery, so it had been either a gun or a knife. She'd need time to recover. Maybe she could find the woman's address and go to her home. "I'll be back to discuss this with Mr. Gordon." Tess offered the woman her hand and they shook.

She met Brett at the exit. He had positioned himself so he could watch her, but be out of the way of customer traffic. After she'd given him a rundown of their conversation, Brett said, "Maybe you shouldn't have warned him you were coming tomorrow."

"She won't tell him. She doesn't believe it was Daniel who held up the store."

"Why do you think that? It sounded like she spouted the party line."

"Gordon is not a beloved boss to the rank and file. Both the women I spoke to have a tone in their voice when they say, 'Mr. Gordon said so.'"

"He's probably an ass. What about the other employee who was a witness?"

"She hasn't been back since the robbery. I'll have to hunt down her info and talk to her at home. It may take some time for me to get her name. I've left my card for the manager and gave one to the girl in produce. She promised to pass my number on to the witness."

"You've done everything you can, Tess. Let's go get the groceries put away and I'll take you to the hospital." He put an arm out to stop her from walking forward. "It would be safer for you to stay here among the customers while I go out and check the car and put the groceries in the trunk. Then I'll park in front of the door and come in and get you."

"Are you really afraid they'd try and do something in a grocery store parking lot?"

Brett's expression grew grave. "If I weren't, I'd allow you to walk out with me. Had one of the guys from my old team been available, I'd have them riding along with us. I'm not taking any chances with you, Tess."

Her stomach and heart spiraled downward and she pressed her hand against her midriff. She'd been trying to block out the seriousness of her situation. Brett would confront whatever they faced head-on. He'd station himself between her and any harm. "I'll go stand right over there." She pointed to a spot close to the registers, out of the way of the customer traffic. "I'll be able to see the car pull up."

"Don't come out. Let me come in and get you."

She nodded. "Okay."

She grasped his arm as he turned away. "I know you deal with things like this all the time, but just knowing you're putting yourself between me and anyone who would hurt me—" Tears blurred her vision. "I should lock myself in the apartment until things are resolved."

Brett studied her face. "You can't give up your life, babe. When you do that, the bad guys win." He kissed her. "I'll be back."

But if something happened to him because of her, she'd never be able to live with herself.

# CHAPTER NINE

**B**RETT SCANNED HAWK'S back yard, taking in the group of people who'd come together to welcome him home. The rush of back slaps, handshakes and hugs had passed and they'd settled down to breaking bread pretty quickly. The smell of grilled meat still hung in the air, though the steaks, hamburgers, and chicken had all been consumed with the speed of hungry locusts. The men had come in off a hard training day with appetites to match. Someone had started up an MP3 player with a personal collection of songs. Blues drifted on a breeze that was just now turning cool.

Langley's three kids, Tad, Anna, and Jessica took Joy, Flash's girlfriend's daughter, inside to play video games while the adults hung out in the back yard.

During a quieter moment, Brett's thoughts lingered on these men, friends he'd served with for nearly four years.

Bowie, the Latin lover of the unit, had surprisingly arrived solo, although he usually had a date for every occasion. He stretched back in a lounge chair talking to Kelsie Tyler and Greenback. Greenback who cuddled his new baby boy, Micah, against his chest and adjusted a blanket around him with loving care.

Langley and Hawk seemed deep into discussion with Jeff Sizemore, the new sniper of their unit, and Jack Logan, their communications specialist. Hawk held A.J. in the crook of his arm and periodically rubbed the toddler's back. The twenty-month-old sucked his thumb while Hawk did what Zoe called his daddy dance, the dip and sway motion he used to sooth his son. The child was nodding his way off to sleep in a hurry.

Where had the time gone? When he'd left A.J. was barely walking, and now he was running around like a speed demon, talking clearly enough for him to figure out what he was saying. His favorite word was *no*.

The makeup of the team had changed with the loss of Brett and Flash, and Derrick Armstrong's implosion. New members had been transferred in to take their places. But it was more than that. Because of Hawk's marriage to his sister Zoe's, he'd have been transferred out anyway. The way the change had come about had delivered more of a punch than a gentle nudge out of this team and into the next. He still had moments of regret, and homesickness hit him hard on occasions like this. Their original unit had a special bond.

Arms slid around his neck from behind and a soft, familiar cheek pressed against his. "Get enough to eat?" Clara asked.

"More than enough, Mom. I'm full as a tick."

"Good. I'm so glad you're home."

She didn't have to tell him. She'd teared up the moment she saw him and held onto him for nearly five minutes. He patted her arm.

"Tess is as tough as you are. She's going to be fine." Clara brushed her lips against his cheek.

"I know. She's doing good. I'm making sure of it."

"If you two need anything, just give me a call."

"Will do, Mom, and thanks. Love you."

She slipped away and settled next to Russell Connelly on the glider. She rested her head against his shoulder and he ducked his head to press a kiss against her temple.

Though being in a coma for two months hadn't been on Brett's to-do list, he *had* survived, and a lot of good things had come out of it. Had Zoe not come to stay with him until he shook free of the coma, she'd have never met Hawk, gotten married and had A.J. Had he not been Russell's patient, he and his mom might never have met. Though they weren't married yet, he could see things were moving in that direction.

And he might have never met Tess.

His gaze strayed to her and the other ladies, Zoe, Trish, Selena, Samantha, and Sizemore's date, Madeline. The women had congregated at one end of the patio in lawn chairs. Their periodic bursts of high-pitched laughter punctuated the rumble of men's voices.

Maybe things did happen for a reason.

"You look thirsty, dude." Doc smacked a beer bottle dripping with condensation into his hand and slouched into the lawn chair diagonal to his. Doc's smile, and his wide, Irish, freckled face triggered an answering grin from Brett.

"I can always use a beer."

"I thought so. How's it going with the new team?" Doc took a swig of his own brew.

He owed this man his life. He had kept him alive until they'd been airlifted to safety. Had he ever thanked him? He'd make damn sure he did at some point. "I'm settling in and getting to know the guys. They're a good team, motivated, professional. You'd like Frank Denotti, our medic."

"I've met him at one training or another. Italian, sings opera, and strong as an ox."

"You got it. Though he didn't do much singing this tour."

Flash wandered out of the house from either a bathroom break or checking on the kids. He pulled a chair up beside them. Brett extended a hand and they bumped knuckles. "How you doing?"

"I'm good. I kind of know what you mean now about working your way back, Cutter. It's a bitch, but I'm getting there."

"What team are you assigned with?"

Flash grinned. "Team seven. Same as you."

Brett punched him on the shoulder. "Excellent. We may get to work together again."

"I hope so. Though I'm still dealing with the repercussions from my…" he paused, "…forced sabbatical, I'm finding my way."

Being on the run for nine months from a drug cartel and a crooked FBI agent had ripped into Flash's career path with a vengeance. But he'd get back, twice as strong.

"One day at a time, brother," Brett said by way of encouragement.

"I hear you."

"Did you get that pay SNAFU worked out?" Doc asked.

Flash dangled the neck of his beer bottle from between his

fingers. The stiffening breeze ruffled his blond hair and threw it forward across his forehead. He shoved it back. "Well it took a while for them to decide I was still alive. Then they voided my pay for the nine months I was gone. Which I understand and accept. I wasn't here to do the job, wasn't here to back up my unit, so I deserved it. Then they gave me back pay for the months I've been back in action, so I'm good." He threw up a thumb. "The only bad thing is, because of how things went down, everything that happened will probably follow me from now on."

Since that came on the heels of his earlier thoughts, Brett felt compelled to say, "There's another way of looking at it, Flash. You did what you're trained to do. You tracked and did reconnaissance on a drug cartel and an FBI agent with terrorist ties...and took them down all by your fucking self, bro. That has to count for something."

Flash ducked his head, clearly embarrassed. "Well, not entirely by myself. By the time I sent the third or fourth report, they'd already set up surveillance of their own which locked Gilbert in a cage. Had I known that, I'd have come in sooner." His facial expression tightened. "That fucking FBI agent Gilbert played me from the beginning. He had orders drawn up that looked legit and I bought into the whole thing. Had I bothered to really look at them, instead of accepting them at face value, I might have recognized they were bogus."

"Is that what the FBI said?" Doc asked.

"No. But—"

"But nothing. If Rick Dobson had approached any of us, we'd have taken on the job," Brett said. "He was a good guy, a good agent. If Gilbert could snow him, his partner, what makes you think you should have suspected anything? You're going to have to lay this down and move on," Brett said. "One foot in front of the other, man."

The smile that stretched across Flash's face held a cockiness more natural to him. "You're right, most wise and powerful sage." He did a rolling motion with his hand and bent low at the waist.

Brett laughed, then raised his beer to him and took a drink. "We're both lucky. We've both gotten second chances. I wonder how rare that is."

"Probably nothing short of a miracle. I really didn't think I'd come back from this. I figured I'd be doing some serious prison time." Flash's gaze wandered past him to Samantha. "There was a chance I'd never see Sam or Joy again." He turned back to them. "Just waking up to them every morning is like hitting the lottery, guys, only better."

Brett was amazed at the way Flash shared his feelings. He'd been the quietest member of their unit and always kept his own counsel. But apparently a close brush with a court martial and prison time could change a man. Or was it Samantha who'd done that?

For a moment Tess's question about how they dealt with the danger, the things they witnessed, played through his mind. They turned to each other because there was a bond between them fashioned through shared experiences, beliefs, and trust. A shared brotherhood. He was going to have to extend that to her, be her sounding board and support, unless she opted to see a professional therapist.

Brett changed the subject. "I have a problem, guys. The restaurant we had scheduled for the rehearsal dinner had a fire and we're SOL on a venue. I called ten restaurants today while Tess was busy at the office and struck out at every one of them. Any suggestions?"

"Antonio's?" Doc said.

"Already called. No go."

The two fired more suggestions at him. Brett took out his phone and noted the ones he hadn't already tried.

"If a better venue doesn't work out, there's always the patio at my place on the beach, though the breeze off the water this time of year can be a bitch," Doc said.

Brett grinned. "So noted. Thanks. But only as a last resort. I'd prefer someplace inside."

The wind picked up a notch, kicking the plastic tablecloth up and out like a tutu on a ballet dancer. The women rose in force to gather the dishes and plates and take everything inside.

Hawk ducked inside with A.J. Doc followed for a bathroom break.

Flash scanned the area around them and then leaned forward in his chair. "I need to tell you something, Cutter, and after I do, if you want to deck me, I'll understand."

An uncomfortable pressure built along Brett's spine, as if a sudden weight rested on his shoulders. "Jesus, Flash. I can't imagine what it is, but it can't be as bad as you're making it out to be."

"While you were in a coma in the hospital, I was trying to juggle the team stuff and the crap the FBI guys wanted me to do for them. The whole time I had this bad feeling in my gut, like I might buy it with every meet I did for them. I was feeling the pressure. Big time pressure, and I really needed to talk to someone. But I couldn't let anyone know what was going on with me.

"So, I snuck into the hospital and into your room. I spilled everything to you, though you couldn't hear a fucking word I said. Or if you did, you didn't wake up. I really needed you to know what was going on, Cutter. You were like the fucking father confessor of the unit. I got worked up and I slapped your cheeks, trying to wake you up. I must have hit you harder than I meant to, and I left a mark. Zoe's probably told you about the mark. Everyone thought it was Derrick for a while, but it wasn't. It was me."

Brett remained silent while he processed what Flash was saying.

"I'm not going to make any excuses. I just want to come clean. Coming back from all the crap I got twisted up in, I just have to make amends for everything that went down before I disappeared and while I was gone. I want everything to be squared away with you and the others."

In the grand scheme of things, what did one little slap matter? The guy had saved his life more times than he could count. "It's okay, Flash," Brett said. "I've gotten worse bruises just horsing around with you guys. You're making a mountain out of a molehill." Had Zoe not told him about the incident when he woke up, he'd have never known it had happened. He'd suffered no lasting damage. But it sounded like Flash had been carrying some big-time guilt about it, and he totally understood how that worked. "Lay this down, too, brother."

"I wish I'd told you everything before our last mission," Flash said.

Brett laughed.

Flash frowned. "What?"

"I wouldn't have remembered if you had."

Flash's face blanked. "Jesus, Cutter."

Brett laughed again. "It's okay. I remember the weeks before." And he remembered the stock of an AK-47 swooping toward his face, and his attempt to jerk out of the way, but not one thing about the mission itself. He believed Derrick Armstrong had been the man swinging that rifle stock, but he couldn't be certain.

"So we're good?" Flash asked.

Brett nodded. "Yeah, we're good." He extended his hand and they shook.

Flash got to his feet. "It's a school night, and Joy has to hit the hay, and Papa Flash is bushed. I'll see you at the wedding rehearsal if we don't get together before then. And If I think of any other restaurant suitable for the dinner, I'll call you."

"Thanks, Flash."

Brett walked over and checked the grill, then paused to shake hands and say good night to the rest of the group as they went into the house to gather dishes and other belongings before they left. He made a point of hugging Selena Shaker. Her resent close brush with cancer had been a wake-up call to most of the guys in steady relationships. Including himself.

"So glad you're doing well, *piccola madre*."

Selena smiled and hugged him. "I'm doing great. I'm even getting my hair back." She swiped at the bangs of her wig, which looked much like her own hair, but short. Though she had always had long, thick hair, the new style suited her. "I won't have to wear this much longer."

"Good. I thought about you and Greenback a lot."

"I appreciate it." She patted his arm. Lucia, their daughter offered him her fist, and he chuckled as he carefully exchanged a knuckle bump with her.

Greenback gripped the baby carrier cradling his son, Micah, in one hand and shook Brett's hand with the other. "I'll see you at the bachelor party."

"I'm counting on it."

His mom grabbed him around the waist and hugged hard. "We're going home. If you need us for anything, just call."

"Thanks, Mom. Love you."

She began to tear up again, as she had when they'd first arrived, but fought it off. "Love you, too."

He shook Russell's hand and murmured good night.

Bowie grabbed him and pounded him on the back. "I'm cutting out. Glad to see you, Cutter. You are missed."

Touched by the other man's sentiment, Brett smiled. "Thanks, Bowie. Homesickness cuts in now and then, but it's good to be back to work."

"I never doubted you'd be back. I'll see you at the bachelor party." He loped up the stairs.

The sentiment triggered by Bowie's words brought to mind how far he'd come since being reassigned. It was time to tell Tess about the promotion. He had to warn her before it came through. Would this current situation cancel things or stall them? He didn't know. But if it happened, it would mean more responsibility, possibly more training, more time out in the field. She was going to love that. *Not*. Dread struck his stomach.

# CHAPTER TEN

**T**ESS PERCHED ON the top step waiting for Brett. All evening, while she'd been laughing with the other women she'd also been gearing up to tell him about the Washington Post job. She'd made up her mind to do it tonight, then reassure him she was good with turning it down.

When he appeared at the bottom of the steps her heart danced into a heavier beat and nerves tightened her stomach. "You've been quiet all night, something wrong?"

Brett shook his head and sat down beside her. "No, it's been good to see the guys. I've just been thinking about how different things could have been and how similar."

Tess looped an arm around his back. "I know this last year and a half has been tough. I also know you still miss your old team."

"Yeah, I do. But I'd have had to transfer out once Hawk and Zoe got married anyway." He planted a soft kiss on her forehead. "And again when I'm leader of my own unit."

She leaned back to look up at him. "Soon?"

"Maybe. Before I left Senior Chief Engle told me I'm up for a promotion. He said the paperwork was in the works. How would you feel about being married to a Lieutenant J.G.?"

A dropping sensation lurched in Tess's stomach. After gearing up to tell him about her own job offer, the pain—and possibly a little resentment—cut deeper than she wanted to admit. His career was moving on while hers would be stalled here. Or would it? She had to make up her mind. She was going to be married in less than three weeks. "Congratulations. I know how hard you've worked for this."

And at this moment, no way could she ask, *and while we're on the subject, how would you feel about being married to a Washington Post reporter?* She'd both steal his thunder and throw him into the same tailspin of guilt and conflict she continued to experience.

Though a lump settled in the pit of her stomach, she cupped his face and brushed her thumb along his cheekbone. "I think you're going to look fantastic at the wedding in your dress whites with your new insignia. And I'll love you just as much no matter what your rank."

Brett's lips brushed hers, then lingered just long enough to give her that buzz down below that melted her bones and made her want to groan. Tears burned her eyes, and she turned her cheek against his shoulder to hide them.

"It'll mean more money. And maybe we can rent a house, so we'll have room for you to have an office, someplace you can work without me underfoot."

If only he wasn't always thinking about how he could make up for his absences, how he could take care of her, it would be easier to be mad. "That would be good." It wasn't his fault her job offer had come at a time when his career was just getting back on track. But it still hurt.

"The lease will run out on my place in a couple of months. I can put my stuff in storage until we decide what we want to do."

Her throat ached. "Sounds like a plan. You don't think you'll go stir crazy living in my small apartment with me?"

"Babe, I live with seven other guys, sometimes more, in close quarters, for days, sometimes weeks. This will be a cakewalk."

Though she'd never felt less like doing it, Tess laughed. "I'll remind you of those words when I'm manic over a story, pacing the room and constantly on the phone doing interviews."

"It's going to be fine. We'll figure it out."

But would she?

Brett stood and offered her a hand up.

They said their goodnights to Langley Marks and Trish, who were still busy gathering their three children's paraphernalia. Tess hugged both Hawk and Zoe and thanked them for hosting Brett's welcome home get-together.

"Any time," Hawk said with a smile.

"I need to check the car, babe" Brett said, and slipped down the hall with Hawk to watch the evening's videos to make sure no one had touched the vehicle.

"He's trying to act cool about all this, but he's worried about you." Zoe lifted her heavy hazelnut-streaked hair from her shoulders and pulled it back into a tail with a scrunchy from the pocket of her jeans.

"Did he say something?" Tess asked.

Zoe shook her head. "He wouldn't say it to me because he knows you'll ask. He'll say it to Hawk."

"And you'll get it out of Hawk?" Tess guessed.

Zoe flashed her a smile. "If it's important."

Tess fought off the urge to tear up. "You're the best almost-sister-in-law a girl could have."

Zoe laughed and hugged her. "We'll soon be sisters. I already feel like we are."

"Me, too." She'd been a rock for Tess the whole time Brett had been gone. When the loneliness and worry had gotten to be too much, Zoe and her mom were there. Which added another special twist to the whole job/family thing. She adored Brett's family.

When they finally walked out the door, the wind had settled down some, but there was a nip in the air. Tess tugged her heavy sweater closer while Brett opened the car door for her, then jogged around.

The silence settled between them for a few blocks.

"How many restaurants did you call while I was at the office today?" Tess asked.

"Ten. I got some more suggestions from Flash and Doc tonight. And Doc volunteered his back patio on the beach."

Tess smiled. "Zoe volunteered their house. Said we could set it up buffet-style in the dining room and bring in more chairs. Or the back patio like tonight."

"That's my sister. But Doc's holds a special meaning. It was there we first danced together."

Surprised by his sentimentality, she blurted, "Guys aren't supposed remember stuff like that."

"I remember every moment. I wanted you so bad—I felt like

93

I'd done a five-mile run full out and couldn't catch my breath."

In the blink of an eye the ache eased and she rested a hand on his thigh. "I thought you were dangerous to my heart."

Brett grasped her hand and raised it to his lips. "Never dangerous, honey. I'd take better care of yours than I would my own."

God, how had she ever managed to resist him back then? And she certainly couldn't now. She laced their fingers and hung on all the way home.

BRETT TRIED TO keep his mind off sex. Tess was still moving slowly, and she didn't need any pressure from him in that direction. But the instant she'd rested her hand on his thigh he was ready. To keep his mind off that, he concentrated on scanning the parking lot until they reached the entryway.

Inside, he stood back and waited for her to unlock the apartment door.

"Let me go in first and check the place out, hon" He pulled out his Sig.

She shot him a surprised glance. "Okay."

He halted inside the living room, every sense alive to movement or scent. Nothing triggered the prickly, hyper-alert feeling he usually got when he sensed danger. Before he allowed himself to relax, though, he did a quick walk-through, then returned to the living room. "It's clear."

Tess closed the door and locked it. "Did you really think they might make it inside the apartment complex?"

"I'd rather be safe than sorry." He laid his Sig on the end table, shucked his jacket, and slouched on the couch.

Tess slipped off her heavy sweater and joined him there. "In case you haven't noticed, it's later."

"Later?" he echoed.

"Yes, it's later."

Understanding shot his pulse into the stratosphere. "It is?" Jesus, he sounded so hopeful it was embarrassing.

Tess laughed. "Yes."

"How does your back feel?" he asked. He wanted to make love with her, but he didn't want it to be painful.

"My back is fine."

She had that tone in her voice he loved, soft, breathy, and sexy as hell. He could almost get off just listening to her speak. Almost.

She ran her hand beneath his brown T-shirt and caressed his stomach and chest. Blood rushed south and he hardened.

His need level went from DEFCON 5 to 1 in a heartbeat as she swung her long leg over his and straddled his lap.

"I love you, Tess."

She framed his face with her hands and looked into his eyes. "Every time you say it I want to tear up. I love you, too. More than words can say." She kissed him. Her lips parted, and his tongue slipped forward to coax hers into playing. He lifted the hem of her sweater and ran questing hands up to cup her breasts. Her skin felt like silk, her breasts, still covered by the gauze, fit his hand perfectly, and her nipples went taut at his touch. Her hips moved against him in a way that made his body hum with anticipation.

Brett skimmed his lips along her throat, then her collarbone, just above the sweater's neckline. "I love it when you do that lap dance thing, but I want to be in a nice bed stretched out with you so I can worship at the Tess shrine for a long, long time."

She laughed and made short work of tugging his T-shirt upward and off. She ran her eyes over his chest and abdomen and focused on the bulge beneath his pants. "Your cammies pants aren't working. They're not hiding a thing."

"You're not the enemy, honey. As a SEAL I can't surrender, but you could try to persuade me."

She grinned. "I've missed you so much." Her arms encircled his neck while she nibbled one of his earlobes.

Her warm breath sent shivers down the back of his neck. His erection strained against his zipper. He raised her sweater higher and pressed his abdomen against hers, relishing the feel of her bare skin against his. "Bed, Tess." Now it was urgent.

"Okay." Her grin was mischievous as she slipped off the couch and offered him her hand.

Careful of her back, Brett nestled her against his side as they kissed their way to the bedroom. He lost no time stripping off his clothes, and then stretched out to watch her disrobe. Tess turned on the bedside lamp, she preferred its softer light, and flipped off the overhead switch before wiggling free of her leggings and sweater. Her long legs and torso gave her body a sleek grace he never tired of admiring.

When she hooked her thumbs under the elastic of her panties Brett sat up. "Let me do that."

SHE'D BEEN SHY about letting him see her without her clothes because of the bruises, scratches and scrapes. But now, with him lying there naked, vulnerable, so completely aroused, all that dissolved. The tenderness and love she read in his face brought a knot of emotion to her throat and a wave of guilt. She needed to tell him about the job offer. But not now.

As he shifted above her and his lips found hers, her heart lifted to meet the soft, brief touch of his kiss. She reached for him, eager for his body to rest atop hers, and to experience the slow slide and friction of him moving inside her.

He rested his hand between her breasts, his touch warm through the gauze. He grazed her nipples with his fingertips while he skimmed his lips across her cheek. "We have to be careful of your back, but I want to be on top this first time."

He positioned himself between her legs. His arousal pushed against her, but the barrier of her panties blocked his entry. She dragged air into lungs suddenly starved for oxygen and bit back a groan.

Though he avoided the bandages, Brett pressed warm, moist kisses along the edge of the gauze while he kneaded and caressed her breasts.

Then he went on to taste and touch his way down her stomach, almost tripping her over the edge before he ever reached the apex of her thighs. She caught her breath as his thumbs slipped under the crotch of her panties to part her nether lips. He blew against the fabric, his breath tickling, warming, arousing, making it impossible for her to stay still. She clutched the comforter beneath her.

"Brett." Had she ever been this aroused?

She hauled in a ragged breath of relief when he tugged her panties down and off. When he rubbed the head of his penis against her, she tilted her hips to urge him inside.

"God, Tess, I'm not going to last a nanosecond," he breathed.

"I'm not either, come inside me." She rotated her hips, forcing him deeper.

He sank into her with a sigh.

Tess caught her breath. The sensation of him filling her, sharing her body, was like finally being complete. It happened every time.

"God, honey. You feel so good." His mouth caught hers for long, slow kisses. She caressed his back and curved her hands over his shoulders, holding him close.

The need to move captured them both. All the hunger of separation overwhelmed them. Tess forgot about her back, forgot everything but him. She cupped his hips and matched his rhythm. The harder he thrust, the wider she opened herself to him, taking him as deep as she could, until they were rocking against each other, fused as tightly together as they could get.

As he swelled and hardened even more, nearing his release, her own climax tumbled over her, projecting a wave of sensation out to her fingertips and toes.

Sensual tingles still lingered when she opened her eyes to look up at him. A slow, satisfied smile crossed his face. Still poised above her, he dropped his head to rest in the bend of her neck.

"Do you know how sexy the sounds you make are when we're making love?" he asked. His lips caressed the soft spot behind her ear.

Heat flared in her face. "I don't make any sounds, I'm too busy trying to catch my breath." She ran a caressing hand over his bare, muscular buttocks. "You're the noisy one."

He laughed and started to ease away.

"Not yet." Her arms tightened around him.

Tess ran her palms up his back and over the back of his head, feeling the texture of his close-cropped hair, then paused to knead the back of his neck.

"I'll give you fifty years to stop that." He groaned when her fingers discovered a particularly knotted muscle.

Tess smiled and kissed his cheek. A few minutes later, Brett eased out of her, and she sighed with regret as their bodies parted. She tugged the sheet up over them both. He lay behind her and pulled her in to spoon with him. Wrapped in his arms, she found security, completion, and so much more.

"It's so good to be home," Brett murmured, and within a few minutes, his breathing leveled out and he dozed off.

Tess turned to study his features in the light from the bedside lamp. The dark circles beneath his eyes had lightened some since he'd had enough sleep the night before, but lines still bracketed his mouth. He'd just come off a mission when he rushed home to be with her. Though he couldn't tell her about any of the things he did, she knew his specialty as a sniper put a great deal of pressure on him.

But he loved what he did. Felt compelled to serve. His father's service as a Marine had impressed him and encouraged him to enlist after college.

Tess pulled the sheet up over his bare shoulder and turned to nestle back against him. She had to make a decision. She either had to talk to him about the Washington job, or set it aside completely and let it go.

Brett's reaction to her mentioning the freelance idea... He would sacrifice his needs for hers. She knew he would. If she wanted to take the job he'd encourage her. But the chances their marriage would survive with him on one coast and her on the other were slim. She knew that.

If she took the job, there would be no need for a wedding.

There. She'd put it out there so she could face it. As much as they loved one another, this would tear them apart. Because as little as they got to see each other now, it would be worse with him in California and her in Washington.

What did it say about her that she was struggling with this decision?

Why was she even tempted?

She'd have to move all the way across the country, to a city she'd visited as a tourist but knew nothing about as a resident. She'd have no contacts to call on when something important happened.

Was she still so hung up on following in her father's footsteps she'd risk her future with Brett? And more important...did her love for him lack some crucial element?

When she thought of how he made her feel when they made love, no, there was nothing that could be better than when they were together. But coming off a ten-month separation, she needed to give them some time to settle back in.

It was the way of it each time he was gone.

"What are you thinking about so intently?" Brett asked, his voice thick with sleep.

She turned to look over her shoulder at him. "A little bit of everything. My mind won't quiet down."

"Want to talk about it?"

"No. I just need to relax." She turned the bedside lamp off. The soft nightlight in the bathroom cast a dim glow, but not enough to disturb them.

"You've had a rough week, Tess. You need to cut yourself some slack." He ran a caressing hand down her lower abdomen and slid her back against his erection, his lips sliding along the crest of her shoulder. "I could help you relax," Brett breathed against her ear, sending shivers down her entire body.

She moved his hand up to her gauze covered breast and pressed her ass back against him. He was a good man, a wonderful lover, and he loved her. Those things were more important than a job.

She kept reminding herself of that while he made slow, thorough love to her.

# CHAPTER ELEVEN

NTERVIEWS LIKE THIS were so hard to do. Had she known Lisa Gooding had been moved from the nursing home to her home, she may have tried to come up with a different idea to talk to her mother. Tess's heart broke for the young woman and her mother. Lisa lay on her side, knees bent, her thin limbs folded into a fetal position. When Shelly Gooding spoke to her, she smiled, as infants do. On occasion her legs jerked, or one of her arms, but beyond that she was trapped in the bed, held hostage by her damaged brain.

After the accident, her physical and mental capabilities had regressed to those of a twelve-month-old baby, no, actually younger, since she was unable to crawl and had to be turned and cared for constantly. The trauma to her body must have stunted her growth as well, for the girl in the bed couldn't have been more than four feet tall or weigh more than eighty pounds.

Shelly Gooding wiped her daughter's cheek where a thin stream of saliva ran to her neck. "She's a good girl. No trouble at all. She loves music, and I play CD's for her all the time. I do PT with her every day to try and stretch her muscles and keep her joints limber. And we take a walk every day." Shelly brushed away a strand of her medium brown hair with the back of her hand and tossed the Kleenex into the garbage can next to the bed. She was an attractive woman of forty-five, but her daughter's tragedy had aged her in ways that were visible, not so much on the outside, but beneath the skin. Her hazel eyes held a look of love and resignation. "Well, she sits in her stroller and enjoys the ride while I push it, of course. I think the fresh air is good for her."

"I'm sure it is, Mrs. Gooding. She's beautiful," Tess said, her voice husky with emotion. Lisa Gooding *was* beautiful. She had large, hazel eyes, and thick black hair tied back in a braid. Her small, oval face had a Madonna-like innocence that scored Tess's throat with raw compassion.

Tess scanned the room, taking in its neutral simplicity. It was a hospital room for all intents and purposes, with all the paraphernalia that went with long-term care. A large machine of some kind sat in one corner. A butterfly mobile hung over the bed and occasionally Lisa's attention snagged on it. There was a picture of her mother and father taped to the railing of her hospital bed within her visual range.

Tess swallowed against another rush of emotion. She had to get on with the interview. "I read back issues of the news coverage about the accident and, of course, the criminal trial of Alan Osborne, as well as the civil suit."

Shelly's expression went blank. "Brian was determined the man would pay one way or another. He was angry for a long time. He's still angry."

"Could some of that come from feelings of guilt that he wasn't hurt but she was?"

"I'm sure it does. He felt so helpless to do anything about it, or for her."

"As I told you, I'm writing this article to document what happens to a family when they're faced with a catastrophic loss. Your family won't be the only one I interview." There was truth in that. Although she'd settled on this subterfuge to interview Shelly Gooding, she intended to write a piece concentrating on the repercussions of drunk drivers. If her editor didn't want to print it, she'd shop it around.

"That will be a good thing. If people can learn they aren't alone it sometimes helps."

"Did you and your husband do any kind of therapy to help you deal with things? Join any kind of support groups?"

"I did. Brian wouldn't go. He was busy trying to get back to work. His therapy was to find ways to make Osborne pay."

"I can understand that. The man was drunk, and he destroyed your daughter's future."

"I understood it. Agreed with it to a certain extent." Shelly touched Lisa's hair. "But he became obsessed. He's better now."

"Now that the object of his rage is out of reach?"

"I guess you could put it that way. When we found out Osborne had died it was like he was relieved it was finally over." A frown furrowed her brow. "I hope they're both at peace finally."

"What does your husband do for a living?"

"He works construction. He's worked for Chanter Construction for fifteen years. Would you like to go into the kitchen and sit down, maybe have some coffee or some iced tea?

Guilt pricked Tess. There was something underhanded about breaking bread with this nice woman, even if it was just a glass of tea, while she dug around in her ex-husband's life. But if she was going to write about what had happened to Lisa, their family, and rule Brian Gooding out of any involvement with the Brittain Development Groups accident, she had to ask questions. "Iced tea would be nice."

They settled in the small kitchen at an oak table just big enough for two. French doors led out onto a back patio and a small yard with a six-foot privacy fence. Well-placed patches of lilies bloomed around the edge of mulched sections of carefully tended landscaping.

Shelly followed Tess's gaze to the patio and smiled. "Brian did that for Lisa. She seems to like the bright colors. He's placed bulbs so there's always something blooming for her. And he bought the lounge so she could lie out there for a few minutes each day during summer months."

"May I take a picture? Tess asked, because she just had to step away to get a grip on her composure.

"Certainly."

Leaving her shoulder bag hanging on her chair, Tess stepped outside, blinking hard and breathing deeply. The sky was a clear blue, without a cloud in sight. The sun had burned off the chill breeze lingering from the night before and the temperature was climbing to seventy. The yard had a peaceful feel to it. Bird feeders stood in the center of an open patch of yard where the birds' activity could easily be seen from the patio lounges. Tess stepped outside and snapped a couple of pictures with her phone.

Though they were divorced, Shelly and Brian Gooding obviously cared a great deal about each other and their daughter. They had gone through hell together. It had torn their marriage apart, but their solidarity in caring for their child was everywhere she looked, here and inside the house.

"It's wonderful out here."

"Yes, it is," Shelly agreed.

"He did a beautiful job, Mrs. Gooding," Tess said.

"Please call me Shelly. And yes, Brian's good at building things, doing landscaping and repair work. He should have been an architect or a landscape artist." She led the way back into the house and busied herself pouring glasses of iced tea while Tess took a seat at the kitchen table.

"May I take notes?" Tess asked and, at Shelly's nod, took out a small notebook. When Shelly sat across from her she began with a question. "You're both so completely invested in Shelly's care..."

"Why aren't we together?" Shelly finished for her.

Tess nodded.

"I had to move on from the accident and Brian couldn't. I had to find a place where I could face the everyday reality that was going to be my life and Lisa's. Brian couldn't do that, either. He was still stuck at that moment when Osborne's car slammed into ours."

"Do you think now that the man is gone, you might find each other again?"

Shelly gripped her glass more tightly but didn't drink. "I'd like to say we will. We've never stopped loving one another. He stops by every day. He's not like some fathers would be. Once the marriage ends, the child is pushed aside or replaced with one from the next marriage." She took a deep breath. "We've both dated other people. But it hasn't taken for either of us. It's also still very difficult for him to see her, accept that she'll never walk or talk again. Never be married and have a husband and children of her own. The pain may never ease enough for him to come back to us."

Tess was amazed at how candid the woman was about her personal life. How horrible for her and Brian Gooding to still love one another and be separated by such a chasm of pain and guilt. It put them both in limbo. Clearly Shelly would take him back, if he could just accept living with his daughter every day.

"Do you think the time Osborne spent in prison was enough?"

"No. If our justice system set up penalties that fit the crime it might be more healing and beneficial for the victims. I wanted Alan Osborne to live. I wanted him to pay for Lisa's care for the rest of his and her lives. I wanted him to have to see her at least once a week and think about her and acknowledge what he had done. But justice isn't really in any lawyer's vocabulary—or the judges', either. They're all about the money and a quick fix. That quick fix ran out a year ago, before Osborne got out of prison."

"What did you do before you had to bring her home?" Tess asked.

"I was a paralegal. I made good money, but I was never going to be a millionaire. As long as the settlement money lasted and her Medicare paid for some of it, we could reach the sixty-five hundred a month necessary to keep her in the nursing home. I was there every day, as was Brian. I was still able to work. But now that the settlement money is gone..." she shrugged. "Private care costs thirty-two thousand a year, which was more than I was making. So I work from home four days a week, doing research, and care for her myself. We're okay."

"Did you like your job?"

"I loved it."

"And your husband? What changed in his life?"

"Brian subsidizes my income and makes the payments on this house. He lives in a small, one-room apartment close by. We live month to month. Lisa gets a small Social Security check, and that helps with her diapers and similar, smaller things."

"What does Brian actually do in his position at Chanter?"

"He's the construction manager. He goes from job to job."

"How supportive where they when this happened?"

"Very supportive. He put in a lot of extra hours after court dates and that kind of thing at first. And now he still does. It takes a lot to keep two households running."

"I imagine his job is high-stress too, dealing with problems on the site."

"Yes, it is."

"What did he think about the recent accident on the Brittain Development Group site?"

"He was upset. He said it was a company's and a manager's worst nightmare when something like that happens."

Would Brian Gooding even make a comment to his wife about it if he was involved? And did he have anything to do with Alan Osborne's death? The death had been ruled an accident, and it was even speculated that it had been a suicide. But Osborne had been sober for the seven years in jail as well as for the one year he had been out of prison. Why would he suddenly fall off the wagon? She'd have to look into whether Gooding had contact with Osborne after he'd gotten out of jail.

After a few more minutes and a few more questions about Brian, Tess asked about Lisa's long-term prognosis. "Her kidneys are failing, and because of her condition, they won't put her on a transplant list. We do dialysis here at home, but eventually it will kill her."

Reeling from the woman's words, Tess swallowed and managed, "I'm so sorry."

"She's not in any pain. If she were, I wouldn't be able to bear it. I'm just making her as comfortable as possible and giving her as complete and enjoyable a life as I can. We both are."

Tess nodded. She gathered her purse and stood to go. "I think I have as much information as I need. I appreciate you seeing me and being so open about your situation and Lisa's. I promise not to share the more private things we've talked about. I'll send you a copy of the article when I'm done with it."

"Thank you." Shelly rose to see her out. "I hope it does some good for other families."

"I hope so, too." Tess shoved her notebook into her bag.

Tess texted Brett, who was waiting outside in the car. When Shelly opened the door, he was standing at the bottom of the wheelchair ramp that ran parallel to the house.

Tess shook Shelly Gooding's hand and said good-bye.

"Tough interview?" Brett asked.

Tess's nodded. Her composure dissolved and her breathing hitched while tears ran down her cheeks.

Brett frowned and hurried her to the car. He held her for a brief moment before opening her door and urging her inside. He went around and got in. "Do you want to tell me about it?"

Tess looked through her purse for a tissue. "In a minute." She kept her head bent to keep Brett from seeing how upset she was.

Brett put the car in gear and backed out of the driveway. He drove down to the next block, then pulled over. She was grateful he gave her time to beat back the sobs and the tears that insisted on falling.

"Their daughter is dying. Her kidneys are failing."

"Jesus!" he breathed.

"She's completely disabled. Like an infant." She told him everything she and Shelly Gooding had talked about. "I don't want Brian Gooding to be involved in the Brittain Group thing. And he may not be. But I really think he had something to do with Alan Osborne's death. He was obsessed with the man, and then, a year after Osborne gets out of prison, he dies suspiciously in a motel room of alcohol poisoning?"

"You can't do anything about the choices people make in their lives, Tess. Especially after they already acted on those decisions. If Brian Gooding did play a part in either of these things, he made the decision to do it."

"You didn't see Lisa Gooding in that bed and you didn't see the heartbreak in Shelly Gooding's face. They never had a chance to move on with their lives after the accident. Gooding was obsessed with the fact that Alan Osborne was still alive, still living a life, while his daughter wasn't. Now that the man is dead, Shelly says he's better."

"You aren't responsible for policing Brian Gooding's actions, Tess. If the police ruled Osborne's death an accident or a suicide, they obviously didn't think there was anything suspicious to follow up on. Just because you have a gut feeling about something, doesn't mean you have to pursue it. You can walk away from this story."

Could she walk away and live with her suspicions about Gooding?

"Lisa and Shelly Gooding wouldn't make it without him. It takes everything both she and Brian have to keep going. If something were to happen to him—" She was silent a moment. "But three people have died because Chanter wanted a bid, Brett." The horrible tug of war inside her cramped her stomach with dread, and she pressed a hand against it.

She needed to do the best job, the most impartial job she could as a reporter and concentrate on covering the story.

Brian Gooding loved his wife and daughter. Though they were divorced, he still cared for them financially, physically, emotionally. The factors keeping them apart were so painful she couldn't even think about them without wanting to weep again.

Seeing their suffering first-hand only pointed out the inconsequentiality of her own situation. Why was she allowing something as unimportant as a job to drive a wedge between her and Brett? And she was doing that. She was holding back from him at a time when she should be reaching out to him for support and comfort. Despite the fact he was operating in bodyguard mode and ready at a moment's notice to step between her and a bullet, a bomb, or any other kind of threat. What did that say about her as his future wife?

She was holding him responsible for a decision that was already inevitable.

It had to end.

But just for a moment she wanted acknowledgement for the accolade the offer represented. She focused on his face. She searched for the words.

# CHAPTER TWELVE

T HE BEST THING to do when you were emotionally compromised during an op was to get right back into the action. He'd been there himself. "Okay. Where to?" Brett put the car in gear and looked over his shoulder to pull into traffic.

Tess hesitated and he glanced in her direction.

She took a deep breath, a frown knitting her brows, eyes moving back and forth as if she was thinking something through. A second later her expression relaxed. "Back to the grocery store." She brushed her hair back from her face. "I did some research on Ronald Gordon in preparation for my interview. He's fifty-five and has worked for the same corporation for the last twenty-five years. He has two grown children. But what is most interesting is he has a nephew who's been in rehab and jail numerous times. The last time he was arrested for robbery but hasn't gone to trial yet. His family bailed him out."

"How did you find out?"

"A social media site."

"Do people—" he stopped, "Why would they put personal info like that out there for everyone to read?"

Tess shrugged. "I went to his wife's page and hooked up with her."

"You have a social media page?" Brett couldn't imagine it.

"I do now. She doesn't know me, but she accepted my request."

Brett shook his head.

"I looked at some of her pictures. She had some of the nephew

TERESA J. REASOR

sitting at a table in the yard. It had a caption with it, so I had his name. With his name, I found a newspaper article about him being arrested several times and charged. So I went on line and accessed public records and got his sentencing details. He's got a record for writing bad checks, has stolen from his family, and broken into homes and businesses. He's just turned twenty-one. If he's arrested again he'll do hard time, especially since this time the guy stuck a gun in someone's face. If he was the one who did the robbery, he's escalating. He might kill someone next time."

"You could get a job as a private detective, Tess."

"No, thanks. The only reason I do background checks on some of the people I interview is a fellow reporter got burned last year when he did a series of interviews with someone who, as it turned out, wasn't who he professed to be. When people started coming out of the woodwork to identify the guy it pushed Max's credibility into the dump. What I'd like to know is why Daniel's public defender didn't even attempt to find out any of these details. He'd have access to more information than I do, and could easily have discovered the same things. If he presented this information plus the mask thing, and the fact Daniel had no money or gun, the cops wouldn't have a case."

"So, you think Gordon's nephew did the job and Gordon blamed Daniel, knowing his brother's a gangbanger and thinking the cops would be on board with that scenario?"

"His nephew is the same general height and build. I'm holding off making a judgment, though, until I interview Daniel and Gordon."

"Confronted by a guy in a mask with a gun pointed in his face, a regular guy wouldn't be looking at anything but the weapon. Unless there was some recognizable identifying mark, or gesture that stood out to help him identify the gunman."

"He either noticed that something or he has some other motive for fingering Daniel. I don't know. I hope I can figure out if Gordon has an agenda, or if he truly believes Daniel did it."

"Do you need me to be bad cop in the room or make myself scarce?"

"I won't know until I meet Gordon." She rested a hand on his thigh. "I kind of like having you as my sidekick to talk things through with. I'm getting spoiled."

Brett laid his hand over hers. She deserved a little spoiling after their months of separation and the lingering aftereffects from the bombing. She was more emotional right now. Or had she always been but hidden it from him? How many times had she cried over the people she wrote about in the safe, isolated, confines of her car and never shared it with him? With anyone?

But he couldn't imagine her doing anything but writing and reporting. She'd even gotten up in the middle of the night and written stories. She loved her job.

How many times had he thrown out a brief, dismissive comment when she shared some detail or observation about a story she was working on? And why had she let him get away with it?

Because she was used to receiving the same treatment from her father. Used to being abandoned for months at a time by Ian, and now by him. On top of it, he had been serving her up the same bullshit Ian did. *Jesus.*

He couldn't do anything about his absences, but he could do better than Ian Kelly about everything else.

And now that he was aware of this huge screw-up, what the hell else had he missed?

He remained silent for a moment. "I think you're doing exactly what you are meant to do, Tess." He glanced at her. "I understand now why you can write about people the way you do. You just take them in while you're talking to them. I know that probably causes moments of pain, like with the Goodings."

"Sometimes. I have to force myself to keep my distance."

"It isn't distance you keep, honey. I don't know exactly what it is. You just reach right in and find the heart of them—of their story. I know I don't say it often enough, but I am proud of you, of your writing."

A smile, slow and warm, lit her face, and he was glad he'd said it. "Thanks, Brett." She glanced away, then returned her attention to him. "Is there some reason you're buttering me up?"

He laughed. "No. But come to think of it—"

"What?"

"I sort of invited all the guys from my new unit to the wedding, if they're back in time."

"Okay."

"We'll probably need to call and let someone know we'll have a few extra."

"No, I settled on an even two hundred to leave us a few more spots just in case."

"Good." He grinned. "Rosenberg thinks you should be a Victoria's Secret supermodel."

Tess laughed. "No, thanks. I like being behind the scenes, not the center of attention."

"You know you'll be front and center on our wedding day, right?"

She grinned. "I guess I can endure it for a few hours."

"You may want to invest in some steel toed high heels. If they come, they'll all want to dance with the bride."

Tess smiled. "I'll try not to maim any of them, either."

Brett chuckled. "They're tough, they'll be okay."

FIFTEEN MINUTES LATER, when they pulled into the grocery store parking lot, Tess attempted to set aside the emotions from the Gooding interview, which were still tying her stomach into knots.

Brett hadn't denigrated what she did for a living, but in the shadow of his own job, he'd never given her reason to believe he thought it was as important, either...until today. In the last couple of days, he appeared to be finally getting it, getting her.

Though the stories she'd written two years ago had helped him and his team, they'd been overshadowed by her father's international scope. She'd been basking in her father's reflected glory for so long, she just wanted some of her own.

The three stories she was working on right now could prove important to her career. If she couldn't do Washington, she could damn sure do San Diego. If she discovered proof Brian Gooding had been involved with a man's death, she'd have to report it to the authorities, as well as write about it.

Brett was right, she couldn't be anyone else's conscience. But damn she didn't want Brian Gooding to be a bad guy.

Brett got out of the car and came around to open her door. He'd left the bulletproof vest behind today and, since he'd finally been able to pick up some clothes from his apartment, had opted for a navy sports coat to cover the bulge of his shoulder holster. Despite the civilian apparel, the way he stood, the controlled way he handled himself, still shouted military, or cop.

Once they passed through the door to the store, two checkers tracked their progress to the customer service department. One was the woman she'd given her business card to the first day. She made a subtle motion with her hand and Tess cut in that direction to speak to her. "Buy a pack of gum," the woman said under her breath.

Tess picked out a pack of gum from the racks at the woman's station and laid it on the conveyer belt. She slipped a dollar bill from her purse. The woman pulled a piece of paper from her pocket and extended it to Tess with her receipt and change. "I've been waiting for you to come back. Rosalie said she would talk to you on the phone. But she's afraid to meet with you face to face. She doesn't want it to get back to Mr. Gordon that she spoke to you."

"It won't, I promise. Thank you."

The woman nodded, then turned to her next customer.

The man crowded Tess, and she glanced behind her with a frown. She caught a flash of dark hair and eyes and a slight build.

Tess tucked the pack of gum, note and receipt into her jacket pocket and returned to Brett. The two of them moved on to the cage-like structure that housed customer service. A heavyset woman with a thick swath of dark hair pushed aside the paperwork she was working on and approached them. "Can I help you?"

"I'd like to speak to the manager, please," Tess said.

"Is it something I can take care of for you?" she asked.

"No. I'd like to speak directly to Mr. Gordon."

The woman eyed Brett with a frown, then nodded. "I think he's at the back of the store, I'll buzz him."

"Thank you." Tess leaned back against the counter and smiled at the set planes of Brett's face while he scanned the aisles for any threat. She slipped her fingers through his and was rewarded with the one-sided quirk at of his mouth.

"I think this is your guy," he said he tilted his head toward a stocky man walking toward them.

"Yes it is," Tess said, recognizing him from his wife's social media page.

Gordon shoved his glasses up his nose as he approached, his gaze shifting from Tess to Brett and back again.

Reaching them, he asked, "May I help you?"

"Mr. Ronald Gordon?" Tess asked, just to make an official identification.

"Yes."

"I'm Tess Kelly from the San Diego Tribune." She offered her hand.

The man's jaw tensed but he shook her hand.

"This is Brett Weaver, my associate. We'd like to interview you about Daniel Delgado, if you have time."

"The police have told me not to speak to anyone about the robbery."

"I'm not asking to speak to you about the robbery, sir. Only Daniel."

Gordon's brown eyes shifted back and forth again. "What is it you want to know about him?"

"What kind of employee was he?"

Gordon's gaze went to the woman working behind them in the customer service cage. "I think we need to move this to my office upstairs."

Though she was focused on whatever paperwork she was working on, Tess noticed the woman glanced up at her with raised brows.

"That will be fine, sir," Tess said.

Tess followed Gordon to a door positioned just behind customer service and then up narrow stairs. Once they reached the landing, the stairway opened into a hall with several offices. He paused outside one of the doors and gestured her inside. Brett waited for her to find a seat and for Gordon to move behind his desk before he took the seat closest to the door. The room was little bigger than a closet, and had a desk and a filing cabinet.

"I'd like to ask some things about you, first, just for background," Tess began before leading him through a series of questions about his own employment with the store. Gordon relaxed in his chair and eagerly talked about his history with the grocery store chain.

"Now about Daniel. How long has he worked here?"

"Since his sophomore year of high school." Gordon folded his hands on his blotter, arranging his face in a pious expression. "He was a good employee. He hasn't called in sick in a year, and he's never late."

"I heard the robbery suspect wore a mask."

"Who told you that?" Gordon demanded, his jaw taking on a pugnacious tilt.

Tess studied his expression. "If the suspect was masked, how did you identify him?"

"I can't talk to you about the robbery."

"Since you identified Daniel, why do you think he would rob the store he'd worked for over a year?"

"Money, I suppose."

"How often do your employees get paid?" Tess asked.

"Every two weeks."

"Since the robbery occurred on a Friday night, on the thirty-first, wouldn't he have just gotten his paycheck?"

"Yes, but robbing the store would have brought him much more."

Interesting choice of words. Would have...or did? "How much trouble do you have from the gangs in the neighborhood, Mr. Gordon?"

"Not much. A lot of their family members work here. That provides some protection from them. Though it doesn't keep them from coming in and spreading a little fear now and then."

"Daniel isn't a member of any gang, is he?"

Gordon slid forward on his seat. "I don't believe so, but it's well known in the neighborhood his brother is. He's been arrested numerous times."

"I looked into his brother. Why do you think he's never done any time?"

"I think his gang buddies cover for him so the cops can't get the evidence they need. I've heard the gang even pays his court fees when he's arrested." An underlying thread of rage hardened his words.

"But up to now Daniel's always walked the straight and narrow. He has a college scholarship. He's on the verge of being able to escape this neighborhood and take his mother with him. This arrest may make all of that impossible."

Gordon's expression hardened and one side of his mouth lifted. "I can't help that."

"Why would he throw all that away, Mr. Gordon?"

"You'll have to ask him." He paused for a moment. "Maybe his brother's gangbanger ways have finally rubbed off on him." Once again a hair-thin touch of bitterness and anger colored his tone.

"Does Daniel's brother deal drugs?" Tess asked.

Gordon's gaze shifted away. "I wouldn't know, but the gangs do have a reputation for doing that as well as robbing, stealing and terrorizing the neighborhood."

She could say the same thing about his nephew. "Do you think Daniel should pay for his brother's mistakes?"

"His brother wasn't the one who perpetrated this crime, but in my opinion he was responsible."

Tess leaned back in her seat and studied Gordon's face, an idea beginning to form.

"Does your nephew belong to the gang, Mr. Gordon?"

Gordon's face flushed red. He shoved his chair back and got to his feet. "My nephew has nothing to do with this robbery. This interview is over."

Tess's gaze swung to Brett and they stood. Brett stepped back and motioned her ahead of him. Gordon came around his desk and grabbed Tess's arm.

Brett caught the man's wrist and shoved him back against the desk. "You don't want to do that." The flat, steady stare he turned on Gordon projected a controlled violence that shot a skittering alarm along Tess's nerve endings. She laid a hand on Brett's shoulder.

"You print anything about my nephew and I'll sue your paper," Gordon threatened as he jerked away and scuttled backwards behind the desk.

"I print facts, Mr. Gordon, not fairy tales. You can't sue if it's the truth," Tess said, her voice quiet. "Thank you for your time."

BRETT TOOK A deep breath to calm the anger-fueled adrenaline flooding his system. The hand he rested against Tess's hip held her close against him all the way to the car.

"What would you have done if you'd been alone and that creep tried to intimidate you into keeping quiet about his nephew?"

"First of all, I'd have never stepped inside his office had you not been with me. I'd have asked him to walk around the store with me while we spoke."

"Why?"

"When I first came into the store, the woman from produce was working a register. She asked me to buy a pack of gum, and when I did, she passed me a note with the other witness's phone number. She didn't want Gordon to know she gave it to me. And the other witness, Rosalie, doesn't want him to learn she's speaking to me either. If he's intimidated them that much, then I knew he'd try something with me. That's why I introduced you as my associate and wanted you to go upstairs with me."

Some of the tension drained from Brett's muscles. "It drives me crazy thinking you might be in danger from anyone, Tess."

"I'm careful, Brett."

As careful as she thought she was, it only took one asshole to take things to another level. "I'm going to buy you some mace and a Taser."

She laughed. "I can see the headlines 'Newspaper reporter Tasers interviewee to get the truth.'" She ran her hand over his arm. "I know you deal with danger all the time, but we women have dealt with it since the birth of the human species. How often do you look under your car before you approach it? Or look in the back seat before you get in? Or carry your keys between your fingers like a weapon?"

Brett held her hand against his arm. Should he be honest with her? And if he was, would she freak out? "I don't do the key thing, but the rest—all the time, honey. Just because I'm not in a war zone right now doesn't mean I don't evaluate the threat level of every place we go. It's as natural as breathing to me right now. It'll ease off after a while, until the next time I'm deployed. But right now I need it, Tess. Your freaking car was blown up!"

She cupped his face and for a long moment met his gaze. "Do you think I don't know all of that already? I know you have to ease into this world when you come home from the other."

For the tenth time today he cursed the console between them that kept him from drawing her close. He leaned over and placed a slow, deliberate kiss on her cheek.

"We're more alike than you think, Brett," Tess said her fingers resting against the front of his shirt. "I deal with people when they're at their most vulnerable, their most volatile. You focus in on movement around you, I concentrate on the emotion."

Was she shining him on to put his fears to rest? It was working, but anxiety still ate at him.

She pulled a piece of paper from her pocket, along with a pack of gum and a receipt. "I'm going to call Rosalie before Gordon has a chance to get to her. If Daniel Delgado did this, he needs to pay for it. But if it was someone else who held up the store that night, she needs to step up and say so."

"I'll drive while you call. Where do we go from here?"

Tess frowned as she read a text message.

"The Brittain Development Corporation. I have an interview with Nicolas Brittain at three o'clock about the accident and how his company is recovering from it. I have to go to the office before the interview, though. Mr. Taylor wants to see me."

She gave him the Brittain Corporation address and he keyed it into the GPS system and saved it while Tess dialed a number on her phone and waited for it to ring.

With a sigh, Brett started the car and whipped out of the grocery store parking lot.

He listened to Tess's side of the conversation while she questioned Rosalie about the robbery. Though the police had told her not to talk about it, Tess kept circling around the facts until the woman admitted the robber had worn a ski mask and she had seen a tattoo on the man's forearm. Tess spent the remainder of the time boosting the woman's sense of right and wrong to encourage her to withstand Gordon's intimidation tactics. By the time Brett drove in and parked in the lot next to the newspaper office she had concluded her conversation.

Brett exited the car and came around to open her door. "What do you think Taylor wants to talk to you about?"

"I don't know. I emailed him my schedule early this morning before we left the house. Something may have come in that he wants me to cover."

They entered the building and rode the elevator up to the newsroom. The space was alive with other reporters at their desks, phones ringing, and movement.

Taylor looked as if he'd been watching for them and left his glassed-in office to meet them. "What the hell is going on, Tess? I just spoke to an editor from the Washington Post. When did they offer you a job? And why haven't you told me about it?"

The noise in the room died for a second, all but a persistent ringing telephone. For a brief moment Tess froze. Then she jerked her eyes up to Brett's face.

Brett felt like he'd just been sucker-punched in the gut. The Washington Post. *The Washington Post* wanted Tess. One second, two passed and he still couldn't breathe. He cleared his throat and dragged air into his lungs.

"Jesus, Tess!" Fuck Taylor. *Why hadn't she told him?*

# CHAPTER THIRTEEN

TESS FOUGHT THE urge to glance at Brett through the glass that partitioned Taylor's office from the rest of the newsroom. She could feel his eyes on her. She'd wanted acknowledgement for the job offer, but she'd wanted to share it with Brett first, before anyone else. She'd wanted to cushion the sharing with the reassurance that she wasn't going to take the job.

Elgin Taylor had stolen both those things from her.

The shock on Brett's face kept replaying through her mind, even as Taylor's voice cut through the panic bubbling up from the pit of her stomach like lava. Brett was so pissed, so hurt because she hadn't told him.

"When did they call you?" Taylor asked.

"A few days before Brett came home."

"Why didn't you say something?"

"Because I wanted time to think it over, and I really wanted to share it with my fiancée before I told anyone else."

"You hadn't told him yet?"

"Uh, no." It was hard for her to keep the sarcasm and anger out of her voice. "He just got home from a war zone. He's been acting as my body guard because some psycho blew up my car. I just wanted a couple of days to hold on to him, to be in the same fucking room with him." Her composure slipped.

Taylor looked away. "I needed to know, Tess. If you leave, I have to be prepared to replace you."

"I can't leave. He's a—" She caught herself before saying SEAL. "He's in the Navy. He's stationed here. I can't live on one side of the continent while he's on the other. I love him." Just saying those words out loud to someone else carved them in stone for her. "If this is all you need, then I have to go. I have another interview in an hour or so, and I need to prepare." And she needed to try and apologize to Brett.

"Shit," Taylor breathed. "I'm sorry. I know that couldn't have been an easy decision to make."

Tears burned her eyes. "Are we done?"

"You're one of my best, Tess. You *are* my best. I was upset about the idea of losing you."

Now he wanted to suck up to her, after the damage was done. Tess jerked the door open. "I have to go."

"I'll call you if anything else comes in."

She nodded once and stepped out. She scanned the room, looking for Brett. Where was he? Anxiety cramped her stomach and filtered its way up into her chest.

Seth Maxwell, one of the other reporters, brushed by her to go into Taylor's office. "He's in the break room," he murmured. "Congratulations on the job, Tess."

"Thank you." She hurried between the desks to the narrow hall that led to the small kitchen area and bathrooms. The stark, utilitarian kitchen had a soft drink machine, a refrigerator, a microwave, and a sink. Two small tables with four chairs each provided a place to sit.

Brett leaned against the counter and dangled a plastic soft drink bottle between his index and middle fingers. He looked up when she came to the door.

She'd had an opportunity to tell him in bed the night before, in the car just a few minutes ago. She should have told him. Why was it so fucking hard for her to share herself? This was the man she was going to marry, was going to share her life with—forever.

When the silence stretched for five seconds, six, Brett finally broke it. "This is, like, every reporter's dream job, isn't it?"

She took a step into the room. "Not every reporter."

"It's the fucking *Washington Post*. It's the paper that broke Watergate. The paper that covers all the politics and politicians in the country. This is...*huge*."

"They didn't get the story on Senator Welch using his influence to cut funding to certain military units because of his own personal agenda."

"You'd be a secret weapon in their arsenal."

She took another step closer to him. "Not so secret. Because I wrote about Welch's personal loss and the influence he wielded because of it, every Congressman would be on guard against me before I ever asked them a question. They'd be wondering what I had uncovered in their lives that might smack of self-interest. The deck would be stacked against me. I wouldn't have any sources who would be willing to share information with me like I've cultivated here. And I'd have to live in a place that has snow and bad weather five months out of the year."

In the millisecond between Elgin Taylor announcing it to the newsroom and the look on Brett's face, she'd made up her mind, and relinquished the job. She loved Brett. She wouldn't leave him. And she couldn't have both.

"But most important, I wouldn't have you there. Or your family. Or my own. I'd be isolated and alone…and lonely for you."

RELIEF STORMED BRETT'S system, then just as quickly changed to concern. If she passed up this opportunity—it was the *Washington Freaking Post!* He swallowed again, his heart lodged somewhere between where it should be and his throat. "Are you sure this is what you want to do?" He couldn't believe he was asking that. If she did want it, their lives would suddenly become unbelievably complicated. Could their relationship even survive living on two different coasts? They'd never see each other. That thought gave him another kick, and an ache settled in the pit of his stomach.

Tess crossed the space between them. She cupped his face and looked deep into his eyes. "I'm sure, Brett. Completely sure."

A knot settled just beneath his collarbone. He leaned in to capture her lips, then pulled her in close, hugging her. He understood what kind of sacrifice this was. And he'd bragged to her about his own promotion—Jesus! His career was taking off while she had decided to take a huge hit so they could be together.

"Honey—" He ran his fingers beneath her hair, cradled the back of her head and held her as close as he could. Pain made his voice thick. "This offer is amazing. Now that I've gotten to see you in action, know more about what you do, how you do it, it isn't surprising they want you, Tess. Any paper would be better for having you."

There was stress in her tone when she quipped, "I'll use that line on Mr. Taylor when I hit him up for a raise."

Brett smiled, though the ache persisted. "I'm sorry, Tess."

"It's okay. I'm young. There's time for me to do a lot of things with my career. This is just one of them. One I don't want to pursue. I may write a book one day. Work for a magazine. Share a byline with my father like we did last time. That's probably what inspired this offer."

"I don't think they'd have offered you a job on the strength of you sharing a byline with your father. It was your work that made this happen, honey. When did they call you?"

"A few days before you came home. I wanted to wait until you were here and we could discuss it before making a decision. I've been waiting for the right time to share it with you."

"But we haven't talked about it," he said.

She remained silent for a moment, and her eyes dropped to his chest. "We don't really need to, do we? We both know if I took the job there wouldn't be any reason for us to get married. As much as I love you, and you me, there wouldn't be any purpose behind a marriage if we never got to see each other or be together." Her throat moved as she swallowed. She leaned against him and rested her head against his shoulder, more for comfort than in celebration. "I love you, Brett. I don't want what we have to end. So, I'm telling them thanks for the offer, but no thanks."

Heat raced into his face and left his ears burning. Her blunt assessment of the situation sounded distant, analytical, but beneath it there was pain and disappointment. Military spouses had to sacrifice so much. For the thousandth time he wondered why she was willing to surrender her ambitions and dreams to be with him when he was gone so much of the time.

Would those decisions come back to haunt them both later?

An insidious inner whisper broke in that offered him no comfort, *They always do.*

His arms tightened around her. "I'm sorry, Tess."

"I'm not. It's a great honor, a feather in my cap that they wanted me, but I want you more, Brett."

Had he not been a tough as nails Navy SEAL he'd be crying like a baby about now. "I know my job gets in the way, but you're everything to me, Tess."

"If I wasn't certain of that, if I didn't feel the same way about you, I'd give that job a shot." She leaned back to look up at him. "You're so much better at sharing your feelings than I am."

"Honey—" He swallowed against the softball-sized knot in his throat. "I think you just did a damn fine job of it."

# CHAPTER FOURTEEN

**B**RETT PULLED THE car into the parking structure across the street from Brittain Development Group and Tess looked up from studying her notes. That Nicholas Brittain had agreed to meet with her had come as a surprise. Lawsuits had already been filed on behalf of both men who were killed in the accident, and the entire building site shut down until inspectors could analyze and discover what had caused the third floor section to collapse.

"You're not planning to drop a bomb on this guy to see if he'll go after you, too, are you?" Brett asked as they walked to the parking structure elevator.

"No, I'm just going to go for a positive piece and get a feel for this guy. He employs a lot of people. I'd hate to see his company go down because of what someone else has done." Despite the sixty-five degree temps outside, the air felt damp and chilly inside the parking structure, so she pulled her cream-colored jacket closed and buttoned it at the waist.

"Or he could be responsible, Tess."

"Yes, he could." She looped a hand through his arm. "I'm trying to keep an open mind about everything and just get a feel for the players."

Brett glanced at her. "Hard to do when you have everything Mary Stubben told you going through your head."

"Yes, it is." They paused at the elevator, and she pushed the down button. "It's the hard part of being a reporter, keeping your opinion out of things and just reporting the facts."

"Newspapers state their opinion all the time. That's how presidents get elected," Brett said.

"Well, this reporter tries to stay objective about stories. Not so much about the people involved."

"Which was lucky for me."

They'd been through so much already as a couple. Her life would have been so different without him. "You were so passionate about your innocence, I couldn't write you off. And you were already carrying enough emotional weight without my adding to it."

Brett pressed a kiss against her temple. "Lucky me."

They walked across the street to the twenty-five story glass and concrete sky scrapper, headquarters for the Brittain Development Group. "They built this ten years ago and have been housed here ever since," Tess said as they entered the facility and crossed a wide, blue-tiled foyer. The flooring reflected light, almost as though they were walking on glass all the way to an information desk. The space looked modern, bright and very impressive.

The receptionist had them sign in and directed them to an elevator. Tess paused to look up the hollow center of the structure to the skylight twenty-five stories above, giving her a brief glimpse of a cloudless San Diego sky. Each floor had what looked like glass framing surrounding the core, but which was probably clear acrylic. It reflected the light from above and directed it downward.

"Beautiful place," Brett said as they waited for the elevator.

"Yes. I've studied some of their work. I need to look at the designs done by the other companies involved in the bidding." She took several pictures of the lobby and the skylight with her phone.

The elevator opened and they waited until a group of seven got off and then took their place.

The top floor was a long way up but the ride gave her the opportunity to glimpse each floor as it went by. They exited the elevator to the open reception area of the company itself. Decorated much like the lobby downstairs, shaped chairs surrounded a chrome and glass coffee table. Tess approached the blonde receptionist seated behind a mahogany desk, but was intercepted by a tall woman emerging from a long hall to the left. Her hair was pulled into a smooth ponytail at the nape of her neck, and she was dressed much like Tess, in dark slacks, a silk blouse, and a jacket.

"Welcome, Miss Kelly. Reception downstairs called to say you were on your way up. I'm Karen Ackerman, Mr. Brittain's assistant." She offered Tess her hand and they shook. "Mr. Brittain is looking forward to meeting you."

Nonplussed by the woman's greeting, Tess introduced Brett and, after a brief handshake, they fell into step behind Miss Ackerman. The long hall they traveled down ran along the clear acrylic wall, allowing them to look out into the core. Elevators ran up and down, smooth, efficient. They passed several closed office doors, each with the person's title displayed on them. At the corner, the receptionist paused before a set of double doors.

"Please wait here for just a moment." After a brief knock the woman opened the door on the right and slipped inside. She announced Tess and Brett, then stepped back to invite them to enter.

Despite having made an appointment, Tess had expected resistance, suspicion, and the waiting games most executives played. It was a surprise to breeze into the owner's office as soon as they walked into the building.

Nicholas Brittain rose from behind his desk, a glass-topped creation which was as much a piece of art as a functional structure. He stepped around it to greet them. With only a smattering of gray threaded through his dark hair, and though Tess knew he was mid-fifties, he appeared fit and trim and had the bearing of a younger man. His hazel eyes met hers, then moved to Brett. He extended his hand to Tess then to Brett.

"Would you like something to drink while we talk?" he asked. "Water, a soft drink, coffee?"

"Water will be fine," Tess said.

"The same," Brett agreed.

"I can get it for you, Mr. Brittain," Karen said.

"I'll take care of it, Karen, thank you. I know you have some things to finish up."

The woman nodded and left the office.

Brittain led the way to a striped couch and two solid chairs that made up a seating arrangement nestled in the left corner of the room. "Please have a seat." He strode to a large cabinet that ran a quarter length of the wall and opened a mini fridge hidden by a veneer that matched the cabinetry and blended into the unit. He retrieved two bottles of water and a bottle of some kind of deep red juice. "Would you like it over ice or just the bottles?"

"The bottles will be fine, sir," Brett said and Tess nodded.

Tess sat in one of the chairs. The modern, sculpted style of the piece cradled her body like a caring hand. "Did someone in your firm design these, Mr. Brittain?" she asked as she stroked the curved arm. She accepted the bottle of water he handed her and set it on a coaster on the glass-topped end table next to her.

"I did. I designed them as an engineering student but didn't sell the prototype to a furniture company until I graduated and needed seed money to start this business."

"They're very unique and comfortable. And your desk, it's amazing."

"Thank you, that's a one-of-a-kind design." He took a seat on the couch across from them.

Tess studied the man's face for a moment. Getting a feel for someone required more than analyzing their conduct when they spoke to her. The fact that Brittain branched out on his own to do creative projects, had actually financed his business through one of his own designs, spoke volumes. He served them himself instead of having his assistant stay to do it, which told her he valued Karen Ackerman's work and didn't expect her to do menial jobs. He probably made his own coffee as well. She cleared her throat. "Brett isn't a reporter, he's acting as my protection detail."

"Because of the car bombing?"

"Yes."

He frowned. "Have they found who's responsible yet?"

"No." Actually, she hadn't heard a word from any of the agencies investigating the incident. The police officers who'd interviewed her about Mary Stubben had been as silent.

She segued into the business at hand. "Brett won't repeat anything you say to me, but if you'd feel more comfortable, he won't mind stepping out."

Brittain eyed Brett a moment. "Military?" he asked.

Brett nodded.

"Still active?" Brittain asked.

"Yes, sir."

"I don't mind if he stays."

Tess leaned forward. "Do you mind if I take notes?"

"No, of course not."

Though he attempted to hide it, tension tightened his shoulders and face. Tess set the pad aside on the table next to her. "Mr. Brittain, I'm not here to dish dirt or try and trick you into admitting any wrongdoing. I'm here to see how your company is weathering the storm."

Brittain twisted the top off his bottle and took a sip. He set the bottle aside and leaned forward to rest his elbows on his knees and cup his hands together between them. "I'd be lying to say we're not still reeling from the accident and the loss of the two men who died. And the investigation is creeping along slow as molasses."

"I'm not surprised. These things seem to have two speeds, slow and slower."

A brief, wry smile touched his face.

"Have they been able to tell you what happened?" she asked.

"I told them."

Tess shifted and rested her elbows on the arms of her chair. "Can you share that with me?"

"We've always dealt with a specific company for all our concrete installations. The grade has to be a specific weight and mixture, and it has to cure for a specific length of time after it's poured into place. The two men who were killed were removing some machinery from beneath the area, unaware anything was wrong. There were already a couple of tons of concrete layered into the forms when one worker signaled the foreman something was wrong. The rebar in the structure should have held the weight, but because too much water had been added to the mix, it wasn't curing as quickly as it should have. Then the supports failed, the concrete dropped to the floor below, and the men were trapped in it. It was still wet. They were either instantly crushed or smothered to death before the crew could reach them."

His jaw tensed. "We make it a practice to do constant quality checks of everything that goes into our structures. The investigators have done thorough tests to make sure no other area of the structure is compromised. The only materials that were affected were those flooring slabs at the west corner of the third floor."

"What could have happened if this accident hadn't occurred?"

"Exactly what happened, which was horrible enough. Had the substandard concrete remained in place, part of the floor could have collapsed at a later date, possibly after the building was finished. It could have been an entire family and the one beneath them who were killed." He shook his head. "Every inch of the apartment complex has been looked at by several inspectors, both from the state as well as ones I hired myself. Nothing else in the structure has been compromised."

"But the delays and the bad press are probably eating you alive."

"Yes, it's running into thousands of dollars a day. We've been told their investigation will be completed by the end of this week. But there's no guarantee."

"What company delivered the concrete?"

"Gross and Miracle. We've been buying product from them for years and never had an issue before. But this is already affecting their business as much as it is ours." He took another sip of his juice. "Any time we're doing a high rise, pouring the concrete is like a ballet of sorts. You put the steel up and build the frames, then they pour the concrete. Depending on the schedule, you can pour a floor every other day and complete the entire frame within three months. There are chemicals added to the mixture to make it cure faster, so it can be walked on within a few hours. The analysis came back indicating it had too much sand, and too much water, as well as more of those curing chemicals than would normally be used."

"Didn't any of the workers recognize there was something wrong with the support structure while it was being poured?"

"No. They were working above it and didn't know there was a problem until it fell. The alarm to clear the area had just been sounded when it happened."

"Were there any new workers on the site that day? Workers your foreman had just hired or didn't recognize?"

Brittain hesitated, his gaze resting on her face for a long moment. "One of the men who died was a new hire. He'd only been on the job for a few days."

"Terry Mitchell?" she asked.

He nodded. "There are always new workers on a site. People

hire in and can't handle the work, then leave after a week or even a few days. But most of my workers have been with me on more than a few sites. You don't just hire in to do concrete work. You have to have experience, expertise. Terry wasn't involved in the concrete work. He was just removing some machinery close to the area. It was—" Brittain shook his head, his throat working. "A horrible tragedy."

She noticed Brittain's use of the man's first name instead of his last. This man cared about his workers. Tess settled back in her chair to think over what else she could ask him. "The investigators. Do they believe this was just an accident?"

"They haven't said yet. That day was the only day on the site the foreman had an extra truckload of cement delivered. But it does happen. You only have ninety minutes between the time the concrete is loaded and mixed to deliver it and get it poured. No one thought anything of it."

"Were you on the site that day?"

"Yes, earlier in the day, while the cement was being poured in another section. Though I'm supposed to be the pencil-pusher around here, I try and make it out to every site once or twice each week. Then when Granger called, I went out again to help deal with the accident." His throat worked again as he swallowed. "Construction accidents are among the worst by far."

"You put in a bid for the Ellison Project. We heard you had withdrawn from the bidding because of this accident."

"We haven't withdrawn as of yet, but it's a serious consideration."

Surprised, Tess glanced in Brett's direction. Mary had said their bid had been withdrawn.

Brett spoke for the first time. "I'm not the businessman, or the reporter, here, but I wouldn't pull out. I'd stick it out. If you can afford to."

Brittain turned to look at Brett. "Why?"

"To pull out now will look like an admission of wrongdoing and imply your company is struggling. From just an observer's viewpoint, this sounds like an accident. There's always a possibility something more was going on, too. They may try to prove negligence on your part, but I don't see how they can, since you were in the process of calling a halt to the work and clearing the area when the structure failed. You may have to settle with the families of the men who lost their lives, but your professional reputation will come out of this untarnished. That's what you're hoping for by allowing Tess to interview you, isn't it?"

"Yes, partly."

"How would you feel if I interviewed the investigators and some of your other employees?" Tess asked.

"I'm open to that. I can set them up for you, if you'd like."

"I'd rather pick and choose from a list, just to keep things impartial. Then when you're ready to make an announcement about the investigators' findings, I can add that information to the piece just before it goes to press."

Brittain hesitated for a moment. "We've done everything we can to cooperate with every agency that's come in to investigate. I truly believe our practices are safe."

"It sounds like you were doing everything right," Brett said. "But I'd increase security at your other sites and put the word out for your foremen to stay extra-vigilant."

Tess met Brett's look.

Brittain's attention shifted from one to the other. "Do you know something I'm not aware of, Ms. Kelly? If you do, you need to contact the investigators who are in charge of this."

There was a mix of emotions in his voice she couldn't quite decipher. Hope? Concern?

"If there's any information I become aware of during my interviews, I promise you, I'll share it with the investigators, Mr. Brittain." Tess changed the subject. "Who are your closest competitors?"

"Hamilton, Chanter, Rigs, and Connor-Jakes."

"I was told Hamilton has dropped out of the bidding," Tess said.

"Yes, he did, just before the accident."

"Who do you think might be closest to you for the Ellison Project bid?"

"Chanter, or possibly Rigs."

"So it stands to reason if you drop out, one of them will benefit from it. They may both have a relationship with the concrete company you use."

"Yes, but the people we deal with at the company—they wouldn't risk their business to help some other company to get a bid. They do work for all of us. Regardless of who gets the bid, they'll be involved in the building process, and it will benefit them."

"Would there have been any way for the support structure to be compromised without anyone noticing?" Brett asked.

"We have security guards who patrol each night. I'm not aware of any reported disturbances. And the structures are checked before the concrete is poured."

But had they been? They were pouring an entire floor of an apartment complex. Had every square inch of structure been checked during that process? With all the activity in preparation for the concrete being poured, and other work continuing in other areas of the structure, probably not.

Tess moved away from questions about the accident to concentrate on the number of people who were employed by the company and the company's achievements.

Nicholas Brittain took another sip from his juice container. "You're asking about things that throw a different light on my company than what the other reporters were interested in. Why?"

"I've researched your safety record. This is the second accident in ten years, which is a better safety record than any other company in the area. I've also done some research about the different buildings you've designed and constructed. A company doesn't just suddenly drop their standards unless something major has happened to them financially. I've studied the information you had to provide to the board when you submitted the Ellison Project bid. There was nothing there to raise a red flag. I'm not out to crucify you or your company for this accident. I'm more interested in the people who work for you," she gestured expansively, encompassing the office, the building, "and how all this works together, and how it can continue to do so."

Brittain settled back on the couch for the first time since they'd walked into the office. He shook his head. "I don't know why you're doing this, but thank you."

# CHAPTER FIFTEEN

**B**RETT GLANCED AT Tess as he merged into traffic. She had tilted the seat back and closed her eyes. "You've already put in a full day's work and it's past lunch time. What do you say we get something to eat and then go to my apartment for a short nap?"

"That sounds wonderful, but I have to report in to Taylor first." She straightened the seat and reached for her bag.

She was as driven as he was. He'd always known that. But she'd just experienced a trauma. She needed to pace herself. Yeah, like he had after waking from the coma? He'd been manic about getting back into shape and back to his team.

When Tess ended the call she said, "Taylor's more interested in the pieces I'm doing than anything current. He told me to stick with what I was doing for a few days."

"Good. You have the list Brittain gave you to work on tomorrow. I located a restaurant that can take us for the rehearsal dinner, if you're up to looking at it."

"Oh my God, I can't believe you found a place. Was that what you were working on while I interviewed Lisa Gooding?"

"Yeah." He rubbed his fingernails against his shirt. "Piece of cake."

Tess narrowed her eyes. "How many restaurants did you call?"

"Today or in all?"

"All together."

*Too fucking many.* "Thirty."

"As much as I appreciate your finding a place, if you tell me a SEAL never gives up, I'm going to punch you."

Brett laughed. "I don't have to, babe. You just did it for me."

She groaned. "I can't believe you got us a place."

Relief slammed through him at her enthusiasm. There had been a moment in the newspaper break room when he'd had doubts the wedding would go forward. "Well, we need to check it out first and choose what we want them to serve. It could be a total dump." He glanced in her direction. "We could go there for lunch. It's past time for the noon crowd."

"Okay."

He drove to South Park. The restaurant was nestled in the midst of an older community of one-story houses. Parking was limited to a small area in back of the restaurant and along the street. The exterior wasn't much to look at, and the outside seating was very limited, but the interior was neat and clean. The bar was small, but one entire wall behind it was dedicated to a wide variety of wines, and they had several good beers on tap. Despite it being late for lunch, there were more than twenty people still dining.

After the waitress had shown them to a table, they studied the menu. Brett asked for the manager. The waitress went to the phone at the bar and after a few minutes a slightly built man with graying hair and a mustache appeared from the back of the restaurant.

"How may I help you?"

Brett stood and offered his hand. "I believe we spoke on the phone this morning, Mr. Rizzo. I'm Brett Weaver and this is my fiancée, Tess Kelly."

"Yes, we talked about your rehearsal dinner. I'm so glad you've come in. Why don't I go get the menu we reserve for parties and see if you find it satisfactory?"

"Thank you."

Brett reached for Tess's hand. "I know this isn't fancy, more family-oriented, but if the food's good—"

"The food's all that matters…and the service, of course."

The manager returned with the menu, sat at their invitation, and went over the wine list and dishes in depth.

After a few moments discussion, Brett suggested, "Let's both order two things from the menu and do a taste test."

Rizzo laughed. "That's an excellent idea, Mr. Weaver. You order the entrees you'd like to try, and I'll have the staff prepare a sampler of the different salads and our desserts, free of charge."

"That would be great."

"A very small sampler," Tess added. "I don't want to have to be rolled out of here like a meatball, and I do have to fit into my wedding dress in a little over two weeks."

The man laughed again and Rizzo went off order their sampler while they settled on the entrees.

Brett settled on the *osso buco* and ravioli. Tess chewed her bottom lip as she looked over the choices and he smiled. She took everything so seriously. But then her job dealt with serious issues, more serious than he'd ever expected.

After she ordered the risotto with grilled salmon and the lasagna she handed the menu back to the waitress.

Brett grasped her hand. "When's the big bachelorette party?" he asked.

"Oh, God!" She raked fingers through her hair, looking like she was tempted to pull it, and it tumbled out from between them in a copper waterfall. "I had hoped I could talk Zoe out of it, but she's got a whole list of things planned, all guaranteed to be excruciating for me."

Brett laughed. "Like what?"

"Well, at least we aren't going to do the club thing. We're doing a full day of manicures, pedicures, hair treatments, a massage, lunch, and some kind of party at the house with finger foods."

The waitress brought their drinks and left.

"That doesn't sound like too bad a day. You won't have to face a night of drinking, gambling, and the general mayhem that follows a group of Navy SEALs when they get together to party."

"I can't imagine Hawk getting too wild. He seems Mr. Controlled-and-Responsible."

"You've never seen him when he drinks." Neither had he, come to think of it.

"I didn't even know he did. Well, other than an occasional beer."

"Since he hooked up with Zoe he sticks to beer and he never drinks hard liquor." God, he was such an asshole, playing her like this.

"So, it's going to be a night to tie one on." Her brown eyes settled on him with a look that said, *are you kidding me?*

"No, I'll want to at least know where I am when we get to the strip joint."

Silence reigned for at least five seconds while her eyes narrowed. "Does Zoe know Hawk is going to take you to a strip joint?"

He controlled his smile for another five seconds, then laughed. "Hawk would never take me to a strip joint, even if I begged him to. He's too," he started to say pussy-whipped and thought better of it. "He'd never do anything to hurt Zoe. I think we're going night fishing on Doc's boat."

She leaned back in her seat and her dark eyes searched his face. "I never know when you're kidding me."

"I was kidding about the strip joint. Truly. We really are going fishing on Doc's boat. Just the eight of us."

"It would be a real tragedy if all of you get drunk and drown."

Brett threw his head back and laughed. "Nobody's going to drown. You're welcome to try and talk the guys out of bringing beer, but it won't happen."

Tess frowned.

Noticing her frown, he said, "You can come to the dock and see us off. Doc will even let you come aboard and check the boat so you'll know we're not bringing any women with us. With eight of us there won't be any room left for anyone else."

Tess covered her eyes. "Oh, my God, it's getting worse every moment."

"Tess." He grasped her hand and eased it down to look into her face. "I know SEALs have a reputation for being cowboys and wild men, but if we get arrested, they can bust us down in rank or shit-can us altogether. None of us wants any of that to happen. So we're careful. I may tease, but I'll never lie to you. All we have planned is a fishing trip where we can relax, drink beer, and play poker."

After a deep breath, she said, "Okay." But she still looked concerned.

Luckily the waitress chose that moment to arrive with their salad sampler and two plates, and for the next hour and a half, while their different courses arrived, they concentrated on eating. And eating. And eating. They discussed the food and family. By the time Brett took the last bite of tiramisu, his eyes nearly rolled back in his head and he decided he must have grown a second stomach, like a cow. Tess hadn't done too badly either, though she'd flagged at the end and only taken one bite each of the desserts.

They narrowed it down to two entrees, two desserts and a single salad. The waitresses boxed up the remaining food for them to take home while they settled the bill. The manager appeared to confirm their reservation for the rehearsal dinner and to note the menu they'd chosen. He shook both their hands and wished them well.

TESS RODE A romantic high as she watched Brett settle their bill. They'd talked and shared bites of each other's food. They were falling back into the groove of being a cohesive unit. Now that she'd made a decision about the job, despite those moments of disappointment she experienced every time she thought about it, she felt lighter. The invisible boundary she'd felt between them was gone. They were looking forward to their wedding. Working toward that goal together.

A man came into the restaurant and sauntered past them to a table. Something about the shape of his face, his hair, struck a chord of familiarity. Where had she seen him before?

"I need to check the car before we leave, honey. Stay here and I'll pull around front." He picked up the bags and walked out the door.

Reality was a bitch. And Brett's words brought Tess back to the here and now with a vengeance. They were no longer a couple planning their rehearsal dinner. They were targets again. Who had set the bomb? Were they terrorists targeting Brett? Or was it directed at her because of the information Mary had shared with her?

She believed the latter, but until the FBI came back and told her definitively, it was still up in the air. The car had a burglar alarm on it, but Brett insisted on checking it each time it was left unattended before he'd allow her get in.

A car pulled around the corner, but it wasn't the rental car. It glided by and she watched it for a moment. A flash of orange caught her attention, an orange sticker with a logo was curved around the right-hand bumper. Was there something familiar about the sticker? A niggling feeling of anxiety settled in her gut and radiated out. Where had she seen it before?

Seconds ticked away as her emotional level spiraled. How long did it take for Brett to walk around and check the car and then drive it to the front of the restaurant? Through the front window, she scanned the row of older homes stretching diagonally away from the restaurant and the businesses directly across from it. She focused on the corner where Brett would have to brake before turning toward the front of the restaurant. One minute passed, then two. Her heart beat against her eardrums. The pressure built as she strained to hear every sound on the street. Her muscles tightened in alarm. When the rental car came into view she rushed out of the building before Brett had come to a complete stop. She jerked open the door and slid into the passenger seat.

"You were supposed to wait until I came in for you, Tess."

"Screw that. What took you so long? Weren't you gone longer this time?"

"I had to wait for a couple of customers to maneuver out of their parking spaces before I could back out."

Her breathing was coming in gasps and she tossed her purse onto the floor at her feet and folded her arms across waist.

Concern tightened Brett's features. He rested his hand on her linen-covered thigh just above her knee and gave her leg a reassuring squeeze. "Easy, honey. I'm fine. You're fine."

With her heart racing out of control, it was hard to get a full breath. Was she having a panic attack? She gripped his wrist and held on, because touching him seemed to help.

Brett pulled away from the curb and drove in aimless circles. The motion of the car seemed comforting, and eventually she calmed.

"Why don't you put your seat back and just relax until we get to the apartment?"

She did as he suggested, because she needed to lean on him

right now, to feel coddled and safe. To just look at him and know he was safe, too. By the time he parked in the lot reserved for residents at his apartment complex she was drowsy.

"How 'bout that nap, meatball?" he asked, his smile endearing and tender.

"I don't think I'm so far gone you'll have to roll me into the building," she teased, offering him a smile. "I'm sorry I got so out of control."

Brett shook his head and released his seat belt so he could reach across the console and tuck her hair behind her ear. "I've walked in your shoes, Tess. You have to cut yourself some slack. Nobody expects you to jump through hoops four days after—being knocked off your feet. Not even Taylor. Okay?"

She understood why he avoided saying "after your car blew up," and appreciated his attempt to steer away from the visual that popped into her head every time she thought about it. She laid a hand against his cheek, then ran a thumb over his lips.

He pressed a kiss against it.

"Why do you suppose they make cars with this damn console thing now?" she asked.

Brett's eyes lit with humor. "I think to cut down on teen pregnancy. It definitely puts a cramp in trying to make out in the front seat."

With a sigh she sat up and readjusted the seat. Her phone rang and she fished it out of her bag and answered.

Brett got out of the car and gathered the carry-out bags from the back seat.

Mrs. Delgado sounded breathless, excited. "The new lawyer says he may be able to get Daniel out."

"I'm happy for you, Mrs. Delgado."

"Daniel has agreed to speak with you, and his lawyer has approved it."

"Will he be with Daniel when I come to speak with him?"

"Yes. He didn't want Daniel answering questions without him."

"That's fine. It's always a good idea for Daniel to be protected, no matter whom he's talking to. Because he's a juvenile, you'll have to sign forms allowing me to interview him there at the facility."

"I have already done so, and Mr. Niles has set up the interview.

He said he could come to the prison at five o'clock Thursday."

"Okay, I'll fill out my paperwork as soon as I get to a computer and then drop it by the facility. With you and your lawyer both submitting paperwork, I'm sure there won't be any issues."

"Thank you, Ms. Kelly. Thank you very much."

Brett opened her door but leaned against the side of the car and waited.

"You're welcome. I'm glad Daniel has better representation."

She hung up, collected her tote and stepped out of the car. "Daniel has agreed to talk to me with his lawyer on Thursday at five." She shoved the door closed.

Brett hit the key fob to lock the car. "The same lawyer who tried to get him to confess and make a deal?"

"No. The one I suggested to Mrs. Delgado."

He nodded. "So you've bought into his innocence?"

"Not yet. I want to talk to him face to face. And I'm going to check out his arms and see if he has any tattoos first. Rosalie said the man who held her at gunpoint had a tattoo on the inside of his arm between his wrist and elbow. But by now his lawyer has had time to read the witness statements, so Daniel may be out before I can interview him."

"I'd prefer you interview him outside of Metropolitan Correctional. Just the thought of you behind bars with a bunch of criminals has all my protective instincts going into hyper drive."

Tess looped her arm through his and ignored the butt of his gun pressing into her shoulder as she leaned into him. "If he's free, and his mom and brother are present while I interview him, if he does have something to hide, it won't come out. Interviewing him at the facility will work better for me. Should I take one of those?" she asked, indicating the takeout bags.

"This one." He handed her the one that would free his right hand, the one he needed to draw his Sig. They walked toward the apartment building. "Come to think of it, maybe you'd be safer there at the facility. Having you in the room with Miguel Delgado—" He shook his head.

The apartment smelled musty, and Brett opened the sliding glass doors and turned on the ceiling fan to help the air circulate.

"I stripped the bed before I left. I'll have to make it before we climb in. While you put away the food, I'll take care of it."

"Okay."

"Stay away from the balcony, Tess."

"Okay." Anger tangled the excellent food she'd eaten earlier into a tight ball. The attack—and it had been an attack, physically and emotionally—had disrupted their lives long enough. It had been four days and the hypervigilance they'd been forced to maintain was getting old. How did Brett live like this for months at a time?

She put away the food and joined him in the bedroom. The corners of the sheets were as tautly aligned as any hospital bed. He spread a lightweight blanket over them.

"If ever you retire from being a SEAL, they'd hire you in a New York minute to make beds at Scribe Mercy or Balboa Hospital."

Brett chuckled. "First thing you learn in training, besides to jump to attention and salute, is to make your bunk."

"It looks good enough to sleep in." Tess slipped off her shoes. While Brett put pillowcases on the pillows she slowly and methodically shed her clothes. She hung her jacket on the bedroom doorknob, folded the rest, and placed them on one side of the dresser. Dressed in nothing but a camisole and a thong, she slid onto the blanket face down.

"Jesus, Tess," Brett breathed behind her.

She looked over her shoulder to find him bailing out of his clothes like they were on fire. She laughed, then caught her breath as, completely naked, he crawled up on the bed. Dear God. Every inch of him, muscular, lean, and conditioned from physical training, looked masculine and fit, and so damn sexy heat flared in her face and worked its way down her body. He nuzzled one cheek of her ass, then gave the other a quick nip. She gasped and ran her hand over his head and turned to loop her arm around his neck as he eased down beside her, allowing every inch of his bare skin to rub against her.

Laying a hand against her bare backside, he tugged her in close against him, his arousal an adamant pressure against her stomach.

"How can you think about sex after all the food you ate?"

"I'm a guy. I think about sex every thirty seconds." He nuzzled her neck and his hand slid beneath her camisole to find her breast.

She laughed again. His fingers toying with her nipple and titillating sensations trailed down her body. There was something to be said about having to go braless, injuries or no injuries.

He pulled back to flash her a smile. "I think you may have the most beautiful ass on the planet."

He plucked and toyed with her nipple until it tightened. Rivulets of sensation ebbed and flowed from her breast to more intimate areas of her body.

"I thought that was reserved for J-Lo or someone." Her voice sounded wispy and soft. She swallowed.

"Only because the world hasn't seen yours." His touch trailed down her side and he caressed said ass in such a way her breathing grew uneven. His lips covered hers and their tongues meshed. A sweet, sweeping wave of tenderness and love tumbled through her. Everything he'd done for her, for them, during the course of the day, every loving look, every patient word came back. She fought the urge to weep and held him as tight and close as she could.

Tess groaned when his fingers slipped beneath the thong's ribbon of fabric and followed it to her moist, aching core. He circled the opening with the tip of one digit, teasing her, tempting her, entering her just enough to drive her crazy with need.

She slipped a hand between them to cup his balls and gently kneaded and caressed them. Brett hummed beneath the kiss and parted his legs. Sliding down, she traced his collarbones with her lips and tasted the warmth of his skin with her tongue. She pressed soft, moist kisses down his chest and followed the thin line of hair down the center of his stomach with a fingertip. She grasped the taut shaft of his erection and stroked it. His muscles tensed and relaxed with the up and down movement of her hand.

She raked her gaze up his body to his face to find him watching her, his blue eyes almost iridescent with heat. Her gaze met his face as she touched the bulbous head with her tongue then laved it, relishing the salty taste of the fluid that beaded there. When she lowered her mouth over him, taking in as much as she could, and sucked, he dropped his head back on the pillow and made a choked sound of pleasure that shot her own arousal higher. She settled into a rhythm, tempting him, teasing as she nipped, licked and sucked.

With every thrust of his hips, her own need grew.

His fingers tangled in her hair and he sounded out of breath when he said, "Come up here baby, I want to be inside you when I go off."

She was more than ready for him. She trembled as she shimmied out of the thong. When he lay between her legs and rose above her, she reached down to guide him home. "Now, please now."

With one quick thrust he became a part of her. They both caught their breath. "God, Tess. You've got me so ready."

The heat and hardness of him inside her was nearly enough all by itself. Brett thrust deep once, twice, an intent look of concentration on his face, as he tried to beat back his own release before he fell into a rhythm laced with desperation. The drag and flow of his movements hit the spot deep inside her that drove her pleasure to a peak. Her pulse thundered in her ears, and her breathing went ragged. When they tumbled over the edge together, the feeling was so intense she cried out.

For a time the uneven rasp of their breathing was the only sound in the room. "I love you, Tess." He never failed to say it, and she had the same breath-catching response every time.

Brett rolled to lie beside her and turned on his side to rest a hand on her stomach. Drawn to him like a magnet, Tess turned onto her side to face him. She cupped his cheek and her thumb moved over the light brown beard stubble shadowing his chin.

Those few moments of panicky fear at the restaurant came back to haunt her. "I want you to promise me something."

"So you've buttered me up with mind-blowing sex so you could talk me into something?" he teased.

She grimaced. "No, it's just…I don't want you trying to get between me and a bullet, Brett." Tears blurred her vision. "I'd never be able to recover from it if something happened to you because of me."

His smile died and he remained silent for a moment, his eyes, so alight with passion moments before, turning dark. "I can't promise that. If I didn't do everything in my power to protect you, I couldn't—" He threw up a hand and shook his head. "I can't make that kind of promise."

Tears ran across her face onto the pillowcase, and she turned into it.

Brett stroked her hair, her back. "Nothing's going to happen to either one of us, honey. The FBI will find out who the hell fucked with your car and we'll move on from this."

When she had herself under control again she wiped her face with the edge of the blanket. "From now on we go to and from the car together. Not knowing if you were okay at the restaurant—"

"Okay. We'll figure something out."

The tight knot of anxiety that had twisted beneath her rib cage eased. She nodded.

He tucked a long strand of hair behind her ear. "As long as we're discussing things, I want you to do something for us both."

"What?"

"I want you to go to Washington and check out the job, Tess. If you don't, you'll always have regrets. And if you decide you want to try it, we'll figure out a way to work things out."

She shook her head. "I've made my decision, Brett."

"I don't want to be the reason you've settled for less when you can have more. Part of loving someone is looking out for their happiness. I can make you happy when we're together like this, but when I'm not—you have to make your own happiness. If Washington might be part of that, then you need to at least look at it more closely so you'll know for certain."

"But I love you." She read the struggle in his face, and a deep, heart-wrenching ache of love filled her.

His throat worked as he swallowed, and for the first time she thought he might lose his composure. "If I wasn't certain of that, I wouldn't be encouraging you to do this."

"I have to think about it." Tess scooted in close to him and lay her head on his shoulder. Giving it consideration was more telling than she wanted to admit. It was some time before she could close her eyes and relax.

HAD BRETT NOT tagged along with Tess for the past few days, he might not have even considered encouraging her to go to Washington. She seemed too involved with the people she interviewed. And she had no tough outer skin to keep her from getting hurt. Or did she?

She seemed to have an empathy with people that made them want to open up to her. She'd used it on him, and he'd fallen in love with her so deep he couldn't break the surface…didn't even want to.

He eased from the bed and slipped on his boxer briefs. Though they were several stories up from street level, the balcony could be used as a point of entry. He closed the door, locked it and placed the security bar in place. He stared out at the surrounding buildings, the patch of gray-blue sky divided by the wispy trail of a jet.

Would the sharks in Washington, D.C. eat Tess alive? Or would she be able to swim with them? She wouldn't know until she went there and got a feel for the job, the people.

If she didn't come to the understanding herself to take it or say no, without other things standing in her way, it would always lie like a broken promise between them to fester and cause resentment.

He turned away from the door and wandered back to the bedroom. The soft rise and fall of her breathing eased his worry and tension. She hadn't slept much the night before and, being so fresh from deployment, neither had he. His gaze rested on the delicate slope of her cheekbone, the tiny freckles sprinkled sparingly across the bridge of her nose, the smooth, creamy curve of her hip. He fought the desire to kiss the hollow spot in the bowl of her shoulder, to wake her and make love all over again. He slipped beneath the covers and aligned his body to spoon with her.

He'd done the right thing about the job, though it was killing him. Now all he could do was hope and pray she'd decide she didn't want it.

And if she decided to take it—?

They were going to have a whopping big credit card debt each month when they flew back and forth to see each other. But they'd find a way.

# CHAPTER SIXTEEN

T ESS WOKE TO the soft, warm brush of Brett's hands and lips against her cheek, her throat, her collarbone. Dusk had settled across the slice of sky she could see from the bedroom window, turning it a deep, powdery periwinkle.

"What time is it?" she croaked even as her hand cupped the back of his head, encouraging him to continue what he was doing.

"It's almost nine," he murmured.

He nuzzled her breast and she slid her fingers down to caress the slope of his neck. "I've slept nearly four hours."

"You needed it." He eased up to look down at her, his face in shadow. The dull, reflective light coming from between the blinds limned the strong lines of his cheek and jaw. "Let's stay here tonight. We can get up early and run over to your apartment in the morning. I'll make a trip to the store for some snacks and drinks. We can hang out in front of the TV and watch a movie."

"Are you trying to manage me, Brett?"

"No. I just thought a change of scenery might help you stay relaxed."

She appreciated his concern, but she didn't need to be coddled. "I'm okay. Really I am."

He remained silent a moment. "What set you off at the restaurant, Tess?"

Still lethargic from sleep, she paused to shift thoughts, and a picture took shape. "There was a man at the restaurant who looked familiar. Then a car went by. It was a dark blue sedan with an orange sticker on the right rear bumper. I've seen it before, but I can't get it to—" She messaged her brow with her fingertips. A low-grade headache throbbed behind her eyes. She'd slept too long. While she focused on the memory, her heart hammered against her breastbone and fear thrust upward to close her throat. "It was in the parking lot at the paper. A man got into the car and drove away."

"The day of the bombing?"

"Yes." She folded her arms against her atop the sheet. Brett brushed his fingertips back and forth across her forearm in a soothing motion.

"What shape was the sticker?"

She sat up and held the sheet against her. "It was a rectangle, because it wrapped around the side of the bumper. But it was so faded I couldn't see any of the details."

Brett sat up to loop an arm around her. "You need to contact the FBI and tell them about this."

"They have the parking lot video feed. They'll know about him and about the car."

"Good. But it wouldn't hurt to touch base with them. This may be a detail they don't have."

"Okay." She dreaded calling. They were always arrogant, dismissive, and never willingly shared information. And every time she spoke to them it brought every second of the explosion back. When it came to this, her reporter's instinct remained suppressed.

"How about a soak in the tub? I can run you some water. Bowie's home, and he may even have some wine."

He *was* managing her. But at least it was in a helpful, caring way.

"I'll take a shower instead, but I'd like that glass of wine."

"Okay. I'll take care of it." He slid off the bed.

Something occurred to her. "How did you know something had triggered my panic at the restaurant?"

"For a while after I woke up, I went through periods I'd react like you did. Something you see, smell or hear sparks a memory or an emotion. It's as if your subconscious recognizes something and revs up your feelings."

Well it certainly had hers. "How did you know to ask me now?"

"When you're first waking up, your defenses are down. And it's easier to remember things."

She leaned back to look up at him. Strips of light from the blinds streamed across his face. "Have you recovered memories from the attack, Brett?"

He'd said he believed Derrick Armstrong had attacked him and left him for dead during his last mission with his old unit. If he could remember what happened for certain, it might help him move on.

He fingered the scar at his temple, as he often did when talking about the lost memories. "I've only experienced one flashback, but I keep trying to remember more. One day I will." He left the bedroom.

Tess slipped out of the bed, retrieved her clothes from where she'd folded and left them on the corner of the dresser, and shuffled into the bathroom. She felt stiff and heavy from too much sleep. She flipped on the bathroom light and flinched from the harsh glare. Her eyes looked puffy and her hair fuzzed into a rat's nest on the right side of her head. It must be true love if he'd braved waking her with kisses as bad as she looked.

She twisted on the water and, while she waited for it to warm, found a bottle of shower gel under the sink where she'd left it months before. She lathered up and then stood under the hot spray for a good ten minutes. By the time she shut off the water she felt almost human again.

She towel-dried her hair and dressed. Discovering a new toothbrush in the medicine cabinet she made use of it, then finger-combed her hair.

When had Brett said his lease was up? They really needed to consolidate their living arrangements. It was ridiculous to go back and forth. She should say something about that when she left the bedroom.

He stood in the kitchen, drinking a beer. Seeing her, he grasped the bowl of the wine glass sitting on the counter and held it up. "You like red, don't you?"

"Yes." She gripped the stem of the glass and raised it to her lips for a sip. She looked up to find Brett frowning.

Had something else happened? "What is it?"

"I wanted to wait to tell you when you were more awake. Your editor called while you were asleep. The coroner released Mary Stubben's body for burial. The funeral will be tomorrow at noon."

THE NIGHT SKY had taken on an amethyst hue by the time they left the apartment. The balmy breeze that had stirred earlier in the day had turned chilly. Brett carried a clothing bag over left shoulder with his one dark civilian suit to wear to the funeral. He tossed the bag into the back seat and moved around the vehicle in a search for explosives. Finding nothing, he opened her door for her.

He'd have preferred they remained at his apartment, but Tess had some research to do, and he hadn't yet retrieved his laptop from his mom, who was holding it for safekeeping. He hadn't made time to stop by her and Russell's place. He still couldn't believe his straitlaced mom was living with a man. Captain Russell Connelly was a good guy, and a good doctor. Hell, he'd brought him out of a coma and gotten him back on his feet. The guy was a miracle worker. He seemed to make his mom happy. Brett was sure they'd eventually tie the knot, but neither seemed in any rush. At their age, what the hell were they waiting for?

He wove through the streets toward Tess's apartment.

"What are you thinking about?" Tess asked.

"Mom and Russell. Why do you suppose they haven't gotten married yet?"

"You've been out of the country. She may want you there to attend the wedding and walk her down the aisle."

Brett glanced at her. "You think so?"

"Possibly. But they seem content the way things are. Maybe neither of them wants to get married."

"Maybe they're waiting for us to do our thing. Think I should say something to Mom?"

Tess was silent for a moment. "Maybe you could just say you want her to be happy, no matter what she and Russell decide about their living arrangements. We're basically living together. What difference does it make if they're doing the same?"

The difference was, it was his mom. "As a son, I feel like I need to be defending her honor or something."

"Yet you've been sleeping with me for months."

"If I could kick my own ass, I'd do it to defend your honor, too."

Tess laughed. "You don't think Russell treats her with respect?"

"I know he treats her good. I'm sure he loves her. Maybe it's a Southern, Bible-belt thing. I felt the same way when I realized Zoe was sleeping with Hawk. I wanted to pound on him for messing with my sister even though I knew he was crazy about her."

Tess laid a hand on his thigh and gave it a squeeze. "It's a different century, Brett. Women are strong, independent creatures, and we're capable of fending for ourselves. We don't need men for the same reasons we did fifty years ago. We don't look to marriage to provide financial security or a home. We can work and get those things for ourselves and not have to live with the threat of them being taken away if the marriage doesn't work out."

Her words reflected a remnant of insecurity she still lived with, since she herself was from a broken home and had been abandoned by her father. Brett had experienced those insecurities, too, after his dad had died and left his mother alone to support and raise three kids. He gave her hand a squeeze.

"If you asked a group of American women today what they hoped to get out of marriage, they'd probably say all they're looking for is love and a good father for their children. After thousands of years of cultural evolution, we still can't live without the things that feed our emotional needs. Or the biological imperative we're born with."

Geez, sometimes she could be unemotionally analytical to the tenth power. "Glad to know you need me for something," Brett quipped, hearing the edge in his tone. "I was beginning to feel a little redundant."

Tess laughed. "I was waiting for you to tell me I was full of it. You've grown very PC since you've been away."

He glanced at her. In the intermittent flash of the streetlights, she smiled.

She'd played him. Payback for the strip club thing.

She leaned across the console to rest her hand against his chest, and he felt the warmth of her touch through his shirt. "You'll never be redundant, Brett." Her voice took on that soft tone he loved. "There's a moment after we've both climaxed, when you're still inside me, and you say, 'I love you, Tess.' Nothing can beat the way you look at me when you say it."

Heat flared in his face at the same time blood rushed south and his cock hardened. He brought her hand to his lips, though he was tempted to direct it elsewhere. "You forgot the protection thing."

"Yes, I did. You're very good at protecting me, your family, your country."

"And I'll be around to fulfill the biological imperative when you're ready."

Tess laughed. "See? Not redundant at all."

He wheeled into the apartment lot, threw the car into park and reached for her, screw the console between them. She tasted of wine and her. For all of two seconds he forgot they were exposed, at risk. The flash of headlights brought him back to the here and now. "Later," he promised, his voice husky.

He hustled her out of the car and into the apartment building. Tess's cheeks looked flushed as they got on the elevator with another couple. The man and woman exited on the same floor and they followed them down the hall.

Tess dug in her purse for her keys and handed them to him. Brett extended the key toward the lock, then froze. The door lacked an inch of meeting the facing. He'd locked the door himself this morning before leaving. Adrenaline surged, and he grasped Tess's arm to urge her away from the apartment and at the same time drew his gun.

He paused at an apartment across the hall and midway down toward the elevator. "Do you know who lives here?"

Tess's cheeks had lost their rosy glow. "Yes, it's Mrs. Howard. She's a widow. She lives alone."

"Knock on the door while I cover the apartment." He aligned his body to protect her. But he couldn't protect her from a bomb blast. His heartbeat skyrocketed and sweat pooled beneath his arms.

An elderly, white-haired woman answered Tess's knock. "Tess, it's good to see you."

Brett interrupted her. "Mrs. Howard, I need Tess to stay with you for a few minutes. Someone has broken into her apartment. Lock yourselves in and dial 911."

The woman's eyes went wide. "Oh, my God!"

Tess latched onto his arm, her nails digging in. "Don't go in there, Brett. Let the police check it out when they get here."

He laid a soothing hand over hers. "It's okay, honey. I'm not going in. Tell them to send the bomb squad, Tess. Tell them I'm here standing guard at the door and I'm armed."

She went into the woman's apartment, reluctance in every step. When she shut the door and he heard the lock engage, he breathed a sigh of relief. He couldn't focus on anything but her when he believed she was in danger. He shook off the tension and turned his attention to the apartment door. He paused outside to listen. Whoever broke in wouldn't use a timer. They couldn't be certain when he and Tess would return. Was there a trigger around the door?

He debated about whether to pull the fire alarm to clear the apartment building when he heard sirens approaching from a distance.

A couple of minutes passed, then police in full tactical gear exited the elevator, their weapons drawn. An officer at the head of the team spoke. "Ensign Brett Weaver?"

"Yes."

"I'm Officer Stan Mackey from the Metro Arson Strike Team, sir. I'm going to ask you to put your weapon down, sir."

Though he'd expected the request, he still had a *what the hell?* moment. "I'm ejecting the clip and clearing the chamber."

"Yes, sir."

He cleared his weapon and laid it and the clip on the floor.

"Do you have any other weapons on your person, sir?"

"No." Brett removed his jacket and turned to prove it.

"Thank you, sir." The officer approached him and bent to retrieve the pistol. The tension of the other officers ratcheted down. He posted an officer at the apartment door and gave an order for the rest to start clearing the floor.

"I've been made aware of your fiancée's situation, sir. Where is she?"

"She's inside a neighbor's apartment down the hall."

"Good, let's step inside with her for a moment."

Brett led the way to Mrs. Howard's apartment. At his knock, Tess opened the door and threw herself against him. She was trembling. "It's okay, honey."

"Is there a bomb?" Her skin looked white and the freckles across her nose stood out. Mrs. Howard on the other hand looked flushed with excitement.

"We don't know yet."

Mackey spoke. "Ms. Kelly, we're clearing the apartment building and bringing in a couple of dogs to sniff for explosives. Detectives Hart and Buckler are on their way. They'll meet us out in the parking lot." He turned his attention to Brett. "You have a permit to carry, Ensign Weaver?"

"Yes, I do."

"May I see it?"

Brett retrieved the permit from his wallet and handed it over. The officer used his radio to verify the permit and returned it to Brett. "We should have verification by the time we're downstairs. I'll return your weapon as soon as we're outside, sir."

Mackey hustled them and Mrs. Howard out of the apartment. He bypassed the elevator and went directly to the stairs.

Brett took Mrs. Howard's arm to steady her as they descended the three floors with a stream of other residents.

"I'm so sorry, Mrs. Howard," Tess said.

"It's all right, Tess. Nothing this exciting has ever happened to me before."

Tess glanced up at Brett, her reaction plain. They could both do without this kind of excitement.

AN HOUR LATER Tess leaned her head on Brett's shoulder as they sat in an interview room at the station. "Tell me again why we're sitting here?"

"Beats the fuck out of me, but if they don't show up within the next five minutes, we're leaving."

As if on cue the door swung open and Detectives Mackey, Buckler, and Hart all entered the interview room. Hart carried a large paper bag.

Fuck, this couldn't be good. Not when they were triple-teaming.

Mackey started off. "The good news is that there was no bomb on the premises."

"Good," Tess said and rested a hand on Brett's chest.

"The bad news?" Brett asked. His gaze trailed from one to the other of the detectives.

"Ms. Kelly's apartment was broken into. We'll need you to walk through and identify anything missing."

After two hours of waiting, Brett was out of patience with their drawing this out. "And?"

Detective Hart opened the paper bag and removed something white from it. Tess caught her breath as he unfolded the item then she cried out.

Though he hadn't seen it, Brett recognized what he was looking at. It was a wedding dress, a dress Tess would have looked a vision in. Red paint defaced the gown and looked like bloodstains. The circular spots looked like bullet holes.

# CHAPTER SEVENTEEN

T HE CHURCH IN the Mission Hills area had a curved sanctuary done in white and stained oak. Great wooden beams crossed the ceiling, moving from a central hub like wagon wheel spokes. Padded pews organized like pie wedges pointed toward the pulpit. Mary's copper-colored casket lay in state to the right surrounded by flower arrangements.

Tess settled in a pew midway down the section behind Mary's family. She reached for Brett's hand and laced their fingers. Since last night she'd bounced back and forth between the urge to weep and barely contained surges of rage. Though there hadn't been any explosives in her apartment, or anywhere else in the building, her apartment had been violated and trashed. Her computer was stolen—as well as her external hard drive, which was an inconvenience, but replaceable. Thankfully her files were backed up to both an online storage program and to the servers at the paper. All the thieves had was access to stories she was working on.

The worst blow was her beautiful wedding gown had been reduced to a paint-spotted threat. She and the SEAL wives, her closest friends, had taken hours to find just the right dress and now she was back to square one. Not to mention the expense.

Her half-hour meeting with Mary Stubben had triggered a sneaky, dangerous malice the police seemed helpless to combat. She had come to this service as a way to soothe her conscience, but anger warred with her guilt. Would Mary still be alive if Tess hadn't spoken with her, hadn't encouraged her to send her more information? Or had she been doomed from the moment she'd copied the files from her boss's computer? There was no way of knowing until the homicide unit completed their investigation. And the police were being reticent about when that might be.

Brett's hand tightened on hers, drawing her attention. His jaw had hardened, his eyes sharper as he leaned close to murmur in her ear. "Frye just showed up."

Tess scanned the rows of pews until she located the CEO of Chanter Construction speaking to one of Mary's family members. She wrestled back the urge to leap to her feet and confront him. She wanted to beat at him with her fists and scream and rant.

Brett put an arm around her as if he'd sensed her thoughts.

"I'm okay," she murmured.

Jonathan Frye's iron gray hair, cut short, lay close against his head. He had a long, narrow face, a slender nose which seemed almost effeminate compared to the sharp, aggressive thrust of a chin dented by a shallow cleft. As he turned to take a seat his blue eyes swept the crowd.

Had he paused for just a second on her and Brett? It seemed so. But how could he recognize either of them from among the other strangers here? She searched for Henry Sullivan, the private detective Frye had hired, but he wasn't present. Had he been the one to break into her apartment? The police wouldn't share their findings until later.

Organ music swelled, signaling the beginning of the service. Tess forced herself to focus on the moment. She owed it to Mary Stubben.

After a couple of songs, the minister climbed the two steps to the podium and gave a sweet eulogy about Mary, who had been active in the church as a Sunday school teacher and as the head of one of the church's charities. He spoke about how quiet and unassuming she had been. How dedicated to trying to help those less fortunate than herself. He mentioned how she always carried cloth handkerchiefs she'd embroidered herself because they were more feminine than a flimsy tissue.

Tess remembered the shreds of paper left behind after Mary's nervous frenzy. Emotion blocked her throat and she swallowed against it.

One of Mary's sisters took the podium and read her favorite

poem by Keats, *A Thing of Beauty*. Then the minister gave a brief sermon about God's grace offering comfort.

The service painted a picture of a woman longing for romance and being ignored by it. The pity of it was there had been far more to the petite woman than her brown, bobbed hair and cornflower blue eyes. For Mary to come to Tess with the information about her boss had required courage and conviction.

Through it all, Tess watched Jonathan Frye. He had been Mary's employer for ten years, but there was no evidence of grief on his face or in his body language. At one point he checked his phone and even sent a text. Anger stampeded through Tess at his arrogant callousness. Mary had been a loyal employee for ten years, and he refused her the respect of thirty minutes of his undivided attention.

Though he was probably responsible for Mary's death, Tess had expected Frye to at least put on a hypocritical show of grief.

When the minister opened the floor to anyone who wanted to share, Mary's two sisters stepped up to speak of family moments. The longer she listened to their grief-shaken voices, the more her anger built. When Frye walked up to the podium, she was both fascinated and offended.

"My name is Jonathan Frye. I was Mary's boss for ten years. She was in her early twenties when she came to work for us. She became my secretary five years ago. I will miss her calm presence, her efficiency in fielding phone calls and proofreading contracts, her organizational skills, and her excellent coffee. She should have been an engineer, she knew that much about what we did at Chanter. She kept me on track at work and brightened my day with her dry sense of humor. On behalf of myself, and all the employees at Chanter Construction, we're sorry for your loss. She will be missed."

Tess shot to her feet. Brett's hand momentarily tightened on hers, a *what the hell?* frown on his face. She tugged free and marched forward.

"My name is Tess Kelly. Mary and I met for the first time at a coffee shop last week, the day she passed away. She and I shared a drink and talked." She scanned the faces of the mourners and spotted Detective Buckler at the back. "It was just a random conversation between strangers, a thirty-minute exchange that became more meaningful, more sparkling clear because of her sudden death."

"I interview people for a living, but Mary's and my conversation wasn't really an interview." The similarities between Mary Stubben and Shelly Gooding clarified in her mind. Both were strong women, stronger than they appeared on the surface. One hoped to right a wrong while the other lived with the devastating consequences of one, but both faced their situation with courage.

"Mary shared a small portion of her life with me that day. We talked about our jobs. The personalities of the people we worked with, some of our challenges and what we hoped the future might hold." Tess focused directly on Jonathan Frye.

"In the few minutes we spent together I learned she was a responsible person of moral strength and character, one who was interested in righting wrongs. Though her physical being was petite, her voice soft, I recognized a core of strength in her. We exchanged contact information so we could keep in touch."

Frye's jaw tightened.

Tess leaned forward onto the podium and focused on Mary's family. Her eyes stung with sympathetic tears, but also tears of guilt and loss. "Sometimes I feel we're like drops of rain in a barrel knocking into each other. But those momentary bumps in time always leave an impression, and we may not realize what kind of effect they'll have until later. Mary touched you all, emotionally, intellectually, physically. Maybe it was a brief kiss, a nudge, a pat, or a kick." Take that, Jonathan Frye.

"But she left a lasting emotional impression, otherwise none of us would be sitting here right now. That's the only legacy any of us can hope to leave behind." Her breathing suddenly constricted as the full weight of her guilt came to bear. She was eager to find her seat and feel Brett's reassuring touch. "I would have liked the opportunity to know her better. I won't forget the moments we shared. I won't forget her. I'm so sorry for your loss."

Though Brett's jaw pulsed with anger, he slid an arm around her when she scooted in beside him and clutched his hand in both of hers. After the minister's brief prayer, the mourners began to file out. On the steps outside, Mary's family waited to greet each person as they left. While she and Brett waited to exit the building, she saw

Frye had been cornered by Mary's sisters and had not yet broken away from them.

Tess urged Brett closer to them so she could listen to their conversation.

"Mary will be missed. She was a member of our Chanter Family. Those of us in the office who knew her best have been grieving her loss."

"She liked her job," Her sister said. "She always said since she didn't have the experience to be useful in the creative process of design and building, she could at least keep everything running smoothly so the rest could move forward."

Frye turned and his piercing gaze rested on Tess, then narrowed. "Mary was more imaginative than she took credit for. Just recently she offered a suggestion that was very helpful to one of our projects."

Tess had never heard so much fork-tongued bullshit in her life. He was making complimentary noises without an ounce of sincerity behind them.

"I'm sorry, but I have to go. Chanter will be thinking of you, and we'll be in touch soon." He shook each woman's hand and hurried away, around the corner of the church to the parking lot.

Mary's two sisters approached Tess. "My name is Trudy Riders and this is my sister, Beth Cummings." The family resemblance between Mary and the two women lay in the shape of their face and the color of their eyes. Unlike Mary's chin-length bob, Trudy's hair was long, pulled back into a tail, and Beth's was cut short and feathered around her face.

"Mary talked about you. She read all your articles and was a fan. Meeting you must have made her day," Trudy said.

Mary had been too frightened to enjoy their encounter, but, unable to think of a reply, Tess merely smiled.

"We appreciate your sharing that small part of her last day," Beth said, her voice stifled by tears. She leaned in to hug Tess. Then the two left to join the rest of the mourners for the ride to the cemetery.

Brett guided Tess down the sidewalk to the parking lot.

Detective Buckler brushed by them on his way to the car, his expression a mirror of Brett's. "Meet me at the Starbucks on Linda Vista. We need to talk."

WITH THE PRESSURE of his hand against her back, Brett hurried Tess to the car. Though rage threatened to erode his control, he managed to keep his tone to a hoarse whisper…just barely. "What the fuck do you think you're doing, Tess?"

"I'm poking the bear. Frye was so fucking smug. Couldn't even stay off the phone long enough to pay attention to the service. Then gave that canned speech. And everything he said to her sisters. How can he be so unemotional about someone he saw every workday for five years? How can he face her family?"

"You're allowing your emotions to cloud your judgment, Tess. You need to be calm and smart, not emotional and rash. You're allowing your sense of responsibility and your anger over last night to get in the way of your objectivity."

Was she objective about any story? Just because she had good instincts didn't mean everything she believed had happened was the truth.

Brett sucked in a deep breath in an attempt to force back his anger. "You wouldn't go to press with the proof of one witness. You haven't uncovered anyone who can corroborate the information she gave you." Brett checked the car, even opened the trunk while Tess followed him.

"That's why I have an interview with Jason Hamilton on Thursday and another one with Todd Warren, one of Mary's coworkers, at five-thirty tomorrow. If Mary's suspicions were true about the blackmail, I'm one step closer to proving she was right."

"Jason Hamilton isn't going to own up to that, Tess."

"If I can get him to react to my knowing about it, I'll have my answer."

Brett shook his head. "He won't."

"You didn't think I could get Nicholas Brittain to cooperate with me either."

"You're covering his ass, Tess. Of course he's going to jump on board when everyone else is trying to fry it."

Tess stalked away and plopped into the car.

Brett slammed the trunk with more force than was necessary.

She was following the course of the story through pure instinct, and her feelings were leading her into trouble. Why couldn't she *see* that?

"I'm not covering Nicholas Brittain's ass," Tess said as soon as he got into the car. "The county building inspector I spoke with on the phone, who has no dog in the fight other than protecting the workers from unsafe building practices, said exactly what Brittain did. I told you that. There was no neglect or incompetence on the construction company's part. They were right in removing the substandard concrete. It could have caused major issues with the building later on if they hadn't."

"And they still don't know what caused the cement forms to give way. Besides, you told me all that last night." He whipped out into traffic and followed the stream of cars. They traveled several blocks in silence.

"The story I turned in this morning reported only the facts. How am I covering Nicholas Brittain's ass by reporting the truth?"

She was relentless when she got something into her head. "All right. You reported the truth. But you're also trying to spike Jonathan Frye's guns by targeting the stories you release."

"All I did was decide not to draw blood and smear a company to gain more readership," Tess said, her voice settling into a stubborn quietness.

"What did you gain by pulling that stunt at the church?" Brett asked as he watched a car that wove through traffic behind them.

She was silent for a moment. "I was angry. At him. At myself. At everything that happened last night. If he's behind it, he deserves to rot in jail."

"And if he is responsible for Mary Stubben's death, you've just made him think you know more than you do. You could have just painted a target on your back."

"If he's responsible for the break-in at my apartment, he already knows everything I know." Instead of talking to the window beside her as she'd been doing, she turned to face him. "And if he had nothing to do with anything, then who blew up my car, destroyed my dress, and stole my computer?

She was on a roll. "And why do you think I haven't written my article yet? I'm waiting until I have more information, or some kind of corroboration. I'm not going to put my reputation on the line for anything other than the truth." Her phone rang and she bent to dig it out of her bag.

While she spoke on the phone Brett tracked the dark blue car trailing them. Had Buckler sent an unmarked vehicle to follow them? Naw, the car was too nice for that. The driver wasn't trying to crowd them or make any aggressive moves.

Brett turned onto Morena Avenue and the car turned behind him. His mind worked through different defensive scenarios. If they were out to do harm, they'd had more than enough time to make their move.

"That was the warden's secretary at the corrections facility. My request has been okayed for Thursday."

Reluctant to voice a warning, he debated for a moment before saying, "Look in your rear view mirror at the dark blue car behind us. Does it look like the car you saw yesterday?"

Tess looked into the mirror then twisted in her seat to look behind them. "No, it's too new a model and too shiny. The car I saw was an older one, still nice, but you could tell it had some mileage on it."

"Okay." He continued onto Linda Vista and swung into the strip mall parking lot in front of Starbucks where Buckler would meet them, giving the car behind them little warning.

The dark blue car cruised by without stopping.

Tess relaxed noticeably. "False alarm, I guess."

Brett nodded, the taut muscles in his neck and shoulders relaxing. "I guess so."

They exited the car and spotted Buckler and Hart sitting outside the shop beneath one of the umbrellas, nursing their coffee. Brett motioned toward them. "Go ahead and have a seat. I'll get us some coffee."

THE DETECTIVES ROSE to their feet as Tess joined them. She motioned them back down.

"I was surprised to see you and Brett at the funeral," Buckler said.

"I feel responsible somehow for what happened to Mary. I felt compelled to pay my respects."

"And metaphorically poke Frye in the eye?" he asked.

"Wish I could have blackened it," Tess said doubling her fist. "He couldn't stay off the phone long enough to pay his respects."

"I saw him. But texting during a funeral isn't a crime, just bad manners. Thus far we have nothing to tie him to Mary's death. Only to someone in the city Planning Commission."

"Have you figured out who leaked the bids to him?"

"We're trying to keep the investigation as low-key as possible."

"I understand, Detective. I won't write anything until you give me the go-ahead."

"Good."

Brett came out onto the patio carrying two cups of coffee in a holder and a bag. He set the bag in the center of the table with a stack of napkins and popped first Tess's coffee free of the holder, then his own. "There's muffins in the bag if anyone's hungry."

Tess reached in, grabbed a muffin, then passed the bag on.

Detective Hart ran a hand over his face. "We've approached the head of the commission, and he's given us authorization to search emails to see who might have done it." He accepted the bag and dug out a muffin.

"I'm sorry you were dragged out until all hours last night," Tess said. She broke the muffin into bite-sized pieces on a napkin.

"It's part of the job." He turned to Brett. "Some of the guys on the MAST team worked the other incident. You were smart not to enter the apartment, and to treat it as if it might be wired."

Brett nodded. "Better safe than sorry."

"It was stupid to take the laptop," Tess said. "All they'll get from it are stories I've written for earlier editions and the research I've compiled for the stories I'm working on now. And I have everything backed up on the server at work and to an online storage."

"Assuming it was Frye and associates, they'll have all the information Mary gave you."

"Which is what I gave you, Detective. There's only the bare facts." And some she'd compiled herself since. Just her suspicions. Those wouldn't matter much unless there was information floating out there to back them up. There was a part of her that hoped her speculations scared the shit out of Frye.

Detective Buckler leaned forward to rest his elbows on the table. "They can always make your life miserable by using any personal information on it to screw with you."

"Not going to happen. I don't save passwords or personal info on it. I have it set up to delete my history immediately. The only thing that's on the computer is research. If Henry Sullivan wants to find out about me, he has the means to get my personal information in other ways. He did a pretty thorough job of reaping what he could about Brittain and Hamilton."

"Mary has to have found more dirt on them to elicit this kind of response," Hart said, more thinking out loud than asking a question.

"If it's Frye," Buckler countered. "Are there any other stories you're working, or have worked in the past, that have angered someone? Have you gotten any hate mail in the past few months?"

"I just finished a human trafficking story. Some of the girls gave interviews, named names, that kind of thing. But sex crimes and the FBI are working that together and they have the same information. It's the only other controversial story I've worked in the last few weeks. And I haven't gotten hate mail. Some weird letters from time to time, but most of my mail is from readers who want to tell me they enjoyed the stories or family members who wanted to thank me for writing about their loved ones. I think the paper keeps a file on the weird ones, if you want to ask to see them."

"And the stories you're working on now?"

"I just did a piece on the Brittain Development Corporation. A positive piece to encourage them not to drop their bid for the Ellison project."

Buckler leaned back in his chair and exchanged a glance with Hart. "We both read it. After having your car blown up, I'd think you'd want to lay low and stay away from controversy."

"It isn't my job to lay low, Detective. It's my job to step right into the middle of things."

Brett's hand clasped hers. "Tell them about the car, Tess."

Buckler and Hart perked up. "What car?" they said together.

Tess smiled despite the seriousness of the situation. "It's a dark blue sedan. I don't know what make or model. It has an orange, rectangular sticker on the right rear bumper, faded and indistinct, like it's been there a long time. It was parked in the lot outside the paper when the security guard and I came out to get into the car the day of the explosion. A tall man in a suit got into it and drove away just before I hit the button on my key fob. I thought I saw the same car outside a restaurant Brett and I went to yesterday." Was it only yesterday? It seemed like at least a month had passed since then. "You have the security tapes from the newspaper parking lot. You're bound to see the car."

"We don't have them, the FBI does." Hart grimaced. "We can request them, but it may take a while to get a copy."

"I thought there was supposed to be interdepartmental cooperation on this," Brett said. "Or are the feebs and Homeland shutting everyone else out?"

Hart and Buckler shared another glance. Hart leaned forward and he gaze went from Tess to Brett then back again. "Why is Homeland sitting on this one?"

Tess laid a hand on Brett's thigh.

He wiped his mouth and took a sip of coffee. "A little over a year ago, a terrorist named Tabarek Moussa came into the United States and went after some military personnel he believed killed his brother. My CO and I were his targets."

"Shit!" Buckler breathed.

Hart took a deep breath. "So they really think this is terrorist's taking another swipe at you?"

"They're ruling it out. I don't believe that's what it is. Tabarek and his network are history. If they weren't killed, they're being housed at Guantanamo." Brett laced his fingers together. "This isn't related to terrorists. If it were, we'd be dealing with a whole fucking building, a bus, a plane. Not a car. Not unless it was a target high-up politically. If you can get access to the forensic information about the bomb, you're going to find it's domestic."

As their silence stretched, Tess said, "I'll go online and look at makes and models and try to figure out which it was. It's an older model, not *old* old, but probably between five and ten years."

Hart seemed to recover. "The guy that got into the car, can you describe him?"

She'd had time to think about this. "He was Caucasian. Olive-skinned. Light brown hair with gray threaded through. Tall, really big, but with a little pooch starting around the middle. He wore a gray suit and black shoes, no hat. I only saw him from the back and side and never got a look at his face. He was quick to get in the car and drive away."

Everything in their demeanor had changed. They were going to go through the motions now and had jumped on the terrorist bandwagon.

Brett reached for her hand and his eyes met hers.

"Have you found the car or driver responsible for Mary's accident?" Tess asked.

"We've found the car. It was a stolen Hummer, thoroughly burned," Buckler said.

Tess nodded. "I suppose the forensic evidence went up in smoke."

"We're still hopeful they might find something."

When she stood, the detectives did as well.

Tears pressed behind her eyelids and she looked away. *We're on our own now.* "I have another appointment. You'll keep me posted when you can?"

"When we can." Buckler said.

Brett gathered the trash and tossed it in a receptacle, his movements jerky with seething frustration. Somehow watching him expend that emotion helped Tess find her composure.

"Where were you when the car bomb went off, Ensign Weaver?" Hart asked as Brett brushed by him.

"I was finishing up a tour downrange, dealing with assholes a lot worse than any you've seen on the streets of San Diego. If you want any more information you'll have to talk to my platoon commander, Lieutenant Commander Jeffrey, on the Coronado base."

"We may have to do that."

"Knock yourselves out."

"Stay away from Frye, Ms. Kelly. We don't want our investigation compromised," Hart said.

"I'll stay away from him as long as he keeps his distance from me, Detective."

They had only taken a step or two when something occurred to her and she turned back. "Why would terrorists paint bullet holes on my wedding dress, Detectives? Though it smacks of terrorism, it feels more homegrown than Middle Eastern. You might want to think about that."

BRETT LOOPED AN arm around her waist and they walked away. All he could say was, "It's going to be okay, Tess."

Her attention focused on a man walking across the parking lot.

"What is it? Is that someone you recognize?"

"I can't see his face, but, yeah, I think I've seen him somewhere before."

Brett's steps slowed and he rested his hand on his Sig as he studied the car parked next to theirs. It looked like the car following them earlier.

A door swung open and Miguel Delgado stepped out.

"Relax, soldier boy. I'm here to thank your girl, not cause any trouble."

"You have her number."

Miguel's gaze turned flat and dark. He reminded Brett of the South American snakes they'd run into on occasion. He and his teammates had dispatched them quickly. Better they were dead than to have to worry about where they might show up the rest of the day. Every time he faced Miguel he got the same quiet feeling he did before taking a kill shot.

"Easy, *ese*. Some things require a face-to-face," Miguel said.

Brett studied him for a long moment. "Tell your driver to stay in the car with his hands on the steering wheel and not to make any sudden moves." Miguel bent and spoke to the man behind the wheel.

"Move out from behind the door and lean back against the driver's side window."

Miguel sauntered over to the other side of the car and leaned back against it.

Brett scanned the parking lot and, seeing no movement, urged Tess forward, out of the way of a car going by. "Stay close to me and as far away from him as possible," he murmured in her ear.

She nodded. Brett turned his attention to Miguel.

Tess seemed more at ease with the man than he. "What is it, Mr. Delgado?"

"I heard you are still having problems, *chica*."

Brett's shoulder muscles tightened. What the hell? How had he learned about the break-in? Since nothing was found, the police had decided to issue a brief story about a bomb threat being called in at the apartment complex.

"You could say that."

"I may be able to help you."

Tess's gaze met Brett's, then swung back to Miguel. "What do you have in mind?"

"Your man is stretched thin. And I have many friends from our neighborhood I could reach out to help you find a solution."

"Your—associates?" Tess asked.

Miguel's smile was wolfish. "I will tell my men what you called them. They will be amused. But no, not my men. Two of the neighborhood men need work. One has been a security guard for many years. He has retired now, but is having trouble making ends meet. The other man worked as a bouncer at a local bar until the bar closed. They could keep watch over your car while you go about your business, keep an eye out for anyone who might follow you."

"And report back to you?"

"No, *chica*. Report to you. These men have no association with my people. But they owe me a favor. Just as I owe you one now. It is a way for us all to clear the slate."

"Why would you owe me a favor?" Tess asked.

"The lawyer you recommended. He is doing well for Daniel."

"Good."

"I pay my debts."

# CHAPTER EIGHTEEN

T HURSDAY STARTED WITH an early-morning call from Captain Jackson. Brett was the least superstitious guy on his new team, but he had a bad feeling about the meeting. He'd moved on from his old team nearly eighteen months ago. Why was he being called to his old CO's office?

After arranging for Hawk to pick her up, Brett dropped Tess at the Metropolitan Correctional Center and turned the car toward Coronado. He passed through the base gates, and his stomach tightened as he neared his CO's office building.

The last time Brett had been there was for a personal one-on-one with Jackson. He'd felt uncomfortable facing the guy who'd endured three days of brutal beatings and more because of him. The terrorists who'd taken over Jackson's house and imprisoned his family had delighted in pounding on him while torturing his wife with threats. All because Brett, their real target, had been out of town with Tess in Washington. Could that be what the meeting was about? Had Jackson discovered something about the bombing that linked it to terrorists?

Jackson's aide hadn't given him even a hint as to the purpose of the meeting.

He parked in front of the one story brick building. It was blocky and utilitarian, and the only landscaping consisted of a few shrubs and sidewalks edged with military precision. He stepped out of the car and gave his cammies, the uniform of the day, a quick inspection. They were the least faded of the much used and abused uniforms he'd worn for the last year during training and deployment. Though their color had weathered, they were clean and pressed, and his insignia in place.

He glanced at his watch and strode down the sidewalk to the main entrance. He opened the door, then stood back as three men hustled out of the building, pausing to snap to attention before him and offer salutes. He returned the salutation, then entered and continued through the lobby and down a long hallway.

Seaman Crouch had been replaced, and Brett had a moment to wonder where he had moved on to before the apple-cheeked aide sitting outside Jackson's office rose to his feet in greeting. The guy had a round baby face that made him look about fourteen. The tag on his uniform read Seaman Chad Vincent. "Captain Jackson said you were to go right in, sir."

"Thank you." He breezed by the aide's desk and knocked on the door. At the Captain's brief command of "Enter," he pushed it open.

Jackson stood at the double window behind his desk as Brett crossed the threshold, nudged the door closed, and saluted.

"At ease, Cutter." Jackson came around his desk and studied him for a brief moment, then offered his hand. "Welcome home."

"Thank you, sir." As he shook his hand, Brett studied Jackson in return, noting the small scars around one eye, where the one socket had been crushed during the beatings. All in all the man had healed remarkably and looked much the same as before. His prematurely gray hair was almost completely white, though his features were that of a man in his prime.

"Have a seat," Jackson motioned to the two chairs in front of his desk.

Brett took the one furthest from the door and Jackson took the other.

"I heard about the car bombing. How is Tess?"

Was that what he was here to discuss? Was Jackson concerned he'd be targeted again?

"She's dealing, sir. We're still waiting for someone—either the FBI or homeland security—to tell us what they've learned."

"I wouldn't hold my breath," Jackson said, his tone dry.

Brett smiled. "I'm not. Neither of us thinks it's terrorist related, sir."

Jackson quirked a brow. "Bombing the car of a newspaper reporter wouldn't send a big enough message. It sounds like something homegrown to me."

"That's what we both believe as well."

"Any suspects in mind?"

"Yes, sir. Tess was approached by a woman about a week ago with information about some illegal activity at the construction company where she worked. Shortly after that the woman was killed and Tess's car was blown up. But I suppose the FBI and Homeland have to work through every possible scenario and rule out suspects. The San Diego police are involved with the investigation into the accident that led to the woman's death."

"Sounds like Tess stumbled knee-deep into shit."

Brett nodded. "That's about the gist of it."

"If there's anything you need, or she does, all you have to do is pick up the phone."

Too bad he'd offered after the two men Miguel suggested had already come on board. "Thank you, sir. You got your invitation to the wedding?"

"Yes, and we'll be there. Marsha's disappointed she can't accept Tess's invitation to be part of the wedding, but her mother's surgery will keep her from being involved."

"I'm sorry to hear that. I know she and Tess and the other wives have become close."

"Yes, they're a force to be reckoned with."

For the first time since he'd walked into the office Brett smiled. "I'm glad Tess has back up while I'm gone." He grew serious. "Now are you going to tell me the bad news? Has something happened to one of the guys on my team?"

"No. As far as I know they're fine and will be returning ASAP. Hopefully in time for your wedding."

"Good. But…" Brett urged.

"Lieutenant Commander Jeffrey was called out of the country unexpectedly and asked me to speak with you, since I was involved in writing recommendations for your file. Your promotion may be delayed until after the FBI and Homeland investigation is completed."

*As slow as their wheels turned, that could be a year—or two—or never.*

*Fuck!* "Do they think Tess or I have something illegal going on?"

"No, nothing like that." Jackson ran a hand over his hair. "I can't give you any reason that makes sense to me, Cutter. All I can tell you is Lieutenant Commander Jeffrey, Lieutenant Harding, and I are all pushing for you to get the promotion. You've worked for it, and you deserve it. But because HQ is stalling, I wanted you to be aware that it might not come through in the near future."

He didn't do what he did for medals, or the money. He did it because he was called to do it and he loved it. But it wasn't just disappointment that tightened like a vise inside him, but a sense of betrayal, too. It seemed like whenever something happened in their personal lives, it affected their military career.

Hawk had done the right thing, and had saved lives when he'd intervened when Derrick Armstrong had gone nuts. And because of it, Hawk had been deployed for six months and missed most of Zoe's pregnancy. What the hell was up with that?

And now, because the FBI was investigating Tess's car bombing, his promotion had dried up. What did one have to do with the other?

He wished Senior Chief had never told him he was up for it. He wished he'd never told Tess. *Shit!*

"This bump in the road isn't a reflection on your ability, Cutter. We both know you deserve this."

Man, this guy had done a one-eighty since Brett had been under his command. But it didn't help the tightness in his chest one damn bit.

Brett got to his feet. "I appreciate you calling me down here to tell me face-to-face, Captain."

Captain Jackson stood and offered his hand. "Lt. Commander Jeffrey and I are both in contact with Homeland and the FBI on a regular basis. I'll keep you posted as we learn things, Brett."

He nodded. "Thank you, sir."

Jackson returned the gesture. "I'll see you at the wedding if not before, Cutter."

"Thank you, sir." He turned to leave then stopped to face Jackson again. "Tess has been offered a job with the Washington Post."

"The Washington Post!" Jackson's brows shot up. "That's—

amazing."

Brett saw the wheels turning in Jackson's head. "Yes, sir. If she decides to take it, I may put in for a transfer." He'd been kicking the idea around ever since she'd told him about the job. This would be the right time to do it. He could start fresh. He'd done it before. "We'd be able to see each other more if I was on the other coast with her. It would only be a little more than a two-hour drive from Little Creek to DC."

Jackson's expression became grave. "I'd hate for us to lose you, Cutter. But if you decide to do it, I'll try and grease the wheels for you."

"Thank you, Captain. I'll let you know. We're going to fly out in a few days so she can check the job out and make a final decision."

"When did this happen?"

"A couple of days before I came home. She was going to turn it down, but I wanted her to try the place on for size first. We've both been there, but really checking the area, her work place—Our families have to make so many sacrifices already, I just thought—if she wants to give it a shot, we'll work it out."

Jackson studied him for a moment. "Cutter, I wish I'd been as wise as you at the beginning of Marsha's and my marriage. I think it's a damn good idea. Our wives deserve as much success as we do."

"Yes, sir."

"Congratulate her for me."

"Will do."

All the way to the car, Brett kept telling himself if Tess took the job, a transfer would be in his best interest as well as hers. It didn't ease the anger that leapt to life and made him want to pound on something. Maybe things would be better in Virginia. Or would things still ebb and flow at the whim of political winds there too? Probably.

Had Tess experienced these deep feelings of disappointment and frustration? If she had, she'd dealt with it with more grace and control than he was. *God damnit!* He jerked the car door open, got in, and slammed it shut.

At least she was going to get the opportunity to look at Washington as a potential home instead of just a fun place to visit.

He'd take care of that travel paperwork right now, and go by and get some new uniforms. Then he'd run by the PX and see if they had anything close to what he wanted to buy Tess for her bride's gift. And maybe while he was at it, he'd concentrate on what it was going to be like married to the love of his life instead of worrying about this promotion bullshit.

# CHAPTER NINETEEN

T ESS SHIFTED ON the hard seat outside the interview room. She had only been waiting there fifteen minutes and already her butt was getting numb. The long hallway stretched into the distance. Cream-colored tiled floors shone clean and waxed, reflecting the florescent lighting overhead.

From where she sat on the second floor, several secure elevators, steel doors, and more than a hundred guards stood between her and the prisoners on the twenty-three floors of the Metropolitan Correctional Center above her—but her hands still shook with nerves, and she caught her breath at every sound. Part of her feelings stemmed from the claustrophobic pressure of the structure itself, claustrophobia she was sure the population housed here also experienced.

At the sound of approaching footsteps Tess glanced up. Clarence Niles, Daniel Delgado's lawyer, strode toward her. She'd met Clarence at the scene of a shooting and had interviewed him later about his client who, after a brief trail, was declared innocent. She got to her feet and shook the hand he offered.

"What's going on, Tess?" His hair was a little thinner, his teeth a little whiter, but he still reminded her of a young Bruce Willis. The only unattractive thing about him was the clients he represented. He specialized in gang members, prostitutes, and drug dealers.

"I'm here to interview your client," she said, stating the obvious.

"Because?" he asked.

"Because he's a honor roll student from a poor neighborhood

with a full scholarship to the University of California and an exemplary work record at the store he's accused of robbing."

"And?"

"And I know his brother has probably run interference to keep him out of the gang he's affiliated with. The district attorney may be using Daniel to try and get to the brother."

"Sounds like you have a pretty good grasp of the situation. Let's sit for a minute before they bring Daniel down." He pointed to the chair she'd been sitting on and took the one next to hers. "This kid is getting a raw deal. It's guilt by association. They found no drugs, no money, no gun, no mask, but they're still holding him because one of witnesses is adamant it was him."

"His boss, Mr. Gordon."

Clarence studied her face. "I see you've met the asshole."

"Yes." Tess paused a moment debating. "I was not impressed, nor are several of the women who work for him."

His brows lifted. "Sexual harassment?"

"No. I don't think so. I think it's just an all-round assholery rather than a criminal one."

Clarence laughed. "I can't go into court and say 'your honor you need to release my client because the man accusing him is an asshole.' That isn't against the law, otherwise I'd probably have a cell upstairs myself."

She remained quiet for a moment. "What kind of charges can be brought against a person if they purposely identify the wrong person for a crime?"

"Criminal conspiracy and perjury if they identify them on the stand during trial. But in either instance, to prove they're purposely identifying them for their own gain would be tough."

"You've dealt with quite a few defendants and probably have a sense of guilt or innocence about each one you've represented. Do you believe Daniel's innocent?"

He narrowed his gray-green eyes as he studied her. "Yeah, I do. No bullshit. I think he was a few blocks from the store, fit the description, and the cops thought they had their guy—at first. Then when they learned who his brother was, it solidified the idea in their minds. They believe he dropped the money, gun and mask off somewhere along the way. But they haven't been able to find them."

"Lack of evidence would be enough for a dismissal, even with Gordon's ID."

"Yeah. But by the time this case goes to trial Daniel will have missed graduation and the scholarship he's earned will have gone away. Without that college money, he'll be stuck in the neighborhood he comes from."

"And I believe that's exactly what Gordon wants to happen."

Clarence's brows went up again. "Why?"

She needed to get a feel for Daniel's innocence herself. "I want to meet Daniel first, and then I'll tell you."

Clarence frowned and started to say something when the clang of the barred door at the end of the hall interrupted.

Two large guards led a shorter handcuffed man toward them. Clarence stood and offered Tess a hand up. One guard unlocked the interview room directly in front of them while the other stood watchful and expressionless next to Daniel.

The two led him inside, handcuffed him to the table in the center of the room, went over the rules that they were to have no physical contact with the prisoner, and they were not allowed to hand him anything, then departed and locked the door behind them. Through the narrow window on the door, Tess could see the edge of one of their shoulders where a guard leaned against the wall outside.

After having met Miguel Delgado, Tess was surprised by how completely opposite Daniel was from his brother. Where Miguel was all hard, ropy muscle, Daniel leaned more toward a stocky, less muscular build, yet he wasn't fat. Where Miguel's features were sharp and angular, Daniel's were more curvilinear without being effeminate. But what surprised her even more was the well-modulated depth of his voice when, after Clarence introduced her, he said, "Nice to meet you, Ms. Kelly." He could have been a radio announcer.

She and Clarence took a seat opposite him. Clarence immediately asked. "How are you doing, Daniel?"

"I'm okay." He clenched his hands and tugged at the loop that held the handcuffs in place. "I'm keeping my head down and working on my school work so I can graduate on time."

"Good."

His dark eyes, so much like his mother's turned to Tess. "What was it you wanted to ask me, Ms. Kelly?"

"First, is it okay with you if I tape this interview?" she asked, producing a small digital recorder from her pocket. "They wouldn't allow me to bring in my notebook and pen."

Clarence laid a hand on Daniel's arm. "If they subpoenaed you, you'd have to hand over the interview, Tess. I won't allow Daniel to answer any questions detrimental to his defense."

"I don't intend to ask any that would be." At his nod, and Daniel's, she started the recorder. "I'd like to hear from you directly what happened the night of the robbery."

Daniel's gaze swung to Clarence and, at his nod, took a deep breath. "The same thing that happens every night I work. I rotate around the store doing what needs done. That night I worked in the dairy department stocking the refrigeration unit. When I was done in dairy, I bagged some groceries, cleaned the conveyor belts on the checkout lanes, and did some sweeping. When my shift was over at eleven, I walked home. I was almost there when a police car came screaming around the corner, pulled over, and two cops jumped out of the car with their guns drawn. They screamed at me to get on the ground, so I did. I kept asking them what was happening, but neither of them would tell me."

"How long does it take for you to walk home from the store?"

"Twenty or twenty-five minutes. I guess it was more like twenty minutes that night."

"Did you see anyone along the way you recognized?"

"No. It's eleven-thirty at night. People don't walk around that late in our neighborhood. My mom works the late shift for a cleaning company, and she can't pick me up because she doesn't get off until midnight."

In the last two days, Tess had walked the distance from the store. Brett, after enlisting Bowie and Doc's help, had accompanied her. All three men had been in hypervigilant SEAL mode the entire time. She'd stopped at several neighborhood houses, spoken to rough-looking young men, their bodies marked by tattoos. Since she'd had three obviously armed men with her, none of them had attempted any aggression or intimidation. All of them knew Daniel, and none of them had seen him that night. And if they had, the district attorney wouldn't have thought them credible anyway.

Everyone on Daniel's street had seen the arrest. From the moment the lights of the police car had flashed, the neighbors had been glued to their windows. All of them were adamant Daniel was innocent.

"Did you happen to notice the time, Daniel?" Tess asked.

"No, but it would be on the cops' dashcam. I usually get home a few minutes before eleven each night."

Tess exchanged a look with Clarence. His assessment of the time was what several witnesses had told her. If it took him twenty minutes to walk home every night, then he wouldn't have had time to leave work, come back, rob the store, wash off the tattoo, stow the cash, gun, and mask, and make it home in the same length of time—unless he'd run like the wind. Or had an accomplice who'd given him a ride and dropped him close to his house. She'd asked about a car but no one had seen him get out of one. And there'd never been any mention of a partner in the crime. And how the hell had the cops gotten there so quickly?

"What kind of relationship do you have with your boss, Mr. Gordon?"

Daniel was silent for a moment. "Well, I always thought it was okay. He's not exactly the touchy-feely pat you on the back for a good job kind of dude. Sometimes he can be short when he tells me to do things. Like he's pissed off about something. But he's like that sometimes with everyone who works for him."

Tess bit her lip. "Do you know any of Mr. Gordon's family?"

"No. I've seen his wife a time or two when she's stopped by to speak to him." Daniel leaned forward to rest his arms on the table, an awkward position when his wrists were bound to the ring. "I don't know why Mr. Gordon thinks it was me who held up the store that night. I've never done anything to him to piss him off enough for him to do it out of spite. He must really believe it was me. But it wasn't. I swear it wasn't."

His earnest confusion was plain to read. Tess thought for a moment. If she brought up Gordon's nephew by name, and Daniel mentioned it to his brother... "Have the police asked you about your brother and the gang?"

"They did when they first brought me in. They offered me a deal if I'd tell them things about Miguel and the others. I kept thinking, why would I take a deal for something I didn't do?" For the first time anger seamed his lips together in a taut line and his nostrils flared. "I wouldn't do it. I asked for a lawyer, then he tried to get me to talk to them. And every time I told him I was innocent, he just kept saying, give them what they want, and they'll let you go."

Tess said, "They couldn't just let you go if you were being arrested for armed robbery, Daniel."

He shrugged. "That's what the lawyer said they'd do." His dark eyes settled on her face. "I know you met my brother. I know what you think you see when you look at Miguel. But he's more than the tattooed gangbanger you think he is. He's done a lot to keep the others off my back, to keep me and Mom safe."

"I know he loves you and your mother very much. But I also know he probably lives his life by different rules than most of us. I don't hold you responsible or look in judgment on you because of your brother's lifestyle. You have no control over the decisions other people make about their lives. Only the ones you make yourself."

She was repeating the words Brett had said to her only a couple of days before when discussing Brian Gooding and her suspicions. If she felt torn about what might become of a man she didn't even know, she could only guess how Daniel must feel. "Who was your other lawyer?"

"I have that information, Tess," Clarence said. "But he can't talk to you about anything. Attorney-client privilege extends beyond my replacing him."

"I'd still like his name."

Clarence glanced in Daniel's direction.

"His name was Eli Carter. He was court appointed."

Tess nodded. "Do you have any tattoos?"

"No. Mom went off on me about them. She said Miguel had enough ink on his body for the both of us."

From what Tess had seen she had to agree. And the area between Daniel's wrist and elbow, the place Rosalie said she'd seen a tattoo, was free of any images.

For fifteen minutes she guided Daniel through questions about school, and his interests. "What is it you hope to study in college?"

"I want to be a doctor. But that won't happen if I have a felony conviction."

"Mr. Niles is really good at his job. I can't see him allowing that to happen."

Daniel's gaze rested on his handcuffs. "Ms. Kelly, they're not interested in looking anywhere else, they think they have their guy. And I won't give them anything on my brother, and that pisses them off. They won't care if they convict me, even if I'm innocent. They just think they're getting another gangbanger off the street. That's the way things work in my neighborhood."

The sad acceptance in his eyes tugged at Tess's sympathies, no matter how objective she tried to be. "We'll see, Daniel. Mr. Niles has investigators out looking for other evidence. Something may pop up."

He jerked his head in Clarence's direction. "Do you have investigators looking for the real guy?"

"Yes, I have an investigator looking at the evidence against you."

Hope flared in his face, his eyes. "Good. I'm glad. They have to find something to prove it wasn't me."

Tess scooped up the recorder and stood to leave. "I appreciate you seeing me, Daniel."

"Thanks for coming and getting me off the floor for a little while."

"Keep studying."

"I don't have anything else to do."

Clarence knocked on the door and the guard opened it. Tess stepped outside the room and took a deep breath. It seemed they'd been in the small space for days when it had only been an hour.

They waited until the guards had freed Daniel from the metal ring and walked him down the hall.

"What were you looking for, Tess?"

"I know you probably have some of this information, but I'll share it anyway. One witness saw a tattoo on the inside of the holdup man's arm between the guy's wrist and elbow."

"It could have been a temp and removed after the robbery."

"There would have been residue, and he'd have had to go somewhere to wash it away. They don't come off easily. There would have been a red area where he'd had to scrub. And doesn't it seem he accomplished a lot in twenty minutes?"

"Yeah. Is that it?"

"Ronald Gordon has a nephew with a drug problem. A nephew who's been arrested in the past for breaking and entering. And who has a history of violence. His name is Jay Gordon. It's Gordon's sister's boy. She had him when she was a teenager and has raised him by herself. He may either be a member of Miguel's gang or may buy his drugs from them. In any case, Gordon got this look of rage on his face when I mentioned Miguel. I think he holds Miguel Delgado responsible for his nephew's drug problem. And I believe he named Daniel as the suspect on purpose to both protect his nephew, who I believe may have held up the store, and to get even."

"Holy hell!"

"I couldn't ask Daniel if he knew Jay. And I can't ask Miguel either. Miguel might kill him before he can be arrested. But if I were you, I'd find out if Jay has a tattoo and try and light a fire under the DA's office to pick him up for questioning before he gets rid of the money, the gun and the mask. If he hasn't already. And before Miguel goes after him."

"The DA's office has to know Gordon has a nephew with a record."

"Yes, since they're the ones who probably prosecuted him in the past. But they think they have leverage against Miguel as long as no one else is brought in as a suspect in the robbery. As a last resort you can let them know I have all this information, and that I'm digging into this story. It might move things along. Every day they don't pick Jay up is a day he's in danger and another day Daniel remains stagnating in here."

"So you believe he's innocent, too?"

After a calming breath, she said, "I hope he is, since I've just given you information that might free him."

"You may be burning some bridges here if I mention your name to the DA's office. The lawyers who work there tend to have long memories when someone throws a poison pen and disrupts their bargaining strategies."

"If you find evidence that they are purposely stonewalling to gain leverage against Miguel, I'd like to know. It would make my story even bigger. Besides, if Daniel's innocent, what they're doing is wrong, you know it as well as I do."

"You know this take-no-prisoners attitude might cause you some problems."

"Says the man whose defends some pretty shady characters."

Clarence shrugged. "Everyone is entitled to a good defense. Besides, my clients always pay their bill."

He grinned and Tess couldn't tell if he was serious or not.

"What do you need in return for all this?" he asked.

"Just let me know ahead of the other media outlets when he's cleared and released. I already have a partial story ready, I just need an ending." She glanced down the hall, eager to leave.

Clarence motioned for her to precede him. "With no weapon, no money recovered, one eye witness identifying a masked hold-up guy—this won't stand up in court. I can get him off, Tess. Just not in time for him to keep his scholarship."

"I know, and I'm sure the DA does, too. I don't know how in good conscience they're keeping him in here."

"The lines get blurred when they're after a bigger fish. And Miguel is a piranha."

That was a fitting description of Miguel. She just hoped he didn't devour Jay Gordon before he could be arrested.

# CHAPTER TWENTY

**B**RETT LIFTED THE bottle of water to his lips and took a large swallow. His gaze stayed on Tess as she played with A.J. several yards away. The afternoon sun struck her hair and turned the dark strands to copper, her skin glowed smooth and pale, though her cheeks had taken on a light pink tinge.

God, she was beautiful. It was probably a good thing they were hanging out in Hawk's back yard right now, because every time he looked at her he wanted to go caveman and carry her off to a bedroom, lock the door, and make love until he was too exhausted to move. But it went deeper than that. She fed something in him no other woman had ever touched. He thought of her every day. Wanted to hear her voice every morning.

What would he do if she took the Washington job? How would they survive the move from one coast to the other? They'd only get to see each other when they were both free. Which would be pretty much never. He cut the thoughts off. He'd deal with that part if and when he had to.

Tess stretched to the right and caught the Nerf ball A.J. threw, more a wild, out-of-control swing than a toss. The kid was going to have a powerful throwing arm if he ever learned some control. She pitched the ball underhand back to him and A.J. laughed when it bounced off his chest and landed at his feet.

"Did A.J. go with you to pick up Tess?"

"No. Zoe dropped him off with your mom this morning while I did the yard work, then Clara brought him by after I picked her up. I'll have him the rest of the afternoon. We'll hang together and take a nap." Hawk flipped the burgers over and closed the lid on the gas grill. He pointed a finger at the water bottle. "You're guzzling that water like you wished it was something stronger."

His brother-in-law knew him well. "Before I left—places south to go CONUS, Senior Chief told me I was up for a promotion. Captain Jackson called me in today and told me things have been put on hold until the investigation into the car bomb is completed."

"Why Captain Jackson and not Lieutenant Commander Jeffrey?"

"Jeffrey had to go out of the country. And maybe they thought I'd take the news better from someone I'd had more contact with."

Hawk hiked a hip up on the picnic table situated close by the grill. "Wish I could say I'm surprised about the stall, but I'm not."

"Neither was I, not really, but I'm still fucked up about it. I was mad as hell at first. Still am. I was counting on the extra money so Tess and I could get a bigger place."

Hawk frowned and nodded.

"It hits you in the gut," Brett muttered. "That feeling of betrayal."

"Don't rush to judgment, Brett, I know you think I got a raw deal when they deployed the team back to Iraq, but it kept me and the others involved with Derrick's take-down from doing time, and losing our careers. It wasn't the perfect solution, but it worked. I'm here with Zoe and A.J. where I want to be, need to be. It was worth the six months."

"At the time you didn't feel that way."

"No, I was mad as hell, felt just like you. But I learned something from it. When we're in combat we're focused on following a plan and getting a series of things to go the way we want them to, one at a time. It's all right up front. But behind the scenes at HQ nothing is as it seems. Sometimes there's other maneuvers going on in the background, things we're not aware of, and we have to let them play out before the whole picture comes to light."

Hawk was right. Even in the SEAL community, despite the good press and a supportive nation, there was still politics involved in every mission. "Had you not returned to Iraq, the kid I was accused of killing might never have been found, and Tess's dad might not have survived to cover the story and clear me. So, I know good came out of it. And I'm grateful for it."

"The mandate came down from on high for us to find the kid, Brett. HQ wanted your name cleared as much as we did. So they did have your back. They may still have it right now, they're just not showing their hand."

Brett nodded. For a moment he was tempted to share Tess's job offer and his thoughts about a transfer. But it was her news to share, and the transfer wouldn't become a reality unless she decided to give the Times a shot. And it might not even then. It depended on a lot of different variables whether he'd qualify for a transfer to an east coast team. The Navy's needs came first.

Brett's gaze shifted to A.J. and Tess again. "Tess and I are going to take off for a few days. She has some research she wants to do in Washington for a story, as soon as this grocery store robbery thing winds up."

"It might do you both good to get out of town and away from things."

"Yeah, it might."

Hawk flipped the burgers and closed the grill again. "How are the two watch dogs working out?"

"Actually pretty good. We did background checks on them and got references from their last jobs. Alonzo's real quiet but stays on the ball. Armando packs some serious muscle. He could probably take us both on with one arm behind his back. I talked to him a little about what special ops might have to offer him. He seemed interested, but he's gearing up to do some amateur boxing."

"If we weren't so tight for time right now—" Hawk said.

"Hey, you don't have to say anything, bro. I know you'd be there if you could be. But you're doing what needs to be done right here. Zoe and A.J. come first. That's the way it should be."

When they sat down to eat at the kitchen table a few minutes later, Brett's attention was snagged by the relationship Tess had developed with A.J. The kid wanted to sit beside her in his high chair, wanted to share his food with her. She pretended to eat the tiny bite of hot dog he offered her and nibbled at his hand instead, the kid roared with laughter. Brett realized he had no relationship with his nephew. He'd been gone most of the little man's twenty-month-old life on training missions and deployment, and had never had any one-on-one with him at all after he was about six months old.

When Hawk started to clean up, Brett wandered over to the high chair and released the tray. A.J. seemed okay with him picking him up, but his eyes went to Tess for reassurance. His nephew was sturdy and tall for his age. He frowned at Brett, and eyed him, sizing him up, his features and his expression such a miniature of Hawk's, Brett had to grin.

A.J. laughed, then pointed at Tess. "Tiss," he said.

"Yeah, that's Aunt Tess. I'm Uncle Brett. You want to try and say Brett?"

A.J. shook his head and pointed toward the living room.

"He wants to go to the picture wall Zoe made for him down the hall," Hawk said.

While Tess loaded the dishwasher, Brett wandered out of the kitchen and was immediately confronted by clusters of candid photos of friends and family stretching along the entire wall. He'd noticed it the other night during his welcome home barbeque, but hadn't thought to ask about it.

"Where's Momma?" Brett asked.

A.J. pointed to Zoe's photo.

"Where's Daddy?"

A.J. twisted around to look back toward the kitchen and pointed. Brett laughed. "Yeah, he's right here, isn't he?"

Tess leaned against the kitchen doorjamb.

Brett spoke to her though his attention was on his nephew. "Where's Hawk? He needs to see this."

"He's bringing up some toys from the weight room. And he's done this more than once with A.J."

"Where's Brett?" Brett asked.

A.J. pointed at his picture.

"I'm Brett, little man." Brett pointed to himself. "Brett."

A.J. frowned, his gray gaze so much like Hawk's focused in on him as if he was working through a problem. He poked a stubby finger into Brett's chest. "Bet."

Brett grinned. "All right! You know how to do high-five?" He held up his hand. A.J. slapped his palm.

Tess laughed. "I hate to break up this party, Brett, but I have an interview scheduled with one of the building inspectors investigating the Brittain accident. Alonzo will be here any minute."

"Okay."

Hawk stepped into the hall from the kitchen, a box of toys in his arms. They followed him into the living room.

"Smart kid," Brett said as he passed A.J. off to Hawk.

"Damn straight," Hawk replied.

"Damn!" A.J. said with feeling.

Hawk's head whipped in his son's direction, his eyes wide.

"You are *so* in trouble if that ends up being the new word of the day," Tess said with a smile. She brushed her lips across A.J.'s cheek and then Hawk's. "Thank you for lunch and for picking me up." She patted Hawk's arm.

"You're welcome." Hawk's concerned frown hadn't abated.

"Dude, they're like sponges," Brett said with a laugh. "Katie Beth used to repeat things we didn't even know she'd heard."

Hawk shot him a steely-eyed look. "I'll remind you of that when you have some of your own."

As soon as the door closed behind them, Tess laughed. "Hawk's expression was priceless."

Brett shook his head. "If you'd told me two years ago he'd be so—" he searched for an appropriate word, "—domesticated, I'd have said, no way."

"Marriage changes you. It takes over your life, more than your work does. Are you sure you're ready for that?"

All the technical training he'd done as a SEAL, the harsh physical conditions he'd worked in, even the stuff he'd done to overcome his speech issues when he was recovering from his head injury, didn't compare to this. He understood that. This was long term, together—forever.

"I'm used to working as part of a team, doing my part, sharing the load. You and I, we pull together even when we're apart. I know we're going to do just as well after the 'I do's.'"

Alonzo pulled up in his white Altima. Tess wandered over to say hello while Brett went over the rental car, looking under the hood, under the chassis and along both bumpers. Satisfied everything was okay, he joined Tess.

In his early sixties, Alonzo Garcia looked younger. His dark eyes had a steady regard, Brett had liked from the first. Though he'd only spent four years in the Marines, he still had the military bearing and walk. He was licensed to carry his firearm and did. Brett filled the man in on where they were going.

Once Brett and Tess were in the car, his thoughts returned to their earlier conversation. They'd talked about kids in the abstract, but not specifics. "Think you might want a little guy like A.J. someday?" he asked after he got in and fastened his seat belt.

Tess smiled. "Someday. Maybe even a couple."

He started to make an offhand comment like, 'Let me know when you're ready, I'm up for it.' But knowing the bulk of responsibility would rest on Tess's shoulders, he wasn't sure either of them was ready for that kind of stress in their relationship. Their marriage needed to be well established before they brought another person into it.

"You're not in any rush, are you?" Brett asked.

Tess remained silent for a moment. "To have a baby?"

"Yeah."

"No. Why?" Her answer carried a thread of adamancy.

He relaxed. "Just checking." He smiled. "I wouldn't mind practicing some before it counts. They say practice makes perfect."

Tess chuckled. "We may have to do that later."

"Good idea."

# CHAPTER TWENTY-ONE

THE OFFICE BUILDING of Hamilton Construction was only a couple of blocks from the Café Curiosité, where she had met Mary Stubben. They parked in a parking structure, left the car under Alonzo's careful observation, and took the stairs down to street level to catch the trolley.

Every time Tess thought about Mary, a sick ache hollowed out her insides. She'd played the voice mail over and over, and it sounded like someone had happened upon her while she was on the phone.

"After this meeting with Hamilton I'd like to make a quick stop at the café down the street."

"Okay. I'll call Alonzo and let him know."

Having help with her security must have taken some stress off of Brett, because he seemed more relaxed. Saving the time it took him to check the car each time they left it was well worth the money they were paying Alonzo and Armando. The two men did it in shifts, so they had a flexible schedule.

If they were reporting back to Miguel Delgado, so be it. They were following her from one appointment to another, but weren't privy to any of her interviews.

Brett's hand rested against the small of her back as they crossed the street. The gesture was so natural to him and inspired a feeling of being cared for each time he did it.

"When are you going to shop for another wedding dress?" he asked.

The anger over the defacement of her dress had passed, leaving her with a sick pain in her stomach and the urge to cry every time she thought about it. She turned her thoughts to dealing with the situation. "I called the shop where I bought the first one and explained what happened. They're pulling several dresses my size from their stores so I can try them on tomorrow. I probably won't go with the same dress. It just feels like bad karma to me."

"I agree." His hand tightened at her waist in a gesture of comfort, then slid away as they reached the entrance to the building.

Hamilton Construction was housed on the seventh floor of a high-rise home to several other businesses. The lobby held none of the special design elements the Brittain Development Corporation displayed, though there was a hip, modern feel to the space. Tess and Brett stepped onto the elevator with a small group coming back from lunch and got off with three of them. In the elevator her phone rang and she scooped it out of the pocket inside her bag and glanced down at the screen. It was Clarence Niles.

"Daniel was released early this morning. And the police put out a BOLO on Jay Gordon yesterday."

"Yes! That's wonderful news, Clarence. Thanks so much for calling." She hoped she'd done the right thing. She wanted to feel excited and relieved for Daniel, but having Miguel involved, and the uneasiness she felt about him, leached some of it away.

"I thought I'd better give you a heads up. I don't know how he knew about your involvement, but Miguel Delgado knows you had a hand in Daniel's release."

She'd expected it. "Well, I guess it's better to have a gang leader owe you than for him to be pissed."

"I guess so." Niles didn't sound too certain. "Be careful Tess."

"I'm staying as far away from Miguel Delgado as possible. Once I release my story, it will be the end of it."

"That would be wise."

"How many bridges did I burn?" If the cops felt like she had crossed the line, it might make it more difficult in future to get information. But sitting on the knowledge they had arrested the wrong boy in order to get to his brother might have backfired.

"I didn't have to use your name, but when you release your story they may have some idea who connected the dots."

She took a deep breath. There was no way around it. "Were my suspicions relevant?"

"Yeah. They're looking into Jay Gordon's uncle, too."

Sometimes it sucked to be right. "Thanks for calling me, Clarence."

"You earned it."

Tess caught Brett's arm and pulled him off to one side to give him a quick rundown on what had happened.

"I never realized what a political balancing act your job could be."

"When you're dealing with people there are always unexpected variables."

Now she had to deal with interviewing Jason Hamilton. Tess focused for a moment on the metal wall decoration welded with sheets of copper fashioned into skyscrapers and twisted wire that represented clouds. Worked into it with creative flare was the name Hamilton Construction.

With Hamilton's reputation for being less than faithful to his wife, she'd decided to go in for the interview alone.

She'd told Elgin Taylor she'd never use her looks to get a story, but she wasn't above using her legs.

"Are you sure about this?" A frown was ready to form between his brows.

"If, after I meet him, I feel uncomfortable, I'll come to the door and invite you in. Hamilton doesn't have a reputation for being a letch, only a hound."

He narrowed his eyes. "I don't like the idea of him sniffing around you."

"I still remember all the self-defense moves you taught me, Brett."

"But you don't have the bloodlust to use them, honey."

"I will if I feel threatened."

Tess walked to the reception desk, stretching the length of the wall. A tall brunette rose from behind it. "May I help you?"

"My name is Tess Kelly. I have an appointment with Mr. Hamilton at four."

The girl checked something on her computer and picked up the phone. When she hung up, she said, "He's waiting for you. His office is the third door on the right, just down that hall." She pointed to the left.

"Thanks."

Brett fell into step beside her. When they got to the correct door, he took a parade rest stance against the wall.

"Do you intend to stand outside the whole time?"

"Yeah."

She rested her hand on his chest. "I'll be okay."

The firm muscle worked beneath her palm as his fingers stroked her hip, his eyes gray-blue and intent. "You know how you were talking about degrees of lechery in the car?"

"Yes."

"All men are lechers. Some of us have more self-control than others, or are more willing to abide by social expectations, but we're all about opportunity. You don't want to give this guy an opportunity, Tess."

Stunned by his words, all she could think was, *Wow*. He projected a smartass, cocky SEAL persona, and a playful lover persona, but when Brett decided to get serious, he didn't mess around.

She swallowed. "I won't. I promise." She skimmed his cheekbone with her lips and stepped away when someone turned the corner and walked toward them. She knocked on Hamilton's office door and it opened after a moment's pause.

Gary Hamilton was in his late fifties but looked younger. His dark hair swept back from a masculine, square-jawed face with a touch of stubble.

"Miss Kelly, please come in."

He raised his brows when he noticed Brett.

Tess motioned to Brett. "This is my fiancé, Brett Weaver. He's doing double duty as my security detail."

Hamilton stepped forward to offer his hand to Brett but his gaze remained on Tess. "Oh, yes. I read the article about your car. So glad you weren't hurt."

"Thank you. I'll only be a short while, Brett."

"Should you need something to drink, eat, anything at all, don't hesitate to ask Kella at the reception desk," Hamilton said, indifference in his voice. He motioned Tess into the office and shut the door.

"What does your fiancé do for a living?" he asked.

Because of the man's dismissive attitude toward Brett, Tess suppressed the urge to tell him he was a SEAL, and instead said, "He's in the Navy."

"I could tell he was military of some sort."

Tess took in the office space as, with his fingertips against the back of her arm, Hamilton guided her toward a seating group to the right. The plush gray carpet beneath her feet felt like sponge. With Brett's warning playing through her mind, she bypassed the overstuffed sofa and sat in the maroon chair diagonal to it.

Hamilton offered her a smile, then took a seat on the couch, but leaned toward her.

She had been wrong. Gary Hamilton was a lecher of the first order, and he was in full-on letch mode.

"What can I do for you, Ms. Kelly?"

"I'm doing a series of interviews about the construction companies in our area. I wanted some history on your company to flesh out the article."

"Well, I started the company in 1979 with my father and brothers, Michael, David, and Corey. My dad died ten years after the business was established. Then the rest of us took over. My brothers take care of the daily construction schedules and sites, while I deal with bringing in more business."

"Do you concentrate mostly on commercial construction?"

"That brings in the most money, but on occasion we do residential as well. It depends on the client."

"I noticed you dropped out of the bidding on the Ellison Project. It's a huge project. Can you tell me why you decided to pull your bid?"

"We had another big project that was going to conflict with that one and decided to pull out."

Tess remained silent for a moment. "Mr. Hamilton."

"You can call me Jason."

Tess caught herself in an eye roll. "My paper isn't a gossip rag, and we're not interested in spreading rumors or causing you any personal embarrassment. But I have run across some information during my research for this article."

"What kind of information?"

"Do you know a woman named Sherry Faulkner?"

Hamilton's smile grew edgy. "I don't believe I know anyone by that name."

Tess removed a file folder from her bag and extended it to him.

Hamilton flipped it open and his cheeks grew dangerously red while his hazel eyes turned dark. For a moment, he looked on the verge of losing control. He took several deep breaths, then slid back in his seat. "Where did you get this?"

"It was given to me by someone who was actually trying to do you a favor. She lost her life trying to bring attention to, not the affair, but the purpose behind the report."

Tess scooted forward in her seat. "I'm not interested in causing you any grief, sir. But I am interested in one corporation using blackmail and other strong-arm tactics to win lucrative contracts, by taking out their competition—any way they can. And so is the San Diego Police Department. Have they been to see you?"

Hamilton's jaw worked. "No, no they haven't."

*Why the hell hadn't they talked to him? There was keeping an investigation low-key, and then there was not investigating at all.* "Do you know who it was who pressured you into dropping out of the bidding?"

"I have a good idea."

"Who do you think that person might be?"

"If I had to guess, it would be either Jonathan Frye or Nicholas Brittain."

"I don't believe it was Mr. Brittain, Mr. Hamilton. He had his own issues to deal with after the accident on one of his sites."

"Are you saying—?"

"Since you've dropped out of the running, I'd say you're probably safe. But it might be in your best interest to maintain a higher level of security until things are resolved."

Hamilton stood and moved restlessly toward the large cherry wood desk. "Do you mind if I smoke?"

"No."

Producing a cigarette and lighter from a box on his desk, he lit it and inhaled deeply, then leaned back against the desktop.

Tess rose to her feet. "Mr. Hamilton, I think it might be a good idea if you approached the police and discussed with them how you were contacted and—warned off." Tess wrote Detective Buckler's number on a piece of paper from her notebook and tore it off.

"They're already aware of the report compiled on you and Ms. Faulkner."

Hamilton took the piece of paper. "You took it to the police?"

"Yes. After the woman who gave it to me was killed."

He shook his head. "Was this woman's death connected to all this?"

"The police are investigating the possibility." Tess moved back to her seat and retrieved her purse. "I believe it was. The Ellison Project means big money, Mr. Hamilton."

"You could have used the dossier to embarrass me and my corporation."

She turned to look over her shoulder. "I cover the crime beat, Mr. Hamilton. It isn't criminal to cheat on your wife." Though his wife might see it differently if she found out. "But it is criminal for someone to blackmail you."

"And this whole interview was—"

"So I could get confirmation you were actually pressured into withdrawing your bid."

He stubbed out the cigarette. "Are you going to use my name, our name, in the article?"

"You should be the one to seek criminal charges against the person who wronged you. It isn't my place to pressure you into doing so. If you don't go to the police, though, and these people aren't stopped, what's to keep them from using the same information against you again?"

"If I don't go to the police, you aren't going to use the report?"

"No. It isn't news. It's just a family affair. The news I'm after is a corrupt construction company boss who is manipulating the system and winning bids through illegal means for projects he might not win legally."

His expression relaxed somewhat.

"If you don't do anything to take him down, Mr. Hamilton, the next time might cost you even more. And if the police find evidence of blackmail, they won't be as considerate as I am about how they go about investigating. It's going to be out there for everyone to see eventually. I'd try and get out in front of this, if you can."

"You didn't tell me who you got the report from."

"It was a woman named Mary Stubben. She was a secretary who worked in Nicholas Frye's office. The report was compiled by a private investigator named Sullivan."

Hamilton breathed an oath.

"Call the police, Mr. Hamilton."

Tess moved to the door and opened it. She smiled at Brett still standing right where she'd left him. "I'm through here."

BRETT STUDIED TESS'S smile. She'd cracked Hamilton. He could tell from the swing of her hips. "Are you going to tell me about it?"

"Outside."

"Did you have to use your legs?"

"No. In fact you were right. He's a letch, big time.

"But you busted his balls."

She cocked her head. "Figuratively speaking."

Once they were outside, she looped her arm through his and shifted her bag higher on the other shoulder. "I'm sorry for the way he treated you. He's not only a letch, he's an asshole."

Brett laughed. He'd dealt with worse. He'd been more concerned about her being alone in the office with the guy.

"Once he knew I had a copy of the report about the affair, he was so upset all he could think about was whether or not I was going to use it in the paper." She frowned. "The police haven't contacted him. What do you think that's all about?"

He shook his head. "Sullivan having compiled the file for Frye doesn't prove he blackmailed Hamilton with the information."

"But Hamilton admitted to me he has been blackmailed. He said he believed it was either Frye or Brittain. I encouraged him to call the police, but I doubt he will."

"Are you going to call Hart and Buckler?" he asked.

"I haven't made up my mind yet."

He understood the impatience laced with anger in her voice. After their last meeting with the detectives, and his conversation with Captain Jackson, he'd had more than a few periods of frustration himself.

"I got a message while you were in with Hamilton. Homeland has signed off of the investigation, but the FBI is still involved."

Her hand tightened on his arm. "Progress, for what it's worth. Who texted you?"

"Captain Jackson. So at least we know terrorists aren't involved."

"I've called repeatedly and they won't tell me anything. Will you call and check the status of the investigation? They might be more willing to tell you something." She jerked her chin up. "And what the hell is up with that? I'm the victim, here. It was my car blown up and they've been hiding out, refusing to talk to me."

"I'll call them and Jackson once we get to the Café," Brett said, looking both ways before urging her across the street.

"How did he hear?"

He'd avoided telling her about the freeze on his promotion. There was a certain amount of embarrassment in admitting to your fiancée you wouldn't be promoted. "He and Lieutenant Commander Jeffrey are close friends. That's not something I know for sure, it's the impression I got. They've been in contact with Homeland and the FBI since the investigation started."

"So they'll talk to SEAL command, but not to the victim?"

She was steaming and rightly so. If she were anyone besides a reporter, the powers that be would be more open with information.

Her phone rang and she paused to check the screen on her cell phone. "I have to take this." She spoke for a moment with her editor then hung up. "There's been a double homicide in San Carlos, Brett," she said. "I have to see the information officer at the station for a statement before I interview Mary's office mate."

He nodded. They caught the trolley back to the parking structure.

They took the stairs to the third floor and walked up the incline toward the car. At the shuffling sound of a footstep behind them, Brett spun, his hand going to the Sig beneath his jacket.

A bang echoed through the structure. An all-too-familiar ping just ahead of them triggered Brett's instant survival response. As two more shots were fired, he pushed Tess between the cars and at the same time he pulled his weapon.

Gunshots came from above them. Alonzo was returning fire.

Alonzo called out, "Are you hit?"

He scanned Tess for any injury. Her eyes were wide, her cheeks pale, but she wasn't hurt. "We're okay," he yelled back. He chambered a round in his weapon. "Get back against the wall, Tess, behind the car as far as you can. Dial 911."

She scrambled to do as he said. With her covered, Brett eased forward and looked around the car bumper for any movement. Everything remained quiet. Nothing moved. A few seconds later the sound of running feet came from down the incline, and a thin figure in jeans ran around the curve. The stairwell door they'd just come through clattered shut below them.

Brett came up to a half crouch and started around the car. Tess gripped his jacket from behind.

Alonzo ran from his car to join them, gun in hand. "It was a man, dressed in jeans, a T-shirt, and a ski mask. He ran back down the slope."

"Stay with Tess. I'll see if I can catch him."

"No. Brett. Please." She was white, shaking like crazy, and clung to him, her grip tight.

With difficulty he quelled the nearly irresistible urge to follow the shooter and—. He reached for her instead. "Okay, honey. It's okay."

He guided her behind the cover of the closest vehicle and held her. Once she'd calmed, he looped an arm around Tess's waist and urged her into the rental car.

Alonzo followed them and took up a defensive stance just behind the rear quarter panel, gun in hand.

Brett gave him a grateful nod.

Adrenaline continued to zing through his system, and his heart pounded. He tried a deep, slow, in-and-out breath.

"Are you okay?" Tess asked.

He nodded. "Are you?"

She shook her head and averted her face. "Every morning when you start the car, I wonder if it's going to go up in flames like mine did. Just walking from the apartment to get into it, I break out in a cold sweat. I want this to end, Brett."

He reached for her. "I do too, honey."

"He could have killed either one of us." She sounded close to tears.

"But he didn't." He brushed her temple with his lips. "This will pass, Tess. You just have to get through this moment to the next."

"That's what you do when you're in SEAL mode?"

"Yeah. That's what I do." God, he hated that she had to experience this.

She leaned forward and rested her head in her hands, her elbows braced on her knees. "The only easy day was yesterday."

He rubbed her back, offering the only comfort he could. "That's what we say."

She looked up at him, her brown eyes almost black against the creamy smoothness of her skin. "Well, it sucks."

THE POLICE IN this district were going to know them both by name by the time they caught the person or persons after her. Detectives Hart and Buckler had shown up as the patrol cops were taking their statements. Alonzo surrendered his weapon, since he'd returned fire.

"We'd like for you to come have a seat in our car so we can talk about some options, Ms. Kelly," Buckler said, his tone quiet.

Tess exchanged a glance with Brett. He gave a shrug. They settled into the back seat of the detective's unmarked car and closed the doors.

"It's clear this man, whoever he is, isn't going to go away until he's caught. And we just learned that Homeland has bowed out of your investigation. So I guess you were both right about terrorists having no part in your attack."

She stifled a sound of impatience. So *now* they wanted to get involved. "The FBI is still investigating."

"They aren't investigating this. We've already called the parking structure owner and requested a look at the camera footage here and the level below. We're already pulling footage from street cameras. And we're canvassing the area for anyone who saw the shooter inside the structure or leaving the building."

Tess nodded. At last someone was sharing something with her.

"We'd like to put you in protective custody until we catch the shooter, Tess," Hart said, his dark brows drawn together in a frown.

"No. It could take weeks for you to catch this guy, and I'm not sitting inside my apartment going crazy while you do it. I'm going to Washington D.C. tomorrow with Brett, and we're getting married in ten days and going on our honeymoon. I have a life."

Hart frowned. "You got lucky this time, Tess."

Brett shifted beside her, and gave her knee a gentle squeeze. "We're going to D.C. tomorrow morning. We'll be gone until Friday. No one knows we're going except our families, Tess's boss, and my commanding officer. We'll take precautions to make sure we aren't followed to the airport. That gives you guys almost seventy-two hours to catch this fucker before we're back. If you haven't caught him by then, we'll revisit this discussion."

The detectives exchanged a look. "Okay," Buckler answered for them both.

Brett nudged her with his elbow. His blue gaze insistent.

Tess grimaced. "I interviewed Hamilton today. He admitted to me he'd been blackmailed into dropping out of the Ellison Project bid. I encouraged him to contact you. I'd let him stew a few hours, then give him a call."

"It wasn't against the law for Frye to investigate his competition. Morally repugnant, but not illegal," Buckler pointed out. "And we didn't have evidence he had used the information in an illegal way. If Hamilton calls us, it will create a link between him and Frye that will allow us to investigate."

"A phone call and a little pressure aren't an investigation, Detective," Tess said with an impatient sigh. She ran fingers that still shook through her hair, pushing it back from her face. "It occurred to me this might not be the only time he's done this. You might want to check the records of other building projects he's been involved with and put out some feelers."

"We'll take care of Hamilton and Frye." There was a strained note of patience in Buckler's voice. "We can provide you a couple of uniforms as a protection detail until you leave for the airport in the morning."

Tears threatened again. When would all this end? "I'd appreciate it. I think Alonzo deserves a day off after getting shot at."

"We'll need a detailed statement from both of you about what happened here. You can come by the station and write it when you get back from D.C.," Hart said.

The sooner she got it down on paper the better. She didn't want a single detail to slip her memory. "I'd rather go to the station and do it now."

"Tess—" Brett started.

"No, I want this behind me." She wanted the son-of-a-bitch to go down for attempted murder.

"Now, is there anyone else you can think of besides Frye who might have a reason to do this?"

"No," she said."

"What about Gordon?" Brett suggested.

"Gordon who?" Buckler asked.

"Ronald Gordon. I'm doing a story about Daniel Delgado."

Silence reigned for ten seconds.

"Shit." Brett breathed the word. "I guess we know who's been investigating the grocery store holdup."

# CHAPTER TWENTY-TWO

'M GOING TO *lose her to this place*. From the moment their plane touched down in Washington D.C., dread took root and wound its way through Brett's gut. They picked up their rental car and took the scenic route to the hotel to get the lay of the land though traffic was heavy. The late March weather was crisp, and the cherry trees D.C. was so famous for were only at bud stage with a few blossoms here and there.

How could California compete with the national capital? The place had a regal feel to it. Huge buildings, stretching a block each, emulated ancient Greek and Roman architecture. The business of their nation was conducted within the walls of many of them. History was carved into every street corner.

He'd get through this somehow. He'd transfer to Virginia, and they'd only be two hours apart. They'd meet in the middle somewhere as often as they could. As much as he kept repeating those things, a sense of loss clung to every thought.

"I've been here three times and I'm always awed by the Capitol building," Tess commented.

"We'll have to go to Rome someday, so you can see where the idea for the design came from. St. Peter's Basilica is unbelievable."

"I'd love to go to France and Italy. I've never been. I turned down an opportunity when Dad invited me to meet him in Paris. But at the time he was covering a story and I was only seventeen. Mom was worried I'd end up in a hotel room alone or wandering the streets while he went off on the trail of something big." She turned toward him. "Can you do that? I mean go out of the country?"

"Well, I have to fill out paperwork. Uncle Sam wants to know where I'll be and when I'll be back, just in case. But yeah, I can apply for leave if I've built it up, and go as long as things aren't running hot or we're not up for a deployment."

"Doesn't having Uncle Sam control your every move aggravate you sometimes?"

It was the first time she'd said anything negative about his job. Coming on top of this trip and the interview and tour she'd be doing tomorrow, he felt more than a pinch of pain. "Yeah, it does sometimes, honey. But I signed up to be there if I'm needed."

He parked beneath the hotel portico to unload the baggage. The fifty-three degree April temperature seemed more like thirty as the wind whipped through. They rushed to unload the trunk. "Go on inside and I'll deal with the car," he urged as Tess stood by clutching her sweater tight around her.

"Living in a moderate climate has made my blood thin," she complained, and rolled her suitcase inside.

He filled out the paperwork and accepted the slip to have the vehicle parked, then wheeled his bag inside. Tess stood at the check-in desk, signing the paperwork and accepting their keycards.

She hooked her bag and tugged it along behind her to join him. "Let's change into some warmer clothes and get something to eat."

"Sounds like a plan." While he'd taken a power nap on the plane, she'd put the finishing touches on the Daniel Delgado story. "Are you going to send Taylor your Delgado story?"

"Already done. I did that while they were signing us in."

Brett shook his head in wonder. She could multitask with the best of them. But at least she wouldn't have part of her attention snagged on something undone.

They took an elevator up to the seventh floor. After wheeling her suitcase into the cream and blue room, Tess pulled back the drapes and looked out at the city. "It's a beautiful place. Or at least this part is."

Brett stowed their bags on the luggage stand. "I'm sure it has its seedy sections like everyplace else, but it is impressive."

"And cold."

Taking that as an invitation, Brett looped his arms around her and tugged her back against him. He nibbled her earlobe, felt her shiver, and his body responded. "I could warm you faster if you were naked. Skin to skin contact works better to raise the body temperature."

"Opportunity knocks," she said with a laugh. "I wish you hadn't said that about all men being lechers. It's stuck in my brain."

"You're still tempted, though."

She tilted her head back against his shoulder. "Always with you, but I'm also starving. Aren't you?"

"I'm a guy, so I'm always hungry for one thing or another."

Tess laughed.

He nipped the muscle between her neck and shoulder. She caught her breath and pressed back against him in response, and her hand gripped his thigh. Then her stomach growled loudly.

Brett laughed and bent his head to rest his cheek against her. "Where would you like to eat lunch?"

"Hard Rock Café."

"Bundle up and we'll go. Do you want to go to Union Station or take a taxi?"

"A taxi. Then I'd like to be a tourist for a while and just walk the National Mall. We didn't get to see anything last time we were here. I love going to the Natural History and the Air and Space Museum. You don't think anyone followed us here, do you?"

He hated the edge of anxiety in her voice, even though she tried to make the question sound casual. He'd been especially vigilant since the break-in, and hadn't been aware of anyone following them since hiring Alonzo and Armando. Neither had the men. So how had the shooter known where they were? And had it been someone hired by Frye, or was it someone associated with the Daniel Delgado situation?

The two policemen on protection detail had driven them to the airport and dropped them off. Brett had made a point of scanning the cabin on the plane for anyone who looked familiar. "No. No one followed us, honey. You can relax. Okay?"

She smiled and turned to nestle against him. "We could pretend this was a pre-honeymoon trip and order room service."

He wanted to say yes, but, except for going to do interviews for her job, she'd hidden at home, and now she needed to get out. He hadn't figured out a way to talk to her about the nightmares. Having experienced something similar, he understood how hard it was to face PTSD and ask for help.

"Once you said Hard Rock, I had my heart set on some Rockin' Wings and a burger."

She hid her face against his shirt for a moment then looked up at him. "I'm being a coward."

"No, honey. You're being cautious, which is a good thing. Do you really think I'd let you do anything if I thought you'd be a danger? No one but family, police headquarters, our police escort and HQ knows about this trip. And no one followed us to the airport. I'm sure of it."

"Okay." She forced a smile. "I want some spinach-artichoke dip and flatbread, too."

"Maybe we'll order the starter combo and get a sample of each of them."

"I'm going to be that meatball I complained about. I'll never fit into my dress."

"You just tried it on yesterday. You can't become a meatball in twenty-four hours, but I'll still love you if we have to lace you into it."

Tess laughed the sound natural and light-hearted. Good. She was finally beginning to relax.

THE RESTAURANT WAS packed, but they didn't have to wait long for a table for two.

Tess knew Brett kept the conversation light and directed away from any of the conflicts at home. She was grateful for his understanding. Being shot at had shaken her. How did Brett face the possibility of being shot, especially since he'd already experienced a bullet wound? He'd covered her with his own body, protected her while Alonzo had returned fire. And she'd been more terrified for him than she'd been for herself and Alonzo.

Brett ordered the wings and burger and she the spinach-artichoke dip and a burger as well. Replete with good food, they left the Hard Rock Café and walked to Ford's Theatre to do a tour of the building. "I'm always surprised at how small it is compared to our modern theaters."

"And it still has an atmosphere of history and tragedy, doesn't it?" Brett said.

"Yes, it does."

The sun had come out and warmed the late March air, but it still felt brisk as they walked west to the International Spy Museum on F Street. In the Secret History of History section they viewed some of the James Bond-like historic tools of the trade. Brett narrowed his eyes at the rectal tool kit in one window. "I didn't think there would be anything I wouldn't do for my country, but I'd really have to think about sticking that up my ass."

Tess laughed. "You risk your life going into battle and you're worried about that?"

"All I can say is it's great not to live in the sixties."

She laughed again. "I think the lipstick pistol would be pretty cool."

He grinned. "If they ever come out on the open market, I'll make sure you get one."

"You and your guns." Tess bumped him with her hip.

"I only have one gun, Tess."

She laughed. "Weapons."

From there they spent the next few hours wending their way through the Smithsonian exhibits, at the Air and Space Museum, and the Museum of Natural History. There was so much to see and they weren't in any hurry. They held hands and talked. The taut feeling of fear that had plagued her since her car had been blown apart eased, and for the first time in a while, Tess felt safe.

It was nearly four when they moved on to West Building of the National Gallery of Art before it closed. They decided to start at the top and work their way down to the first floor. Tess paused before an Andrew Wyeth painting of a window, the curtains blown inward by a breeze. She was amazed at how delicate the lace looked. "What kind of art do you like, Brett?"

"Realistic stuff. I'm not into abstract, though I like some of the sculptures."

"Classical? Impressionistic?"

"Classical paintings always seem too refined, too steeped in technique. But I do like the Photo Realists. Anyone who can obsess over every brush stroke and come up with a painting that looks like a photograph has to be acknowledged. The Impressionists were okay. The way they experimented with light and movement was interesting. I went to an exhibit of Edwin Roscoe Schrader's paintings in Los Angeles a few years ago. Caught hell from the guys for it. I was impressed with how he could use a brush stroke for a person and you'd just see it. His style was impressionistic."

She was stunned. "Were you dating an artist at the time?"

"No. I was dating one of the caterers who provided food for the reception."

Tess laughed. But she was still surprised he had some knowledge of art. But why should she be? He was a college graduate, had a degree in engineering, and had chosen to serve his country instead of pursuing a job in his field.

With everything she learned about Brett, with everything they shared with one another, the ties between them built and strengthened. Just when she thought she knew him, there was more to discover.

She looped her arm through his and leaned against him. "I'm ready to go back to the hotel, how about you?"

He squeezed her arm. "Yeah. I could go for a beer and a steak, watch a little tube, and relax with you. How does that sound?"

She rested her head against his shoulder. "It sounds perfect."

Brett whipped out his phone and called the cab company.

"You saved the number in your phone?"

"First rule of visiting a strange city, always scope out transportation, shelter, and sustenance."

She smiled. He always prepared for everything like it was a mission, but he could be spontaneous and laid back, too. And he was funny. What more could she ask for?

Neither of them had mentioned her upcoming interview since they arrived. She was trying not to allow what was happening in San Diego to influence her decision. If she changed coasts, she had to do it for the job, not because she was running from something.

Brett had faced worse. Her father had, too, in his job as a foreign freelance journalist. How did they deal with all the aftermath of being under fire? She needed to know so maybe she could get a handle on her own feelings.

BRETT LAY ON the bed and concentrated on the television while Tess ironed the blouse and pants she planned to wear to her interview tomorrow. The steak he'd eaten at dinner sat like a stone in his belly. They'd avoided talking about the interview, but it crouched between them, a wall built of emotion and worry.

He had to embrace this thing. He had to want this for her. If he didn't, it would never work. But he couldn't get the idea out of his head that this would be the end of them.

Tess slipped onto the bed and curled against his side.

"All ready for tomorrow?" he asked, his voice husky.

"Yes. I think so."

"I'll drop you off, then go for a run at Potomac Park. It'll give me a chance to admire the memorials." He'd need to burn off the emotional fallout from the wait. She'd have to be crazy not to take the job, and he had to be prepared to accept and support her decision. He'd call Captain Jackson ASAP when he knew for certain.

She ran a caressing hand beneath his shirt. "I should be done around lunch."

"Just give me a call and I'll drive over and pick you up."

"Okay."

Tess leaned up on one arm to look down at him. "I love you, Brett. I know how difficult this will be for us both if I take the job. And what a sacrifice you'll be making to transfer to Virginia."

A large knot had lodged in his stomach. "No more than you'd be making if you didn't take this shot." He hadn't told her it might be six months to a year before a transfer came through. They'd deal with that when they had to. And he still hadn't told her about the freeze on his promotion. She had enough on her mind right now. He wouldn't do anything to throw her off her game.

He cupped her face his thumb moved over her cheekbone. "One moment to the next, Tess."

She smiled and lay down to cuddle close.

He'd have to tell her everything after this was over.

# CHAPTER TWENTY-THREE

**B**RETT PULLED TO the curb. "That has got to be one of the ugliest buildings in Washington, D.C."

Tess laughed. "Not every building here can carry the architectural classicism of the Jefferson Memorial."

"It looks like a parking structure for people."

She eyed the façade. "It kind of does, doesn't it? They're looking for a new home, and I heard they're close to purchasing it. But this building is iconic. They've been here forever."

"They could take the iconic part, like the name of the paper from over the door, and transfer it to some other building."

"I'll be sure to tell them you said that." She released her seat belt and reached for the portfolio at her feet.

Brett grinned. "Call me when you're done."

"I will."

"Do I say break a leg for something like this?"

"Good luck will be fine."

"Good luck." He leaned over and kissed her.

Tess dragged a deep breath into her lungs and shoved the door open. Aware of Brett watching her cross the street with her portfolio, she strutted her way to the front door to hide the way her legs shook. She felt winded by the time she made it to the reception desk in the lobby and asked for directions.

She stepped off the elevator and was immediately confronted by the circular hub from which the rest of the room expanded. A bank of televisions hung beneath, tuned to different news channels. Closed-caption print scrolled along the bottoms of the screens. The floor plans were open and brightened by rows of inlaid florescent lights across the ceiling. Except for its shape, the space wasn't very different from her own office in San Diego.

She approached the hub and asked for directions to the managing editor's office. One woman at work there came out from behind the hub and actually walked her halfway.

She tapped on the edge of the door. A gray-haired man looked up and came out from behind his desk. "Tess Kelly, I presume."

"Yes. And you're Mr. Arnold. It says so on the door." She hoped her smile looked natural and not as stressed as she felt.

He laughed and approached her, hand out, as she stepped into the room.

They shook briefly. "I thought we'd walk down the hall to one of the conference rooms where no one will interrupt us."

"Okay."

He led the way two doors down and held open a glass panel door for her to precede him into the room. Recessed lights gave off a soft glow and washed down the cream colored walls, while a bank of windows at one end allowed in natural light. The table gleamed a dark cherry. The chairs were upholstered in blue-gray fabric.

Arnold pulled out a chair at the end of the table and waited for Tess to sit before taking a seat himself. She studied him briefly. He had olive skin, heavy features, and a large nose with sharp hazel eyes. Dark hair scattered with gray hugged his head in waves.

"I've been reading some of the stories you've covered for the San Diego paper. The piece you did recently on human trafficking was especially good."

"Thank you."

"Your style is very different from your father's."

Surprised by the comment, she paused before saying anything. "He's the daredevil in the family."

"Not the only one, it would seem. I heard about the car bomb. For all the competition, when one of our own is attacked, it's big news in the journalism community."

Was that why she was here?

He settled back in his seat and rested an arm on the table. "I'd like to hear about it."

Of course he would. He was a newspaper man. "Homeland

Security has signed off on the investigation and said the bomb was not terrorist-related. The FBI and local police are still investigating."

"Who do *you* think is responsible?"

"I was covering several controversial stories at the same time. The human trafficking story for one. There was also a local boy arrested for armed robbery with ties to a gang leader, plus a possible blackmail scheme perpetrated by the CEO of a San Diego construction corporation."

"So you're not afraid to cover tough stories."

*Not afraid?* She couldn't lie. "I'm afraid every day. I've had a body guard accompany me everywhere I go for the past ten days."

"But you're still pushing?"

"Yes, I'm still pushing."

"And your editor there, he gives you the time to cultivate the stories you want to do?"

"In between more immediate demands."

"It's all about getting the news out before the next paper seizes it."

"But it's also about the people experiencing the news and the readers. You can't report a house fire that killed ten people without talking about the people who died. It was their lives that came to a sudden, premature end. They're not just names."

"We can't give individual attention to every person in every story we cover."

"I don't, either. Only the ones where something doesn't completely add up or there's an undercurrent of something more going on that hasn't been uncovered yet."

"And how do you reach that conclusion?"

"By talking to the people involved face-to-face. You get the watered-down version by talking to them on the phone. And it's harder for them to lie if you're looking them in the eye."

"Is that what you did with Senator Welch?"

"Yes."

"But you had inside information, didn't you?"

Was he talking about Brett?

"Actually, no. I researched the Senator because he was coming to California, and only then discovered his persistent attempts to cut funding to the Naval Special Warfare Command. I interviewed a few people to figure out why. That's when I learned about his stepson being killed. Then I put out feelers to some of the guys his stepson was stationed with and got the full story. After that I put two and two together and came to interview him here. The city of San Diego and the state of California depend on military dollars to keep their economy strong. To try and shut down bases wouldn't only be detrimental to San Diego's economy, but to the military itself."

The interview took a turn away from what she'd done in the past to what she expected her life to be like as a reporter for the Post. Instantaneous coverage.

"How do you think you'll feel about working with your father?"

Tess frowned. "What do you mean?"

"He's signed on to work with the Post in our International News Division."

Stunned to silence, Tess continued to stare at Arnold. Why hadn't Ian told her? Her heart plummeted. She swallowed, though her mouth had gone dry. "That's why you extended the job offer?"

Arnold hesitated. "You'll be a good fit here, Tess. You're smart, intuitive, and a good reporter."

Every moment of excitement she'd experienced was wrenched from her in an instant. She couldn't catch her breath. "So he attached this invitation onto his signing on with you?"

"Just the extension of an interview. Once you'd completed the telephone interview, we decided to go through with it. It was up to us to decide whether you'd be the caliber of journalist who'd fit our paper. And you are, Tess."

Why would Ian do this? What had he hoped to accomplish? She'd been all too eager to grab at this carrot, because it would finally prove to him she was a serious journalist. And it had been him dangling it in front of her all along.

Somehow she got to her feet.

Arnold stood with a frown.

It took every ounce of control she had to extend her hand to him. "I appreciate the interview, Mr. Arnold."

"But?"

"I don't ride my father's coattails."

"You don't have to, Tess."

She struggled to hold on to her composure and forced herself to smile. "Thank you for saying that." She swallowed. "But this is a newspaper office. Someone will find out about this, and even if they didn't—with him coming on board and suddenly his daughter does, too—it would smack of nepotism. I don't want to have to fight that battle. When I first decided to become a journalist, I lived in my father's shadow. People expected me to be just like him. But I'm not. I've carved out my own style, my own niche. If he's on this coast and I'm on the other, it's easier for me to do my job and do it well." She swallowed, though it hurt to do so.

Arnold laid a hand on her shoulder. "You'd be a real asset to us, Tess. Are you sure?"

She shook her head. "I'm sure. I'm sorry to have wasted your time."

"It wasn't a waste at all, Tess. I'm sorry you won't be joining us."

She searched his face, hoping to see sincerity there, and was relieved when she did. "Thank you." She gathered her things.

Arnold walked her to the elevator and shook her hand one last time. "I'll be watching for your byline, Tess. Wherever you are, you're going to do well."

She smiled again, though she'd never felt less like doing so. "I'm getting married in a ten days. He was going to transfer to this coast if I took the job."

"It sounds like he believes in you."

Though Brett had tried to hide his concern and keep everything positive, it would have impacted his career. Still he had intended to do it. "Yes, he does. Good-bye, Mr. Arnold."

In the elevator, she searched the number for a cab company on her phone and called it. For five long minutes she had to stand in the lobby and wait for the car to arrive. As soon as it cruised to a stop, she rushed out of the building and hurried to get in.

She gave the driver the name of her hotel and curled into the corner of the back seat. Tears streamed down her face. Ian had belittled her by tying this job offer to his own. He'd robbed her of the joy of getting it through her own merit. He'd relegated her to the shadows. *Again.* How could he think so little of her? She wanted to wail and beat on something to release the emotional maelstrom spiraling inside her. Instead she lost all control and sobbed her heart out.

She searched her bag for something to wipe her face and was grateful when the driver handed her a wad of Kleenex through the slot between the seats. By the time the car pulled beneath the hotel canopy, she had regained some control. She thanked the driver for his help and gave him a tip for remaining silent while she'd had her meltdown.

His, "I'm real sorry, lady," nearly sent her back over the edge. She murmured her thanks and exited the car.

She darted into the restroom in the lobby. In the mirror there she stared at the aftermath of her crying jag. Her nose was red, her cheeks stained with mascara. She bathed her face with cold water and rubbed it away, then took a deep breath to steady herself. She called the front desk from her phone and had them ring the room. After the tenth ring she hung up. Brett was probably still at the park running. At least she wouldn't have to face him until she'd pulled herself together.

She left the restroom and got into the elevator. In the room, she changed into jeans and a sweater and put a cold compress on her face. Half an hour later, the swelling had gone down around her eyes, but the hurt still lay like a hard burning knot beneath her breastbone. She had no choice but to move on.

Thank God Arnold had told her about Ian's contract with them. It would have been a disaster if she'd accepted the job and ended up in the awkward professional situation she'd described during their meeting.

The editor's last words to her had clarified something. Brett did believe in her, support her. He'd been willing to sacrifice his own happiness for hers. He'd have left his family, his team behind. *And she'd been willing to let him.* Jesus! She was more like her father than she'd ever dreamed.

Realizing how she might have hurt him was worse than what Ian had done. Tears streamed down her face again. She was a fool. His willingness to put her needs ahead of his own proved how much he loved her. And she'd done nothing to prove hers to him.

What she had with Brett was more important than a career or anything else. It was time she started appreciating it.

BRETT MOPPED HIS face with the hand towel he'd borrowed from the hotel. Dressed in net jogging pants and a T-shirt, he paced back and forth beside his car in the Jefferson Memorial parking lot to cool down from the five-mile run. He'd gotten a late start after being caught up in wandering the memorials in the park. He'd spent some time at the Vietnam Memorial, reading the names on the wall, and studying the statues of men on patrol, covered in rain ponchos, at the Korean War Memorial.

By the time he'd completed the circuit and the run, he'd re-signed himself to the move. He'd also acknowledged the resentment he'd felt about playing second fiddle to a job. Admitted it and set it aside. Tess had done it for nearly ten months, was signing on for a lifetime of it. Or at least the next twenty-five years. He didn't have a leg to stand on.

Marriage was about compromise. He knew and understood that. But had he really ever had to compromise about anything with her? His being a SEAL, his enlistment in the Navy was set in stone. She had to live with that. He'd learn to live with this.

They'd go for a drive tomorrow and check out the landscape between D.C. and Little Creek, Virginia. It was a two-hour drive but if they split that they'd each just have an hour. They'd take their time to explore the area and get back in time to fly out at ten tomorrow night.

His phone rang and surprised to see Tess's number hit the button. "Hey."

"Are you almost through running your SEAL ass off?"

He laughed. "Yeah. What's up?"

"My meeting ended early and I wanted to eat lunch with you."

He couldn't tell a damn thing from her voice. "How did it go?"

"It went fine. We'll talk about it when you get here."

Did that mean she wanted to celebrate? Was there an issue? "I'm on my way."

"I'll be waiting."

He shut off the cell phone and slid in behind the wheel. All the way to the hotel he wondered how he needed to play it. Would she need comfort? Would she want to celebrate? She'd sounded calm on the phone, so did that mean it was a done deal? If she'd said yes, he was prepared. If she'd told them no he'd be—relieved. But he couldn't let her see that. *Ah, damn it!* He'd just have to wait and play it by ear.

At the hotel, he slung the towel over his shoulder, handed the valet the car keys, and half-jogged through the lobby to the elevator. He used his keycard to open the door instead of knocking.

Tess stood at the window looking out at the D.C. horizon. She turned to look over her shoulder at him. "How were the cherry trees?"

"A few blossoms, but for the most part just buds."

"We'll have to come back next year to see them in full bloom. I hear D.C.'s at its prettiest then."

The importance of what she said stunned him. He'd been prepared for the worst. He crossed the distance between them in an instant. Was that a hint of redness around her eyes? "Tess?"

She moved to lean against him. "It was enough they wanted me. That I was good enough to work for them."

There was an air of fragility about her he'd never felt before. Something else had happened. But he'd have to wait for her to share it with him when she was ready.

"Mr. Taylor gives me time to expand on stories, do more in depth investigation. I'd have to start all over building trust in order to do that here."

He cupped the back of her head and held her close. "You can kick journalism west coast butt and show these Easterners up any day, Tess."

"Yeah, I can." She leaned back to look up at him. "Thank you for encouraging me to come here. I'd have always wondered."

"Are you sure, Tess?"

"The move was going to cost us both too much. After all the hype, it just wasn't worth it."

He scanned her face for answers.

"I love you, Brett. You mean more to me than any job, any anything. The fact that you were willing to put everything on the line for me...not many men would do it."

"I love you, Tess. Besides, you're probably going to have to put up with a lot more—"

She placed a hand over his mouth. "We're not going to do that. We very nearly did already. We're just going to love each other as much as we can, and be together as often as we can."

He was glad to hear it. But something major had happened here, and he still needed to know what it was.

But she sidetracked him. "Do you think we could call and see about an earlier flight? Now that all this is behind me, I'd like to go home."

Shit! Something really major had gone down. "Sure. Why don't you call while I'm in the shower, and if there's something available we can bug out?"

"You won't mind?"

"No. Of course not. If there isn't a flight out, we'll go for a drive."

"Okay."

Brett gathered his T-shirt and boxer briefs and stepped into the bathroom. He had a bad feeling about this.

# CHAPTER TWENTY-FOUR

**D**READ POOLED IN the pit of Tess's stomach. Zoe had assured her it was just going to be a spa day, including lunch, a pedicure, manicure, facial, massage, and then drinks and dinner back at her and Hawk's house, followed by some kind of party. This was beyond her comfort zone. She'd give anything right now to be in the field, interviewing people about their lives. What did that say about her?

In a way she was grateful to have something to focus on besides the D.C. disaster. And since Jay Gordon had not been picked up yet and the construction bid story hadn't been resolved with an arrest, Brett was still sticking to her like glue. Thank God her friends hadn't decided to do the club thing for her bachelorette party. She'd have had to pull the plug on that.

"I think it's time for me to interview Henry Sullivan," she spoke her thoughts aloud to take her mind off of the spa trip following lunch.

Brett took his eyes off the road to glance briefly in her direction. "The police told you to stay away from him, Tess."

"No they didn't. They told me to stay away from Frye."

"You just can't help yourself, can you? You want to beard the lion."

"It's part of my job."

Brett shot her a look from beneath his blond brows. "Bullshit. You just want to stir the pot."

She smiled. "I'm calling him later. It's time we talked."

Brett narrowed his blue eyes against the sun's glare and reached for the dark glasses in his shirt pocket. "Tell me why you dread this bachelorette thing so much?"

She didn't reply for a moment. "I don't like the fuss and bother. I get up every day, shower, shampoo, slap on my makeup, and go. Being pampered and primped just isn't my thing."

"And?"

"I don't like strangers touching me."

Brett frowned. "Does this have anything to do with that guy in college?"

Tess frowned. Had being used by someone who wanted to have an "in" with her father given her trust issues? Probably, but no more than her father's many missed visitation appointments and forgotten birthdays. "I don't know. I suppose I've always been sort of self-contained because my mother and father were never very demonstrative. What made you think of him?"

"I called the Post before we went to Washington to see if he still worked there."

Her mouth parted in surprise. She hadn't given him a thought. "Was Kevin still there?"

"No, he'd moved on to a smaller paper in Oregon." A smile quirked the corners of his mouth.

Tess laid her hand on Brett's thigh. "I love that you're pleased about that on my behalf. That you even remembered to call. But I've put that behind me, Brett. I never even thought of him while I was there."

He covered her hand with his. "You don't hesitate to be touchy-feely with me."

"I love you. Of course I don't. Besides, your family is all about hugging and kissing and showering affection. I've learned a thing or two from them. But I still have a phobia about having someone I don't know lay hands on me."

"If you're too uncomfortable tell, Zoe."

"I think I can get through one afternoon. I've been told that a massage is very relaxing." Since there was no progress to report in either Mary's death or the Brittain Company construction accident, and with Jay Gordon still on the loose, she needed to relax. "Zoe and the others went to a lot of trouble to arrange this. I'm going to make sure I enjoy it."

FROM HIS SEAT in the waiting area of the spa beauty shop, their second stop after lunch, Brett stretched his legs out and checked his phone for the tenth time, just for something to do. He'd done a lot of waiting during his SEAL career. Waiting to deploy, waiting to go into action, waiting to jump out of a plane. He'd even spent eight hours in a depression in the ground in his ghillie suit during sniper training and hadn't been nearly this bored.

"I like the sounds women make," Bowie said from beside him.

Brett raised his brows. "I can tell. The ladies around here think you're a peppermint stick and it's the first day of Christmas."

Bowie laughed. "You're getting your share of looks and stuff too, but you're not paying attention."

"I'm getting married in a week. I'm not fucking it up this close to the wedding."

"You wouldn't fuck it up if you'd been married forty years and there was an eighteen-year-old stripper shaking her booty in your face. It isn't in you."

"That's because I've found the one, Bowie. Even if I look, nothing there can compare with what I have."

Bowie nodded. "Tess is gorgeous, and you two work together like a unit. I'm not sure I'll ever have that. Or if it's in me to recognize it if I did."

Brett tucked his phone into his shirt pocket. "*You're* not ready yet."

Bowie's brows went up.

Brett leaned forward to add, "You know that moment when we're about to go into action, but we haven't committed yet?"

"Yeah."

"You're stuck in that moment. When you're ready to commit, you'll find what you need."

"I get what you're saying." At the sound of the women's laughter, Bowie looked up. "Until I do, I'll just enjoy them all."

Brett was grateful he wasn't still in that boat. "Brother, when you finally fall, it's going to be like a tank dropped on your head."

TESS DECIDED SHE'D dreaded the massage for nothing. That her masseuse was a woman made it easier for her to relax. The woman rubbed and kneaded every muscle in her body until she felt as loose and limber as cooked pasta. She'd even groaned with pleasure a few times.

Halfway through she got a call and reached for the phone she'd balanced on the edge of the table.

Detective Buckler's voice came over the line. "We've found Jay Gordon."

"Great!"

"Not so much. He was dead in a hotel room from an apparent drug overdose. We've recovered some of the money from the store holdup and a gun. It seems you were right. He was our perp."

She was relieved she had judged Daniel Delgado correctly, but Jay Gordon's death tempered her relief. "You're sure it was an accidental overdose?"

"The crime scene techs are still working the scene, but there's no sign of a struggle, so we believe it was self-administered. We'll know more after the autopsy."

"I'm sorry you had to find him like that."

"If you'll submit your interview questions via email, I'll answer the ones I can so you can get a jump on the story."

"Thank you, Detective. I appreciate it. I'll do that ASAP."

"I figured you would." There was a small hint of humor in his tone.

Two minutes after she'd hung up from Detective Buckler, Brett called her.

"I have to meet with Captain Jackson on base at four. But Bowie will be here with you. And one of the ladies has arranged for you to be picked up by the limo and taken to Zoe's house after you're done."

"Okay." She filled Brett in on the news.

"I'm glad things are starting to wind down."

"Me too."

"I don't know what's happening in that room, but the sounds

you were making a few minutes ago were sexy as hell, a real turn-on."

Tess's checks heated.

"Maybe you can give me a demonstration later."

"I hope you're not letting Bowie listen to this conversation, Brett, because I'll kill you if he is."

Brett laughed. "Would I do that?"

"Brett," she warned.

"He's not, I promise. Just relax and enjoy your massage. I think they plan to take you out for drinks and then back to the house. I'll meet you there."

"Okay."

BRETT PULLED INTO Hawk and Zoe's driveway. Dismissed from his meeting at five, he arrived in plenty of time to help set up. The party at Hawk's house promised to be the easiest part of the day. They would set the burglar alarm, and he and Hawk could hang out while the ladies were in the living room doing their thing.

Zoe met him at the door and hugged him.

"Is everyone back already?" Brett asked in surprise.

"No, Hawk picked me up a little early so I could get some last-minute things taken care of. He's running an errand for me and will be right back." Her smile held a hint of nerves. "I have a lady arriving in about five minutes. Her name is Margaret Todd. I'll need you to help her unload her cases and bring them into the house. Can you keep an eye out for her on the porch while I freshen my makeup? And could you ask Trish if she could join me in my bedroom for a moment as soon as she gets here?"

"Sure."

His sister didn't have to beat him over the head with the hint to make himself scarce. He sat in one of the wicker chairs on the porch and propped his feet on the railing.

A sweet fragrance wafted from the large pots of pink flowers Zoe had put out on small tables there. The parrot lilies, with their woodsy stems and deep green leaves, seemed to thrive in the seventy degree temperature and added some color to the front of the house. The porch provided a windbreak, but Brett zipped his jacket anyway.

Hawk's house had been comfortable before, but Zoe had added her own special touches. Tess would want to do that to their house if they decided to rent. A little more space would definitely be nice. She could have her own office.

Would an office make up for not getting her dream job? Probably not. He rubbed the tension along the back of his neck. It wouldn't make up to him for the stall of his promotion. He wanted his own team. He wanted the extra money it represented. But he didn't want to have to deal with the political shit. He was still chewing on the problem when a green Chrysler minivan pulled into the drive.

A woman of about fifty-five with short brown hair and big earrings got out and waved. "Is this the Yazzie residence?" she asked.

Brett sauntered off the porch. "You have the right place. Are you Mrs. Todd?" Brett asked as he approached her car. The woman reminded him of his first grade teacher.

She grinned. "Yes." She offered her hand and he shook it briefly.

"My sister said you'd need some help unloading."

"Yes, I probably will." She dragged open the van's side door. "Are you the fiancé of the lady we're having the party for?"

"Yes."

"I'll try and make certain she goes away with some of our best products."

Products? What the hell was she talking about? "Thank you, ma'am. That would be nice."

All three of the three-foot tall rolling cases were heavier to lift out of the van than they looked. Brett wheeled one down the sidewalk, then backed it up the two low steps onto the porch and into the house. He left Mrs. Todd rifling through the one he'd unloaded and setting out some kind of display cabinets.

He had the other two unloaded and inside by the time the limo pulled up and Bowie emerged, decked out in black chinos, T-shirt and sports coat. With his sunglasses on he looked like a hit man.

Brett rushed up the sidewalk to meet him. Bowie scanned the street before he reached back in to help each of the ladies out of the low-slung car. The fragrances of perfume and the distinctive essence of women accompanied them.

Each woman took a turn hugging Bowie's neck and kissing his cheek, while they thanked him for his endless entertainment at the spa. They greeted Brett in the same way. Then they wandered down the walk and into the house.

Tess stepped out of the car and Brett smiled. Her red hair gleamed with copper lights and her spaghetti strap top beneath her black jacket bared the smooth, creamy texture of her shoulders. She looked good enough to eat. He might just do that later.

She brushed Bowie's cheek with a kiss and thanked him, then turned to Brett. "I've had a wonderful day. Not at all the bachelorette torture I was expecting."

"Good. You look rested and revived."

"The massage was—fantastic."

He'd heard first-hand how good the massage was. Standing outside the room and hearing her moaning like she was in the throes of passion had been enough. He'd been rock-hard and walking funny by the time he left for his meeting at the base.

"We all enjoyed the entertainment you provided too, Bowie."

He tucked Tess in close to his body, putting himself between her and any threat, and shifted his attention to Bowie. "Entertainment?"

"Some of the ladies working at the spa thought I was some television star named Daniel Sun something-or-other. They stuffed phone numbers in my pockets and offered me free massages, so I just went with it."

Brett laughed and shook his head. "Your name will be mud if you run into any of them again."

"No, bro," his smile gleamed white. "Daniel Sun something-or-other's will be. But I do have a date. Unless you need me."

"No, Hawk—" He broke off as his brother-in-law turned into the drive and parked behind the minivan. "Hawk and I have this covered."

"I'll get the limo driver to drop me back at my car. What time do you need him back?"

Brett looked to Tess.

"Ten o'clock," she said.

"You heard the lady. Thanks, Bowie. I owe you one." The two gripped hands and shook.

Hawk joined them, a plastic bag of something dangling from one hand and a twenty-four pack of diet soda from the other. Eager to get Tess inside, Brett left Hawk talking to Bowie and escorted her down the walk and into the house.

The ladies were in the dining room putting out platters of finger foods and pouring drinks. Their banter and laughter filled the house.

After everyone had eaten their fill, Zoe, Tess, Trish, Selena, and Angela wandered into the living room with Mrs. Todd and took a seat.

"Looks like it's time for us to make ourselves scarce," Brett said.

"Want a beer?" Hawk asked.

"Yeah, I could use one."

They settled at the kitchen table. Mrs. Todd's voice carried from the living room. "Ladies, we're all women, and we all have a clit, and what I'm about to show you will make you a very, very happy woman."

The word "clit" seemed to vibrate down the hallway like the feedback from a bad PA system. Brett's head snapped toward Hawk and the two eyed each other.

Hawk half stood, a frown on his face. Then he shook his head. "I don't want to know." He settled back in his chair, but beneath his breath said, "U-uh, don't want to know." He raised his beer and took a long swallow.

Five minutes later, Brett went to get another bottle and then sneaked over to the kitchen door. Margaret Todd's voice carried down the hall. "This model can vibrate and rotate at the same time."

Female laughter, high-pitched and musical, reached him.

He sensed Hawk behind him, and turned to say something. The look on Hawk's face would have made him laugh if he hadn't been certain he had the same expression. "Your sister..." Hawk growled.

"Your wife…" Brett said, pointing a finger.

"Now, ladies," Margaret continued her pitch. "This model comes in several interesting colors."

Overcome by curiosity, Brett stepped out into the hall. In full SEAL stealth mode he eased down the hallway, hugging the wall, his steps light, almost silent. The living room opened up before him. Margaret Todd, the woman he'd thought of as grandmotherly, gripped a bright red dildo the size of a club in her fist. Tess was gazing at it with rapt attention. And worse, Zoe, his beautiful, Madonna-like sister, held a blue one and actually caressed the head with her palm.

Brett pivoted and bumped into Hawk. He used urgent SEAL hand signals to direct him back the way they'd come. They double-timed it through the kitchen to the screened-in sunroom and shut the door.

"Oh, Jesus—Oh, Jesus." The image of Zoe stroking the neon blue rubber cock played through Brett's mind in a horrifying loop.

Overcome by laughter, Hawk collapsed into the cushion-lined glider.

"What the hell, Hawk? I'm scarred for life. I may never be able to look at my sister again."

Hawk chuckled.

"Oh, shit!" Brett exploded and paced back and forth.

"What is it?"

"That Todd woman said she'd be sure Tess got some of their best products."

Hawk threw his head back and the sound of his laughter rumbled through the room. Every time he wound down and almost stopped, he looked at Brett and started all over again. He rolled off the glider and lay curled on the floor, hugging his sides while tears streamed down his face.

Brett fought the urge to plant a swift kick up his brother-in-law's ass. He plopped down on the glider and rested a foot on Hawk's hip. "The only thing that would be worse would be if Mom was here."

"Stop." Hawk waved a hand. "Don't make me laugh anymore. My stomach's killing me."

"You won't be laughing when Zoe whips that thing out in the

bedroom and wants a three-way with Big Blue."

Hawk gripped his stomach once again overtaken by mirth. He wiped his eyes with the back of his hand and asked, "Are you having a moment of insecurity, Brett?"

Was he? "Uh—no. A piece of plastic doesn't say 'I love you' after the show's over. And women need that. It's just…Zoe's my sister." Brett covered his eyes with the palms of his hands and rubbed. "Geez, I think that image is permanently burned onto my brain."

Hawk chuckled. "Have you thought about how hungry for sex they must get when we're not around for months on end?" His expression became contemplative. "At least as much as we do when we think about them, and we're hundreds of miles from home. Wouldn't you rather compete with Mr. Blue than some real-life asshole trying to take your place when you're not here to put up a fight?"

Brett thought about that. How often had he worried about Tess getting fed up with his absence and moving on? Especially when, for days on end, he couldn't even call and tell her he loved her. When he lay in his bunk at night and his deployment stretched before him, with one delay after another keeping him away from her, those doubts kept him awake more and more.

"Yeah. I think about it," he told Hawk. It ate at his gut, his heart. He didn't have to worry about some faceless man, but something he couldn't compete against. She loved being a reporter, was good at it. Would she grow to resent him because she hadn't followed her dream? He had to know why she'd turned the job down before he could be certain, and thus far she hadn't told him what happened during the interview.

Forcing a smile, he got to his feet and offered Hawk a hand up off the floor. He had to believe in his lady. If she said the job wasn't as important as what they had, he should believe her. Tess was true, honorable. And until she'd met him she'd been pretty untried sexually. The look of amazement on her face as she stared at that neon red cock popped back in his head, and he flinched. "Come on, let's get in there."

Regaining his feet, wariness crept over Hawk's features. "What do you mean?"

"If Tess is going to have a Mr. Blue to keep her company while I'm gone, I'm at least going to pick it out myself."

Hawk laughed. "What—you going to buy her one for a wedding gift?"

"Naw. I don't want the competition until the honeymoon is over. I'll give it to her before my next deployment."

"Oh, Jesus," Hawk breathed, holding his ribs again.

The porch door opened and Tess stuck her head into the room. "What are you two up to?" she asked.

Hawk straightened and smiled. "Nothing. Just talking and drinking a beer."

She opened the door further and Brett spied the short robe she was wearing. What the hell? Were they getting naked now?

"Zoe wants your opinion about something, Hawk," she said.

Hawk's brows shot up.

Was that apprehension he saw in his brother-in-law's face? Hell, he'd seen the man take on armed insurgents without hesitation. Hawk had gone into a building about to blow at any minute and dragged Brett's own ass out within seconds of it going up. He'd saved his life. He wasn't afraid of anything.

Brett shot him a thumbs-up. "Go, Big Blue."

Hawk shook his head and, as he walked past Brett, he murmured, *"Asshole."*

TESS BIT HER lip to keep from laughing at Brett's expression. What thoughts had gone through his mind when he and Hawk had peeked into the living room? She'd known the two men wouldn't be able to resist. How could they, with Vera Todd announcing each product as if she was in an auditorium instead of the small living room? The gang had gotten such a kick out of the men's hasty retreat.

Tess took Brett's hand and tugged him toward the living room.

"What's going on?" he demanded.

"Zoe did something today to surprise Hawk when we were at the spa."

His brows climbed. "My sister's full of surprises today."

Tess chuckled. They rounded the corner and paused just behind the couch.

Dressed in a floor-length robe, Zoe pulled Hawk toward the couch. "Have a seat, Adam," she said and flipped her ponytail over her shoulder in a nervous gesture.

"What is it?" Hawk asked, a touch of wariness in his expression as he did what she asked.

She slid between his parted legs and sat on his thigh. "They had this special makeup at the spa today. It's for covering tattoos and scars. I bought some, and Trish helped me put it on." She reached for the belt of her robe.

Hawk caught her hands. "I love you, Zoe. Scars and all. You don't have to hide anything with me."

"I know. I just want to be pretty for you."

"You already are, honey. The most beautiful thing I ever laid eyes on, from the moment we first met."

Tess's eyes glazed with tears at the sincerity in his expression, his voice. The comment earned him a kiss from Zoe.

"It's just my legs." She tugged at the belt and parted the robe. The T-shirt and shorts she wore were modest, but the latter bared her legs from high up on her thighs. She stood and tossed the robe over the ottoman.

The drunk driver who had hit Zoe when she was seven had left a legacy of scars. She walked with a permanent limp, because part of the calf muscle on her left leg was missing. Skin grafts had further scarred her body. But the makeup did a good job of covering the damaged areas' reddish discoloration, giving her legs a clear, smooth look. They appeared normal except for the back of the left one.

"I thought I'd use the makeup to cover my legs for the wedding."

The other women seemed to hold their breath while Hawk studied Zoe's legs for a long, slow moment, then stood and reached for his wife. "You look beautiful." He slipped his arms around her waist, and then lowered his lips to her shoulder. His voice was just a rumble as he whispered something in her ear. Zoe colored prettily. "I didn't marry you for your legs. I married you for your perfect, heart-shaped ass," he said loud enough for everyone to hear.

All the women in the room groaned.

Hawk laughed, then went serious. His expression transformed into a look so tender and passionate when he focused on Zoe, Tess had to look away." And because I couldn't imagine life without you."

"Good save, Hawk," Trish Marks said with a laugh, though her eyes glittered suspiciously, as did several of the other women's.

The party started to break up.

Brett hooked a finger beneath the belt of Tess's robe. "Have you got anything on under this, you want my opinion about?"

"No."

His grin widened and her cheeks grew hot.

"I do have something on, but it's for after the wedding. The others wanted to see it. But you don't get to peek until after the ceremony."

When he reached for the hem of her robe she smacked his hand. "Not until after the wedding."

His smile did special things to her. His gaze swung to the display of sex toys on the table. "Is there anything over there you're interested in?"

The heat in her cheeks climbed to scorch level. "No."

"What about for when I'm deployed?"

She studied his face. "A piece of plastic can't take your place, Brett."

"I know." He pulled her close. "But it could tide you over until I get home."

How long would they have before he was deployed again, or went on another training? "No it can't. It isn't the same." She lay her head against his shoulder. "I need the whole package."

His lips homed in on the special place just below her ear that sent chills all the way to the bottoms of her feet.

"Not nearly as much as I need you, honey."

# CHAPTER TWENTY-FIVE

SITTING AT HER desk, Tess rolled her head and felt the stiff pull and tug of the muscles stretching. She could use another massage. Since the bachelorette party she was overwhelmed with work. But she'd cemented the last of the wedding arrangements. All she had to do now was wait for the big event.

Family and friends would start to arrive in five days. She really wished she could put the Brittain Construction accident to bed and see Jonathan Frye arrested. What if she was on her honeymoon when it all went down? All the work she'd done would be passed on to another reporter to compile in a short article. Screw that. She'd write one based on her research, have Brittain call her if anything came through, and shoot it to Taylor from their honeymoon suite.

Brett came out of the bedroom. His shirt was open, baring a long strip of lightly furred chest and his sculpted abs. His pants were unbuttoned, but zipped so they hung on his lean hips. Every nerve in her body seemed to stand at attention. He rubbed his hand over his close-cropped dark blond hair. She was going to live with him, sleep with him, make love with him as often as she wanted. Well, whenever he was home. The idea made her get tingly in all her most intimate places.

"How did you sleep?" she asked to distract herself from the hormone rush.

"Like the dead. Staying up all night on an op and staying up fishing and drinking beer are definitely two different things."

Tess grinned. "Beer and any kind of activity, other than eating, doesn't mix well."

Brett went to the kitchen and poured a cup of coffee, then raised the pot, offering her one. Tess shook her head. She'd already had more than enough.

"Hawk is the poster boy for that observation. He's a six-foot-four-inch badass SEAL operator until he gets about six beers in him, and then all he wants is to go to sleep. And he can't play poker worth shit if he's drinking."

She laughed. "He didn't lose the car or house in a poker game, did he?"

"No, just his shirt."

"It sounds like you had a good time."

Brett smiled. "Yeah, it was great!"

Tess laughed. He'd come in at 5:30 a.m., more than a little drunk, and now, after five hours of sleep and a shower, looked fresh as a daisy. How the hell did he do it?

He wandered into the living room and paused to press a kiss on the curve of her shoulder, triggering a shiver of response.

"We didn't see a single mermaid the whole time we were out there, though at one point I think Doc was looking for one."

"It almost makes me jealous that I wasn't there to see it."

He laughed and slumped back into the chair closest to the computer.

"Think you'd be up for a drive later?"

He groaned. "It's Sunday, Tess."

"And I have five days to put all the things I'm working on to bed before the wedding."

Brett shot her a narrow-eyed look. "All right. But it depends on who we're going to see."

"I thought we'd visit Brian Gooding. I'd like to finish the story I was writing about the repercussions of drunk driving. While you were gone last night, I did a couple of phone interviews and some research.

Brett studied the coffee in his cup. "If you discover that your suspicions about him are true, what will you do?"

"He's not going to admit to any wrongdoing. He has too much to lose."

He tilted his head. "I didn't think Hamilton would admit to being blackmailed, or that Brittain would be so open about the accident, either. I wouldn't rule anything out."

Had her father made any kind of sacrifice for her, like the sacrifices Brian Gooding had made, and still made every day, for his daughter? She couldn't remember anything her father had done that she hadn't paid dearly for. She hadn't answered any of Ian's calls since coming home from D.C. She didn't know or care if he was coming to the wedding. All she knew was that he had hurt her for the last time. She was through playing second fiddle to him. She was going to concentrate on her career here and her life with Brett. To hell with Ian.

But despite her bravado, the ache still throbbed too deep to heal.

"I'm not going to push Gooding, Brett. I don't think I want to know."

Brett focused on her for a moment. "Okay."

"But I am going to finish the article."

"Okay."

"I'll fix us something for lunch and then we'll drive over his apartment."

"I could use some food. I'm a little hung over."

She studied him more closely. His eyes were a little bloodshot, but other than that he looked fine. Good enough to jump. She just might do that later.

BRIAN GOODING HAD aged since the employee picture Mary had sent her. His dark hair was more salt than pepper and thinning in front. He looked older than fifty, his square jaw already sagging. The small one-room apartment he invited them into was little more than an efficiency, and in a rough section of town. They had passed a sign for weekly or monthly rentals in the window of the office downstairs.

"This is Brett Weaver, my fiancé, Mr. Gooding. I hope you don't mind if he sits in. If you do, he can step outside and wait for me."

"I don't mind. Come on in." Gooding gestured them into the

room. Plastic tubs of belongings were stacked against one wall.

"I read about the shooting in the parking garage," Gooding said.

Tess raised a brow in surprise. Her name hadn't been used in the article.

"It didn't take much of a leap to put two and two together, Miss Kelly. I don't have time for much else, but I do read the paper every day. The article said a reporter, but when your car blew up they identified you," he explained. He frowned. "I hope they catch whoever is after you."

Was Gooding toying with her, or was this a real show of empathy? She couldn't put aside her instant suspicions, but murmured a thank you.

He pulled a chair out at the small kitchen table barely big enough for two. Tess took the seat and Brett the other, while Gooding dragged a chair over from beside the bed.

"Thank you for seeing me on Sunday."

"It's probably the only day you'd be able to catch me. I'm usually on one construction site or the other during the week."

"Your wife said you worked for Chanter Construction as a project manager."

"Yeah. I've been with the company twenty years now. Since just after Shelly and I got married."

"Is it a good company to work for?" Tess asked.

"Yeah. It's paid the bills, and my insurance is good. It covered Lisa's surgeries and care until we got other medical coverage through the state."

"What is it exactly that you do at Chanter?"

"Mostly I schedule material deliveries, equipment, and manpower when and where they're needed."

Did that mean he could have arranged for the cement deliveries at Brittain Construction?

"It's mostly logistics. When I need plumbers at two sites, and only have one crew available, I have to figure out how long it will take them to complete the first job and what the rest of the workers can do until the crew can come in. Time is money, so you can't have people standing around waiting."

"I learned a little about concrete deliveries having to be timed so you can pour floors."

"Yeah. Pouring the floors is a balancing act. It's dangerous work, too, so you have to have skilled workers do it. I read your article about Brittain Development. That was a real tragedy. We've had a few close calls, too. So I can sympathize."

"Recently?" she asked.

"No. Early last year."

Tess nodded. "Was the company supportive after your accident?"

"Yeah. Mr. Frye even came by the hospital to see how we were doing."

What a surprise. He certainly hadn't seemed to care that much about Mary.

"Did you know Mary Stubben?"

Gooding's expression turned solemn. "Yeah. Mary was a sweet lady. Her death was a big shock to everyone in the head office. I had dealings with her all the time. She was always on the ball with anything you needed done."

Could he look so concerned if he'd had some part in Mary's death? She glanced at Brett to see him studying Gooding with a frown.

Tess pulled out her notebook. "Is it okay if I take notes?"

"Sure."

"Did your wife tell you what kind of article I'm doing?"

"Yeah. Sort of a life after a drunk driving tragedy type thing."

Tess nodded. "How exactly has your life changed since the accident?"

He was quiet for a moment. "My wife and I divorced. It was my fault. I had all this rage inside me over what happened. It spilled out onto everything. Shelly couldn't live with me, and I couldn't blame her. I didn't want to live with myself. You see, when Osborne swerved into our lane, I turned the wheel to avoid him. It should have been my side of the car he hit, not Lisa's. Had I turned the wheel the other way, it would have been me. I wish it had been me." He clenched his hands on the table, and looked away, his throat working.

"It was a split-second reaction, Mr. Gooding. It's instinctive to turn away from something coming at you," Brett said.

"I've told myself that again and again, but life would have been so different—" he shook his head. "It was easier for Shelly to let *me* go." He pointed to himself. "When it's your child, you just can't."

"The man responsible for Lisa's condition committed suicide. Did that give you any kind of closure?"

"When I heard he was dead, for half a second I was satisfied. Then I was angry all over again. He took the coward's way out. He should have had to live with what he'd done as long as we will. The only positive thing that came out of his passing is I no longer had a target for my anger. I just felt hollow inside, and I had to finally deal with my guilt. I started seeing a therapist about two months after his death. Something I probably should have done right after the accident."

"But you're doing better now?"

"Yeah. It's been slow going, but my blood pressure has started to ease down and I'm actually able to go a night or two without the nightmares, and get through a day at work without blowing up."

That accounted for his sudden change in attitude with his wife. The tight feeling of anxiety, Tess had carried around every time she thought of Gooding and his wife eased.

And she could identify with what he was going through. She had her own nightmares to deal with. When she woke Brett, he was always calming, comforting, but he'd also encouraged her to see someone instead of trying to tough it out.

"I'm glad you're doing better. Shelly told me about Lisa's kidney failure."

He folded his hands together and studied them. "I'm a match, but I have diabetes, so they won't take one of mine. Lisa will die before they find a match. She's not high enough on the list."

How would he and Shelly deal with being freed by their daughter's death? It would have to be a relief and at the same time the most terrible of losses.

"I'm so sorry."

He nodded.

Tess looked toward the plastic containers. "It looks like you're moving."

"Shelly's agreed to let me move back in. I want to be as close to Lisa as I can for what time she has left." His chin quivered and he looked away.

Tess leaned forward and placed a hand over his. "You and Shelly have done everything you can for her. She's as comfortable as you can make her. I think she knows that, and feels how much you love her."

"But she'll never go to college, never get married, never have children. Her life stopped that day, and ours did, too."

Everything he said was true. But maybe one day he and his wife would start to live again. "You have an opportunity, Mr. Gooding. I know your wife…the way she talks about you, I can tell she still loves you. I'd use this time together to start again. Show her how far you've come."

BRETT HELD TESS'S arm just above the elbow as they ascended the rickety exterior stairs to the parking lot. "I felt damn sorry for him."

"I did too.

"But he could have arranged the truckload of cement to be delivered to Brittain Construction."

"But how would he arrange for the cement to be a substandard mix?"

Brett shook his head. "He liked Mary Stubben. As protective as he is about his wife and child, I can't see him harming a woman or being a part of killing her."

"Me either."

"Despite the link to his job, I just don't see him taking part. But he does need money to help with expenses."

"Hart and Buckler will have to be the ones to decide. I never sent them my research on the new hires and the other employees involved in operations."

"You need to do that, Tess." As they crossed the parking lot, Brett waved to Armando. The bouncer/bodyguard waved back with the all clear. It was costing the nest egg they'd saved for their honeymoon to pay for security, but it was worth it. Reaching the car, Brett opened Tess's door.

"I haven't done it because I didn't want to point to Brian

Gooding as a possible suspect."

"I think we've had this conversation before. You can't protect people from their own bad decisions. They have to take responsibility." He went around to the driver's side and got in, started the car, and pulled out of the parking lot. Armando fell in two cars behind.

"Where are we going from here?" he asked.

Tess shrugged. "Home, I guess. I'll work on this story and get it in tomorrow." Her phone rang and she fished it out of her bag. Her gaze leapt to Brett's face. "It's Armando. A dark blue sedan with a faded orange sticker on the bumper just passed him." They stopped at a light. The dark blue car pulled up beside them.

Every instinct fired and Brett drew his Sig and held it just below the man's eye level. He was a big man, filling the seat of his car, his head almost brushing the top. Henry Sullivan looked past Brett to stare directly at Tess, his expression stony. He raised a cell phone to his ear.

Tess's phone rang. She pushed the button for speakerphone.

Sullivan's voice sounded gravelly over the connection. "Stop fucking calling me. I did a report for Frye, and that's all. I don't want any part in that crazy fucker's business."

"What do you mean, Mr. Sullivan?"

"You know what I mean. You keep interviewing his employees, and asking questions, you'll have him on your ass again. Just let it go."

"A woman's dead, Mr. Sullivan. If you know anything at all, you need to contact the police."

"I don't know anything, and I don't want to know anything."

"Yes, you do. It was you in the parking lot of my paper when the bomb went off. What were you there for, if not to blow up my car?"

The light changed and Sullivan shot forward in front of them.

The phone went dead.

# CHAPTER TWENTY-SIX

**B**RETT'S ATTENTION MOVED from Buckler and Hart back to Tess. Had he done the right thing in calling them for this powwow?

"We don't have a direct tie from Frye to Mary's death, the car bomb, or the Brittain company accident. We've looked for one. We have to find something or someone to link him to the bombing before we can demand a warrant to look through his business files and financials."

"You have Mary," Tess said. Brett fought a smile at the intent expression she turned on the two detectives. They had no idea how determined she could be. "And you have Sullivan. He's tied to a woman who was killed under suspicious circumstances and was at the scene of a bombing moments before it happened. It's circumstantial, but there is a connection there."

She half stood, then sat back down. "You have to talk to Sullivan. The way you two behaved when his name came up, I can tell he's either slimy, or dangerous, or both." Tess's tone sounded as impatient as Brett felt. "And, based on the research I did on him, he doesn't seem the type to scare easily. Something's spooked him. I'm thinking he's bitten off more than he can chew with Frye, and he's trying to distance himself so he won't be considered an accessory."

"You're sure he was the man in the parking lot."

"Yes, seeing him in profile inside his car clinched it. I'm certain of it. It was his car in the parking lot that pulled away before the bomb went off."

Hart and Buckler exchanged a glance.

"So you think he set the bomb?" Hart asked.

"No. I think he knew what was going down and was there to try and figure out a way to stop it. If he was in on the bombing, he'd be covering his ass and keeping his distance, not trying to warn me off. And he's been following us. He may have evidence about who Frye's hired to come after me. He may be trying to figure out a way to slither out of the whole mess."

Hart sat forward, rested his elbows on his knees, and laced his fingers. "He's not the kind to suddenly grow a conscience."

"I don't think his conscience is bothering him, I think his sense of self-preservation may have kicked in," Brett said. "And why hasn't the FBI picked him up and questioned him about the bombing?"

"They did. He said he parked there, but walked to a nearby office building to see a client whose wife was having an affair. The guy confirmed he came by his office."

"Believe me, we've gone around in as many circles as you have about this," Buckler said. "The DA won't give us a warrant to search his office, either. He has no history with explosives, no training in using them, and had a legitimate reason for being there. And the report he compiled for Frye wasn't against the law."

Brett ran a hand over his head, roughing up his hair. "What about the bidding on the Ellison project?"

"Frye's dropped out of the bidding."

"And that ends the investigation?" Tess asked.

"No. We found out who sent him the information, but the guy quit his job and is in the wind. We're still looking for him," Buckler said. "If we can find him, we might be able to build a criminal case if he was paid for the info."

"So Frye gets away without any kind of punishment?"

"Well, we did prove he had access to the information, and the commission has voted that he won't be permitted to bid on any city-sanctioned projects for the next four years."

Brett shifted in his seat. "Four years is just a slap on the wrist."

"We couldn't prove Frye had solicited the information." Buckler shoved his fingers through his hair. "This guy is sheathed in Teflon. Everything rolls right off of him."

"And Hamilton has refused to talk to us about the blackmail."

Hart's expression was as downcast as Buckler's.

Tess stood and paced back and forth. "Mary lost her life because of this. There has to be something we can do. You have to talk to Sullivan. Put some pressure on him. He knows something."

"What about Marcus Kipfer?" Brett asked.

"Kipfer fits the profile. He's a drug addict who knows how to blow stuff up," Buckler said, a hint of bitter frustration in his voice. "But he has an alibi."

"What kind of alibi?"

"A girlfriend."

"Is she an addict, too?" Tess asked.

"No. And she's very protective of him."

"Meaning she'd lie for him?"

Buckler raised a brow.

"So what are you going to do?" Tess asked.

"Keep looking." Buckler stood and beckoned to Hart. "And talk to Sullivan. Who knows? He just might work with us for once. And we'll wait for Kipfer to screw up with the girlfriend so she might change her mind and tell the truth. All we need is one break."

Brett worried the one break they needed might involve Tess. After the wedding and the honeymoon, he'd have to go back to work, and they couldn't afford to pay for added security indefinitely. It was already eating a hole into their joint savings and their honeymoon fund. Tess would be left unprotected, vulnerable.

He shut the door behind the detectives. Tess's arms went around him from behind and she pressed close against his back. "You were awfully quiet. What were you thinking?"

Brett caressed her arms and relished the feel of her breasts pressing into his back. "I'm thinking the reason this whole thing started is they think you have whatever Mary took from work that last day. It has to be proof positive against Frye. If we find it, it will end the problems."

Tess stepped away. "But where would she have hidden it? The cops have searched her car, her house, her desk at work. They had to have."

"Then it has to be somewhere else."

"The only place we had in common was the Café Curiosité, where we met." Tess's eyes widened. "Saraphina would have called me if Mary had left anything at the shop for me to pick up."

"Maybe Saraphina doesn't know it's there. Isn't that the place with all the antiques?"

"Yes." Tess's mind race through possibilities. "It could be hidden anywhere."

"We won't know until we go look around. Maybe it will be right there at the counter."

"I'm sure the police have gone there and asked about our meeting. But I'm up for a treasure hunt. There's certainly nothing to lose."

SMALL FOLD-UP CHAIRS and tables with wooden slats sat in the shade of brightly-colored red and white-striped umbrellas out on the street. It looked trendy and artistic. Though the weather was pleasant, Brett guided Tess inside.

"This constant vigilance is getting old," Tess said, eyeing the tables. "I miss being able to sit out in the sun and enjoy an afternoon."

"I know. But it will be over soon."

She leaned her head against his shoulder in response.

They were met at the door by the scent of coffee and fresh baked goods. Brett breathed in the fragrances and, though he'd just eaten, his sweet tooth kicked in.

"I'm going to go to the restroom," Tess told him. "Order me a coffee with cream."

"I'm getting something sweet. I'll get two forks so we can share it."

"You and your sweet tooth. How can you even think of eating anything else after the lunch you scarfed down?" She threw up her hand before he could answer. "Never mind…" the corner of her mouth quirked up before she continued. "'I'm a guy, Tess, and we're always hungry for one thing or another.'"

Brett laughed at her imitation. "You need to deepen your voice a little to get it just right."

She shook her head and sauntered away.

The woman behind the counter took his order and Brett found a table near the back of the room. A moment later Tess slipped into her chair.

A stunning African-American woman, who was in the process of a glass cabinet with fresh baked desserts, smiled and waved to her.

"That's Saraphina Rollins, the manager. I covered a burglary here. The store was broken into in the middle of the night, and some of the higher-end coffees were stolen, along with quite a bit of other inventory."

"Why would someone break in to steal coffee?"

Tess shrugged. "Maybe they were caffeine junkies."

Brett chuckled.

"It's good to see you again, Tess," Saraphina said as she approached their table.

Brett shoved back his seat and stood automatically, acknowledging the woman as she came to stand next to their table.

"Saraphina, this is Brett, my fiancé."

The woman smiled and offered her hand. "You made it back in time for the wedding."

"Yeah." He shook her hand briefly. "Six more days and Tess will make an honest man out of me."

She laughed. "She said you wouldn't let her down."

Brett glanced in Tess's direction. Would he have made it if her car hadn't gone up like a demolition project? He hoped so. "I do my best."

"I'm glad to meet you." She turned back to Tess. "I'm sorry about your friend. It was a shock when the police stopped in and asked questions about your visit."

"Mary was killed later that day in a hit and run. They were trying to establish where she might have gone and what she did that day before the accident."

"So they suspect murder?"

"Yes, I'm afraid so."

Saraphina's lips pursed in an "O" of surprise. "How horrible."

"Did you happen to see Mary later that day, after we'd met for coffee?"

"I didn't, I'd already left for the day. But one of the wait staff did."

"Is she here today?"

"Yes. I'll ask Janet to come over and talk to you."

"Thanks, Saraphina. I appreciate it.

"In the meantime, enjoy your coffee before it gets cold."

Brett sipped his java, then forked a bite while Tess fiddled with her silverware, her actions fraught with nervous impatience.

"How can you be so calm?" she demanded in an accusing tone.

Brett chuckled. "I've waited longer for an MRE to heat, Tess. Eat a bite of this and get your mind off of things." He held out a forkfull of double chocolate brownie with whipped cream and caramel sauce.

"Oh, my God, I'm going to waddle down the aisle at the wedding."

"You'd have to eat more than one bite for that to happen."

She opened her mouth and he fed her the morsel. Tess groaned and he immediately got hard. Jesus, he was like one of Pavlov's dogs. All he had to do is hear her make that sound and he was ready.

"We could start looking around," she suggested. Her gaze scanned the antique glassware displayed on nearby shelves.

Brett offered her another bite, but she shook her head. "No, let's wait. Janet might have seen what Mary did while she was here. It will save us time in the long run if we talk to her first."

Five minutes later a young woman dressed in jeans and a button-down shirt came from behind the counter and approached their table. "Hello, I'm Janet Green. Saraphina said you wanted to ask me some questions."

"I'm Tess Kelly, Janet. And this is my fiancé, Brett. I was in here two weeks ago with a friend, and she was killed in a hit and run accident later that same day."

Janet nodded. "I remember. I waited on you that day. You seemed an unusual pair. She was like a small wren and you're more a swan."

Brett smiled at the quick flush of color that crossed Tess's cheeks.

Janet went on. "The police came in and talked to me about her. She came back in about five-thirty and ordered a Chai Tea Latte to go. Her car was parked on the street. She was as nervous then as she seemed when you were in here together that afternoon."

"Did she do anything besides order the tea?" Brett asked.

"She wandered through the displays for a minute, then left."

Tess exchanged a glance with him.

"Did you see her pause at any particular spot?" Tess asked.

Janet shook her head. "I was busy with other customers."

"Do you have surveillance cameras set up in that area?" Brett asked.

"Yes. But I'm not sure how long the feed is kept. You'll have to ask Saraphina about it."

Brett was on his feet immediately. "I'll take care of it." He strode toward the counter.

"THANKS FOR ANSWERING our questions, Janet. We appreciate it." Tess said, extracting a business card from her wallet. "If you think of anything else, call me."

"I'm sorry about your friend."

She and Mary hadn't had time to become friends. She wasn't certain they'd have remained a part of each other's lives after Tess had published her story. But, now she was gone they'd never know. There was an undeniable sadness in that. "Thank you."

Tess slipped out of her seat and wandered over to the displays on the right. A gramophone provided the centerpiece of one display cabinet. Had Mary been interested in music? Tess regretted not having asked her more personal questions. Besides getting to know her better, she'd be better able to guess what item Mary might have been attracted to. If she'd left something behind for Tess to find, it would have to be something small, like another flash drive.

Glass display cabinets shaped like houses held small items. She scanned each one carefully on the off chance Mary had opened one and slipped something inside. A player piano with its paper roll of music sat butted up against one of the tables where a woman sat reading and drinking tea. Tess strolled over and lifted the wooden lid protecting the keys. Nothing.

TERESA J. REASOR

She moved on to a shelf of china cups. She tilted each one and looked inside. Nothing more interesting than dust. Damn it. Where could Mary have hidden it, and why hadn't she given it to the girl behind the counter?

Because someone had been following her, watching her.

Brett came toward her from a hall leading from the back of the business. "I think I know where we need to look," he said.

Tess glanced up...and her gaze was caught and held by a man standing at the counter. Dark hair, dark eyes, slight build. And for what seemed like a lifetime, the world paused. She knew that face. But it had been covered with tattoos and a beard. She caught her breath and her lips parted.

Marcus Kipfer had covered his tattoos with something and shaved his beard. He reached beneath his workout jacket for something at the small of his back.

"Brett." His name came out in a whisper, her breath stopped by the sudden panicked rush of her heart. She pointed.

In a swift, practiced move, Brett drew his Sig and twisted to face the threat.

The man pulled his weapon and leveled it at him.

# CHAPTER TWENTY-SEVEN

S OMEONE SCREAMED. BEDLAM broke out as customers surged
to their feet. Two women ran toward the door and out. Four
other customers crawled for cover. A man and women cowered
behind the piano at Tess's right.

Tess wanted to move, needed to, but her limbs were frozen,
locked in place. All she could see was the barrel of the gun pointed
at Brett. The fear for him was numbing. *OhGodohGod*, ran through
her mind like a mantra, then tripped over into *don't let anything happen
to him.*

Kipfer's eyes shifted back and forth between her and Brett, his
breathing ragged and out of control. "Give it up and I won't have
to start shooting people."

Brett's features were taut, his eyes flat and focused. His stance
shouted *I mean business and I will kill you* as he aimed his weapon at
Kipfer. "We don't have anything to give up. We don't have it.
Lower your weapon and get down on the floor."

"You know where it is."

"Yeah, I know, and if you shoot, you'll never find it, but the
police will. You might shoot me, but, make no mistake, I'll take you
out. Put your weapon down."

A momentary indecision flickered across Kipfer's face. "Not
happening." He shook his head. "I've been following you for
weeks. You're giving it to me." Though he didn't take his eyes off
Brett, he addressed Tess next. "I know you don't want anything to
happen to your boyfriend, do you, Tess?" Sweat trickled down the
side of his face. His eyes kept shifting back and forth, though he

concentrated mostly on Brett. He had to be on something.

God, they were trapped here by a homicidal addict with a gun. Unable to speak, Tess shook her head.

"Start looking for it, and once you give it to me all this will be over. Tell her where you think it is, SEAL boy."

Brett never wavered from his stance. "Not happening," Brett said in exactly the same tone Kipfer had used. "The police are on their way, you know everyone in here with a cell phone has already called them. Give it up."

Kipfer's face hardened, and he tightened his grip on the gun. What if he pulled the trigger by accident? Oh, God. If she could divide his attention between the two of them, Brett might have an opportunity to take him out.

Tess swallowed. "I'll find it. I'm looking now." Her voice, stolen by fear, sounded weak. She shuffled sideways past the man and woman behind the piano to the next set of display cabinets. She scanned the items on the shelves. Looking for a weapon, looking for anything that might end this. Glass trinkets and jewelry were everywhere.

A glass sphere about the size of a baseball caught her eye, and she gripped it and dropped her hand to her side. If she threw it would she be able to hit him, distract him? She motioned to the woman cowering beneath a table, urging her to move away. The woman crawled past her and lay down behind a heavy wooden cabinet.

Sirens wailed in the distance.

"Hurry up," Kipfer shouted, his tone agitated.

Tess's gaze fell on an antique typewriter and she knew. That had to be it. Mary had only been in the shop for a few minutes. She'd pick something that would have meaning to her and to Tess. The typewriter made perfect sense, since they both used a keyboard for their work. She continued down the café, farther away from the rest of the patrons.

"I can't find it. There isn't enough time. The police are coming. You should get out of here before they arrive."

Kipfer was sweating profusely and his agitation was getting worse. A siren screamed outside. "You nosy bitch. If you'd died in the car like you were supposed to, I wouldn't be here now." He screamed with frustration at the same time he swung his gun toward her.

The Sig in Brett's hand barked twice in quick succession at the same time Kipfer's gun discharged. A glass panel in one of the display cases shattered and Tess jerked in reaction.

Kipfer's pistol dropped to the floor. He wove on his feet, then collapsed like a puppet whose strings had been cut.

Brett moved forward, still in shooting stance, and kicked the gun out of Kipfer's reach. Brett looked over his shoulder, his eyes frantic. "Tess, are you okay?"

"Yes." Her voice was hoarse, like she hadn't spoken in weeks. She leaned against a wooden shelf beside her, lightheaded with relief.

Kipfer gasped for air. "You fucking shot me." He strained to get the words out, as if the air had been knocked out of him. Two circles of blood spread slowly across his shirt high on his chest.

"Lie still until the cops get here."

Janet popped up from behind the service bar, cell phone in hand. "Call nine-one-one and tell them we need an ambulance," Brett ordered.

Customers started rising from their crouched positions. Some of them clung together in groups. One woman was sobbing.

The woman who'd hidden behind the piano touched Tess's arm. "You're bleeding."

Blood dripped from Tess's fingertips onto the wooden floor.

BRETT PACED BACK and forth just outside the ambulance while the paramedic bandaged Tess's wound. His head was about to explode. He'd been so fucking cocky, riding high on having taken down the fucker. Relieved that she'd still been standing. And she'd been shot! "Are you sure you're all right. Jesus, you were hit and I didn't even know it." He glared at a driver rubbernecking while he passed the ambulance. Yeah, be sure to get a good look, asshole.

"I wasn't shot, Brett. I was grazed."

"Grazed is shot, Tess."

"You'll probably need a tetanus booster, but no stitches," the paramedic said. He taped the bandage in place. "And he's right, you were shot. You are very lucky."

Brett raked his fingers over his hair. "I could have gotten you killed. I should have pulled the trigger sooner."

"Are we done here?" Tess asked the EMT.

"Yeah, unless you want to go to the hospital."

Tess threw him a look. The paramedic grinned. "You'll need to see your regular doctor sometime today. He may want you to take a round of antibiotics just to be sure you don't develop an infection."

*How the fuck could the two of them act so fucking calm?*

Tess signed a waiver releasing the EMTs from transporting her to the hospital. Brett stepped forward to offer Tess a hand as she climbed down from the ambulance. He gathered her close, his arms tight around her. He was still shaking from a combination of adrenaline and fear for her.

Tess hugged him back. "You saved my life, your own, and possibly several other people's, Brett. Marcus Kipfer didn't care about himself or anyone else. The only thing he cared about was getting whatever it is that Mary took from the office and his next hit of cocaine. The other paramedic said he was high. And he had a vial of cocaine in his pocket."

"How the hell did you recognize him? He sure as shit didn't look like his mug shot. He must have used that stuff Zoe got from the spa to cover his tattoos."

"And shaved his beard. I've seen him before."

Brett frowned. "Where?"

"In the checkout lane at the grocery store, the day we went there to interview Gordon. At the restaurant when we did the sampling for the rehearsal dinner, and I thought I saw him at the coffee shop when we met Hart and Buckler after Mary's funeral. Each time I was distracted by other people. He was hiding in plain sight. Without his tattoos he just blended into the background."

"He had to be the one who shot at us in the parking garage. He must have followed us to Hamilton's office." Brett shook his head. "Damned if I've ever noticed him before. But today? How did you recognize him today?"

"He heard what you said as you came toward me and his expression changed. Something about his eyes—I just knew who he was. And he was drawing his gun." She shuddered.

Jesus, he'd walked right past him. The guy could have shot him in the back. "You saved my life. I wouldn't have known he was there if you hadn't warned me."

"I didn't. I couldn't even speak. I just froze."

Brett's arms tightened again. "We need to work on that, Tess. When someone's waving a gun around, you're supposed to take cover."

She laughed. "I promise to do better next time."

*What was he saying?* "Jesus, honey. I can't believe I even said that."

"If you're finished with the EMT, we could use some help in here," Detective Hart said from the doorway of the café.

*Seriously? That was definitely a first.* "We better take him up on the invite before he changes his mind. Or have you lost interest after all the excitement?"

"Not a chance. I want *us* to find whatever it is that Mary hid here. You haven't told them where to look yet, have you?"

"Nope." She deserved her moment of discovery after everything she'd been through. "Let's double-time it in there before they change their minds."

As they entered the shop a crime scene tech handed them each a pair of latex gloves.

"How's your arm?" Buckler asked.

"It's just a flesh wound," Tess said with a smirk.

"Tess!" Brett couldn't believe she was so fucking cavalier about it all.

"What? If it was you with the nick, you wouldn't be able to stand it until you said the same thing."

Buckler laughed. "She's got you there."

Brett cradled his head in his hands.

Hart sidled up to them. "Kipfer is in surgery. We'll know something soon. The docs give him a good chance of survival." He eyed Brett. "You could have killed him. You'd have been justified if you had."

He was trained to kill. A double tap to the head and take them out. "It was something someone said in an interview with Tess recently. I figured Kipfer deserved to think about what he'd done for a long, long time, instead of taking the easy way out. With the police car out front and me in here, he knew he wasn't getting out for free. He wanted me to kill him. I didn't want to let him off that easy."

"Since you two laid the foundation for the case, we thought you'd want to be in on recovering the evidence. If there's evidence to find," Detective Buckler said. "I've okayed it with my Captain, but we're bending the rules, so this is off the record, Tess." He flashed Tess a frown.

"Okay."

"Where did you think Miss Stubben might have hidden something, Brett?"

"I bet I know where it is," Tess said.

Brett nodded. "Lead the way, honey." Tess moved around a glass display cabinet and went directly to the heavy antique typewriter.

Tess looked up at him. "It's the only piece in the room that would have meaning for us both."

He nodded. "You're one smart lady. And tough, too. I'll raise it for you."

Buckler motioned to one of the crime scene techs. The man rushed forward to take photos. Brett grasped the front of the typewriter and lifted the heavy machine.

"There's an envelope underneath," Tess said, her eyes suspiciously bright.

The technician took pictures again.

Tess reached under the machine and pulled out a wrinkled business envelope. She peeled back the flap carefully, then tugged some papers free. Between the layers lay another flash drive. She slid it out into her palm and then slid it into the plastic sleeve the crime tech held out to her. "Will you let me know what you find?" she asked.

"We'll let you know," Hart agreed.

Tess opened the sheets of paper and read a few lines. "They're emails printed from Frye's business computer arranging payment for services. Not construction services, but intimate services performed by a prostitute named Cher. He's asking her if she's

264

approached her boyfriend Marcus about the job." She glanced up at Hart. "You never said anything about her being a prostitute."

"There is supposed to be a divide in the information shared between the police and the press, you know."

She raised a brow. "I'll remember that next time." She returned her attention to the emails.

Brett crowded close and read over her shoulder. He placed a comforting hand on her when he read the next message.

Tess folded the sheets carefully and placed them back in the envelope. "He solicited Kipfer to use his driving skills to get rid of a problem."

"You're not going to read them all?" Hart asked.

She shook her head. "I've read enough." Tears ran down her cheeks. "Mary obviously didn't realize it, but she printed out the evidence that Frye arranged her murder."

# CHAPTER TWENTY-EIGHT

T HE AIR WAS lush with the rich scents of coffee, garlic, tomatoes, and herbs. The small banquet room off the main dining area of the restaurant barely contained the wedding party. But their friends and family seemed to be enjoying themselves, and the food had been wonderful. It was a twofold celebration. Frye had been arrested, and Marcus Kipfer was singing like a bird about everything to try and avoid the death penalty. All of Mary Stubben's suspicions about her boss had proven to be true. Frye was going down for her murder and also the death of the two men on the Brittain construction site.

But still Tess fought the urge to massage her throbbing temples. The moment Ian had shown up, *late*, for the rehearsal, the headache had kicked in. It was so typical for him to be late and make an entrance. The pain had worsened the longer she'd had to suppress the urge to strangle him during the practice ceremony.

And she still hadn't gotten beyond how he had humiliated her professionally before an editor of the Washington Post. Why would he do it?

Ian leaned forward to talk across the table to her mother and stepfather, Milton. Now they were no longer married, her parents seemed to have buried the hatchet. Despite the fact she'd like to bury one in Ian's head herself, she was glad they were getting along, and seemed determined to do everything they could to make her wedding about her instead of the past.

Zoe and Hawk sat beside Ian, Clara and Russell on the other side. They seemed entertained by whatever he was saying. He knew how to mesmerize people. He was magnetic, self-centered, and completely thoughtless.

Brett's hand moved up and down her back and he leaned close. "What's going on, Tess?"

She'd been too hurt, too embarrassed to tell him about the Washington Post fiasco, though she was certain he'd sensed something had happened. And now wasn't the time to tell him.

"I'm a little bummed you have to stay somewhere else tonight. I've gotten used to you being there anytime I want to jump you."

His slow smile reached right around her heart and gave it an intimate squeeze. He brushed her lips with a kiss. "It'll only be for a few hours, then we'll be joined at the hip again."

"I was thinking of being joined somewhere much more intimate." It was so much fun to flirt with him. It helped take away the stress, especially when Brett's eyes turned a bright, vibrant blue and his cheeks grew flushed.

Tess sighed. "I suppose we need to get up and mingle a few minutes before the party breaks up."

"I suppose."

They left their place at the head of the table and worked their way down opposite sides, sharing a word with each of their guests. Tess hugged Selena carefully. She had just gone through some reconstructive surgery and was still tender. "I can't wait to see you and the other ladies in your dresses tomorrow."

"We're going to be gorgeous. But we'll tone it down so we won't steal your thunder," Selena teased.

Tess laughed. "I appreciate it."

Greenback brushed a kiss across her cheek and whispered, "Thanks for this. She really needed something to focus on besides the surgery."

"*I* needed *her*."

Tess's mother was emotional but too reserved to show it. She cupped Tess's face and kissed her. "I love you. And this family you're marrying into is something special."

"They are, Mom."

"I'm so glad you have them here to support you. I've always worried about you being here so far from us, without family."

"Every one you see at this table has my back. I know I can call on them any time. So you don't have to worry about me anymore."

"I still will—it's my job, after all—but I'm more at ease now."

Tess moved on to hug Milton from behind. "I'm so glad you'll be walking me down the aisle tomorrow, and that you're willing to share the limelight with Ian."

Milton patted her arm. "I wouldn't miss it, princess."

Doc and Bowie had come stag, and Tess gave them each a hug. "We appreciate you two acting as ushers.

"Our pleasure," Doc said.

"Anything for you and Cutter," Bowie said. "And if ever you decide to dump his ass, you have my number."

"Bowie, I appreciate the offer but—it ain't gonna happen."

He grinned.

Langley and Trish sat on the other side of the table with Flash and Samantha. As the girlfriend of a SEAL, she and the other SEAL ladies had taken Samantha under their wing. Though she still owned a house in Nevada, she'd left her home to move to California with Flash, and had no family other than her little girl, Joy. Samantha, Zoe, Trish, Selena, Marsha and Clara acted as a network of support for each other when their spouses, boyfriends, and, in Clara's case, her son was deployed. By marrying Brett, Tess was becoming an official member of this SEAL family.

She'd finally made it around the table, given Ian a brief hug, and reunited with Brett, when the clink of a spoon against a glass heralded an announcement and she looked up. Ian was rising to his feet, a glass of ginger ale in his hand instead of a wine glass. His red hair had dulled a little with age and was sprinkled here and there with gray, but his long-limbed body was still lean and athletic. "I want to make a brief announcement."

Tess's muscles tensed. She could never guess what her father might do or say. But if he said one word about Washington D.C. she was going to leap across the table and stab him with her butter knife.

"Brett," Ian began. "I'm going to make you a list of everything I did wrong while I was married so you'll have a 'what not to do' list. It may help you to avoid the pitfalls." Laughter spread around the room. "The main thing I never learned to do, that I can tell you already have done, is to love my daughter more than yourself. You keep doing that and you'll make a great husband."

He looked down into his glass and cleared his throat. "Tess. I've made more mistakes than I care to think about as a father, but I do love you."

Was that a tear she saw in her father's eye? Tess refused to cry over a declaration he should have been more willing to make in the past. But the urge to weep was still strong.

"From the first moment the nurse handed me this tiny, screaming bundle with carrot-red hair in the delivery room, I knew you were going to dent my heart. Thank God the hair was the only thing you got from me. Otherwise we might not be sitting here tonight." The group laughed again.

Ian grew serious. "I was never willing to make the right kind of sacrifices or compromises. Those were two of my biggest mistakes. You have something special with Brett, worth doing both. Lean on each other. Share everything with each other. Make sure there's never an insurmountable distance between you, even when you're physically miles apart. Because a love built on a willingness to share, not just troubles, but yourselves, is indestructible. You can do all that. You already have these last ten months while Brett was deployed. You're both much wiser than I have ever been."

He raised his glass and everyone stood and raised theirs. "To you both. Long life and happiness together."

After a few more toasts, less serious, the party started breaking up. The hugging and kissing started all over again. By the time everyone was gone, leaving her and Brett alone at last, Tess leaned against him, exhausted.

They left the restaurant and walked around to the parking lot behind the restaurant. "Tell me why I decided to do a wedding."

"Because as her only child, and a girl, your mother guilted you into it?"

Tess laughed. "Yeah, she did. But once I started making arrangements I sort of wanted it, too."

He kissed her temple softly. "One more day and it will be over and you'll be Mrs. Brett Weaver."

"Tess Weaver sounds pretty good, doesn't it?"

"It definitely has a ring to it. You're going to keep Tess Kelly as your byline, aren't you? Since your readership knows you as Tess

Kelly."

"Yes. I'll be able to maintain my privacy more if I'm Tess Kelly online and Tess Weaver everywhere else."

Once in the car Brett paused before putting the key in the ignition. "What's happened between you and Ian?"

She wasn't surprised he had noticed the coolness between them. Tess was quiet for a moment, considering the best way to explain it. And realizing she should have told him before. "He was responsible for the Washington Post offer. He's signed on with them to be head of their international news group. I think he attached my offer to the deal." She tucked a strand of hair behind her ear. "So they didn't offer me the job because they were impressed by my work, but because he encouraged them to."

Brett was so still, his hands resting on the wheel, she turned to look at him. "Why would he do that?"

Tess shook her head. "I don't know. I couldn't take the job under those conditions. Arnold, the editor I spoke with, was very kind. He kept saying he was sorry I wasn't going to be a member of their staff. I think he really meant it but…" she threw up her hands, "…I'll never know for sure."

In the dull illumination from the streetlight, Brett's jaw rippled. "I'm sorry, Tess."

"I'm not. I feel hurt and betrayed by Ian. But, after it's all said and done, it was just a *job*, Brett. I think I was more excited about them wanting me than the position itself. Once that was taken away—" She shook her head. "I'd have been miserable there, and you'd have been miserable in Virginia. At least here we're really *together* when we can be. Our family is here."

"Yeah, they are. I can't say anything that will make up for this. But you are good enough to be on the staff of the Washington Post, The New York Times, any national newspaper that comes calling."

"It's enough that you believe in me, Brett, and I believe in you. After I left the interview, I realized how selfish I'd been. I put you through so much for a *job*. I'd risked *us* by even thinking about it." She gripped his arm. "What we have is more important to me than anything else."

Brett leaned across the console and she met him halfway for

the kiss. "You're everything to me, Tess."

Her hurt eased every time he acknowledged his love for her. How could she have risked that? She cupped his face and lingered over the next kiss.

"We could go home and have a quickie before I have to go bunk at Zoe and Hawk's," Brett suggested.

Tess laughed. "You're such a man." It was fun to make him think she was turning him down and see the small grimace of disappointment.

Twenty minutes later, they pulled in the parking lot at her apartment. Tess looped an arm around Brett's waist and nestled in against his side in the elevator. "It's going to feel strange not having you here tonight."

"You could change your mind and I could stay." He ran his fingers up beneath the edge of her sweater and caressed the bare skin along the waistband of her skirt.

"You're not supposed to see me tomorrow until the wedding. It's a tradition." The elevator door opened and they walked down the hall.

"I can leave after you go to sleep."

She had no willpower where he was concerned. She waited for him to unlock the door, then slid her fingers around his belt and pulled him into the apartment. She tossed her purse on the floor just inside the door. Brett crowded her back against the wall, his mouth seeking hers. One long kiss blended into the next. He released the button and zipper on her skirt and it fell to the floor at her feet. He caressed her hips, sliding her panties down. There was something fantastically erotic about him remaining completely dressed while she was naked from the waist down. He cupped her bottom and lifted her. Tess kicked free of her shoes and wrapped her legs around him. She wiggled against the pressure of his arousal while he rocked against her. So open to him, yet only feeling the promise of him moving against her, Tess groaned.

"Every time you do that it drives me crazy," Brett murmured against her throat, his breath hot on her skin.

"I promise to do it again if you come inside me."

It was his turn to groan. He hiked her higher against him and walked down the hall to the bedroom.

He lowered her to the bed and froze for a moment. It was too dark in the room to see anything but the shape of his face and the gleam of his eyes, but she knew what he was thinking.

"This will be the last time we make love until we're married," she said, sitting up to caress the back of his neck, then run her hands down his shirt in a quest for the buttons.

"Marriage will only make it better," he murmured, his lips brushing her cheek. "I promise not to fall down on the job."

He smothered her laughter with his mouth. Their tongues tangled, intensifying the slow, heady rush of need that throbbed through her body. He tugged her sweater and camisole up to cup her breast and knead it. She caught her breath when his mouth covered her nipple. He feathered the underside with his tongue, then sucked. The drawing sensation triggered rivulets of pleasure that flowed downward to the intimate heart of her.

She attacked his shirt buttons again and fumbled some of them open.

Brett dragged it up over his head, T-shirt and all, and tossed them to the side of the bed. He balanced on his knees between her thighs, and the jingle of his belt as he unbuckled it triggered a heartfelt sigh. Her body clenched, waiting for him, needing him.

But instead of entering her, he lowered his mouth to her breasts again. He pressed open-mouthed kisses over her stomach while she traced the taut muscles of his shoulders. A sudden memory of Kipfer's gun pointed at him made her shudder. He'd have taken a bullet for her. He almost had at the parking garage. He was so precious. Did he know how much she loved him, needed him?

"Brett, kiss me," she pleaded. He slid upward, allowing every inch of his naked torso to brush against her before his lips caught hers. She ran her hands down his back to his partially unclothed buttocks and pushed his pants down. She squeezed his muscular ass.

"I love you." The words weren't enough. Never enough. With a tilt of her hips, she guided his erection inside her. The heartstopping moment of physical intimacy made her sigh.

"I know you do," the assurance in his voice eased her last bit of anxiety. "And you're always so impatient."

Tess chuckled. "I love it when you're inside me and we're as close as we can get."

He rocked forward, sealing the connection between them. That one quick movement triggered a tidal wave of pleasure and she groaned again.

"Oh, honey," Brett moaned.

He gave up on control and began the intimate dance they'd perfected together. The sweet, sweeping give and take, push and pull, overtook them. Tess had a few moments to wonder at how the act mirrored their relationship. How they fit together in a hundred seamless ways, physically, emotionally, and how blessed they were to be together.

When they lay panting and spent a few minutes later Tess caressed his back and held him close.

Her cell rang in the living room and Brett made a noise very close to a growl. "I'll get it." He rolled free and reached for the bedside lamp.

Tess laughed at the sight of him. His pants were inside out and caught on one foot, which was still wearing a shoe. The other foot still sported a sock and his boxer briefs were half-mast at knee level.

Brett grinned, completely unabashed by his nudity or his clothing's condition.

Her cell phone rang. "I'll get it. You pull yourself together." Tess rolled out of bed, grabbed a fresh pair of panties from the drawer and a pair of sleep pants. She wiggled into them while Brett straightened out his clothes.

Finding her skirt and panties in the living room, she picked them up and fumbled inside her bag for her cell. "Hello."

"Tess, it's me. I'm downstairs. Can we talk?" Ian's voice was the last thing she'd expected to hear. She'd known they were due for a reckoning, but the night before the wedding was probably not the best time. But then, when? She sighed. "Yes, come on up."

She returned to the bedroom. Brett was in the bathroom, and she tossed her discarded clothing onto the bed, exchanged her sweater for a T-shirt and gathered her hair into a scrunchie at the nape of her neck.

She answered Ian's knock and stood back to allow him into the living room.

"I didn't interrupt anything?"

"No, Brett's getting ready to go to his sister's to spend the night."

He nodded. His body radiated tension, his expression concerned. He clenched and unclenched his fists inside his pants pockets. "I know you're angry with me."

"Not anymore, Ian. At first I was and just—"*so hurt I couldn't breathe.* "You've done a lot of shitty things to me in the past. Said a lot of shitty, hurtful things. But this time you fucked with my professional life. My professional reputation. And I am done. I'm done."

"It wasn't like that, Tess. I showed them your articles. Told them you were my daughter, sure, but said you are also a damn fine journalist. And they were missing out on one of the best." He threw out a hand in a gesture of entreaty she'd never seen from him before. "There was never any tie to my contract. Just a suggestion they check you out and see what you were doing. How strong a writer you are."

Brett came down the hall and paused at the entrance to the living room.

She didn't know whether to believe Ian or not. "Why? Why would you want me there? So I could live in your shadow some more?"

"You don't have to, Tess. You have strengths of your own. I wanted you there because I wanted to work with you. I wanted us to be a father-daughter team." He stepped forward and tried to take her arm, but she pulled away. "I missed out on your life as a child and a young adult because I had my head up my ass. I wanted to make up for as much of that as I could. I knew as soon as they saw the work you're doing now they'd want you. And they did. Arnold and all the other editors were damn impressed. That was the only reason they contacted you and made the offer. Not because I demanded they give you a spot. They wouldn't have gone for that even if I had."

Maybe one day she'd believe that. But right now none of it mattered anymore. "I've made my decision, Ian. I didn't turn them down because of you. I turned it down because of what I have with Brett. My job is my job. But Brett and I are building a life together."

She brushed away the fine wisps of hair that had escaped the scrunchie and lay against her cheek. "You missed out on my life. I was almost tempted to miss out on my own."

"Will you at least think about doing some freelance stuff with me?"

Tess laughed and shook her head. A knocked sounded at the door and she automatically moved to answer it.

Surprised, she frowned at the man who stood in the hall.

Ronald Gordon looked thinner, almost haggard. Deep lines of grief etched each side of his mouth.

"I just wanted you to know my nephew is worth more than the paragraph you gave him in your paper. Did you know he and Daniel Delgado were friends? That he became an addict after he met Miguel at their house?

Gordon stifled a sob. "And now he's dead and Miguel will live on to poison more teenagers with his dope. To cause more parents the pain my sister is feeling because she just buried her son. But you won't." Gordon raised his hand and plunged it downward.

Seeing something sharp descending at her, Tess threw up an arm to try and block it. Gordon shoved her back and she staggered, his greater size and strength pushing her, knocking her feet right out from under her. She went down hard onto her back. A piercing pain shot into her shoulder.

Ian and Brett rushed forward.

Brett dragged Gordon off of her as she tried to roll onto her side, but her arms wouldn't work, nor her legs. Warmth spread through her, and a weightlessness that was not unpleasant. Her eyes refused to focus.

"Dear, God." Ian knelt and reached for something sticking out of her shoulder.

After a moment of confusion, she recognized it as a syringe.

*Am I going to die?*

Her eyes rolled back in her head and darkness claimed her.

# CHAPTER TWENTY-NINE

**"S**HE'S THROWING UP, Brett," Ian shouted from behind Brett. "She's having trouble breathing."

"What did you give her?" Brett plowed his fist into Gordon's face again and again. "What was it?"

Gordon's head lolled back, held up only by Brett's grip on his shirt collar. "Heroin." The word sounded garbled coming from Gordon's busted mouth. "I gave her heroin."

Brett's heart thundered up through his chest and into his throat. "Oh, God. Jesus." He released Gordon's shirt and the man fell flat, then rolled onto his side.

Brett scrambled to his feet, sprinted to the phone on the desk and dialed 911."

Gordon staggered to his feet and out into the hall. Brett let him go. He wouldn't get far. The cops would pick him up.

Looking at Tess, so helpless and still on the floor, escalated his anxiety to panic proportion. He could barely breathe, barely think. He had to concentrated on what needed to be done.

The sound of busy signal nearly drove him out of his mind. He yelled in frustration and fought the urge to throw the phone against the wall. He shoved it at Ian. "Keep hitting the redial button until they answer."

With hands stained with Gordon's blood, he dragged his cell phone out his pocket, rushed through his contacts and pushed the key.

Miguel's voice sounded as cocky as always, "Sailor boy."

"Gordon came to Tess's apartment and stabbed her with a

hypodermic filled with heroin. 911 isn't answering. She's dying. Please tell me you have something you give your guys if they O.D."

Miguel's tone turned flat. "We're on our way. We'll be there in five minutes."

Five minutes! Five minutes was a fucking *lifetime*! He shoved the cell phone in his pocket.

Ian had finally gotten through to the emergency operator, his frantic voice was high-pitched with stress and punctuated with open sobs. His green eyes looked wild, and he was tearing at his hair with one hand while he gripped the phone with the other. The international reporter who had dodged bullets and been abducted by terrorists was falling apart.

Brett dropped to his knees next to Tess, then just as quickly rushed to his feet again. He couldn't touch her with Gordon's blood on his hands. He scrubbed his hands, then got a dishtowel from the kitchen and wet it. He hurried back and kneeled to bathe her face and clean the vomit from her chin. He made sure her airway was clear and rolled her back onto her side in case she threw up again. Her pulse was weak, her skin pasty and white. If he had to, he'd do CPR until it killed him. He wasn't losing her.

"Don't leave me, Tess. Keep fighting, baby. I'm here." Tears blurred his eyes. He kept his fingers on her pulse and monitored every breath. "Fight, Tess. Keep breathing, honey. I love you, Tess." He didn't think she could hear him, but it helped him to tell her.

"Get a blanket from the bedroom, Ian."

The big man struggled to his feet with the phone still clamped to his ear, staggered into the bedroom, and returned with the blanket from the bed. Brett covered her. As he met Ian's frantic gaze he realized Tess's father had aged ten years in the minutes since the attack.

Brett had never prayed so hard in his life. He offered God every bargain he could think of in return for Tess's life. Time crept by. He strained to hear the sound of an ambulance's siren, and fought the urge to scream and rail. The cell phone in his hand sounded and he punched the button to answer it.

"I am here," Miguel's voice came across the connection. Brett gave him the apartment number.

It seemed an eternity before Miguel appeared at the open apartment door. He hurried to Tess's side holding what looked like a syringe. He stabbed it into Tess's thigh and pushed the plunger. "This is Narcan and will neutralize the drug in her system. When the ambulance arrives, tell them what I've given her." He shoved the syringe into Brett's hand. Then he lifted Tess's eyelids and felt her pulse.

"How long does it take to work?" Brett asked.

"It is already working. They will give her more throughout the night." The sound of a siren whispered in the distance, and Miguel stood. "Where is Gordon?"

"He stumbled out the door. I beat him until he told me what he gave her."

"Good. Tell Ms. Kelly we are even and that Gordon will no longer be a problem for her."

"Don't let him off easy. Let him face what he's done here."

Miguel's expression remained flat, unreadable. He strode back out the door without another word.

Had Brett just signed a man's death warrant? Did he even care? Brett searched his heart for some pity for Gordon, and found none.

He gripped Tess's wrist and felt her pulse again. It felt a little faster, a little stronger. He pressed his ear to her chest and listened to her breathing. It didn't seem as shallow.

"Just a little longer, baby. Help is coming."

# CHAPTER THIRTY

THE BEEPING NOISE was driving her crazy. Growing louder and louder, pounding a nail of consciousness into her sleep-dulled mind. Was it a delivery truck outside backing up? Surely it didn't take that long to—Tess opened her eyes.

The room was shrouded in twilight. A long wall lamp over the bed reflected a soft glow off the ceiling.

*Shit!* She was in the hospital. She rolled onto her side and the sticky pads attached to the heart monitor pulled at her skin.

Brett sprawled loose-limbed and sound asleep in a chair by the bed. His six-foot frame overwhelmed the small seat, and his head tilted at an angle guaranteed to give him a crick in his neck. Light brown lashes fanned against his cheeks. His hair, having grown since his return, was actually attempting to lie flat, but not quite making it. Even with beard scruff darkening the lower half of his face, he'd never looked more handsome.

Tess moved her arm, felt the tug of the IV and frowned. Oh God, what about the wedding? Would she be able to walk down the aisle?

Before she'd been overwhelmed by the heroin's affects she recalled she'd wondered if she was dying and hadn't cared if she did. The drug, the heroin Gordon had injected her with...Had leached her will to live. Drained it from her consciousness. How insidious and scary was that?

She'd awakened to the brightly-lit bedlam of the emergency room with an IV in her arm and a doctor asking questions she felt too tired to answer. All she'd wanted to do was return to the floating euphoria where nothing mattered. Until she'd seen Brett standing off to one side. She'd never forget the look of anguished worry on his face.

The door opened and a nurse came into the room carrying a basket filled with the paraphernalia to draw blood. Her pale scrubs looked dull gray until she neared the bed and stepped into the dim light, and they turned blue. She offered Tess a smile, and after a glance in Brett's direction, whispered, "How are you feeling?"

If she said 'like shit' they'd make her stay and she'd miss the wedding. "I'm good."

Brett shifted in his seat, straightened, and then arched his back and stretched. He came to the bed and rested a hand on the railing to watch while the nurse took her temp, vital signs and checked the IV bag.

"The doctor's ordered another tox screen and a few other tests."

Tess stretched out her arm where a bruise had already formed from other blood draws and flinched when her shoulder moved. She knew she had a bruise on her thigh where Brett had told her Miguel had injected her. But she also felt sore in other places as well. She looked away while the nurse inserted the needle.

Brett grasped her free hand and ran a calming thumb over her fingers. Dark rings discolored the skin beneath his eyes. Exhaustion dragged at the corners of his mouth. As soon as the nurse finished and left, Tess patted the bed beside her.

After a brief pause, he lowered the side railing and slid onto the narrow mattress to spoon with her.

"How are you really feeling?" he asked.

"A little shaky. And sore in spots."

"Me too."

She ran her fingers over his red knuckles. "I'm sorry."

"For what, honey?"

"For…everything."

Brett let out a sigh. "None of this shit was your fault."

She guided his hand up beneath her cheek. After a few minutes of silence she asked, "Did they find Gordon?"

"Buckler called my cell phone last night about one. Gordon was dumped out of a car in front of the police station downtown."

"He was still breathing, wasn't he?"

"Yeah. A little beat up, but okay. He's confessed to everything. He'd been looking for his nephew for days when the cops found him dead. He blamed himself for not finding him in time."

"His nephew had a two-year history of drug addiction. He's been in and out of jail and rehab." But things could have been handled with more consideration at the paper. "I didn't write the piece in the paper about his nephew. It was done by another staff writer. I should have done it."

"He was just looking for some kind of payback, and you were the only one he was brave enough to take on."

Tess turned to look over her shoulder. "Is Ian okay?"

"Yeah. Once you were out of the woods. He was in pretty bad shape before."

"My mom?"

"Luckily by the time I called her, things were turning around. Don't you remember her coming in?"

She rubbed her forehead. "Vaguely." She hugged his hand to her. "They are going to let me out in time for the wedding, aren't they?"

"If the doctor says you're good to go."

She was going to be at the church if she had to crawl there. Surely by three o'clock she'd back on her feet. She wasn't about to miss her own wedding. Not after all this.

"I don't ever want to go through anything with you ever again like I did last night, Tess." Brett said, his voice breaking. Her heart sank, but when she attempted to face him his arm tightened.

She hastened to reassure him. "I'm okay. This was just a random thing. It's never going to happen again."

After a few minutes his arm relaxed and she turned to brush away the tears still wet on his face. Emotion gripped her throat at seeing them and answering tears blurred her vision.

"Maybe we should move to D.C.," he said.

"Screw D.C. It's the Post's fault I went on the interview with Mary to begin with. I'd just done the phone interview with the editor and I was gung ho to sink my teeth into something controversial. If I hadn't met with her, she'd still be alive, and none of this would have happened. I wouldn't move to Washington D.C.

if you paid me."

Brett laughed. "Okay."

When he pulled her close to snuggle against him, she relaxed. "Did you really wipe puke off my face?" she asked.

Brett snorted and his chest shook. "Yeah."

Tess cringed at the thought of him seeing her like that. "I suppose you really have to love someone to do that."

"In sickness and in health, honey."

Tears glazed her eyes again, but she smiled. "I have a weak stomach, but I'll do my best."

FROM ALL THE stares and good wishes tossed her way as she left the hospital, Tess was pretty certain Scripps Mercy had never had a bride leave its halls in a wheelchair, already dressed to walk down the aisle. Her mother carried her belongings, while Clara held the short train up from the side of the chair.

"Are you sure you're okay?" her mother asked for the tenth time in two hours.

"Yes, I'm fine." In truth she felt much better now she was on her way to the church, but still shaky. It had been sixteen hours since she'd been injected. With all the medications they'd given her to neutralize the heroin, she was on her feet. She still needed to take things easy. Still felt like she'd been stomped on by an elephant.

But her kidney and liver functions were normal. And, because she'd been attacked and injected, and not considered a real drug user, they decided not to send her to rehab. *Hallelujah!*

Milton stood out front waiting for them, his car pulled up with the doors open. He helped her out of the wheelchair and into the back seat with Clara. Her mother took a seat up front.

Clara folded the train of her dress over her lap to keep it from wrinkling. She gave Tess's hand a brief squeeze and actually smiled when she looked as if she really wanted to cry.

Twenty-five minutes later, as Tess stood outside the entrance to the Crown Room, surrounded by her bridesmaids and their escorts, nerves hit her. She'd never seen so many men in dress white uniforms. But the navy blue bridesmaids' dresses she'd chosen contrasted nicely. Greenback and Selena would start the procession, followed by Langley and Trish, Flash and Samantha, then Bowie and Zoe.

Ian took her arm and brushed a kiss against her forehead. "You look beautiful, Tess." His voice shook and he cleared his throat.

"Thank you, Daddy." She'd had time to think about everything he'd said last night before the attack, and she couldn't stay angry with him. "I think I'd like to do some freelance stuff with you." It was her way of accepting his apology and telling him she forgave him.

Ian laughed.

Milton flashed her a smile and took her other arm. "Most beautiful bride I've ever seen."

Tess leaned her head against his shoulder for a moment. He patted her cheek.

Zoe tucked Tess's bouquet of white and pink-tinged Calla lilies into her hand. Tess savored their fragrance.

The music began. Nerves and a rush of excitement set off the sensation of bats playing badminton in her stomach. Greenback and Langley opened the doors and took their places. The room glowed gold in the light of the overhead lamps and wall sconces. The space resembled the belly of a Victorian ship with its spine-like beams and wooden coffered ceiling. The men looked more masculine against the background, the women more feminine.

This was the place she and Brett had first met, and a fitting place for them to seal the ties between them.

The bridesmaids and escorts disappeared through the doors a pair at a time. Then the music changed and Ian and Milton stepped forward, supporting and guiding her. Rows of chairs arranged for the guests created the aisle.

Brett stood at the end waiting for her. As soon as she saw him her nerves settled. Sunlight spilled through the bank of windows that curved around the end of the room. A small two-step platform had been erected, and an arbor of white and pink Calla lilies, matching her bouquet, had been placed where they would stand. Hawk stood at parade rest on Brett's left, acting as his best man, the minister on his right.

She had never been more certain of anything as she walked toward Brett and her future. She had never felt such love for another person. He had been willing to die for her, had saved her life three times. Had fought for her. She was so lucky to have found him. So lucky they had found each other.

BRETT HAD NEVER seen Tess look more beautiful. The heart-shaped bodice of her gown followed the curve of her breasts, while lace covered her shoulders and arms, emphasizing the natural grace of her figure. Her auburn hair flowed free over her shoulders beneath an elbow-length veil.

Everything they'd been through in the last three weeks played through his mind. It was a miracle she was walking toward him at this moment. When she made it to the steps and her father placed her hand into Brett's, the symbolic meaning behind the gesture brought a knot to his throat.

He gripped her hand as she climbed the platform. Milton stepped forward to help with the train that spread out behind her. Zoe stepped forward to take her bouquet.

Tess paused to look up at him and smiled. "I made it."

After all the worry about his being AWOL for the wedding, it was she who'd nearly missed it—permanently. Brett slipped an arm around her and held her close. Emotion nearly overwhelmed him. Lord, if he cried in front of this crowd, he'd never hear the end of it.

"That's supposed to come at the end of the ceremony," the minister said.

The wedding party and guests laughed.

"I couldn't help myself," Brett quipped and they laughed again.

"Did your team make it?" she asked.

"They're directly behind you on your right."

Tess turned to look over her shoulder at them and wave. Brett laughed when the guys grinned like fools.

He pointed to his insignia and her eyes widened. "Your promotion came through? I'm marrying a Lieutenant."

Lieutenant Commander Jeffrey had shown up with the rest of his unit moments before the service with the shoulder boards and his collar insignia. They'd had a brief promotion celebration in the room Brett had reserved for the night.

Pastor Grant cleared his throat. They sobered and turned to face him. He smiled and began the service with a prayer and went directly into the traditional service. "Dearly beloved, we are gathered here in the sight of God and this company to join this man and woman in holy matrimony…

Tess's voice was strong as she repeated her vows, but her hand trembled a little when she slipped the plain gold band over his finger. He spoke his own vows from memory, without prompting, and slid the ring on hers.

The pastor finished the ceremony with, "The sanctity of marriage and the bond between a husband and wife are built each day through love and respect, and, when nurtured, become as strong as this silk cord." He looped the silk cord around their hands in the Irish custom they had rehearsed, and then tied it.

"You don't have to tie it too tight, pastor, we've already got this part covered." Brett said. He looked deep into Tess's eyes and saw the same love and joy that crowded his chest.

Tess smiled. "Yes, we do."

## THE END

# BREAKING TIES

## A SEAL TEAM HEARTBREAKERS NOVELLA

Teresa J. Reasor

Navy SEAL Oliver 'Greenback' Shaker is used to making sacrifices in service his country. Yet he's blindsided when he returns from a training rotation and learns his wife, Selena, has kept a terrible secret for weeks, as she waited for him to come home—a secret that may require a sacrifice he's not prepared to make.

Faced with a life threatening illness, Selena wants to follow the same code of strength and perseverance her husband does as a SEAL, but she can't go it alone. She needs a team, headed by her husband, to see it through. But in Oliver's line of work, duty comes first.

Still reeling from her first diagnosis, they learn Selena is pregnant. Now with two lives hanging in the balance, the emotional and physical toll stretches the ties that bind their marriage to the breaking point. But as a SEAL, Oliver never gives up. And Selena proves valor and courage don't just live on the battlefield, but in every person's heart.

# DEDICATION

To Joyce Brown, breast cancer survivor and Certified Breast Patient Navigator for the Baptist Healthcare Oncology Services of Corbin, Kentucky, for your help in clarifying the medical procedures needed by my character.

Any mistakes I've made are totally my own.

God bless all those brave women and men who face the battle with cancer every day with courage and humor.

And to all you ladies out there: Please do monthly exams, yearly clinical exams, and mammograms when your doctors recommend them!!

God bless our military men and women. Your sacrifices do not go unnoticed.

# CHAPTER ONE

**E**NSIGN OLIVER 'GREENBACK' Shaker used the dense shadows to hide his position, easing into the narrow, masonry-clogged alley between two battle-scarred buildings. His body armor trapped the heat and reflected it back against his skin, and sweat poured down his back and sides like he was being sautéed inside his BDUs. He'd experienced heat before, but Iraq was surely like being trapped in the third circle of hell.

The distant sound of a baby crying came from one of the dark buildings. Through his night vision goggles he detected the dim glow of a light barely visible across the street. Some of the structures still housed families just struggling to survive while terrorist and military forces battled around them for control of the area. They had nowhere else to go, so they hunkered down and hoped the violence would pass.

What would he do if he were faced with such a terrible dilemma?

For a brief moment he allowed his thoughts to stray to Selena, waiting for him at home in San Diego. She had just sent him a short video of the doctor's most recent scan of their baby, showing how much it had grown. He'd never seen anything as beautiful as his wife's belly swollen with their child. He wanted to reach through the computer screen, to run his hands over it and feel the baby move.

He was here doing his job so no one would have to face such choices on American soil. *But, God, how he missed her!*

The civilian presence in the area was one of the reasons his team was here, risking their lives, doing this mission old-school instead of raining down ordnance.

He gripped his SCAR rifle and scanned the street for movement. It was his job to guard the team's back door, their route of escape. As soon as they finished wiring the building to blow, they'd fall back and double-time it out to wait for the structure to blow.

The first click came over his com system, signaling Hawk, his commanding officer and leader of the mission, had gained entry to the building. Next came Bowie's signal, then Doc's. Cutter's and Strong Man's clicks soon followed.

Greenback glanced at his watch and mentally marked the time. They had seven minutes to get in, set the timer and get out. Derrick Armstrong aka Strong Man would be the last man out and would set the last timer.

Greenback didn't know which was worse, being two blocks away, alone, and surrounded by insurgents. Or being inside a structure filled with explosives and occupied by terrorists. Pick a fucking card. Both sucked. But at least things had remained quiet at his...

The sound of approaching footsteps froze his thoughts and movements. He shifted, finding cover behind a jagged clump of masonry which partially blocked the alley. He waited to identify whether the person was armed or not. If he carried no weapon, Greenback would hold his position and allow the man to pass.

The baby's cry from above and across the street drew the guy's attention. He paused, the barrel of the AK-47 slung over his shoulder, pointing heavenward.

The tango was armed and on foot patrol. Possibly one of the terrorists.

The man pivoted. The glow of his flashlight swung toward the alley, reflecting off the wall opposite Greenback. Still wearing his NVGs, the light blinded him, leaving dots seared on his retinas. *Shit!*

The tango shuffled into the alley. Greenback froze as the man eased past him, so close he smelled his sweat and the faint hint of garlic.

The tango halted, looking up as though he heard or sensed something. "Who is there?" he demanded in Arabic.

With the aftereffects of the flashlight still obscuring his vision, Greenback could only guess the man's location. Should the tango shout a warning to the rest of the patrol, there would be no escape for him or the team. With all his strength, Greenback swung his heavy rifle stock and connected with something solid. A hollow thump like a melon cracking open echoed through the alley. He sensed more than saw the tango's head whip back and a dull thud followed as he dropped to the ground. Greenback followed the sound, lending his weight to pinning the sentry and keeping him quiet. He gripped the man's head, the spongy feeling of crushed bones making him gag. The tango's choking struggle to breathe lasted an agonizing thirty seconds, and then his efforts ceased.

Fear and relief tangled in Greenback's gut, triggering a wave of nausea. His heart pumped hard from the surge of adrenaline, his vision slowly cleared, and he felt for a pulse. There was none. He scrambled to his feet and rolled the man against the wall.

He turned to study the street again. Had anyone heard the brief struggle? Nothing moved. How long before the next tango on patrol wandered by? There had to be more than one. What were the chances the next guy would use the alley as a shortcut? Greenback steeled himself to do whatever came next.

The baby across the street started crying again, louder and louder. Why didn't someone pick it up?

"OLIVER? OLIVER?" SELENA bounced Lucia on her hip in an attempt to soothe her. The toddler's cheeks were flushed with fever and her tiny body radiated heat. Her two-and-a-half-old daughter had never been this ill. She'd run low-grade temperatures when she was teething, and once with an ear infection, but this one was still creeping up and refused to stay down, even with children's Tylenol. Several hours later, Selena's concern had turned into full-fledged fear.

Though the room was cool, Oliver's curly, dark brown hair clung to his forehead, damp with sweat. His eyes darted back and forth beneath his lids, a sign of REM sleep. She knew better than to touch him while he was under so deeply, because he'd react like he was in danger.

His hands twitched and his breathing became uneven. What was it he dreamed about? If only he would tell her. He'd sometimes come half off the bed if she startled him awake.

"Greenback!" she said, using his SEAL handle in as commanding a tone as she could manage, since she was pretty sure he was dreaming about a mission. "Lucia is sick."

His eyes flew open and he sat up so quickly she gasped.

"What's wrong?" he asked.

Her heart flew into a wave of fast contractions, exhaustion intensifying her reaction. "Lucia's running a high fever and it's not coming down as it should, even with Tylenol. I think we need to go to the ER."

He threw back the covers and was on his feet in one smooth move. How did he go from deep sleep to wide-awake in seconds? It was a skill she could use. She was groggy from being up with the baby off and on all night. Had he not just gotten home from a training rotation she'd have asked him to help earlier. But he'd been so exhausted he'd slurred his words.

While he yanked on a pair of jeans and a T-shirt, she gently rocked Lucia and bathed her face with a cool cloth. Instead of soothing her, the damp rag seemed to make her scream louder.

"Let me take her, so you can get dressed." Oliver plucked Lucia from her arms and cuddled her close while he did the dance and dip movement that usually rocked her to sleep. His dark hair, so much like the baby's, clung in ringlets where he'd splashed water to smooth it down.

"Daddy-daddy-daddy." Lucia strung the syllables together in a monotonous chant while Selena got dressed, but at least she was no longer screaming.

Selena hurried into a pair of jeans and a blouse and stuffed her feet into slip-on tennis shoes. She dragged her long hair into a scrunchie to pull it back from her face.

Oliver frowned, his concern clear in his brow and compressed lips. "Jesus, she really is hot. Why didn't you wake me sooner?"

Defensive and worried, she said, "I gave her some children's Tylenol, thinking it would bring the fever down until I could take her into the pediatrician's office this morning. It obviously didn't work."

She gathered the diaper bag and her purse. Oliver carried Lucia, followed her to the van parked alongside their small house, opened the back door, and secured Lucia in her car seat.

"I'll sit back here with her while you drive," Selena said, climbing in next to the baby seat. She fished in her bag and found the keys and handed them to him.

"Daddy-daddy-daddy."

"Daddy's driving, baby. We'll be there in a minute," Oliver said while he quickly backed the vehicle out of the driveway.

Of course Lucia would want Oliver. She'd had a steady diet of Mama for the last six weeks. Tears blurred Selena's eyes at her unexpected resentment. He swung through just long enough for her and Lucia to rain their affections on him, then he swooped back out again.

She snapped the seat belt on and laid a soothing hand on Lucia's chest as she began to struggle against the restraints of the car seat and cry.

Lucia had been more fussy than usual for the last few days. And her nose had run a little. Selena scolded herself for not noticing sooner, but it was so hard being responsible for everything on top of her work at the bank. The house, the yard, the van, Lucia. *Everything.*

Being married to a SEAL was like being single nine months out of the year, with no companionship and no sex. As much as she'd wanted a family, she hadn't realized she'd be raising Lucia mostly on her own.

She'd kept everything together until last Friday, though. But now fear cramped her stomach. Every time she thought about it, a gut-clenching dread swamped her.

She needed to tell Oliver. And she would. As soon as Lucia was better. She couldn't worry about it while her baby was ill.

Oliver looked up into the rear view mirror at her. "How long has she been sick?"

"Just this evening. She's been a little fussy the last few days, but nothing I could put my finger on."

He turned into the Balboa Medical Center parking lot. "I'll drop you at the ER entrance and go park the van. I'll be back as soon as I can."

"Okay," Selena murmured, already busy releasing Lucia from the car seat. Selena lifted her free and grabbed her purse and the diaper bag from the floor. As soon he stopped the van, she got out and shoved the door closed. He drove away immediately.

While Selena sat in a small privacy cubicle and provided the woman checking them in with all the necessary information, Lucia clung to her and cried. The sound bounced off the sides of the small space, magnifying it. With each second, the tension headache pounding at the nape of Selena's neck intensified.

Finally Oliver appeared at the mouth of the cubicle. His hair, now dry, lay in heavy curls, accentuating his olive-skinned Italian good looks. The girl behind the computer flashed him a smile and sat up straighter. He nodded to her. His biceps flexed against the short sleeves of his T-shirt as he lifted Lucia. "I'll see if I can entertain her until we're called back into an examination room."

Selena watched his progress down the hall to the waiting room. Carrying forty to sixty pounds of gear during every mission, and the constant physical training he and the team did, had honed his five-eight frame into muscular perfection. Her desire for him had never waned. All he had to do was look at her with his heavy-lidded, chocolate brown eyes, and she was hot for him. And he reacted the same way to her. Would he still feel that way after she told him?

She collected her insurance card and identification from the girl and walked back to join Oliver and Lucia in the waiting area. Four other people waited ahead of them.

Since Lucia seemed to prefer the hall to the waiting area, Oliver walked her up and down, doing his dance, bounce move. Her throat closed just watching him. Loving him and Lucia was the one thing keeping her together, keeping her strong. But she didn't feel strong right now. She felt shaky and afraid. Afraid for herself, but afraid for Lucia and Oliver, too.

The waiting area cleared out quickly, and a nurse called them back to the examination room. The claustrophobic closeness of the space was stifling, and she struggled to push the air in and out.

"You okay, hon?" Oliver asked, a frown working its way across his face.

Lucia reached for her, giving her an excuse to focus on their child instead of the walls closing in around her. "I'm fine." She cuddled her daughter close and grabbed a tissue to wipe Lucia's nose. The doctor came in before Oliver could probe any further.

Lucia screamed at having a strange man touch her. Selena answered the doctor's questions while Oliver held the toddler during the examination. At his diagnosis of another ear infection, Selena frowned in concern. "She just got over an ear infection last month."

"Do you know if she has any allergies?" he asked.

"No."

He studied the chart. "How often have the infections reoccurred?"

"Just in the last four months she's had three."

"Is she in daycare?"

"Five days a week, while I'm at work."

"Children in daycare are more susceptible to bacterial infections. Children indiscriminately spread germs. Any pets?"

"No."

"Any stuffed toys she sleeps with?"

"Her lamb."

"I'd recommend washing it as often as possible, or slipping it out of her bed once she's asleep. Toys harbor bacteria.

"With children this age," the doctor continued, "the Eustachian tubes are flatter and narrow. They don't drain as easily as adults. That allows bacteria to build up and causes fluid to gather behind the eardrum and cause the pain.

"It's too soon to tell, though, because that last infection might not have responded to the first antibiotic she took, and it lingered. I'll give her something a little stronger and see if we can't wipe it out. But if she continues to develop them, your regular pediatrician may want her to see an ear, nose, and throat specialist. If she doesn't respond to the antibiotic quickly, take her in to see your regular doctor immediately."

"Thank you. I will."

Half an hour later they were out of the ER, with prescriptions for some drops to numb Lucia's pain and the antibiotic.

Although they rushed through an all-night pharmacy and picked up the prescription, the sky was already lightening as they reached home. Selena gave Lucia, now exhausted from crying, a dose of the antibiotic. Oliver administered the ear drops and got the baby down while Selena made coffee.

Their small, bungalow-style house had been a labor of love. They remodeled things when they could afford to, and the kitchen had been their first project together. The terracotta tile floors glowed with warmth. They'd painted the cabinets a pale sky blue and distressed them. The glass doors shone. Fresh herbs filled the room with fragrances from a window box garden in the small breakfast nook next to the round kitchen table. Selena stacked the bills and letters spread across the table and set them aside. She settled there while she waited for the coffee to brew and for Oliver to join her.

Though exhaustion dragged at her limbs and she longed for sleep, they needed to talk. She needed to tell him, though the dread of it made her want to throw up. Just saying the words would make things real for her, for them both. And change things for them—between them—forever.

Ten minutes later, Oliver wandered into the room and paused at the coffee maker to pour them each a cup. He added cream to hers, then sauntered over to the table. The deliberate way he placed his feet, the measured distance between steps, was a SEAL thing, perpetuated by their training. She would recognize him in a crowd of a thousand other men just by the way he walked.

He slid the cup in front of her. "Are you sure you want to drink coffee? Since you've been up with the baby all night, I can hold down the fort while you sleep."

"I may in a bit." She concentrated on the cup in front of her to keep from tearing up. "There's something I have to tell you. I couldn't while you were on your training rotation, but now you're home—"

Oliver frowned and placed a hand over the one she clenched on the kitchen table. "What is it?"

She studied his features...so strong, so masculine. She'd seen him smiling like a fool all the way through their wedding. Seen him grimace in release when they made love. Seen him luminous with pride and joy when he'd first set eyes on Lucia when he'd come home from a deployment. What would his expression reveal when she told him?

She swallowed. "Three weeks ago I found a lump in my breast and went to the doctor. I may have cancer."

# CHAPTER TWO

**W**HILE SELENA TOOK a shower, Oliver sat at the kitchen table. He stared rigidly at his clenched fists. He wanted to pound on something. Pound it until his fists were bloody. Anything to rid himself of the gut-wrenching fear. If he lost it, it would frighten Selena and wake the baby. He forced his fingers to relax and pressed his hands flat on the tabletop.

While he'd been having a blast practicing defensive driving skills, she'd learned she might have cancer. She'd had to deal with the aftermath of hearing those words *alone*.

Guilt crashed into him with the punch of a breaching ram. The black coffee in his stomach burned like battery acid. *Sweet Jesus.* Nausea rolled over him.

He couldn't catch his breath. He ran five miles a day. Hit the weight and exercise equipment three times a week. Did PT when he needed it and, in certain instances, just to pass the time. But sitting across the table from his wife and hearing those words had punched the air out of him. Though he'd held her, told her everything was going to be okay, he hadn't recovered. Not yet. He hadn't drawn a full breath—and probably wouldn't until the results from the needle biopsy were in—and only then if he knew for certain she didn't have cancer.

She couldn't have cancer. *Please, God, don't let Selena have cancer.*

He shot up from the table and strode down the hall to Lucia's bedroom. The combination of medication and exhaustion had finally overtaken the toddler, and she'd fallen asleep, her tiny limbs sprawled in boneless abandon, her hands curled into loose fists.

Even in sleep she was taking on the world. Which was when his daughter was most like him. When awake and well she was never still, never quiet. She hustled through her day like she wanted to discover and absorb everything she could in as little time as possible.

If Selena was sick, how would she be able to keep up with Lucia?

At the sound of the water being turned off, Oliver left Lucia's room and wandered into their bedroom. He hadn't done enough to comfort his wife, to bolster her courage. How could he accomplish it? What could he do to show his support?

Selena opened the bathroom door. Her dark hair was bound in a towel, her body wrapped in a long terrycloth robe. He had seen her that way—all bundled up in robe and turban after a shower—a million times, and never felt closed off from her. But something in her posture, her expression, warned him to keep his distance this time.

The first time they'd made love had been after a trip to the beach. She had just showered off the sand and salt, and had worn a similar robe, with a bright red towel wrapped turban-style around her hair. He had led her over to sit on the bed, loosened the heavy weight of her wet hair, and buried his fingers in it. He'd cradled her face in his hands and kissed her until she opened her lips to him, and then her body.

"What can I do, Selena?" he asked, his voice husky, echoing his emotions.

"Nothing." Her voice had an edge to it, then softened. "I'm tired. I've been up all night with Lucia. I just need to sleep."

"We both do." He kicked off his shoes and stripped off the brown T-shirt and cammies. In his boxer briefs he stretched out on the bed. When she climbed into bed, he'd hold her.

She went to the dresser, tossed the wet towel in the hamper next to it and reached for her brush. She brought it with her to the bed and, sitting on the edge, ran the bristles through her hair, her movements sluggish with exhaustion.

Her glorious mass of hair had a life of its own. Even wet, it lay in heavy waves down her back and across her shoulders. Would chemotherapy strip her luxuriant symbol of vitality away and kill it while it killed the cancer?

How would she deal with it? How would he?

A new wave of anxiety struck him. He needed to hold her. "Come to bed, Selena. Lucia will be back up before you have time to close your eyes."

She set aside the brush and lay upon the cover, but turned her back to him.

Fuck that. Never in their married life had there been any kind of emotional distance between them. Even when a bit of resentment lingered following an argument, they reached for each other. He wasn't letting this take hold. Not now. He looped an arm around her waist and tugged her back against him to spoon.

A tense silence stretched between them, until she guided his hand beneath her robe and held it cupped around her bare breast. Relief flooded him, and he drew his first full breath since she'd said the C word. Her skin was silky smooth, warm, inviting beneath his palm. She had beautiful breasts, full, round, more than his hand could hold, but not so much she looked out of proportion. Instead of sex, his thoughts turned to the way Selena had nestled Lucia against her and offered the baby her nipple for the first time. Selena's face had literally glowed with love and purpose while Lucia latched on and nursed.

Selena turned, her shoulder pushed against his chest and her tear-glazed eyes, bruised with pain, raised to his. "I'm scared, Oliver," she whispered.

Though her tone was soft, it might as well have been a shout. He could protect her from terrorists and other bad things in the world, but he couldn't do a damn thing to shield her from this. The raw emotion on her face, her tear-filled eyes, intensified his helplessness. He tried to swallow but his mouth was dry. "I am, too, *tesoro*." His fingers lingered around her breast in a soothing caress. "We need to stay calm until we know what we're dealing with. Then we'll decide on a plan. And if it is breast cancer…well, the docs cure it every day." *Didn't they?* "It's going to be okay."

It had to be.

He would not accept any other outcome.

SELENA WOKE WITH a start, her heart racing. What happened? Had she heard something? Had she forgotten something?

The house lay quiet around her. The bedside clock read 11:35, its ticking as loud as the rhythmic hammer of drumsticks beating time.

Fear surged over her, bringing with it the reason behind her roiling gut and panicky heartbeat. It was as if her survival mode was stuck in first gear, already at full throttle every time her eyes opened. She wanted to run, but where? Where could she go and not hear a constant replay of the words, "I think we need to do a biopsy."

Silence closed in around her, making her thoughts too strident to bear. She rolled off the bed and shuffled down the hall to Lucia's room. Her daughter's yellow comforter with purple butterflies was smoothed over the bed, and the stuffed lamb she slept with lay propped against the pillows. The clothes basket, usually filled with clean clothes waiting to be folded, sat empty.

Selena wandered on to the living room. The toys Lucia kept scattered around the room had been tossed into the wooden box behind the sofa, and the room was straightened.

She needed a cup of coffee and some aspirin to offset the hungover feeling from sleeping too long. The kitchen looked as clean as the other rooms, and even the few dirty dishes left in the sink earlier had been washed and left to dry in the drainer.

Though she should have been grateful Oliver had worked so hard to clean up the messes left behind by an active toddler, she wasn't. She had hours to fill and nothing to fill them with. Nothing to keep her mind off of the lump in her breast. She clenched her hand at her side to keep from touching the spot, now tender from being examined, stuck by a needle and probed by her own compulsive fingertips. Every time she touched it she prayed it would be gone. It had to be some awful mistake.

She set up the coffee pot and, finding a bottle of aspirin in the kitchen cabinet, took two. She sat down at the table and noticed the note propped against the small ceramic pot kept on the windowsill over the sink. They used it to store small odds and ends—paperclips, pencils, rubber bands, screws—anything which might be a choking hazard for a busy, curious, two-and-a-half-year-old girl.

Selena wandered over and retrieved the note. Oliver's square, masculine script said, *Don't cook. Lucia and I have gone out to get a late lunch. Be back in thirty minutes.* The time on the note was 11:15.

She'd spent fifteen minutes walking through the house and making coffee. She needed to get dressed. She would not allow herself to lie around in a depressed funk. She wouldn't allow Oliver to see her like this...or Lucia. She had to get on with the business of living.

Everyone died. What counted was was how you spent the time you had.

Oliver faced death every time he went into battle. He'd done it again and again every time he'd been downrange in the six years he'd been a SEAL. She could at least face this small lump in her breast with as much courage as he faced his duty.

She shoved her fingers though her tangled hair and squeezed her throbbing temples. Telling herself these things and living them were two different things.

But she *had* to do this. She had no other choice.

Bringing the cup of coffee to fortify her, Selena went into the bathroom. She grimaced at her reflection. Her hair was a wild snarl and her face puffy from sleep. She ran a cool basin of water and bathed her face, tamed her hair by pulling it back into a ponytail, brushed her teeth, and put on a light smattering of makeup.

By the time she heard a car pull up outside, she was dressed in white capris, a top with tiny flowers printed on it and slip-on tennis shoes. She met Oliver at the door with a smile and held it open for him.

Oliver brushed a kiss against her cheek as he shouldered past her with bags of Chinese food in both hands. "Lucia's right behind me. Her fever's down, the drops are working and I think the antibiotic has kicked in."

Lucia climbed the two steps up on the small porch by clinging to the railing. She greeted Selena with, "I want eggroll."

"I hope daddy got eggroll." Selena stepped out on the porch to help her up the last step into the house.

"Daddy got six eggrolls," Oliver said from the kitchen.

Lucia laughed. "You're funny Daddy."

Just hearing her speak in a sentence instead of the daddy-daddy-daddy mantra she'd done at the hospital was a relief.

By the time she had lifted Lucia onto her booster seat at the table, Oliver had placed an egg roll, fried rice and some sweet and sour chicken, chopped in small pieces, on a plastic plate. He set it in front of Lucia, and she dug in with her spoon.

"Are you feeling better?" he asked as they sat down at the table together.

"Yes. I got some sleep and I'm better."

She turned to brush a dark curl back behind Lucia's ear to keep her from getting food in it. "I noticed how you and daddy cleaned up the living room and your room. You both did a good job."

"Toys go in the box."

"Yes, you're right. When you're not playing with them, toys go in the box."

Lucia nodded adamantly. She gripped her egg roll in a tiny fist and gnawed on one end.

"I'm always surprised she likes cabbage," Oliver said.

"She'll actually eat anything you or I do. And I'm glad to see her appetite's back. She's been a little finicky the last few days. I should have realized something was brewing."

Oliver paused, his fork midway to his mouth. "Selena—you're already a super mom. To catch every nuance, you'd have to be psychic."

She nodded. Hearing him say it did help a little. Silence fell between them and she concentrated on her food.

"When will we know?" he asked.

"Tomorrow or the next day."

He nodded. "After we eat, let's go for a drive. We can stop somewhere for dinner."

"Okay." She understood his need for action. If you kept on the move, time passed more quickly. For the last two weeks, she'd been in a state of hyperactivity, rushing from one thing to the next.

She was relieved to have a task to complete. She packed a tote bag for Lucia, storing the medicine in a small cooling bag, then added extra clothes, wipes, drinks, snacks, and toys. Once they were in the car with Lucia secured in her car seat in the back, Oliver pointed the van north.

"Where are we going?" she asked.

"Laguna Beach. I thought we'd walk the beach. Maybe go to the museum if it's still open when we're through."

"We can eat at Las Brisas next door," she suggested. "We haven't been in a long time."

"Sounds good."

Silence lingered. Oliver rolled down the windows so the breeze blew through, bringing with it the rush of the wind and scent of the sea. Traffic was light, but the drive to Laguna would take anywhere between two and three hours, depending on the traffic. By midway Lucia grew restless, so Oliver pulled over at Oceanside and they all got out to stretch their legs.

The breeze off the water was chilly, so Selena bundled Lucia into the sweater and hat she'd packed earlier. They walked down the long stretch of concrete sidewalk, both of them holding Lucia by a hand while Oliver pushed the empty umbrella stroller.

They reached the pier, and Selena experienced a twinge while she strapped Lucia into the stroller. She was a petite child, in the bottom twenty-five percent for height and weight, understandable since neither of her parents were big people. But she had almost outgrown the small, portable stroller. Her baby had become a toddler overnight. Where had the time gone? She wanted to roll it all back and relive every moment with more clarity, more attention.

Her eyes blurred with tears, and she shoved her sunglasses on and turned to look out to sea so Oliver wouldn't know. Cirrus clouds shaped like ostrich feathers fluttered across a clear blue sky. The Pacific Ocean stretched to the horizon, its color darkened to ultramarine.

Her gaze settled on her husband while he pushed the stroller and pointed out things to Lucia. Though he only stood five foot eight, he was muscular and fit. Because of his broad shoulders and back, he always seemed taller, and bigger than his one hundred sixty-five pounds. His movements were relaxed, but every step he took radiated purpose and drive.

Should something happen to her, he'd grieve, but he'd move on. He'd formulate a plan to fulfill Lucia's needs and see it through.

He'd make sure their daughter was cared for and loved.

Just as she would have to, should anything happen to him.

But would he sacrifice his calling, his job, for Lucia? And who would he find to care for her while he was out of the country, as he often was?

Gulls screeched overhead and Lucia pointed upward as she followed their flight. As though sensing Selena's absence, Oliver stopped and looked over his shoulder, searching for her. She hurried to catch up.

"You, okay, *cara*?" he asked.

She nodded. "Yes. Just admiring the scenery."

Another couple, pushing a double stroller with twins strapped in it, strolled by and exchanged a smile and a nod with Selena.

She experienced another wave of anxiety. If she took chemo for a long time, she'd never be able to have another child. She'd be sterile.

She and Oliver planned to have another baby, had been semi-trying for the last six months, in between his training rotations. Their dreams of another child would end.

"Have you called your mom to talk about any of this?" Oliver asked.

"No, I didn't want to worry them until I knew something for certain. Maybe not even then."

"Your mom and sisters will be hurt if you don't tell them, Selena."

"Not yet, Oliver." Every time she said the C word it made it more real, more certain. If she told her family, they'd call her constantly. Their questions and good intentions would undermine what little control she had over her fear. She had to get a handle on everything before she spoke to them.

"You haven't told anyone?"

"I told you."

His dark eyes searched her face, then he slipped an arm around her and rested his lips against her forehead. She wrapped her arms around him and held on. Her anxiety eased.

"Go, Daddy." Lucia's voice, impatient and demanding, interrupted the moment. She rocked back and forth as though she could move the stroller with her will alone. Oliver grabbed the handles and pushed her along again while they continued up the pier.

# CHAPTER THREE

S ELENA'S FRENETIC UNLOADING of their laundry basket of beach paraphernalia convinced Oliver she was on the brink of implosion. One minute she threw herself into an activity, the next she dropped so deep into her thoughts he feared she'd never surface. How long had she been like this?

The thing was, he felt the same way…and he didn't like it one damn bit. He was used to action, but there wasn't a damn thing to do right now but wait. The waiting he did as a SEAL was long and boring, sometimes fraught with danger, but at least they saw an end to it. He couldn't see an end this time. There were too many unknowns. The tight band around his chest was suddenly unbearable.

There were only a few clusters of people on the beach, and the tide would be in soon. He decided to let Selena finish unloading and led Lucia by the hand to a tide pool tucked in an outcropping of rock at one end of the cove. The water was rising, and he was surprised when the toddler ignored the splash of the breakers and concentrated on settling her small feet on the slick rocks.

She squatted down eagerly when they arrived at the pool. Starfish and sea anemones of a variety of colors clung to the pitted surface, and small fish wove their way between them in the shallow water. A hermit crab scuttled between two submerged rocks and paused to feed on the brown algae coating the shallow pools.

"Peach," Lucia declared, squatting and pointing at a sea star.

Oliver shook his head. "It's a starfish, baby."

"Peach."

"Peach is a character in her current favorite cartoon," Selena explained from behind them.

"I'm relieved." He was also relieved she'd decided to join them. "I was trying to figure out how to set her straight."

"The story also has a shrimp in it. I fixed shrimp one night for supper and she cried for an hour. It took me half an hour to figure out what she was upset about. I explained that Jacque, the shrimp character, was not on her plate, and then she was fine."

Oliver chuckled.

They tiptoed around a mussel bed and spied a small octopus clinging to the rocks.

"Look at this little guy, Lucia. Isn't he something? He's an octopus." He spent several moments getting her to say the word and finally settled for ocpus. "Our girl is really smart," he said over his shoulder.

"Yes, she is."

After a few more minutes of exploration, he lifted Lucia on his shoulders and carried her back to the strip of beach where her toys waited. Lucia ran to her bulldozer and began making motor noises while she pushed sand around with the vehicle's toy scoop.

Selena said, "I can't make up my mind whether she's going to be a construction worker or an engineer." She sat on the blanket, stretched out her legs, and crossed her ankles.

"Let's hope an engineer." Oliver sat beside her. "She'll be doing something creative and earning good money."

Selena smiled. "You know you'd have just as much pride in her no matter what she does."

He would. His baby girl was his angel. "As long as she's happy. Speaking of happy, how are plans going for Brett and Tess's wedding?"

"Tess gets together with me and the other wives once every couple of weeks for dinner. We talk about the progress and brainstorm for places she can call to get things done. She's pretty much arranged most of the wedding, since Brett went wheels up right after he popped the question. We even went along while she shopped for her wedding gown. It's beautiful. She's beautiful."

"Not as beautiful as you, *cara mia*. I still remember how you looked on our wedding day." He caught the flash of doubt in her eyes. "I do. You had tiny pink roses in your bouquet and in your hair. And your dress had a rose pattern in the lace. I kept thinking you'd decide at the last minute you didn't want to take a chance on a guy who wasn't even out of college. Especially one who had plans to go into the Navy as soon as he graduated."

"I can't believe you remember the lace on my dress. We were so young and fearless back then." She smiled, and for once no melancholy lurked beneath her expression. "Do you think Brett will make it back in time?"

Oliver shrugged. "There's no guarantee. He had to fill out the paperwork to notify HQ and his commanding officer of his intent to marry. If he's not in the thick of things, he'll make it."

"I don't know what she'll do if he doesn't get back."

"They can always Skype the ceremony and have a private one once he's home."

Her eyes rounded in amazement. "Ohmygod! Skype the ceremony? Would it even be a legal marriage?"

"Well, not if he isn't here to sign the marriage license. I think in the state of California you both have to be present during the ceremony. But he'd be there to say his vows and the I do's, so she wouldn't have to cancel the whole thing.

"Oliver, you have no romance in your soul. Skype the ceremony!" She shot him an exasperated *men!* look.

He grinned at her. "We'll see how much romance I have once we get back home tonight."

Her eyes widened.

He covered her hand with his. "You have to live each moment as it comes, *cara*. You can't let this take you out of the fight."

Selena remained silent for a moment. "Is that how you think, feel, when you're—doing what you do?"

"Yeah. And I do whatever I have to so I can come home to you and Lucia."

Her fingers tightened around his. Her eyes glazed with tears.

"My job is my job, Selena and it's important. But you and Lucia are my world."

She looked out to sea. "Do you think it's any different for me?"

He frowned, his throat tight with emotion. "No. I know it's the same."

The continued to hold hands while their daughter played.

Meantime, the tide crept closer to the blanket and to Lucia's small section of beach.

Selena seemed calmer now. "Is Lucia hungry yet?" Oliver asked, loud enough for his daughter to hear.

"Yes!" She struggled to her feet, covered in sand with the bulldozer in hand.

Oliver grimaced. "We need a built-in shower for the van. I picked the only beach in Laguna without a bathroom."

"No worries. I brought fresh clothing. We never leave home without at least three outfits."

Selena did so many things he'd never noticed. He needed to start paying attention in case he had to help out later.

THEY ATE AT Las Brisas as she'd suggested. The popular restaurant was crowded and noisy and made up for the quiet at their table. They shared a bit of the food from both their plates with Lucia, and she surprised them both by eating guacamole.

On the way home Lucia valiantly fought sleep as she watched a cartoon on the iPad Selena kept in her bag. As her eyes closed, it slid from her grasp to balance precariously on her lap. Selena caught it before it could hit the floor and unplugged the earphones.

Oliver's words earlier at the beach replayed in her mind. He was right, she owed it to him, and to Lucia, to embrace her life the best she could. She was alive right now. Not dying. She tilted her head back and watched the light fade from the horizon and turn to a velvety purple. She had to find her way around the fear and move on.

When Oliver pulled into their driveway and parked, he said, "I'll get Lucia if you can get the bag with her medicine. I'll unload the other stuff in the morning."

"Okay." Selena got out and opened the side door to get the tote bag she'd stored behind the seat, then stepped back so Oliver could get Lucia. She lay limp against Oliver's shoulder, deeply asleep. Selena eased the van door closed and hurried to open the front door, then lock it behind them. She followed Oliver down the hall to Lucia's room and folded down the comforter and sheet so he could slide her into bed.

Selena eased Lucia's sneakers off, then her socks, and brushed the sand from her feet before tucking them beneath the sheet. A bath and clean sheets would be the first order of business in the morning.

Oliver drew the sheet and comforter up over the sleeping toddler and leaned down to brush his lips against her cheek.

He straightened and breathed against Selena's ear, "I'm going to take a shower. Want to join me?"

She turned to look up at him, and he kissed her. Warm and soft, his lips moved against hers, tempting her to lean into him and increase the pressure.

He was her light, her world, just as he said she and Lucia were his. She needed to be close to him. He made her feel stronger.

She ran her hands up under his T-shirt and caressed the flat planes of his shoulder blades as she nestled in close and felt the immediate response of his body to hers. Would he still react the same way if they took her breast?

Desperation took hold and she tugged her hands free of his shirt, encircled his neck with her arms. She needed to forget everything but them for a little while. She broke the kiss. "How about that shower?"

Oliver took her hand and pulled her toward their bedroom.

As THE ONLY child of an Irish American father with Native American roots and an Italian mother, Oliver had believed he knew all about love until he met Selena. She had been shy at first, but seductive at the same time. He'd wondered about those mixed signals until he figured out she was as inexperienced as he was about real passion, and neither of them had any idea how to handle the fact that they couldn't keep their hands off of each other. All they had to do was be in the same room for it to combust. It had taken them by storm, and they married before either of them graduated.

She loved with the hot, passionate nature of her Mediterranean heritage. In the shower, the brush of her soapy hand along his rib cage, the sweet scrape of her teeth against his shoulder, made every nerve sing. His cock hardened, and when her hand encircled it, running up and down its length, he thought he might explode.

"My turn, *cara mia.*"

He turned so the shower spray would stream over his shoulder and down between them. He filled his hand with body wash and guided her to turn so she could lean back against him. He soaped her throat, her shoulders, careful not to put any pressure on her breasts. He wanted to give her pleasure, but to feel the lump himself would destroy him. Instead he cupped the underside of both and kneaded them, then toyed with her nipples.

Her bottom moved back against him, his erection sliding between the cheeks of her ass while her hands gripped the outside of his thighs. Looking down on her soapy, water-slick breasts, Oliver had to count backwards from twenty-five to keep from going off right then.

When he was certain of his control, he pumped more bath wash into his hand and continued down the slope of her ribs to her belly. He nipped the smooth skin of her shoulder and tasted the water and the lingering essence of the soap as he caressed her upper thighs, then moved inward till his fingers found the moist heat between her legs.

Selena braced a foot on the edge of the tub, giving him complete access as she moved beneath his touch. Her throaty groan echoed against tile and tub while he caressed the tiny, sensitive nub of flesh at the top of her nether lips, then slid a finger into her. Her channel felt hot, and the ripple of her body drew it in further.

It was his groan that bounced around the shower then. He needed to be inside her. Resting a hand against her belly he dragged her back beneath the spray and let the water run down their bodies and rinse the soap away.

He stepped out of the shower and, grabbing a towel, offered her a hand. He looped the towel around her hips and, walking backward, guided her toward the bed.

"We've left the water on," she said, her voice breathy and soft.

"I'll get it later."

"We're still wet."

"So?"

They fell upon the bed together, and, for the first time since he'd arrived home, Selena laughed. The sound, throaty and hoarse, was the biggest seduction of all. He loved her laugh. He kissed her and she hooked a leg over his hip, urging him on. He rolled between her thighs and gave them both what they wanted. The sweet, moist heat of her welcomed him, and he stilled, savoring the sensation as their bodies meshed. "I love you, Selena."

"Per l'eternità?" For all time?

"Per l'eternità," he agreed.

"Then I am whole."

Forever. He moved, filling her, then drawing almost free, and her hands gripped his hips. Her body tensed and pulsed, bearing down on him, then opening for his next thrust. This erotic dance they had performed for eight years together had never seemed more intense, more passionate. Her hand slid between them to cup his balls, and her thumb rested at the base of his erection, putting more upward pressure on his thrusts, giving them both more pleasure.

She murmured his name, her voice breaking with emotion. Her hips rolled and she contracted around him as she found what she sought, so he buried himself in her and welcomed his own release.

Though he'd never before been emotional during sex, tears clouded his vision now, and he turned his face into the strands of wet hair curling across her pillow. *Per l'eternità.*

# CHAPTER FOUR

S ELENA KEPT A tight grip on her purse strap. She rarely carried
more than a small clutch, but today needed something more
substantial to cling to. She scanned the waiting room one more
time, for lack of anything else to do, but the landscape hadn't
changed in the past five minutes. Women sat around the room in
various postures and stages of pregnancy, along with women like
her waiting to see the doctor for other reasons.

Like all doctors' waiting rooms, the patients spoke in subdued
tones, but there were laughter and smiles as well. *How far along are
you? Don't you just hate it when your feet swell?* All the discomfort and joy
of pregnancy was bounced back and forth, though the women were
often strangers. A young woman sat two seats down from them, her
baby, tiny, carefully swaddled in a carrier/car seat. She was probably
there for her two-week checkup.

Oliver sat beside her and, though he held a *National Geographic*,
and his eyes rested on a page, but he hadn't turned it. In fact, if his
eyes had not been open, she'd have sworn he was taking one of his
power naps. Men were always uncomfortable in a gynecologist's
office, but was he experiencing the same heart-sickening fear and
pain she was?

An older woman, maybe in her early fifties, entered the office,
checked in at the window and sat down near the door. A brightly
colored scarf, pulled tight around her head, followed the round
curve of her skull and ended in a long tail down her back.

Selena fought the urge to brush back a long strand of her thick,
dark hair for fear the woman would notice.

Would she lose her hair, too? Of course she would.

Her heart raced, harsh and sickening. Nausea surged up to coat her mouth with saliva. Sweat pooled beneath her arms and between her breasts.

A nurse came to the door leading back into the examining rooms and Selena's head jerked up along with everyone else's. The nurse's eyes came to rest on her, "Selena."

Oliver reached for her arm. Her legs shook as she stood.

"Doctor Sanderlin will see you in her office now." The nurse led the way past a number of examination rooms and turned two corners before they arrived at a door. The black plate fastened to it at eye level read Captain Alicia Sanderlin M.D. ObGyn. After a brief tap the nurse opened the door and motioned them in. "Please have a seat, Dr. Sanderlin will be with you in a moment."

A large cherry wood desk and desk chair dominated the room, its surface cluttered with paperwork. A bud vase with three pink roses, some baby's-breath, and greenery sat on one corner. Behind it a bookcase stretched, filled with medical texts and decorative knickknacks. Three well-stuffed armchairs upholstered in a rich burgundy fabric sat in front of the desk in a curve. Striped drapes matched their color and the gray carpet.

They'd barely sat down when Dr. Sanderlin rushed in. Oliver stood politely while Selena shoved to her feet.

"I'm sorry you had to wait, Ensign Shaker, Selena." She paused to shake Oliver's hand, then retrieved a file from her desk, and, instead of sitting behind it, she repositioned the third chair so she could face them both.

Her gaze moved from Oliver to Selena and stayed there. The woman had been her ObGyn since they'd moved to San Diego, and Selena trusted her to be both caring and a straight shooter. But God, she wanted to be anywhere else but sitting in front of her in this chair now.

"I have some good news and some not so good news," she said, her pale green eyes steady. "Mixed in with all the other tests we ran last week, we did a pregnancy test, and it came back positive."

Selena caught her breath and her hand instinctively curved around her lower abdomen. Oh, God, what would this mean if she was sick? "I'm a little late, but I thought it was probably because of…of…everything else."

"Well, from your HCG levels, I'd say you're between six and seven weeks pregnant. Before you leave today we'll do a preliminary exam and try and pin it down."

Selena reached out to Oliver, and he took her hand and squeezed it, but his open joy when he'd gotten the news about Lucia was absent, as it was for her. The worry overshadowed everything else. How were they supposed to feel about this?

Dr. Sanderlin drew a deep breath. "Now for the not so good news." She opened the file. "The surgical oncologist we referred you to submitted this pathology report to me. I want to go over everything with you both in depth."

Selena nodded, unable to speak.

"The tissue sample did show a malignancy."

Oliver's fingers squeezed hers almost to the point of pain, then eased off.

Selena curled the fingers of her other hand against her throat as bile rose again.

"From the position of the tumor, we believe it is Ductal Carcinoma. An HER2 test was done. This test detects the proteins in the cancer cells which tell the cells to grow and divide. It came back negative, which is a very good thing. We also tested the tissue to see if it was hormone-receptor negative or positive. It is positive for hormone receptors."

Dr. Sanderlin slid closer to the edge of her seat. "With this type of cancer, the tumor feeds off the estrogen in your system. But, based on the numerous ultrasound images we did, it's fairly small, so we'll be able to tell if it's spread beyond the boundaries of the initial tumor when it's surgically removed and a dissection of your lymph nodes is performed. You'll return to the surgical oncologist for the removal. I've already talked to him and set up an appointment for you. As soon as you meet with him, they'll schedule your surgery."

Selena's face felt numb. "Won't the anesthesia harm the baby?"

"I'll be working closely with Dr. Brooks, Selena, so you and the baby will get the best care." Dr. Sanderlin turned to lay the file on her desk. "The first step in finding out how we need to treat this malignancy is to remove it and see how far it's spread. We don't want to wait to remove the tumor and any affected tissue."

Oliver's expression was wooden with control. The only thing that moved was his throat as he swallowed.

"Once we get the results from your surgery, I'll refer you to a medical oncologist. Dr. Dixon has a wonderful reputation and is a very caring doctor. I think you'll like him.

"Though pregnancy makes it more difficult to treat cancer," the doctor continued, "we can treat it. But we won't be able to start you on hormone therapy or radiation until the baby is born. And we can't start chemotherapy until you're at least four months along. We can't treat your cancer as aggressively as we would if you weren't pregnant, but we can fight it and keep it in check until the birth, and then get more aggressive afterward if we need to."

Her throat ached from the effort not to cry. "What about the chemotherapy?"

"Dr. Dixon will go over the protocols with you, but there are drugs we can use which won't impact the baby. He'll give you medications to control your pain and nausea, but your body will be going through a lot."

"And if she weren't pregnant?" Oliver spoke for the first time.

Selena jerked around to look at him while her heart sank. He couldn't be serious.

"If she weren't pregnant, you could attack this thing full-on, right? Wipe it out." There was an edge to Oliver's voice she had never heard before, a blend of rage and pain that gripped her by the throat and brought tears to her eyes.

Dr. Sanderlin paused a moment to study him. "In years past, termination of the pregnancy was suggested as part of the protocol for treatment. But we no longer encourage that first thing. I recommend you wait for the results of Selena's surgery and make a decision then. There will still be time if that's the course the two of you settle on." There was no judgment in her tone, only compassion. "Breast cancer is survivable, Ensign Shaker. Selena will have three doctors in her corner, making sure she gets everything she needs to overcome this."

Dr. Sanderlin stood. "I'm going to take Selena down the hall and do a brief exam. You can stay here while we accomplish that, and I'll send her back here when we're done."

As soon as the door closed behind the two women, Oliver leaned forward in his chair, dropped his face onto his hands, closed his eyes, and took deep, gulping gasps of air to keep from vomiting. He finally succeeded in quelling the nausea somewhat.

Dear God, she had cancer. Selena had cancer. He had prayed, hoped it wasn't cancer. He'd prayed for anything but that. And gotten a pregnancy in return.

He paced the office, feeling caged, smothered by his rampaging fears and the rage accompanying them.

Had the changes in her hormones triggered the cancer? Would the baby they'd been trying to conceive kill her? And how would he live with that?

His military training said if something was a threat to life, you took it out. End of discussion.

But the baby would delay her treatment, curtail it. He knew Selena would never agree to ending the pregnancy. He'd seen her reaction. That fierce, protective, instinctive response the news had sparked.

How could he fight her maternal instinct? How could he fight his own conscience long enough to argue for termination?

But if it came down to a choice between her or the baby, Selena had to take priority. She had to agree with that. She was everything—to him, to Lucia.

An exam supposed to take a few minutes stretched on to half an hour. Worry set in and Oliver breathed a sigh and rose when Dr. Sanderlin came into the office.

"I thought I'd take a moment to give you an update, Ensign Shaker. May I call you Oliver?"

"Yes, ma'am."

"Have a seat," she pointed at the chair he'd just vacated.

She settled into the chair closest to him. "From the physical exam and the information Selena shared with me, we've determined she's seven weeks pregnant. She's understandably excited and frightened at the same time."

"Could the pregnancy have triggered the cancer?" he asked.

"I don't believe so. From the size and position of the tumor, I'd say it already had a start before she became pregnant."

"She does self-exams every month."

"And that probably helped her detect the tumor before it spread any further but a woman can have a malignancy before it's ever detected, even with a mammogram. When Selena has her surgery, we'll know more about whether it has spread to the lymph nodes. Please try to stay calm, for your benefit as well as hers. Once the tumor has been removed, we'll know where we need to go from there."

He nodded. Her calm settled his roiling gut, but not the fear. He had to get a grip on that himself. "Thanks, Doc."

"Her appointment is on Friday for a preop workup and more tests. We're not dragging our feet on this, Oliver.

He nodded, unable to speak around the knot in his throat.

"I'll be talking to you soon," she said as she stood.

"Okay."

They had never had a quiet marriage. Whether they were making love, fighting, even cooking together, they made plenty of noise. But for the last three days silence had been their language.

And now in the car it resonated between them as loud as a scream.

It took twenty-five minutes to reach home, every second taut with unspoken recriminations. It was almost a relief when she finally asked, "Did you mean it?"

He didn't need her to clarify what she was asking about. "Yeah. I meant it. If it comes down to a choice, I choose you, Selena."

"They're going to take the cancer out and that will be the end of it."

God, he hoped so, prayed it would be so.

"We made this baby just like we did Lucia. It was made with love, Oliver."

He gritted his teeth against a flood of painful emotions. He could turn the tables on her and lay on some guilt, but he wasn't there yet. He'd save that for when it counted. "You said you'd wait and see what they discover during surgery. If it's aggressive, *cara*—" he couldn't say the words.

"This is my body, Oliver. I don't say anything to you when you put yours at risk every time you deploy."

"This is different, Selena."

"No it's not. You put yourself in harm's way to protect those who can't protect themselves. Where is the difference?"

The difference was she was the one who was in danger now. It was only supposed to be him. "I'm a trained soldier. I do everything I can to make sure I come home to you, Selena."

"But there's never any guarantee. I've watched you go to war twice, waited for you to return. I knew there'd be a chance I'd lose you each time. Even when you go somewhere to train, with all the dangerous stuff you do, I know there's always a possibility you could be injured or killed in an accident. That's my reality." She laid her hand on his thigh and his muscles tightened. "This is our family, Oliver. I need you to be as supportive of me as I am of you."

He'd never heard her talk like this before. And whatever he'd planned to say couldn't stand up to everything she'd just dumped on him. So he said nothing at all.

# CHAPTER FIVE

S ELENA PICKED UP the loan application she'd been assessing and scanned the applicant information again. With every word her stomach pitched a little further off-kilter. She dropped the paper and closed her eyes, willing the morning sickness, which had finally kicked in today, to ease.

Two seconds later she lost the battle and darted down the hall to the ladies' room. She'd barely made it into one of the stalls when she lost the breakfast of yogurt and granola she'd eaten an hour before. For ten minutes she heaved until she thought her lungs might come up and her stomach muscles ached. Despite the ick factor, though the floor looked clean, she sat on the tile for another five minutes and simply breathed in and out, resting against the stall door.

She was having a baby. Somehow morning sickness made it more real than even the positive pregnancy test and hearing the doctor say it.

A pair of low-heeled black pumps appeared at one side of the stall. "I've made you a cup of hot tea and scared up some soda crackers." It was Sheila Masters, the secretary she shared with two other loan officers at the bank.

"You are an angel, Sheila. Thank you."

"Do you need me to call someone to pick you up?"

"No. Going home won't help. This isn't a virus."

Sheila remained silent for a moment. "Does it mean what I think it means?"

She hadn't told her family. Or even her closest friends. She was allowing this cancer thing to drain every bit of joy from her life. Was she keeping the baby a secret because of the door Oliver had opened…even though she'd insisted it remain closed? She cupped her hand around her lower abdomen. *Hell, no!*

"Yes, I'm having a baby." The strong sound of her own voice helped her feel more positive, more certain. *The baby Oliver and I wanted.*

"Congratulations!"

"Thank you. I haven't told Mr. Watts yet, so I'd appreciate it if you'd keep it quiet until I have a chance to speak with him today."

"As the English say, mum's the word."

She smiled at the joke. "Thanks."

She'd have to tell her boss everything and let him know she'd also be out several weeks after the surgery. Would they hold her job for her if she had to be out for an extended time? Without her salary, their financial situation would take a big hit. How would they make it?

She realized she was falling back into the pit of worry again and shoved it away. They'd figure it out some way.

She staggered to her feet and leaned against the stall door for a moment, till she was certain her stomach had settled. A cup of tea did sound good. She entered her office to find it sitting in the center of her blotter with the crackers. Once again she breathed a relieved sigh and mentally thanked Sheila for being female and understanding.

She returned to processing the loan application, then called her boss's extension to ask for a few minutes of his time.

Because of her pregnancy, more blood tests and several more ultrasounds had been done of her breasts and armpits. With every test she became more certain the outcome of the surgery might not be what they'd hoped.

She kept her thoughts and feelings to herself, for fear of upsetting Oliver even more. This was up to her to deal with. It was her body. Her life. As much as she loved him, he lived on the periphery of her and Lucia's lives much of the time. He seemed content with the arrangement. He loved them, she was certain of that. But, like most men, he identified so completely with what he did, he was a Special Forces operator first and a husband and father second.

She'd accepted the reality long ago.

But things were different now. She didn't have time to pander to his ego.

Her surgery was scheduled for next Friday. Two weeks from her first visit to the ObGyn. The baby would be nine weeks along and would be about the size of a grape. She was going to count her own progress through the weeks of her pregnancy. She was going to concentrate on having a healthy baby and doing whatever she had to do to stay alive.

Clinging to her resolve, she went down the hall to speak to her boss.

THE DESERT SUN beat against the back of Oliver's neck, despite his Boonie hat. He should have tied a bandana around his neck before he'd taken the controls. Why the fuck was it so much hotter out here? It was the same state, the same sun.

Intellectually he knew all the reasons, but this one small irritation fed the black mood which had festered ever since he and Selena had left the doctor's office. He was angry because it was easier to feel rage than to acknowledge the fear. Rage at God for letting this happen, rage at Selena for being sick, for choosing a fetus over their family, rage at himself for not being home enough, not spending enough time with her, not doing all the things a husband should do.

Coming out to Camp Billy Machen for this updated training was a blessing. He was no good to Selena in his current frame of mind, and when he'd told her he needed to go, she seemed relieved. Or was it because she was resolved his job should come first even now? God, he didn't know how to feel anymore.

Oliver gripped the black control box to the drone like he'd just been thrown a lifeline. It gave him an excuse to concentrate on something else. The electronic screen flashed as he moved the toggle, directing the surveillance drone to fly at a specific speed and altitude.

It was like flying a souped-up model airplane using a flight simulator. The engine was designed to be quieter, and the powerful camera attached to its small fuselage homed in on objects, mapped their location, and could use infrared technology to detect heat signatures. It also sent recorded images to the computer Hawk had balanced on the hood of their Humvee. The drone was an expensive device designed to surveil the enemy and save lives.

Six of his teammates, three two-man teams in Desert Patrol Vehicles, DPVs, were out there waiting to be located Though the DPVs were no longer used as much as they had been during Desert Storm, they still came in handy for training and at times were fun to drive over the rough terrain.

The only down side was they had no air conditioning, and after four hours out in the sun, the guys would be eager to return to base and get out of the heat. But they had to be detected before they could do so. Oliver switched the camera to infrared, swooped the drone down to two hundred feet, and skimmed across the area.

The topographic landscape flying past the drone's lens looked similar to what they'd experienced in Afghanistan and Iraq. For a moment he flashed back to the dry, sandy heat. The smell of the place would be forever locked in his memory. It reeked of poverty, suffering, death and war.

He designed his flight path to cover the grid he'd been assigned. Two red heat signatures, moving west, popped up on the screen and he swooped overhead and took a picture of the armored dune buggy decked out with a gun mount on the reinforced framework. Hawk, his team leader, leaned his six foot four frame back against the front quarter panel of their Humvee and watched the screen from over Oliver's shoulder. Hawk radioed the two men detected in the vehicle that they'd been spotted and to return to base.

Two more DPVs to go and they'd get out of the heat for a while. Three minutes later the drone caught up to the next vehicle moving south and tagged them with a picture. Five long minutes followed until he discovered the next two men, who were parked and working on one of the wheels on their vehicle. Oliver switched off the infrared to identify them.

"Bowie and Doc are having a mechanical issue," he said as he took the picture.

Hawk nodded. "We'll swing by their location on our way back to base and see if we can assist or give them a ride."

"I have their location saved so we can track them with GPS."

"Sounds like a plan."

Oliver pushed the drone to a higher altitude and directed it back to them. He circled to get the lay of the land, and finding a bare strip where traffic from Humvees, trucks, DPVs and the occasional motorcycle had cleared a path, and lined up for a landing. The drone swooped down and he slowed its speed. The wheels extended and the machine settled on the hard-packed, bumpy sand twenty feet or so from their ride.

"Have you thought about taking flying lessons, Greenback?" Hawk asked as they loaded the drone into the back of the vehicle. "Looks like you've already got the landing part down."

"Private lessons are too expensive, but if you can sweet-talk command into paying, I'm definitely up for it."

"I'll see what I can do."

He felt a brief moment of excitement before reality hit. He couldn't volunteer for extra duty or training while Selena was sick. What was he thinking? This goddamn waiting was holding their lives up. He needed to tell Hawk what was going on, but, Jesus, his team leader's mother had died of breast cancer while he was down range. It was hard as hell to bring it up.

He needed to come up with something else to talk about until he figured out what he wanted to say to Hawk.

"Will Brett make it back for the wedding?" he asked.

Hawk frowned. "You've asked the six-million-dollar question. I hope so. Tess is going to be one very disappointed bride if he doesn't."

"Maybe she can cancel at the last minute and have it on the beach or in someone's back yard when he makes it."

"There are a hundred and fifty guests coming. A quarter of them military."

Or maybe not. "I told Selena they could Skype the ceremony, and then have another when Brett hits CONUS."

Hawk glanced in his direction. "If it comes down to the wire, it wouldn't be a bad idea as last-minute saves go. I'll put it out there."

"It was insane to attempt a big, fancy wedding. If Selena and I hadn't already done the deed before I went into the teams, we'd have eloped or had a simple ceremony with our closest friends, like you and Zoe."

"In our case it was good and bad at the same time, Greenback. Good we got hitched, but somewhere down the road, Zoe may regret not having the big show. But there are worse things. I missed her whole pregnancy."

"At least you were there for the birth. I missed it all." He couldn't avoid this pregnancy or Selena's illness. What would he have done if he were out of the states when she'd gotten ill? His breathing hitched.

His own struggles brought Derrick Armstrong to mind. "Any news about Strong Man?"

Hawk remained silent for a moment. "He took a plea. Four years' prison in a military facility and a dishonorable discharge. He avoided facing us, but it also saved the team some unwanted publicity in the SEAL community and the public."

Silence stretched for several beats.

"It was a waste," Oliver mussed.

"Yeah."

"Why would he try and kill his best friend?"

"It had to be him. Doc and Bowie were together during the op. Flash was on the roof across the street. We all saw him exit the structure after the explosion, and besides, he was busy taking out insurgents up there. The others saw the muzzle flashes and the guys above them going down."

"Who did Doc see going back in besides you?"

"Maybe Derrick had a change of heart. But I don't know how he got back out before the place blew. And I sure as shit didn't see him inside."

That last mission with Brett had changed the whole makeup of the team. They'd lost Brett and Flash, first to other challenges, then to other teams, and Derrick Armstrong to prison. What had happened would remain a mystery until Brett remembered what happened or Derrick decided to man up and come clean.

Five minutes later they pulled up beside Bowie and Doc. "We've broken an axel." Bowe announced. "I've called in our coordinates and requested a tow."

Hawk got out of the Humvee. "If the motor pool has the coordinates, they can come out and get the buggy. You can ride in with us."

"Roger that!" Doc's redhead complexion was flushed from the heat and sun, and his freckles looked darker in the strong light. He jogged around the car to get in on the other side.

"Guess he's ready to go back to base," Bowie said, his dark eyebrows quirked. He jerked the door open and climbed in.

Teammates and friends since BUD/S, the two guys could read each other's body language in the dark and instinctively knew what the other was thinking. Oliver had seen the communication between them at work. Oliver wondered why he hadn't bonded with one of the other guys like that.

Maybe because most of them had been single and he was married. After BUD/S, there'd always been beer runs and parties the single guys had organized in between trainings, but he'd gone home to Selena. He'd been a married man of three years before taking on the teams.

He sure as shit could use a friend to confide in right now. His gaze swung to Hawk. He'd been through the breast cancer thing with his mother. He'd understand his need to be with Selena as much as possible.

Hawk's wife Zoe had scars from a hit and run accident and had physical issues from it. He didn't seem to give a damn about her limp or her scars. He was crazy about her. Every guy in the team knew it.

Hawk would identify with what he was going through. He had to tell him, and he was going to need some time off for Selena's surgery and other treatments. Fill out the paperwork.

Anxiety shot heat into his face, nullifying the cold air blowing out of the vents. And his breathing quickened.

Hawk pulled away from the DPV and drove east.

"Stop looking at your cell phone," Bowie said in tune to the click of their seat belts. "You're acting like a girl."

"Shut the fuck up." Oliver caught Doc's movement from the corner of his eye as he flipped a half-hearted backhanded punch to Bowie's solar plexus and Bowie umphed in pain. "You're just pissed because you're between girls right now."

The car seemed to close in around Oliver, growing smaller and smaller, the seat belt too tight over his chest. He tugged at it to relieve the pressure.

"Dude, I'm always between girls." Oliver knew he was smiling from the tone of his voice. "Remember those twins? And they were identical in every way."

As the sound of his own breathing got harsher, his heartbeat louder, pumping through his ears, Bowie and Doc's voices grew muffled.

"Yeah, I remember them. How could I forget? You've been rehashing the details for the past year. Makes me think you're spoiled to multiples and can't man up to a single woman anymore."

The sweat coating Oliver's skin turned to ice water and nausea rolled over him.

"Doc you're not getting the whole picture man. We're talking hands, mouths, tits—"

"Stop!" The word exploded from Oliver. Hawk slammed on the brakes.

The seat belt locked and jerked Oliver back before he hit the dash. He slammed open the door, and the inferno of heat outside rushed in with the dust stirred by their tires. He fought free of the seat belt, rolled out of the car, and barely caught himself before doing a face-plant in the dirt.

He choked on the dust, and his attempts to draw breath turned to hacking coughs interspersed with sobs while tears streamed down his face, as much from his efforts to breathe as from emotion.

"Where's the med kit, Hawk?" Doc's voice came from within the vehicle as the other doors flew open.

"In back with the drone."

Hawk and Bowie grabbed him under each arm and dragged him free of the dust cloud and into the meager shade of a Joshua tree.

Doc squatted in front of him and took his pulse. While he coughed up the grit he'd breathed and swallowed, Oliver focused on his broad Irish face. It took some time to beat back the emotion still clawing at his chest, keeping his breathing tight. He rubbed his shirtsleeve over his eyes and face to wipe away his tears. They'd think it was from the dust, wouldn't they?

"Just take a few more deep breaths, Greenback. Are you having pressure in your chest? Any pain?"

*Any pain?* He dropped his head back and shook it. "I thought I was going to hurl. It must have been the heat." SEALs weren't supposed to have anxiety attacks. He was supposed to be in control. Keep his emotions in hand. He braced a forearm on his updrawn knee and rested his forehead upon it.

Doc rested a hand on his shoulder.

He'd just lied to a friend to protect his ego. He wasn't in control. He wasn't in control of anything. They were going to cut into his wife and take her breast. Maybe both of them. Time to man up. "It isn't the heat, guys." He blinked his eyes furiously when the tears threatened again. "Selena's pregnant and she's got breast cancer. They're going to do a mastectomy next week."

Doc's eyes widened with shock. Hawk and Bowie froze with the same motionlessness they used when terrorists tiptoed close to their location.

Hawk was the first to move, and dropped to one knee next to him. "What the fuck are you doing here? You should be with her."

"She's working, taking care of as much bank business as she can before she has the surgery. We have to stay busy and fill every moment...otherwise we'd both go crazy." He raked his fingers through his hair and squeezed his temples. "I have to get my head straight before I can be any use to her, Hawk. I haven't slept since I found out. I'm just so fucked up right now."

Hawk's face showed all the pain he was feeling. "I didn't get an opportunity to be there for Mom when she was going through this. She didn't tell me she was sick until it was too late. You have an opportunity to be Selena's wingman through all this, Greenback. You need to get your shit together and step up. I'm calling Zoe and Trish. They'll get the ball rolling on that end. She'll need backup while you're out here." Hawk jerked his cell phone out and ran his thumb over the face to open it.

"She hasn't even called her mom and sisters, Hawk. We won't know how bad it is until after the surgery." Oliver scrubbed his face with his hands. Hawk was right. He was making this all about his needs and ignoring hers. He'd been such a shit to her before leaving home for this training—angry, distant, and silent. Like he'd been for days. He was blaming her for being sick when there wasn't a damn thing she could do about it. He'd really fucked up.

"L.T., I'd like to be the one to talk to them."

Hawk handed him the phone.

SELENA DUMPED THE shopping bags and her purse next to the front door and turned to check on Lucia's progress up the front walk. The backpack her daughter wore was almost as big as she was, but she insisted on carrying it back and forth to daycare with her favorite toy for naptime. Thank goodness this last round of antibiotics seemed to have done the trick, and the troublesome ear infection was gone.

She was holding open the door for Lucia when Zoe Yazzie's car pulled into the drive. The doors opened and five women got out—Zoe, Hawk's wife, and her soon to be sister-in-law, Tess Kelly. Trish Marks, the unofficial leader of the wives' group and wife of Langley Marks, Hawk's XO. Marsha Jackson, Oliver's commanding officer's wife, and then Zoe's mom, Clara Weaver, brought up the rear.

She studied each of their expressions while they walked toward her. Had something happened to Oliver? Anxiety hit her like a thunderbolt and her heart rate shot up.

"Oliver called us," Zoe said, setting her fears to rest. "He and the guys will be out there a couple more days, and he thought a little backup for you might not be a bad idea. Just in case."

Selena heaved a sigh. Just what had he told them?

Zoe grasped Lucia's hand, "Hello, Miss Lucia. How was school today?" She walked with Lucia up the two steps and Selena stood back to let them in.

"Nap time sucks," Lucia declared, her words so clear all the women laughed.

"She learned the expression from one of the older children and loves saying it," Selena giggled.

Everyone filed in, but no one sat down. Marsha Jackson stepped forward. "Oliver called us all and told us everything. His exact words were, 'I've already been an asshole, and she's already pissed at me, so it won't matter if she gets mad at me for telling you.'" Marsha swallowed. "We're a family, Selena. We all want to stand with you through whatever comes. We're here to schedule help times for while you recover from surgery. You'll need it, and we want to do at least that much."

The tight ball of hurt and confusion left by Oliver's defection to Camp Billy Machen eased and, though Selena attempted to stem the tears, her eyes still filled. She brushed them aside and offered them all a smile. "I'm not mad at him for telling you. I've wanted to but—it was just too much."

"We understand," Trish said, hugging her.

"Come on into the kitchen and we'll have some iced tea and talk."

When they were settled at the kitchen table Selena looked at each expectant face, opened herself to experience their genuine, heartfelt desire to support her, and spilled it all. After they all cried a little, they got busy making a list of things she might need help with following surgery.

"I want Oliver to save as many of his emergency leave days as possible in case we need them."

"I'm retired and Russell is still working, so I'm available during the day," Clara said as she lifted Lucia up in her lap and handed her a slice of cheese and some crackers from the plate Selena had put out.

They wrote down their schedules, then worked out a rotation for each day.

"Oliver will be here at night as long as they don't have another training."

"He'll want to take off a few days to be with you, Selena," Zoe said.

Would he? After his first rush of support he'd been so distant. Especially since the doctor's appointment and everything she'd said in the car.

"I'm trying to stay positive. Excuse me for a second, please." She stood and went back to retrieve something from the bags she'd dropped by the door that she wanted to share.

She'd designed the baby announcements at work during her lunch break. She'd dropped them by a one-hour copy place on her way to get Lucia from daycare and picked them up on her way home. The women laughed when she saw the grape-shaped cartoon, and immediately set to helping her address the envelopes.

"Is the baby really the size of a grape?" Tess asked, holding up the announcement. Her auburn hair shone with copper highlights and, though she was the closest to her age, Selena felt centuries older.

"It will be by next week," Selena said. "It's about the size of a sesame seed right now."

Tess shook her head. "Amazing. If the baby's a girl you could name her Chablis," Tess said with a grin.

"Oh, my God, that sounds like a stripper," Trish said.

"Or Champagne…no, wait, it would be a stripper's name, too," Zoe chimed in.

"What about Barbera or Margaux? Those are wine terms, but don't sound so stripperesque," Tess suggested.

"Is stripperesque even a word?" Marsha asked as she sealed an envelope.

"And how do you even know Barbera and Margaux are wine terms?" Zoe demanded.

"California is wine country. I had to write a story about one of the vineyards."

"If we're going to name her after a wine, it will have to be an Italian wine," Selena said firmly, desperate to keep the laughter and the feeling of normalcy going.

"Chianti," Clara suggested. When they all looked at her, she shrugged. "It's the only Italian wine I know."

"Rosato, it's a rose-colored Italian wine. Her name could be Rosa," Tess suggested.

"Actually Rosa might work. My mother's name is Rosalie but my father often calls her Rosa."

"That's so sweet."

It was. Just the simple pastime of discussing baby names gave her something to hold onto and made her feel as though her life could go on despite the cancer.

She had to hold onto the life inside her. It was the most important positive thing in her life right now. If only she could get Oliver to see it for the blessing it was, instead of a stumbling block to survival which he believed it to be. Once they took the cancer out and she was well again, he'd see things differently.

# CHAPTER SIX

"**W**E HAD TO take a little more breast tissue than I had hoped, Selena." The surgical oncologist was tall and thin, with exaggerated features which seemed crammed into the center of his face. He projected confidence and a positive attitude.

But Oliver's heart sank. They had been talking lumpectomy, then a modified mastectomy, and now they were talking more. It had been thirty-six hours since the surgery and, aside from being in some moderate pain, Selena seemed to be soldiering up, but he'd seen how her fingers had traced over the area and been worried when he watched her face as she did it.

"I wanted to go back over some of the information I've shared with you before. We had to take the nipple, but we've left you plenty of skin to use for reconstruction later. The border of the tumor was wider than we had at first expected. The important thing is we were able to remove all the diseased tissue. And there was no muscular involvement."

Her features were pale, but she didn't seem surprised.

"We will have the pathology on the seven lymph nodes we removed by next week. I'll discuss follow-up treatment once we have pathology results, so I'll need to see you a week from today. The nurse will set up the appointment for you. I'll want to check the site and make sure it is healing as expected, and we'll also remove your temporary drains. The nurse will show you how to empty them in the meantime. You don't need to change the dressing. I'll do it during your appointment in a few days. Just keep the site dry, relax, and allow yourself to heal. If you see any unusual swelling, or have severe pain, don't hesitate to contact my office or come in to the ER."

Once the doctor left, Oliver sat on the edge of the bed and cradled her hand.

"Did you know it had spread more than they'd first thought?" he asked.

"I suspected it had. They did so many ultrasound images, especially in the area under my arm." Dark shadows were stamped beneath her eyes. With so many nurses and techs going in and out of the surgical rooms, sleep, when it came, was brief. "My breast is gone, Oliver."

"I know."

Her gaze held an uncertainty. "You've always loved my breasts."

"I've always loved the rest of you, too, *cara mia.*"

He knew he'd said the right thing when she leaned in to rest against him. Careful of the tubes, he slipped an arm around her and stroked her hair. "It's going to be okay." What else could he say?

THE PAIN WAS nothing compared to the hollow feeling she got every time she saw the spot where her breast had been. Even with the bandages pulled tight around her, she could see the concave shape of her loss.

She'd read somewhere the surgery severed the nerves so she would no longer experience sensation in that breast anymore. And what if the cancer spread to the other one? If only she could be numb all over right now.

She needed to be home and away from this place where they had disfigured her. She'd had no idea how she'd feel afterward. She'd been concentrating on just getting past the surgery. Nothing else. But now she felt so much pain and anger.

"What matters is, the cancer is gone, *carina,*" Oliver said, his voice soft.

But it might not be gone. She couldn't take radiation therapy to be certain. What more would they do?

Exhaustion rushed up to envelop her, and she settled against Oliver's shoulder and closed her eyes. He loved her. But men were usually squeamish about these things. Would his reaction be different because of his experiences?

And they still couldn't seem to talk about the baby. How long would their silence last?

BACKUP WAITED FOR them at home. Oliver hoped he'd done the right thing. Selena needed to know how much she was loved. And maybe it would make up for some of the shit they were both dealing with right now.

Because the medical staff couldn't use the typical diagnostic tests due to her pregnancy, they were still in the dark about the spread of the disease. No radioactive dye to check the lymph nodes. No radiation until she'd delivered the baby. No hormone therapy to starve the cancer and make sure it didn't come back. Pregnancy tied their hands in so many ways.

The hurt look so clear in Selena's eyes gripped him by the throat every time. A part of her was gone now, and she was grieving... he was, too. But she was alive. Which was all that mattered.

They reached home to find Hawk sitting on the small stoop.

"What's Hawk doing here, Oliver?" Her hand lingered against her blouse, covering the spot where her breast had been.

"I asked him to run an errand for me."

While Oliver went around to help her out, Hawk came over to greet them, but his gaze remained on Selena's face.

Though she was dressed as normal in jeans and a button-up blouse, she moved as though every step was over broken glass.

"Zoe said to call if you need anything at all. Goes for me, too."

She nodded and made an effort to smile. "Thank you, Hawk."

He nodded and turned to Oliver. "The package is inside, Greenback. I'm shoving off so you two can rest."

"Thanks, Hawk."

"What package, Oliver?"

"Just something I thought you might need." He helped her up the stoop.

"I remember how you did this when I came home from the hospital with Lucia," she said, her voice soft.

Her dark eyes, so expressive, lifted to his face.

He wasn't ready for this conversation. "In the teams we plan each step we take with care, but at the end of the day, when we've done all we can, all we think of is home. We've done all we can for the moment, and now it's time to think of home."

He opened the door and shoved it wide. Selena's mother rose from the couch. She appeared to be as nervous as Oliver felt. As she took a step toward the door, her features, so similar to Selena's, crumpled with emotion. When Selena walked toward her and buried her face against her mother's shoulder, Oliver knew he'd done the right thing. He closed the door to give them a few minutes while he went back out to retrieve Selena's small overnight bag.

He was finally starting to get it. As a SEAL he stood alone as a man, but together as a member of his team. And at home Selena did the same, but the other half of her team was usually gone, leaving her stranded. It was hard to reach out to family and friends who lived outside the life and explain the psychology. She carried just as much on her shoulders, and she was used to doing it alone. Then when it came time to ask for help, it made it harder for her to say the words or even admit she needed it. He'd need to be her backup and tell people what she couldn't say herself.

When he re-entered the house, Rosalie, Selena's mother, still held her, but they'd gravitated to the couch.

He dumped the overnight bag in the bedroom and went into the kitchen to fix them all something to drink. Though it was just past noon, he craved a beer, or something stronger, but chose a glass of iced tea instead.

He slid the glasses on coasters in front of them.

Selena's eyes, wet with tears, settled on him. "Thank you, Oliver."

HE SPENT THE day catching up on yard work and fixing a small leak in the storage building roof while Selena slept and was babied by her mother, which was exactly what she needed.

At five o'clock he picked Lucia up from daycare. She'd be excited to have Selena home, for, as much as she'd enjoyed having Daddy's undivided attention for an evening or two, she'd gotten teary at bedtime each night when Momma wasn't there. She'd never been separated from Selena for more than a few hours. He'd lain with her in her tiny twin bed until she finally fell asleep, and then lay awake in their bed, staring at the ceiling and alert for the phone in case the hospital called. It was easier to take power naps in the chair at the hospital than to sleep without Selena beside him.

"Mommy's home and she's excited to see you," he said as he helped Lucia get her backpack off and settled her in her booster seat in the back of the van.

"Mommy's home!" A smile lit her entire face. "I'm e-sighted too."

Oliver smiled at the mispronounced word but didn't correct her.

"Mommy has a sore spot on her chest right here." He pointed to his right pectoral muscle. "We have to be careful not to touch it until it's well."

Lucia's eyes widened. "I won't touch it," she said in a whisper.

"She's missed you very much."

"I missed Mommy, too."

He fastened the seat belt and gave her a kiss.

"Grandma Rose is at the house, too. She's come to visit us."

Lucia grinned. "Grandma Rose?"

"Yes, she came to see you and to help Mommy until she feels better."

"We Skype Grandma Rose."

What did it say when your three year old knew how to Skype? "Yes, I know you do. You'll see her in person as soon as we're home. What do you want to listen to on the radio?"

"*Twinkle, Twinkle.*"

Half wishing he hadn't asked, he put in the CD of nursery songs as soon as he was belted in and cranked the ignition.

He listened to Lucia sing along with the CD. She knew almost every word to the songs. Who cared if, during *Whole World In His Hands*, it was Ho Wood?

For the first time he allowed himself to wonder if the baby

Selena was carrying would be as smart. If it survived. If Selena could carry it to term. *If-if-if.* How was he supposed to feel? How could he promise to lay his life down to protect other people's children and not do the same for his own? But it wasn't his life hanging in the balance, it was his wife's. The guilt and pain of this struggle were constant.

He turned the thoughts off. He couldn't think about it. He had to concentrate on Selena. He was more worried about her emotional state right now. Those few moments of grief at the hospital would not be the last.

Though they'd traveled to New York several times since Lucia was born, and both their families had come to visit when they could, Grandma Rose was someone new in Lucia's world. She was both excited and a little shy for all of five minutes, then gave Rosalie enthusiastic hugs and kisses. She sat on the couch between Selena and her mother and jabbered away, filling them both in on everything she had done at daycare. Her vocabulary was growing through the lessons she was taught at daycare and through music. But her pronunciation was sometimes comical.

For the rest of the evening, Grandma Rose held center stage and did most of the cooking. At eight o'clock Selena ran out of steam and went to bed, and he got Lucia tucked in soon after.

It was as he was checking on Selena for the fourth time and easing the bedroom door shut, Rosalie caught him in a hug. "She's going to be okay. She's strong, and she has you in her corner."

"I know," he said trying to be positive, though the fear was still there.

"You don't have to entertain me if you want to go on to bed. I know you've been running between home and the hospital. I have my e-reader and the television. If Lucia wakes up, I'll take care of her."

He didn't want to go to bed, but he did want to lie beside his wife and just know she was there.

"Frank and I have had a long marriage. And it's because we've leaned on each other we've made it when other friends didn't. You and Selena have that kind of marriage."

"I haven't been home nearly enough."

"But when you are, you pour everything you have into it, Oliver. She knows you love her."

He nodded, though the guilt wouldn't go away. He knew the other married men experienced it too. More marriages ended than survived the teams. "I put fresh linens on the guest room bed and laid towels out for you. Help yourself to anything you need."

Rosalie patted his arm and murmured goodnight. She went back into the living room.

He slipped into the bedroom, took a quick shower, and eased in beside Selena.

Her eyes opened and she studied his face for a moment. "I'm very proud of what you do, Oliver. You have nothing to feel guilty about. I went into our marriage with my eyes wide open."

So she had heard what they'd said. "You didn't count on the teams."

"No, but it was something you needed to do and I understood. I still do."

Just as she needed to carry their baby. He flinched away from the thought. "You've read the code we follow."

"Yes."

"I take it very seriously, Selena."

"I know you do."

"I was thinking you need your own code."

She sifted her fingers through the curls on his forehead, and he sighed, and then lifted her palm to his lips. "Repeat after me. I will *never* give up."

She looked into his eyes for a long moment, and a lone tear streaked across her nose and onto the pillow. "I will *never* give up."

"If adversity knocks me down, I *will* pick myself up."

"If adversity knocks me down. I *will* pick myself up."

"I will use every ounce of my strength to fight."

Her voice cracked but she said the words. "I will use every ounce of my strength to fight."

"I will never stop fighting."

"I will never stop fighting."

He wiped her tears away with the sheet. "I love you. No matter what happens, I'll love you."

She nodded. He wanted to wrap her in his arms and cuddle her, but the tubes were there, and he was afraid he might accidentally hurt her. Instead he laced his fingers through hers and held tight.

# CHAPTER SEVEN

S ELENA STARED AT the huge clump of hair in the drain. There was more and more each day. So much she'd bought a screen for the tub so it wouldn't go down the drain and clog.

This latest loss looked like a small animal had drowned in the shower. She braced herself before turning to face the mirror over the sink. Her heart fell and tears glazed her eyes. She'd thought seeing the flat, nipple-less area where her breast had been removed would be the worst shock she'd sustain, but seeing her hair fall out had a suck factor all its own.

They had been so upbeat about her prognosis until the three lymph nodes had come back positive. Three lymph nodes had made the difference between chemo and no chemo.

And this latest suggestion by her medical oncologist had hit her hardest. He wanted her to have her ovaries removed once the baby was delivered.

She stared at her reflection. She didn't want Oliver to see her like this. Ragged. Unkempt. She stared at her reflection. Would she lose her eyebrows and lashes too? With her Italian features, she'd look like a modern day Mona Lisa. She tried an enigmatic smile. It ended up more a grimace.

She lowered the lid onto the toilet, sat down and gave free vent to the tears for the next five minutes. Only five minutes, because it was all the time she could spare to dwell on this loss. With difficulty, she dragged her composure back into place, mopped her face, and blew her nose. Rifling through a lavatory drawer, she found a pair of scissors, but just did a few halfhearted snips before putting them down. Why do a job when an expert was available?

She picked up her cell phone and dialed Trish and Langley's number.

Langley answered the phone with a brusque, "Hello."

"Langley, this is Selena."

"Hey, pretty lady. You okay?"

"Yes, I just called to ask a favor."

"Shoot."

She explained what she needed. "If I swing by, could you do it before I have to go to work?"

"Yeah, I can do it."

"I can be there in about twenty minutes."

"I'll be here."

She dressed, took her nausea medication, and applied a light makeup to cover the bruise-like shadows beneath her eyes, then wrapped a scarf around her head.

Langley opened the door to her and ushered her into the kitchen. "You lucked out, the clan just left for school with Trish."

"Oliver took Lucia to daycare for me."

Langley put a chair in the middle of the kitchen floor and whipped out a barber's cape from his kit, and then produced scissors, clippers, and a comb.

Suddenly shy, Selena studied his lantern-jawed, homely, handsome face. "It looks pretty bad."

"It'll be okay, honey," he said, his gaze steady.

Her throat tight, she sat in the chair and dropped her bag on the floor next to her. The vulnerability of having such a widely recognized cancer side-effect out where everyone could see was as painful as her aching joints. Everywhere she went people stared.

Langley unwrapped the scarf and laid it on the counter. He ran his fingers over the long strands still hanging in there at the back. Her hair was so thin on top she could see her scalp. She knew what his fingers came away with when he drew a deep breath. "I'll need to use scissors first, take some length off so the clippers won't pull."

Selena swallowed. "Okay."

He got out the scissors. With every fallen strand her head felt lighter, and she decided to equate each one with shedding yet another worry. She relaxed and gazed absently at the small ray of sunshine reflecting off the toaster. This was just one more thing she had to endure to stay well until the baby was born. At the flutter of the baby's kick, she rested a hand against the side of her distended abdomen, enjoying the moment of communion with her unborn child.

Langley turned on the clippers, and, starting at her hairline in front, then going from front to back in long, slow, smooth strips. The fuzz scattered across the barber's cape looked like black feathers. When he turned the clippers off, she twisted around to look up at him.

He cupped her naked head with his large hand, and his Adam's apple bobbed as he swallowed. "All done."

"Thank you, Langley."

"Welcome." He tugged the Velcro catch on the barber's cape free, shook it off, and turned away to fold it and stuff it in the case with the clippers.

"I can help you clean up."

"I got it covered. You better scoot or you'll be late."

"Does it—It looks better this way, doesn't it?"

Langley turned to face her. His smile looked natural and eased the tightness in her chest. "Prettiest G.I. haircut I've ever seen."

Selena smiled. But as soon as her fingers explored the area behind her ear, tears threatened. She dropped her hand, jerked her chin up, and squared her shoulders. "Bald is beautiful."

Langley laughed. "You've convinced me."

Selena shot him her best smile, scooped up her purse, and rose from the chair. "I owe you some double chocolate brownies." She gave him a quick hug.

"With nuts," he added, giving her a gentle squeeze in return.

"With nuts."

She murmured, "Bald is beautiful," all the way to work.

LANGLEY'S CALL WAS only a small surprise.

Oliver rubbed a hand over his jaw and jerked the wheel to

avoid a slow-moving delivery van as it turned in front of him. "How was she when she left?"

"She was holding it together. As she was leaving, she said 'bald is beautiful,' and nearly drove me to my knees."

"I understand." He did. With every new thing she had to face—the treatment, the nausea, sore joints, aches and pains—she just kept going. She clung to her job as a small spot of normalcy in her otherwise cancer-fighting-filled life. But how much longer would she be able to work?

"If you have any ideas how I can help her face this, let me know."

"Roger that. I'll give it some thought."

"Thanks, Lang."

"Whatever it takes, my friend. See you at the base."

"I'm on my way."

There were things about her treatment she wasn't sharing with him. He couldn't go to every doctor's appointment, though he'd made it to every chemo treatment thus far. The first had been terrifying. Though he'd tried to remain calm and reassuring, her anxiety about the baby had spread to him. Watching the fluid flow into her vein and wondering if she would have a reaction, or if it would send her into premature labor, had been the worst four hours of his life.

And now, even though Selena covered the evidence with scarves, he'd seen what was happening to her hair in the shower, on the bathroom floor, even in the clothesbasket. And there wasn't a damn thing anyone could do about it.

And the day after chemo, she was always knocked off her feet by nausea and exhaustion. And he was so fucking helpless to protect her from any of it.

He ran his hand over his own tight curls. He'd shave his hair off, too, but she loved running her fingers through it when they lay in bed and talked each night. What could he do to offer her support? He'd ask the other guys.

He turned the car toward Coronado. They would be transported to Miramar, where they were to fly out for a HALO jump, high altitude, low opening. When in CONUS (the Continental U.S.) they were required to do jumps to keep their skills razor sharp.

Doc and Bowie looked up as he exited the car and moved to meet him. With a quick greeting they entered the storage facility to retrieve their jump gear, so they each could spread theirs out on tables for close inspection. He made himself concentrate on double-checking every strap and buckle. Then inspected his face mask, hose, and oxygen supply, even though they'd done the same thing the day before in preparation.

Hawk entered with the three new guys of the unit—Jeff Sizemore, call sign Bullet, their new sniper; Seaman Jack Logan, call sign Box for his COM expertise; and Seaman Kelsey Tyler, call sign Celt, a member of the fire team. Langley Marks followed behind them.

What if something happened to Selena while he was twenty-nine thousand feet in the air and he couldn't get to her right away? What if something were to happen to him while she was going through all this? He loved what he did, knew the members of his team depended on him. But right now she needed him more and, since they weren't deployed into a war zone, they could do without him, or transfer someone in to complete the team until he could return.

He reached for his phone and stepped away from the group to call Selena. The bank's automated system asked him to key in the extension and put him through to her office. Her voice sounded the same as always when she answered. "Selena Shaker speaking. What can I do for you?"

"I just wanted to check on you," he replied.

"I'm fine. Just working on some paperwork and getting ready for a meeting."

"Feeling okay?"

"Just a little tired."

Of course she wouldn't mention the hair thing until he saw her tonight. "I'll be out of touch for a while. If anything happens, you know the backup plan."

They'd devised a list of people to call who would stand in for him until he could reach her. What they hell did that say about his priorities?

"Yes. But I'm sure I won't need to call anyone. I'm having a good day. Even my stomach has decided to cooperate."

A good day after she'd had Langley shave her head? He smiled. His wife was amazing. "Good, I'm glad, *cara*." She'd been plagued with morning sickness the first few months, and now the nausea from the chemo had kicked in to take over. She must sometimes feel like the problems and physical stressors would never end.

He wouldn't stress her out by telling her what training they were involved in today. She'd worry. "Should you have to call, Langley will be coordinating today. He'll have his cell and he'll know how to get me to wherever you need me, as fast as humanly possible."

"Okay. I have a doctor's appointment later. So I'll be fine. Be careful."

"Roger that. Love you."

"Love you, too."

"Everything okay?" Langley asked when Oliver joined the rest of the team and immediately went back to checking his equipment.

"Yeah. Everything's fine." He was going to enjoy this last jump with his team, then speak with Hawk about a change of duty until Selena came through delivery and treatment.

He needed to have his mind in the game a hundred and ten percent if he was to do justice for the other guys in his team. And as long as Selena was going through this, he couldn't guarantee he'd be able to do it.

The rest of the men were already changing into thermal shirts to go under their polypropylene garments. It could get damn cold at twenty-nine thousand feet at the 126 mph they'd be dropping. They'd wait to put on balaclava face masks and gloves when they were airborne.

An hour and a half later, when they finally boarded the aircraft, they were weighted down with the rest of their gear, including body armor, an oxygen system and mask which snapped to his helmet, plus altimeter, parachute, and goggles. This time, he thought, they at least would not have the extra hundred pounds of equipment usually strapped to them during missions. Which meant more freefall time before he opened his chute.

"You wouldn't believe it. I've never caught a dolphin fish any bigger than twelve to fourteen pounds. This sucker had to be at least thirty," Doc said.

"This is beginning to sound like one of those tall tales you fishermen spin all the time," Sizemore said, the flash of his smile bright white in the dim light of the fuselage.

"I have proof." Doc dredged his iPhone from the right front pocket of his cammies with some difficulty. He scanned through the pictures until he came across the one he wanted. He held it up.

"You know pictures can be deceiving," Bowie said from his seat next to Doc. "Depending on the perspective."

The look of betrayal on Doc's face was almost comical. "Just for that, neither one of you guys are invited to my fish grill. I have enough mahi-mahi fillets to feed the entire team. We'll be eating and partying while you two sit home alone and hungry."

Oliver laughed, then just as quickly sobered. He was going to miss the guys. They were his backup down range, and had shown their support more times than he could ever repay.

"Hey, Greenback." Doc waved a hand to get his attention. He wandered over to where the guys had congregated. "We've been talking about nicknames. We know why Bowie got his, being from Texas. And mine is self-explanatory, as is Bullet's. But none of us know where yours came from." His brows rose. "Care to share and put the mystery to bed?"

Oliver braced a hand against the steel fuselage. He grinned at the memory the question triggered. "I had just made it through BUD/S, and we'd transported out to Machen to do SQT (SEAL Qualification Training). We were sent out to do some night maneuvers in the desert. You know, using compass and the stars to navigate and do patrols. Our lieutenant notifies us we have another team lying in wait to ambush us somewhere out there, and part of the fun is for us to avoid capture and get back to the base undetected. He assigned me and two others to protect our back door in case they approached us from the rear. It's black as pitch with a slice of moon the width of a gnat's eyelash, so we're wearing our NVGs so we can see two feet in front of us and not step on a rattlesnake or each other."

Doc and Bullet nodded a shared understanding in their expression.

"Well, the lieutenant radios back to check on us every so often, and I'm looking through the NVGs turning everything green in front of me, and every time he asks for a status I say, "It's green back here."

The men started to chuckle.

"By the time we got back to base camp, my name had become Greenback."

Doc shook his head with a wide grin. "It's a much better story than the stuff I imagined."

Oliver bumped knuckles with him and wandered over to take a seat next to Hawk. "I need to talk to you about something."

Hawk nodded. "Okay." He frowned. "Selena okay?"

"So far. But I don't think she's telling me everything. She's twenty-two weeks along and the chemo's been hard and is only going to get harder. I think it might be time for me to request a temporary duty change until the baby is born. I need to be on the ground and closer to home right now."

Hawk nodded. "Understood. Captain Jackson and I discussed this a couple of weeks ago. Go in and see him tomorrow. I think he has something in mind for you."

It was a reassuring to know command had his back in this. "Thanks, Hawk."

Hawk's gray gaze remained on his face. "You know this doesn't mean you're breaking ties with us, with this team. We'll still be here when you're ready to come back. And we'll still be there for you and Selena until she's well."

Emotion gripped his throat, and he looked away. "We couldn't do it without all of you. Zoe and Trish, Clara and Tess. Since Selena's mom left, they've been dropping meals by, and taking Lucia for play dates. They're all amazing."

Hawk gripped his forearm in a moment of commiseration. "Selena would be doing the same for them."

"Strap in and prepare for takeoff," the pilot's voice came over the COM. The engines turned over and then roared as they taxied forward, making it impossible to talk.

At ten thousand feet they leveled off and everyone donned their balaclava face masks, helmets, positioned their goggles and went on oxygen to leach the nitrogen from their bloodstreams. The plane circled for forty-five minutes, climbing to an altitude of twenty-nine thousand feet before the cargo bay door opened and the pilot announced they'd reached their diving height. They rose as one and packed together in jump formation near the incline. As soon as the pilot announced they were over the jump area, Hawk signaled, moved forward, and leapt. They all followed him as they'd done a thousand times before, through training, into battle, down ropes, and even out the backs of planes.

The curve of the atmosphere looked like a convex lens along the horizon, and the sound of the wind filled Oliver's ears despite his helmet. Up here at what looked like the top of the world, his heart raced and he came alive. Hurtling toward the earth fed the adrenaline junkie in him.

But down below the woman who nurtured his unborn child was struggling. He could do without this for a time. Until she was well.

At thirty-five hundred feet he deployed his chute. Air filled it and jerked him upward. He grasped the wooden handles used to manipulate the direction of descent. Below him Hawk's chute moved east, and he looked over his shoulder to locate the men behind him, and saw their chutes staggered in a landing formation, one above the other, following him down. His throat tightened with emotion.

Hawk was right. Nothing could break the ties between him and this team. When age or some physical condition made him unable to do this job, he'd still be tied to this life, and the men who lived it with him. He'd lived a lifetime in the five years he'd been a SEAL. He planned to live many more.

Selena was going to get well and he'd come back to his team.

# CHAPTER EIGHT

S ELENA TURNED THE key in the door, pushed it open, then stood back for Lucia to precede her into the house. Had she ever been this tired? Maybe it was just an aftereffect of her doctor's appointment. She couldn't think about it just now. She'd start screaming the way she had as soon as she'd gotten in the car.

When she made it to the couch she kicked her shoes off and slumped back against the cushions. Lucia sidled up to her and Selena lifted the straps of her backpack free and dropped it next to the couch. Lucia climbed up on the cushions next to her.

She'd been unusually silent since Selena had picked her up at daycare. "What's wrong, baby?"

"You're hair's all gone, Mommy."

The tremulous tone in her voice arrowed straight into Selena's heart. She should have taken Lucia's reaction into consideration before shaving off her hair. Why hadn't she? Because she was slipping. She couldn't think of everything, do everything she needed to do and try to deal with everyone else's needs when it was such an effort to deal with her own.

"Mommy took some medicine and it made my hair fall out. So I had it cut." She pulled her scarf free and ran a hand over her scalp. There was a small patch of stubble at the crown and at the nape of her neck, but the rest was gone. "It will grow back soon."

Lucia got up on her knees and ran her small hand over the top of Selena's head.

Selena looped her arms around her to hold her steady. "Would you like it if Mommy wore a wig?"

"Whassat?"

How to explain? "It fits on your head like a hat, but it's made of hair." She pushed herself free of the couch and offered Lucia her hand. They wandered down the hall to Oliver's small office. The space was actually a spare bedroom. Right now a large, heavy plastic storage unit was tucked in the corner where Oliver kept extra military gear, his personal sig and a twelve gauge he'd had as a boy. She automatically checked the cabinet door to make sure it was still locked before sitting down at the computer desk and opening the laptop. Lucia wiggled up onto her lap. As soon as the browser came up, Selena typed in WIGS.

A whole list of companies who created wigs or sold them came up. She clicked on the image listing at the top and pictures of wigs popped up, some on Styrofoam heads and others suspended in space.

"Which ones do you like?" Selena asked. She breathed in the combination of baby shampoo, crayons and the outdoors distinctive to her active child.

"Dat one." Lucia pointed to a bright pink wig made of synthetic fibers.

"You think I'd look good with pink hair?"

"Yes."

"Or do you think Lucia would look good in pink hair?"

A wide smile spread across Lucia's face. "Yes."

Selena laughed and gave her a hug.

"Does my hair have to fall off?" Lucia asked.

"No." God forbid her baby would sink her teeth into the idea. She'd cut it off herself to hurry things along. "Mommy doesn't want your hair cut. I think it looks beautiful just as it is." Selena curled a long, shoulder-length strand around her finger to form a barrel curl. "But you can wear a wig over your hair if you want to."

"If Mommy gets a wig, Lucia will have to have a pink one," Oliver said from the door.

"Daddy!" Lucia wiggled free of her lap and ran to him. He swung her up into his arms. "Mommy's hair is all gone," she announced in a whisper.

"I see. She looks beautiful, doesn't she?"

Lucia turned to look over her shoulder. "Like the Moon Lady."

"It's a Chinese folk tale she learned about at daycare," Selena explained. She walked over to Oliver to lean against him. "The lady isn't bald, but for some reason it's how Lucia imagines her."

Lucia shimmed down and went to the computer to look at the pictures again.

His lips skimmed Selena's eyelids and he lay his cheek against her bare head. "I brought a couple of movies home. One for Lucia and a few for us. I thought we'd have a family night."

"Okay."

"I'm cooking. Doc sent you some mahi-mahi. He caught a thirty-pound dolphin fish. Can you believe that?"

"I didn't know they got so big."

"Bowie and Bullet voiced some disbelief and Doc has uninvited them to his next fish grill."

She laughed. "You know he'll change his mind. He's a soft touch."

"They know it, too. But he thought you might like some before everyone else, as a treat."

"That was really nice of him." The guys were forever doing thoughtful things. "I'll call and thank him."

Oliver ran his hand over her bare scalp. "You look like Sinead O'Connor."

Selena smiled. "With an Italian nose."

"What's wrong with your nose? I think it's perfect." He kissed it. "Why don't you lie down and rest while Lucia and I cook?"

She nodded. She was sure Langley had warned him about her hair, giving him time to adjust before seeing her. But just once she wished he'd come straight out and say she looked like shit. She had dark circles under her eyes and, though she forced herself to eat, she had lost weight. She was just a bald baby bump.

How could Oliver be so supportive about everything else and not about the baby? She wanted to march into the kitchen and confront him, but exhaustion born from two hard knocks in one day dragged at her limbs, and she could hardly keep her eyes open. She had to tell Oliver, but the prospect was just too much for her right now.

She went into her bedroom and pulled the top cover down. She shed her dress, put on a T-shirt and shorts, and slipped beneath the comforter. She was asleep in moments.

She woke to the sound of the television in the living room with an overwhelming need to urinate. She bailed out of bed and went into the bathroom.

When she came out Oliver stood at the dresser, removing his watch.

What time is it?" she asked.

"Nearly ten. You were sleeping so soundly I didn't want to wake you. Lucia and I ate fish and watched *Finding Nemo*. I assured her we weren't eating clown fish or a tang."

Selena smiled. "How did you know what kind of fish Dory was?"

"We had to look it up before she'd eat."

Selena laughed.

"Are you hungry?"

"No." She slipped beneath the covers and pulled them up. She opened with the easier of two pieces of news. "I told my boss today I needed to take a leave of absence."

Oliver strode to the side of the bed and sat down on the edge next to her.

"We knew you'd have to eventually."

"I made a mistake on a big contract which could have cost the bank thousands, Oliver." She started to run her fingers through her hair to push it back and caught herself when she met the soft skin of her scalp. "If Diana hadn't caught it, I'd have probably been fired."

He rested his fingers against the exposed nape of her neck. "I'm sorry, *carina*."

"I should have discussed it with you, but—I couldn't take the risk of being fired. At least this way I might have a chance of going back." So why did it feel like such a defeat?

"It'll be okay, Selena. It was the right thing to do." He remained silent for a moment. "I talked to Hawk today about a change of duty so I can stay more available. He said Captain Jackson already had something for me. I'm seeing him tomorrow."

They were both losing out on important bits of who they were.

"I'm sorry, Oliver."

"It's just temporary for us both, Selena. As soon as you have the baby, and get well, everything will go back to normal."

No it wouldn't. Nothing would ever go back to the way it was before cancer. Their new normal was going to be something else entirely. "The doctor talked to me about what he called another measure of defense." She closed her eyes against the pain. "They want to take out my ovaries once the baby's born. I'll never have another child."

"Two will be enough, honey."

"I'll be thrown into menopause at twenty-eight. I'll have to stay on medication for ten years to make sure the cancer doesn't come back."

"Whatever it takes, Selena."

He clearly didn't understand what she was saying. Everything that made her a woman was being ripped away, one piece at a time. "My sex drive will be gone, Oliver. What if I can't want you anymore?"

He took her into his arms. "You promised me, and yourself, you would fight. Whatever it takes. As long as you survive, we can work on everything else. As long as you survive." His expression was fierce, intent.

She rested her cheek against his shoulder. If only she had his strength.

"If I lost an arm, a leg, you'd still love me, wouldn't you?" he asked.

"Yes." Her arms tightened around him.

"This is the same. These things don't make up the person you are. Your ovaries aren't what make you my Selena."

But it was part of what made her a woman. Because of all the hormones coursing through her, they couldn't be certain the chemo was slowing or stopping the spread of the cancer. The lymph node swelling under her right arm never went away, though she tried to keep the limb elevated as much as possible.

"You want to know what the sexiest thing about you is?"

"What?"

"Your laugh. It was the first thing I noticed about you in college. I'd gone to the party at Joe Rollins house, and the place was packed. Some babe in tight jeans and a barely-there top was putting the moves on me. And I should have been raring to go, since I was just one big hormone then, but I kept hearing your laugh.

"Finally I just walked away from the babe and followed the sound to the kitchen. You were there with a group of girls. You looked like you'd just graduated from Catholic high school. Fresh-faced, young, and less underdressed than most of the other college freshmen there. I asked you to dance and spent the rest of the night trying to make you laugh. Every time I hear it, I get hard."

How could she not love him after that story? She kissed him, then said, "You're so full of it."

He laughed. "I'm serious."

He looked so earnest she had to believe him. She cupped his face in her hands and kissed him again, this time with feeling. "What movie was it you brought home for us to watch?"

"The guys made a list and I got all the ones I was able to find."

If his team had made the list she could hardly wait to see what they'd chosen. "Go get them and we'll pop one in."

She drew a deep breath after he left the room. The tight feeling of pain and frustration had eased, and she was actually able to smile when he came back in. He fanned the stack of DVDs out on the bed. For a moment she was stunned, but then dissolved into a fit of the giggles.

Every movie had a bald heroine: *Alien 3, Empire Records, V for Vendetta, G. I. Jane* and *Star Trek: The Motion Picture.*

"Let's watch *G.I. Jane*," she suggested.

"You don't have to choose one you think I'd like. Contrary to popular belief, military operators do watch things besides war movies."

"I need to watch someone who's ready to kick butt."

He grinned. "Okay." He sauntered over to the small entertainment center angled in the corner of the room, popped in the DVD, and turned on the television. "You want some popcorn?"

She shook her head.

He shucked his shorts and slid beneath the covers in his boxer briefs and T-shirt. She cuddled close against his side and felt the baby move.

She was entitled to a few meltdowns. But she had to keep a positive attitude. The mistake at work, her hair loss, the chemo, the doctor's strong suggestion about her ovaries, and worry over the baby—they had all combined to knock her off her feet.

*If adversity knocks me down, I will get back up. I will never give up the fight.*

The opening credits of the movie rolled forward and she tried to lose herself in the story. At the point, when Demi Moore was doing sit-ups while hanging from a top bunk, Selena slipped her hand into Oliver's boxer briefs and curled her fingers around his penis. He hardened in an instant and a smile curved her lips.

He shifted to look down at her, his brown eyes already darkening with desire. "I thought we were watching a movie."

"We are watching a movie. But I've been asleep for hours and I'm feeling rested and…ready for something more."

He eyed her, his expression serious, as his hand moved beneath her T-shirt and he palmed her growing baby bump. "Are you sure it's okay?"

He might have freaked out about the baby because of her diagnosis, but his protective concern made her smile. His need to keep his distance was constantly at war with his paternal instincts. He might fool himself, but he couldn't fool her. Once the baby was born, he'd be as loving to it as he was to Lucia. She knew he would.

Her hand covered his. "It's okay."

He reached for the television control and turned it off.

She smiled. One of the best things about making love with her husband was on the way he paid attention to detail. He spent at least a decade kissing her, though she wanted to rush toward other things. She finally peeled his shirt up and he got the message and tossed it aside, then wiggled free of his briefs. The spiraling pattern of hair on his chest was soft beneath her hands. His nipples tightened while she toyed with them and tasted the salty heat of his skin. He shuddered in response and caught his breath.

In return, his hand fished beneath her T-shirt and found her left breast and caressed and toyed with the nipple. She had never allowed him to see the area where her right breast had been for fear it would crush any sexual feelings he had for her. But she reveled in the sensation when he touched her.

If he could still want her without a breast, without hair, maybe they would survive cancer as a couple. She trailed her lips to his collarbone and then nipped his shoulder while she looped her knee over his hip and moved against him.

"You're very impatient," he complained. "And you still have your shorts on."

"Carpe diem," she murmured into his ear and sucked on his earlobe.

He groaned and tugged her shorts down and off. There was a tremor in his arms as he moved up over her to wedge himself between her thighs, and she smiled at his excitement. His muscle-hardened stomach brushed hers distended with child. With one slow glide he thrust into her. The pleasure of their bodies joining, being as close as they could get, was both a joy and a relief.

He balanced his weight on his hands, careful not to put too much pressure on her. His slow, easy movements were somehow more sensual because of the care he showed her and because his position allowed her to watch his expression. With every gentle thrust her pleasurable tension built. She let it come, hoping to extend the moments of intimacy for as long as they could last. Oliver's expression of concentration morphed into a frown as he fought against his release. He reached down between them and touched her where their bodies joined, messaging the sensitive area until the slow-growing wave became a tsunami which broke over her and swept him along in its wake.

With the release came a fresh wave of exhaustion. She looped an arm around his neck and drew his lips down to hers for a long, sweet kiss. "I'm going to pretend I'm a man and roll over and go to sleep," she said, her voice breathy.

"I feel so used," Oliver said in an aggrieved tone.

She laughed. "If you want to turn the movie back on and finish it, it won't bother me." She caressed his cheek.

"Okay."

When she turned on her side, he moved to spoon with her, but didn't turn the light off. "I love you, Oliver."

"Ti amo per l'eternità," he said in return.

OLIVER CONTINUED TO hold her until her breathing deepened and slowed. He studied the fragile curve of her cheek, and the slender bridge of her nose. There was a new fragility to her shape, despite her pregnancy, which concerned him. She needed to eat more, for herself and the baby. No matter what kind of job he was assigned on post, from now on he was going to make it his calling to see she ate and slept as she should.

She could only fight effectively if she was in top form. And he was going to make some calls to her doctors and find out if there were things she wasn't sharing with him. He needed to know.

And maybe with a plan of action in place, he could keep the worry at bay.

# CHAPTER NINE

**S**ELENA RUBBED THE side of her swollen belly where tiny toes or fingers poked between her ribs with insistent determination and then pushed downward. If she were trapped in such a tight space, she'd probably be tempted to do the same.

She tensed at the sound of approaching footsteps. The curtain parted and Judy Elmer, one of the nurses, stepped into the alcove with a tray in her hand.

"Hey, Selena. Good to see you," Judy greeted her with a smile and set the tray on the table next to her. Her gaze dropped to Selena's belly. "It looks like your little one is progressing just as he should. Well, he or she."

"Yes. Dr. Sanderlin says the baby's almost nineteen inches long and weighs about six pounds."

"So you're going old school and don't know what you're having?" Judy asked.

"We want to be surprised. But Lucia, our three year old, has decided her/his name should be Gumby."

Judy laughed.

Selena gripped the arms of the recliner as the nurse peeled back her lapel to expose the port running into the vein just below her collarbone. Judy picked up a syringe filled with clear fluid and pulled loose the cap. "I'm just going to check your port for any blockage."

Selena nodded and closed her eyes while the nurse inserted the needle into the port and pushed the plunger. Though the process wasn't painful she held her breath.

"Everything's clear here. I'll check your vitals, then hook you up, okay?"

Selena swallowed though her mouth was dry. "Okay."

Judy took her pulse and blood pressure.

"You're blood pressure's a little high. Why don't we wait just a few minutes and see if it comes down?"

"Okay."

"Go ahead and just raise the footrest on the recliner and relax. I'll be back in a few minutes to check it again."

Selena nodded and tugged her scarf forward a little and smoothed it.

Judy stepped out of the curtained area and walked away.

She'd been told repeatedly the chemicals wouldn't hurt the baby, but her fear kicked in every time.

Everything she did these days was for one child or the other, and poor Oliver got neglected in the crunch. Even sex had been put on hold until after the birth.

He seemed just as focused, had been for months, on making sure she was eating healthy and unstressed. He messaged her swollen arm when lymphedema kicked in and bandaged it for her to keep the swelling down. He was all about her. While she ate, slept, breathed for the baby.

At thirty-five weeks, her maternal instincts were cranked to overdrive. She just needed this one thing to go right.

Judy returned a few minutes later with the bag of Saline and a smaller bag of fluid. She hooked the two together so the saline would feed the chemo into her port a little at a time.

She paused to take Selena's blood pressure again. "It's come down a little. Let's wait a few more minutes.

She left again and Selena tilted the recliner back, stared the ceiling, and wished Oliver were there to calm her. She closed her eyes and concentrated on breathing in and out.

Twenty minutes later Judy slipped back through the curtain. She took a blood sample from the port and once again took her blood pressure. Judy recorded the reading and nodded. "I'll get your chemo started."

Selena rested her hands on her belly, holding it while Judy started the infusion. Once the needle was in place and the liquids were dripping, Judy pulled the curtains back so all the nurses could watch over her and Selena could socialize with the other patients if she wanted.

If only she could sleep through the next four hours, but the constant back and forth of the nurses, and knowing where she was, kept her from being able to relax.

Five other women sat in recliners in similar positions, all hooked up to IVs of one kind or another. When she'd begun the treatments, there had been as few as three and as many as ten other patients at any given time. She recognized a couple of the women and raised a hand in greeting.

"How many does this make for you?" the woman directly across from her asked.

"Treatments or children?" Selena asked.

"Both." The woman said.

"Six treatments, two children."

"Congratulations on both."

"Thanks." The painful tightening of her stomach muscles sent a wave of anxiety through Selena. It was just a Braxton Hicks contraction. She was fine. She'd be hyper-aware of every small twinge of discomfort until the baby was born.

She forced herself to concentrate, to keep talking with the woman across from her. "How many for you?" Selena asked.

"This is my seventh and final treatment."

"I'm so happy for you," Selena said with feeling. She was. And envious. Once the baby had arrived, she still had months of other therapies and surgeries to look forward to.

One thing at a time. As Oliver said.

She shifted in her seat as her back began to ache and once again a contraction hit.

She glanced toward the desk in search of Judy, but an unfamiliar nurse stood there recording something on a tablet. She watched the clock, only half listening to the conversation between the woman and another she also recognized. Five minutes later, when another spasm hit, she timed it.

Braxton Hicks didn't last sixty seconds and hurt like a son-of-a-bitch. Her heart rate soared and she couldn't catch her breath. She looked down the wide aisle to the desk and pushed the call button.

It was too soon. The baby needed the extra five weeks to grow and develop.

Judy hurried over, "What is it, Selena?"

She tried to keep her voice calm but her words came out breathy and weak. She wasn't ready, the baby wasn't ready. "I'm in labor."

"BACK INTO THE surf, get wet and sandy," Oliver yelled. Eighty-two extremely tired men ran toward the water and rolled around in the surf, then returned to the sand and tumbled around in it until they were covered from head to toe.

Five minutes later he was yelling again. "Chainey! Do I see a dry spot on your shirt?"

"Hooyah, Ensign Shaker." The recruit who stood before him was six inches taller, at least forty pounds heavier, and looked about fourteen.

"Get your ass back in the surf and get sandy. And when I say get sandy, I mean every inch of you. The devil's in the details, Chainey. Every detail you miss on a mission can cost your life or someone else's."

"Hooyah, Ensign Shaker." The kid ran back into the ocean and allowed the water to flow over him, then he raced back to the loose sand twenty feet inland and rolled like a log. When he stood, he looked like the sugar cookie he should have resembled to begin with.

"Now give me twenty, Chainey, and do it quick because you're holding up your boat crew. You're putting their lives at risk because you are keeping them in a holding pattern while you take care of bullshit."

"Hooyah, Ensign Shaker." Chainey hit the sand. He counted out the twenty, leapt to his feet, and dashed over to join his boat crew, who stood holding the IBS—inflatable boat, small—aloft as instructed.

The summer surf crashed behind them as eight teams of eight men ran in a shuffle down the beach, their rubber boats balanced over them, and then back again. The breeze coming off the water was stiff. The surf was high and was going to give the boat crews a pounding.

It was the first day of BUD/S and they were weeding out the weak, the ones who didn't have the right mindset to make it through. There was a method to the torture they dished out, a learning curve to every exercise.

He was having a blast, though he kept his facial expression stern.

Oliver noticed a man dressed in shorts and the brown T-shirt worn by the instructors jogging toward them at a steady clip. He narrowed his eyes in an attempt to identify him. It was Seaman Corey Bryant, and Oliver frowned until the man changed course and started toward him. Oliver heart clenched and he sprinted to meet him.

"The hospital called. Your wife's gone into premature labor, during her chemo. She's been taken to maternity. I'm here to relieve you."

Oliver didn't stop to thank him, but broke into an all-out run up the beach to the facility. He was out of breath and shaking by the time he made it to his locker. He ignored the change of clothes and just grabbed his wallet and car keys.

It was just five weeks early. The baby would be fine. Selena would be fine. He'd been telling himself that for months. But what if they weren't? If something happened to the baby, Selena wouldn't be able to handle it. She'd clung to it as a ray of hope during a time of fear, and if it was suddenly taken from her—what then?

He pulled out of the parking lot and wove his way toward the front gate. He had to force himself to watch the speed limit, the urge to floor the gas pedal almost irresistible.

And what about him? How would he feel should his son or daughter's life be snatched away before it had a chance to begin?

He'd been tortured by both pain and guilt since the moment he'd suggested aborting the baby during their first doctor's appointment. If something happened to the baby now, it would be as though he'd willed it. Willed it with his need to keep his distance, in case it happened because of the cancer, the chemo, or just plain bad luck.

Would Selena forgive him for those words, spoken out of fear for her? He'd never asked her forgiveness. Never reneged on the intent behind them. Why hadn't he done so?

He shook with the need to be there at the hospital as he pulled up at the gate and was waved through by the MPs.

It seemed an eternity passed before he turned onto Bob Wilson Drive and saw the hulking shape of the Naval Medical Center. Then he faced the nightmare of trying to find parking.

SELENA TOOK DEEP breaths to steady her racing heart. The room in the maternity wing was empty but for her and the doctor. Thank God. Though the nurses had tried not to stare while she'd changed from her street clothes to a hospital gown, the sight of her mastectomy scar had given them both pause. But it had gotten them on the phone to her ObGyn probably more quickly than otherwise.

"You have to calm down, Selena," Dr. Sanderlin said, her voice steady. "The baby's fine. You're fine. We're giving you something to lower your blood pressure.

"Did someone call Oliver?" Would she ever be able to do anything again without turning to Oliver for reassurance? Since quitting her job, she'd turned into a dependent ninny.

"Yes, they've called him, and I'm sure he's on his way."

"Can we stop the labor? Wouldn't it be better if we waited a few more weeks?"

"Every week is important, but you were already dilated three centimeters at your last visit and you're at six now. I don't think trying to stop your labor is the right thing to do. It will put your body and the baby under more stress. And leave you open to infection. I think our best option is to let nature take its course.

"I've ordered a test on the amniotic fluid we withdrew just a few minutes ago," Dr. Sanderlin continued. "It should be back within the hour. The neonatal intensive care unit will be prepared if there's any issue with lung development. But I just looked at the fetal development on your ultrasound and everything looks fine.

He's just going to be small."

Another contraction hit and Selena tried to breathe with it. She had done this alone last time. She could do it again if she had to. But she really wanted Oliver. The unbearable feeling of pressure in her lower abdomen seemed to go on forever. She had to turn on her side to grip the bar on the hospital bed. When it eased, she drew a cleansing breath.

"I have to lie on my side. I can't lie flat on my back."

"You can lie in whatever position is most comfortable, Selena." Dr. Sanderlin laid a reassuring hand on her shoulder. "The baby's turned in the right direction. Everything is going to be fine. You're doing great."

The baby's steady heartbeat through the monitor reassured her all was right with him/her.

"I've already called down to anesthesia and the nurse will be up to give you an epidural. I've already placed the order in your chart. I'm not expecting any problems, but I'd prefer you had one just in case."

"Okay."

"I'm going to send a nurse midwife in to sit with you until your husband gets here. When you get close to delivery I'll be back." Dr. Sanderlin left the room and Selena closed her eyes and geared up for the next contraction. It was already building.

OLIVER RAN FROM the parking structure to the hospital. Inside the place proved to be a maze, and the longer it took him to find the maternity wing the more his anxiety escalated. When he finally found the door, he had to be buzzed in by one of the nurses.

She handed him a gown to cover up with, then pointed out the room. He jogged to it and pushed open the door. A strange woosh-woosh-woosh sound came from a monitor by the bed. Selena gripped the bar next to her in obvious pain. A blonde woman stood close, offering her encouragement.

The sight of his wife in pain hammered him with a one-two punch. Seeing her curled on her side in a hospital bed, her scalp bare, gave him visions of something worse. His breathing stopped as he absorbed the roundhouse blow. He'd run toward danger his whole SEAL career, but nothing had scared him more than seeing her like this. It was a nightmare he'd done everything to avoid, to help *her* avoid.

Her eyes focused on him. "Oliver."

The sound of her voice broke the spell.

She needed him. This was the birth of their child. It had nothing to do with the cancer.

The first step was the hardest, but once he'd made it, his feet moved forward on their own. He hooked a nearby chair and jerked it close to the bed, his breathing coming in unsteady gasps. He made an effort to slow it, and then leaned over the railing to press his lips to her forehead and run a comforting hand down her back. "How's it going?"

"My water just broke." She glanced over her shoulder at the blonde woman.

"My name is Sharon Rollins, I'm a nurse midwife here at the hospital," she said as she reached for rubber gloves from the bedside table.

He nodded. "Oliver."

She tipped her chin in acknowledgement. "I need to check you, Selena."

Selena rolled on her back and just as quickly rolled back. "Wait-wait."

The look of focused control on her face as she dealt with the pain reassured Oliver a little. She had done this before, knew what to expect. She'd done it *alone. Jesus!* His every muscle tensed with regret and sympathy. When she drew a breath, so did he.

The woman folded back the sheet and did an internal exam. "This baby's in a rush, you're at ten," she announced. "You're going to want to push, but try not to. Try and blow through it." She tugged off her gloves and pushed the paging button on the bed. When a voice answered she said, "Page Dr. Sanderlin, stat, and alert the NICU, they need to get someone down here *now*."

Selena grasped Oliver's wrist and her fingers dug in as she started to blow. "Please, please."

"What do you need me to do?" Oliver asked the nurse midwife.

"When the rest of the crew get in here, she'll want to hold on to you while she pushes." She raised the head of the bed, dropped the foot, helped Serena onto her back, and positioned her feet in the stirrups.

Seeing his wife so vulnerable and exposed, and so helpless to do anything about it, Oliver slipped an arm around Selena and held on through the next contraction.

Suddenly the room was filled with people. Selena's doctor strode in dressed in a gown and gloves.

"We didn't get the epidural, did we?" she said.

Selena just stared at her wide-eyed.

"It's okay. I don't think we'll need it. Let's have a baby."

Oliver had thought he knew what labor was until now. With every contraction, his wife pushed and pushed. He learned to count for her as she bore down, again and again. His arm ached where she clutched it. He blocked it out. The discomfort was nothing compared to what she was going through. Ten minutes turned into twenty. How could one small baby require so much effort to be born? Sweat rolled down his face and hers. A nurse wiped it away for them both.

"The baby's crowning, Selena. One more push."

Dr. Sanderlin had already said the same thing several times. He didn't believe it anymore.

"The head is out. Don't push, Selena. *Don't push.*" The doctor's voice held an edge. Her hands worked frantically below, doing something neither of them could see. Her frantic movements and her tone gripped Oliver by the throat.

"Push one more time, Selena. One last big one."

Her face lined with exhaustion, Selena dragged in one more breath and held it. Her grimace of effort scored deep lines around her eyes and mouth. The moment the baby slipped free he saw the relief in her face.

"It's a boy. Hurry—take him," Dr. Sanderlin said, passing a bundle wrapped in white cloth off to the NICU nurse standing by. She rushed the baby to the small hooded table and was joined there by two other medical personnel.

He barely heard Dr. Sanderlin when she said, "You're going to feel a little pressure, Selena."

The silence in the room stretched for an eon. Selena's gaze swung upward to him, panicked fear stretching her features into a mask. His arms tightened around her as a cry of pain and denial built in his chest.

A high-pitched squeal shattered the terrifying quiet, followed by a trembling cry. The entire room took a breath.

"Sounds like someone's mad," Dr. Sanderlin said, with a quick smile.

Tears streamed down Oliver's face. "I didn't mean what I said in your office the first day."

Dr. Sanderlin set her the medical instrument on the tray the nurse held out to her. "I know."

"I didn't mean it, Selena."

Selena turned her face into his chest and gripped his scrubs in her fists. "I know, Oliver. I've always known. It's okay. We're okay."

# EPILOGUE

S ELENA DRIED HER sweaty palms on her pants legs while she shivered from the doctor's office air conditioning. How many trips to this office had she made in the last six months? At least twenty. Not counting the trips for blood work, X-rays, mammograms, biopsies, all the procedures she'd been unable to have before Micah's birth.

Oliver bounced and weaved in his daddy dance while he gave the baby his bottle. Micah was her miracle baby. He'd not only survived having the cord wrapped around his neck at birth—something they only learned from Dr. Sanderlin after the heart-numbing moment in her hospital room—but he'd also survived the targeting chemo she'd needed while she carried him. He had no lasting effects from either.

Following the birth she'd been bombarded with tests and procedures in a rush to knock out the cancer which had spread to her liver, but not to her other breast. Then came radiation, more chemo, and hormone suppression therapy, all of which she prayed had done the trick. She'd had another MRI just this week and now they were here to learn the diagnosis.

How many miracles could one person receive before God said, "Sorry, but you've reached your quota?" All she needed was one more.

Oliver settled Micah in his carrier, which was waiting on the floor between them, and handed him a set of plastic keys to chew on. He was teething, and he gnawed on the toy with quiet attention while he made a happy humming noise. She bent to put a cloth diaper beneath his chin to catch the slobber. He had Oliver's curly hair, just as Lucia did, and she curled a strand around her finger.

Oliver sat down beside her. She straightened and brushed her bangs back with her fingers, then clenched her hand into a fist in her lap to hide their trembling.

Oliver grasped her hand and laced their fingers. "The wig looks great—natural and sexy," Oliver said. "I like the short 'do on you." His smile would have looked natural to anyone else, but she noticed the tightness at the corners. He was as anxious as she was.

"I thought it looked more like a kick-ass heroine in an action movie. I'm getting well. I wanted to look the part." She had worked hard to regain some of her self-confidence and leave behind the clinging vine she'd become...even though Oliver repeatedly denied any evidence of it.

He bent to brush her knuckles with his lips. "Hooyah!" he said with feeling.

The door opened behind them and they both turned to look.

Dr. Sanderlin walked through first, but she wore no lab coat, and her hair was loose about her shoulders. She smiled at Selena, then Oliver. Dr. Dixon, tall, gray-haired and studious, followed.

Selena dragged air into her lungs, but her breath stuck in her throat. This was either very, very good or—She didn't want to think about it.

"I wanted to be included in this meeting," Dr. Sanderlin said. "Since it all started in my office nearly a year and a half ago, I asked Dr. Dixon if I could sit in."

The tight, anxious ball of nerves wedged beneath Selena's ribs began to ease.

Dr. Dixon cleared his throat. "There is no sign of cancer anywhere in your latest scans. Two other radiologists and I have gone over them. There's nothing there."

Selena's composure dissolved in relief and she covered her face with her hands and burst into tears.

Oliver pulled her to her feet and wrapped her in his arms. They clung, hard, and when she raised her face to him, he kissed her.

"We'll want you to stay on your regimen for a few more months before we switch you over to suppression therapy to maintain your status," Dr. Dixon continued. "You're ready for breast reconstruction now, whenever you feel up to it."

"I can give you a list of Board Certified plastic surgeons your insurance will cover," Dr. Sanderlin added.

A sound of joy, half laugh, half sob, broke from Selena. She'd have her breast back. She'd look like a healthy woman again. It's what she wanted. She left Oliver's arms to hug first Dr. Sanderlin, then Dr. Dixon.

"You did all the heavy lifting, Selena," Dr. Dixon said, patting her back.

"Not without Oliver," Selena said.

Dr. Sanderlin held Micah and admired his new tooth. Dr. Dixon loosened up and held him for a moment as well. They celebrated for a few more minutes, and then gathered Micah, the diaper bag, and returned to the van.

"We need to call everyone and give them the news," Selena said while she paced and watched Oliver strap the baby in and pull the door closed.

"Later, after we've celebrated a little on our own," Oliver said, flashing her a grin. He rested his arms on either side of her and leaned in, pushing her back against the van, and nestling his body in perfect alignment with hers.

Her heart raced and a small tingle settled in intimate areas. It took more effort these days to get her going, but Oliver was patient. At times it must have seemed almost as big a challenge to him as one of his missions. Thank God he was a SEAL. They never gave up.

He kissed her, then rested his cheek against hers.

As though he'd read her thoughts, he whispered, "Hawk once told me I'd never break the ties I have to my team. And I thought, because of everything I'd been through with them, I'd never have as strong a bond with anyone else. But I was wrong.

"When you've shared a life-and-death struggle as we have, it either makes you cling to one another, or it breaks the ties between you." His brown eyes were liquid with love and emotion. "I know there have been times when things were stretched pretty thin between us, especially when I was acting like an ass at the beginning. But, every time, we've rebounded and our ties have just grown stronger. I'm so lucky, Selena. I could have lost you so many times, so many ways."

Her eyes filled and her lips trembled as she whispered, "When I couldn't fight for myself, you helped me fight for you, and Lucia, and Micah. When I believed I had nothing left, you showed me I did. I couldn't have survived this without you." She rested her cheek against his chest until her tears and shakes abated.

He pulled back an inch or two and ducked his chin so he could look right into her eyes. "And you know the saying, the only thing tougher than a Marine is his wife?"

She smiled up at him. "Yeah."

"Well those women ain't got nothin' on me and my girls."

## THE END

# BOOKS BY TERESA REASOR

**SEAL Team Heartbreakers Series**

Breaking Free
(Book 1 of the SEAL Team Heartbreakers)

Breaking Through
(Book 2 of the SEAL Team Heartbreakers)

Breaking Away
(Book 3 of the SEAL Team Heartbreakers)

Building Ties
(Book 4 of the SEAL Team Heartbreakers)

Breaking Ties
(Available in the Hot Alpha SEALs: Military Romance
Megaset and in Building Ties Print Edition)

**Historicals**

Highland Moonlight

Captive Hearts

**Highland Moonlight Spinoffs**

To Capture a Highlander's Heart: The Beginning (Short Story)

To Capture A Highlander's Heart: The Courtship (Novella)

To Capture A Highlander's Heart: The Wedding Night (Coming Soon)

**Paranormals**

Timeless (Paranormal Romantic Suspense)

An Automated Death (A Steampunk Short Story)

**Contemporary Romance**

Caught In The Act (Comedic Short Story)

**Children's Books**

Willy C. Sparks: The Dragon Who Lost His Fire

Haiku Clue (Coming Soon)

**To contact Teresa Reasor or for more information on upcoming books:**

Website: http://www.teresareasor.com/

Blog: http://mymusesmusings.blogspot.com/

Facebook: https://www.facebook.com/teresa.reasor

Twitter: https://twitter.com/teresareasor

Substance-B: http://substance-b.com/TeresaReasor.html

Goodreads: goodreads.com/author/show/2308555.Teresa_J_Reasor

Pinterest: http://www.pinterest.com/teresareasor/

Authors Den: http://www.authorsden.com/teresajreasor

Sign up for my Newsletter: http://bit.ly/I7TtiC

or my Street Team: http://bit.ly/17ww6YZ

Printed in Great Britain
by Amazon.co.uk, Ltd.,
Marston Gate.